KU-270-359

Ken McCoy was born in wartime Leeds and has lived in Yorkshire all his life. For twenty-five years he ran his own building and civil engineering company. During this time he also worked as a freelance artist, greeting card designer and after-dinner entertainer. He has appeared on television, radio and as a comedian on the Leeds City Varieties' *Good Old Days*.

Writing is now Ken's first love – not counting of course his wife Valerie, to whom he has been married since 1973. He has five children and twelve grandchildren.

www.kenmccoy.co.uk

Hope Street

Ken McCoy

piatkus

PIATKUS

First published in Great Britain in 2000 by Judy Piatkus Ltd
This paperback edition published in 2011 by Piatkus

A CIP catalogue record for this book
is available from the British Library.

ISBN 978-0-7499-5693-6

Typeset by Phoenix Photosetting, Chatham, Kent
Printed and bound in Great Britain by CPI Group (UK), Croydon, CR0 4YY

Piatkus
An imprint of
Little, Brown Book Group
100 Victoria Embankment
London EC4Y 0DY

An Hachette UK Company
www.hachette.co.uk

www.piatkus.co.uk

To my wife, Valerie, for helping me with this book.
Thanks for your cleverness, your insight,
your pretty face and your love.

Part One

Chapter One

'It's my turn!'

'It's not yer know. I were here before you!'

'No yer wasn't . . . he wasn't, was he Stewart?'

Maggie Fish and Roy Bradford were jostling for position at the front of the queue. Roy was just one of three short-trousered boys awaiting his turn. All three pairs of trousers were identical, insofar as they were torn and patched and held up by utility braces. Three pairs of knees sported an assortment of plasters and scabs and three pairs of socks flopped around six assorted ankles. Maggie's second best summer frock was as yet unpatched, in fact almost pristine apart from the odd mend here and there. Her five-year-old knees unblemished, save a pink circle left by a recently torn off scab. She'd waited ages for her turn. Stewart Ganton's dad had bought him a pedal car with his demob money. He was the only kid in the street with a pedal car and he was capitalising on his monopoly by hiring it out at a ha'penny a go. This would buy his customers a bumpy ride to the end of the cobbled street of terraced houses, as far as the letter box on Carrcroft Road and back. He held out a grimy hand.

'First come, first served,' he said, by way of arbitration. Maggie had her ha'penny ready. She quickly slapped it into Stewart's outstretched palm.

'Maggie next, then Roy,' announced Stewart, who had the authority to decide such things.

'Hurry up Kevin!' he yelled down the street at the current driver. 'Or I'll have ter charge yer double. Yer only supposed ter go up an' down t' street once. Yer not supposed ter drive round in flippin' circles.'

Kevin grinned the grin of someone who'd got away with something for nothing, and headed back to base. The return journey was uphill and not as exciting as the first part. He came panting to a halt and was helped out with a hefty yank from Maggie, impatient for her turn.

'Leave off, Fishy! I can gerrout meself yer know,' he complained.

High above, Ruby Moffitt had her backside poking from her bedroom window as she industriously cleaned the dusty panes. Window cleaners were as yet an ill-afforded luxury in Hope Street. It was a warm summer evening in post-war Leeds, and it was good to get at least some part of her out of the house and into the sunshine. She was the first to spot him.

'Hey up, Maggie! Yer dad's here.'

Maggie looked up, then followed Mrs Moffitt's gaze to the end of the street, where a trilby-hatted man carrying a battered suitcase had just turned the corner. Tall and slim with a dark moustache, striding down the stone-flagged footpath, with a slightly bow-legged gait.

Greetings were being called out from back yards as the man passed by. The man acknowledging them with a smile and a wave. Maggie froze with indecision. He certainly looked like the man in the photo on their mantelpiece, but she couldn't be absolutely sure. What a time for him to come home from the war, just when it was her turn. Maggie plumped for the best of both worlds. Quickly climbing into the red car, she pedalled like mad down to the end of the street, not dawdling like the other kids had. The yellow bow in her dark brown hair flowing bravely backwards as she raced past the fading insult to Hitler on Janet Shearman's lavvie wall, past Mrs Venison scouring her yard steps with a donkey stone, past the Venisons' yapping mongrel, which set off in pursuit and past little Jimmy Moffitt, who was poking a stick with a piece of plasticine on the end, down a street gulley, trying to retrieve a lost marble. As she approached her dad, his face lit up with a half smile of semi-recognition. Wondering to himself, Blimey! Is that mucky-faced kid really my baby girl? The flimsy wheels bouncing over the uneven cobbles, her feet jumping off the spinning pedals, then

4

catching up with them as the car slowed down. Showing her dad what a really good driver she was.

'Don't go so fast! Yer'll break me car,' yelled a worried Stewart.

'Hiya Dad!' called out Maggie as she hurtled towards him.

'Hiya Maggie!'

It was her dad all right. She remembered him now, although she hadn't seen him since he went away to war and that seemed years and years ago. As she passed, she looked up at him and waved; the dog was barking, inches away from her head, trying to get in front of the car. Her feet jumped off the pedals again. She was wondering why her dad had a look of consternation on his face. The car ran over the dog's foot before hitting the lamp-post outside Kevin Walsh's house, leaving a nasty dent in it. The dog limped off, howling in pain and Maggie fell out, grazing her knee, but not badly enough for her to moan about. A yell of anguish came from Stewart.

'I told yer! . . . didn't I tell 'er? I'll tell me dad o' you, Maggie Fish.'

Maggie abandoned the car and raced up to her dad, grabbing his free hand. He put down his case and swung her up on to his shoulders. His demob suit was new and still smelled of military mothballs, dark brown with a darker stripe and matching trilby. Blood trickled unnoticed from her knee. She removed her dad's hat and put it on her own head, to the delight of the watching children. It covered half her face, leaving below it a smile of smug superiority. The other children looked up at her enviously, especially Alice Greenhough, whose dad had been killed in Holland, so he wouldn't be coming back.

Roy raced down to the overturned car and finished Maggie's ride before offering Stewart another ha'penny for his own ride. Stewart examined the dent, issued another threat to Maggie, then to Roy's disappointment, withdrew the car from hire.

Denis Bradford had been relaxing on the lavatory at the end of his yard, the one facing Johnnie's. He was reading in a two-day-old Yorkshire Evening Post, that the Americans were testing an atom bomb on an island called Bikini in the Pacific ocean. This met with Denis's unqualified approval. Any weapon that could end a war as quickly as that one did, had to be worth having. Denis had celebrated his twenty-seventh birthday, 13 February 1942, in

Singapore. Two days later the base fell to the Japanese in the biggest military defeat in British history. In May of that year, Denis had been put to work on the Thailand–Burma Railway and was one of the few survivors to be there at its official opening eighteen months later. Two hundred and fifty miles of track at the cost of four hundred lives per mile. The Japanese would never be Denis's favourite people.

He'd been home ten months now. Time enough for the war to be fading in his memory. Two stones heavier, but still as skinny as a rail. Hearing the shouts of greeting, he pulled the chain and peered round the door, still fastening his trousers.

'Welcome home, Johnnie lad!' he shouted. His voice slightly obscured by the flushing sound echoing from within.

'Thanks, Denis. Good to be back,' returned Johnnie. His welcome not exactly matching the one he'd pictured in his mind these last few months. No bands, no bunting, no welcoming speeches. Just Maggie riding on his shoulders and Denis Bradford popping his head round the lavvie door. Still it was a better welcome than some . . . and his real welcome awaited him inside. His lovely Jean.

Maggie took off the hat and waved it at her cheering pals, then banged noisily on the tin bath hanging from the yard wall, before she and her dad vanished out of sight into number seventeen Hope Street. It was a good day for the Fish family.

Johnnie stepped through the door into the smothering arms of his beloved Jean. Maggie wavered precariously on his shoulders as he let go his grip of her to embrace his wife. They stayed locked in each other's arms until Maggie got fed up and clambered down from her father's back, picked up his suitcase and tried, unsuccessfully, to heave it on to the table.

Eventually Johnnie released his wife from his embrace and stood back to look at her.

'Beautiful as ever,' he smiled.

Jean just held on to his hands, not ready to speak just yet. Johnnie looked around the back room. It was as he'd left it in 1944 apart from a square of carpet Jean had bought from a rag-man, who'd paid a woman in Roundhay half a crown to take it off her hands. Jean had given him twice that, and was delighted with her bargain, which had cleaned up beautifully and was the envy of the street. The cast-iron kitchen range was empty. During the summer the fire was only lit when heat was needed for the oven. Above it, on the wooden mantelpiece, was a clock, a photograph of Johnnie and a vase containing the rent money.

A scarred, drop-leaf dining table was pushed up against a wall and four dining chairs jammed beneath it, leaving room for a worn, brown settee and easy chair. The holes in the arms camouflaged with homemade fitted covers. A mirror on the wall next to the scullery door had the words 'Welcome Home Daddy', written in lipstick, in a suspiciously adult hand. The room was spotless and smelled faintly of lavender furniture polish. Johnnie nodded his approval, his wife hadn't let things go to rack and ruin.

'Only me! I thought yer might want ter go ter t' pictures tonight. I can babysit if yer want.'

This was the forfeit Ruby Moffitt was prepared to pay for the chance of witnessing the homecoming. She'd knocked and walked in uninvited as she usually did. A pan of potatoes was boiling unheeded in the tiny adjacent scullery, the steam drifting into the back room, where Johnnie Fish had plonked his suitcase on the table and was opening it, eagerly watched by his wife and daughter. All homecoming servicemen brought presents with them. Her Larry had brought her half a dozen pairs of fifteen-denier nylons, and presents for the kids. She was desperate to know if this compared favourably with Jean's husband.

'Not tonight thanks, Ruby,' said Jean, showing her to the door. 'I wouldn't mind tomorrow, if that's all right?'

"Course it is,' replied a disappointed Ruby, backing away to the door, with her eyes fixed firmly on the suitcase. 'I bet there's nylons in there,' she winked at Jean. 'My Larry brought me nylons.' She looked for Johnnie's reaction, hoping for the embarrassed look of a man who hadn't brought his wife nylons back from the war.

'Nylons?' he said. 'Cheap as muck are nylons over there, Ruby love. I brought a couple o' dozen pairs back with me.'

Ruby's face dropped as Jean's face lit up. 'See you tomorrow Ruby.' She closed the door on her neighbour and turned round.

'Two dozen pairs of nylons? Honest?'

Johnnie grinned. 'Did I say two dozen? I meant two. Honestly, they're like gold dust over there. You'll just have ter make 'em last, so that Randy Ruby thinks yer've got two dozen.'

Jean laughed, her disappointment gone in a flash. She held him in her arms. Maggie looked on approvingly, then turned her face away as they kissed, lightly at first, then passionately.

'I've got better plans for you my girl. Better than going ter the pictures,' said Johnnie.

'I should hope so,' laughed Jean. She looked at the clock on the mantelpiece. Half past six.

'Right Maggie,' she said. 'I think we'll have that meal that smells so good, then it's bedtime for all of us.'

Maggie's mouth opened in amazement. Fancy grown ups going to bed at the same time as her. Brenda Howsham would never believe her when she told her at school tomorrow. Still, I bet it's because my dad's tired after being away at the war so long. Her dad had given her a German doll that she'd treasure all her life and a pair of toy clogs that were destined to stand on the mantelpiece for the next few years. Maggie hugged the doll to her, knowing in her heart that it would take the place of the one-eyed rabbit that had seen her through her infancy. It had a real porcelain face with pink and white skin and jet black hair and was dressed in a traditional German costume.

'Oh Dad, thanks, it's smashin'.'

Johnnie handed Jean her nylons. 'You can have yer big present later,' he said with a grin.

Maggie looked disappointed. 'I wanted to see me mam's big present, she's seen mine.' Johnnie and Jean laughed and Maggie didn't understand.

They sat together beside Maggie's bed, watching their daughter fight a losing battle against the inevitable sleep, then tiptoed from her bedroom into their own. Jean took Johnnie in her arms again.

'I've been waiting for this since VE Day,' said Jean. 'I was beginning to think they'd never let you come home.'

'It were all them displaced persons. They needed somebody intelligent ter sort 'em out.'

'Oh aye! So why did they need you then?'

'Don't you be so insubordinate woman. Yer talking to an ex-corporal yer know.'

'Sorry corporal . . . permission to remove knickers, corporal?'

'Permission refused. That's a job for a corporal, not a civilian.'

'Sorry corporal.'

Jean pulled her dress over her head and stood to attention in front of Johnnie, saluted smartly, unbuttoned his trousers and pulled them down as Johnnie simultaneously pulled her knickers down. They stood back to appraise each other. She with her knickers around her ankles, he with trousers and underpants around his ankles. Jean rubbed her chin thoughtfully as she gazed down at his stirring loins.

'And just who do you think you're going to satisfy with that, soldier?' she asked.

'Me,' he replied.

The game restarted with feverish passion until Johnnie pushed her naked on to the bed, knelt astride her and gazed down on the woman he'd pictured in his mind every night since March 1944. That lovely face, his favourite face. Her skin pale and smooth, her eyes dark hazel and full of love for him. The rest of her just right. Not too fat, not too thin. Her breasts full and round and his to touch. He took one tenderly in each hand, as though not daring to hurt her. She pulled him down to her, kissing him passionately, opening her legs and bringing him inside her for the first time in over two years.

The second time was slower and less frantic and much nicer.

Chapter Two

May 1947

Johnnie looked through the curtains. 'Taxi's here love,' he announced.

A heavily pregnant Jean held out her arms to Maggie, who walked into her mam's embrace and rested her head against her bosom. It was warm and comforting and nice.

'It'll not be long, love. Then I'll be back with a little baby brother or sister for you.'

'I hope it's a sister,' decided Maggie firmly.

'We have to have what were given,' laughed her mam. 'Your dad wants a little boy.'

'Well, I'm fed up o' being outnumbered by you women. If it's three to one, I've no chance,' grumbled Johnnie, good naturedly. 'I wouldn't mind another girl though, if she turns out half as grand as our Maggie.'

He picked up the suitcase and walked out to the taxi, followed by Jean and Maggie. Vera Bradford and various other women and children were waiting in curious, chattering, groups. The arrival of a taxi was an unusual event in Hope Street.

'Now you be good for Mrs Bradford,' cautioned Jean, as Maggie took her next door neighbour's hand.

'Don't you go worrying about her love,' said Vera. 'She'll be all right with us. How often are they comin'?'

'Every ten minutes.'

This provoked a murmur of concern amongst the women in the crowd.

'Best get yer skates on Jean love,' advised Vera.

Johnnie helped his wife into the car before instructing the driver. 'Hyde Terrace Maternity Hospital. Quick as yer like, mate.'

The taxi bumped out of the street and sped down Carrcroft Road. The driver had heard of babies being born in the back of taxis. He didn't want first hand experience. The spectators dispersed as Vera led Maggie back into her house where Roy and his dad were listening to Dick Barton, Special Agent, on the wireless. One-year-old Mavis was playing with a rag doll on the floor.

Denis held up his hand to silence any chat from his wife as he caught the vital end of the programme. Dick Barton and Snowy were racing to rescue Jock from certain death at the hands of an evil wrongdoer as the dramatic theme music heralded the end of the episode. The clipped tones of the announcer told listeners to tune in next week to discover Jock's fate. Denis stretched and looked up at his wife.

'Did she get off alright then?'

'Aye – mind you, I don't think it'll be long afore it's born. She were 'aving contractions every ten minutes.'

'What's a contraction, Mam?' asked Roy.

'Summat yer'll never know nowt about lad, worse luck,' grumbled his mam.

'They're what your stomach does just before you have a baby,' explained Maggie, knowledgeably. 'They're like really bad pains.'

'Well, I don't want ter know nowt about 'em then,' said Roy.

'Yer mam'll know about 'em all right. It were bloody torture 'aving our Roy. It were like havin' a baby bloody elephant.'

'Do you think me mam'll be all right then, Mrs Bradford?' asked a concerned Maggie.

''Course she will love,' said Vera. 'Second one's allus easier.'

'Our Mavis shot out like a bar o' soap,' said Denis, reassuringly.

'Oh aye! An' you'd know all about that would yer? Don't talk about things yer know nowt about,' scolded Vera. 'Maggie's mam'll be all right because she's a woman. Now if she'd been a fella, there might have been summat ter worry about.'

'Can fellas have babies then?' asked a confused Roy.

'I wish they bloody could! There wouldn't be so many of the little buggers about if men had to have 'em.'

11

'Now then Vera, watch yer language in front o' Maggie,' said Denis.

'Sorry Maggie.'

'It's all right Mrs Bradford. Me dad sometimes swears.'

'He'll have a lot ter swear about, workin' up at Openshawe's. Bloody sweat shop up there,' remarked Denis.

'Now who's swearin'?' said Vera.

'Oh aye! Sorry lass,' grinned a contrite Denis.

The evening wore on. *Comedy Bandbox* came on the radio. A ball flew into the backyard from the street, rattling hard against the window and drawing a curse from Vera.

'I bet that's Jimmy bloody Moffitt! I'll rattle his ear'ole if he breaks our winder!'

Roy went out and threw it back. Taking great delight in conveying his mam's threat to snotty-nosed Jimmy. Vera put the kettle on for some cocoa, then turned to Maggie.

'If yer dad's not back afore half past eight, I said yer could sleep here love. Our Roy can sleep in t'attic an' you can sleep in his bed. If our Mavis starts crying, just ignore her. Our Roy does.'

'Oh great!' enthused Roy. 'I like it up in t'attic.'

'It's only this once, young feller me lad,' cautioned his dad. 'An' no clumping round in t' middle of the night, wakin' everybody up like yer did last time.'

'I didn't have no po. I had ter come down ter piddle in your po. It weren't my fault,' protested Roy.

'There was no need ter put yer boots on just ter come downstairs for a piddle,' argued his dad.

Maggie smiled, slightly embarrassed.

'Now look what yer've done,' snapped Vera. 'Yer've embarrassed t' poor lass with all yer talk about poes an' piddling.'

'I'm not embarrassed, Mrs Bradford.'

'Well, you've every cause ter be. Talking like that in front o' visitors. It's not right.'

Eight-thirty arrived without her dad returning. Mavis had already been put to bed. Maggie would have much preferred sleeping in her own bed, but accepted the alternative arrangements without a fuss. Her mam came first tonight . . . and the new baby. She and Roy got washed in the scullery sink before modestly taking it in turns to shut the scullery door and change

12

into their pyjamas. She'd brought her German doll, Betty, with her. Vera picked it up admiringly.

'Did you ever see such a bonny dolly? . . . Look at this, Denis.' She showed it to her husband, who gave a grunt of admiration without looking up from the *Yorkshire Evening Post*.

'Right lass,' said Vera. 'You get yerself off ter bed an' when yer wake up, yer'll have a brand new baby brother or sister . . . you mark my words.'

Maggie and Roy went up together. 'Yer can use me po if yer like,' he said magnanimously. Maggie nodded, wishing he wouldn't talk about poes so much. When she grew up she'd have a house with its own inside lavvie, like in the pictures. Even Laurel and Hardy had an inside lavvie. Closing the door behind her, she looked around Roy's sparsely furnished bedroom. Mavis was already sound asleep, one chubby arm dangling through the wooden slats in her cot. Apart from a small chest of drawers and a chair, the bed and the cot were the only items of furniture in the room. Coats were hung on two pegs at the back of the door and other garments draped across the chair. The ubiquitous chamber pot poked its handle out from beneath the bed. Maggie pushed it out of sight with her foot. To her, it was an emergency vessel, to be used only in the direst of circumstances. The curtains were drawn, but still let in a good deal of daylight. Her own bedroom, in the house next door was much the same, except she had a small wardrobe and her wallpaper was newer. Climbing into Roy's bed she fell asleep within minutes.

A loud banging on the back door woke everyone up. It was dark now. The middle of the night. Maggie heard Denis grumbling as he went downstairs. At the side of Maggie's bed was a candle in a tin holder with some matches beside it. She struck one and lit the candle, illuminating the small room with an eerie light. Mavis murmured something but went back to sleep. Long shadows dancing on the walls. The coats on the back of the door looked like a man in a dark cloak, moving in the flickering light. Maggie shivered with apprehension. She heard the bolt being drawn downstairs and someone came in. Then nothing, just silence. She was sure it was her dad, but she couldn't understand the silence. After a while she picked up the candle and went to the bedroom door. Roy was already there on the tiny landing, his finger to his lips. She could see his mam descending the stairs, turning into the back room. Curious to see what was happening.

'Oh my good God!' they heard her say.

Roy looked at Maggie. 'I reckon summat's up.'

Maggie's heart started thumping fast, not quite knowing why. She followed Roy down the stairs, step by tentative step. They stood at the entrance to the back room, Maggie with her candle still burning, its light exaggerating the fear in her face. Her dad was sitting at the table, with his head in his hands. She couldn't see his face but he was crying. Sobbing noisily. His shoulders heaving up and down. She'd never known her dad cry. It must be something awful. She put her candle holder down on a low wooden stool. Vera turned and saw her.

'Johnnie, Maggie's here,' she said quietly, placing a gentle hand on Johnnie's shoulder. He looked up, across the room, into Maggie's big, brown frightened eyes.

'What's up, Dad?'

He couldn't answer at first. He tried to speak, but couldn't control his sobs. This had happened to Maggie loads of times, but never to her dad. She walked slowly towards him. Her dad was breathing deeply, trying to take control of himself. Her last couple of steps saw her fling herself into his arms. He hugged her to him, almost too hard, as if he never wanted to let go of her. Then his arms relaxed and he gently held her away from him, his face was sad and wet with tears and somehow a lot older. He looked at her, as if trying to find the right moment. Trying to assess if she was ready for what he had to tell her. She'd have to be, he couldn't keep something like this from her.

'Yer mam died, Maggie.' It was an effort to force such a terrible statement out. His eyes dropped, not wanting to see the effect his words had on his daughter.

Maggie didn't understand. Things like that don't sink in when you're six years old. Not straight away anyway. Unable to contemplate the enormity of what her dad had just told her, she asked . . .

'Has she had a baby?'

He looked back up at her, wondering if she'd heard him properly. Then he looked up at Vera and Denis. 'She had a little boy,' he said, his voice unsteady, on the verge of breaking down. Vera's lips quivered and she burst into tears. Denis put his arm

14

around her and Johnnie hugged Maggie to him again. Roy went into the scullery, wondering if he should make everyone some cocoa. He put the kettle on just in case. Upstairs Mavis started crying, but no one could hear her.

Chapter Three

May 1951

It was Danny's fourth birthday. Not that you'd know it. He'd got a birthday card and a Dinky Toy, a Humber Super Snipe, from Grandma and Grandad Roberts in Nuneaton. Maggie had given him a card she'd made herself and that was the extent of his presents. Grandma and Grandad Fish were both dead and there were no uncles or aunts to speak of, unless you counted Uncle Stewart and Auntie Beryl in Australia, who they never heard from. It was a Saturday and his dad and Maggie had gone off to visit mam's grave. Danny had asked Maggie if he could go with them, but she said best not, the way dad's feeling, you might not come back. His dad had been in a funny mood, smacking him for spilling milk on the tablecloth. He'd been playing with his Dinky Car and had knocked the milk over with his elbow, saturating the tablecloth and earning himself a clip around his ears which had reduced him to tears. Maggie had reminded Dad that it was Danny's birthday.

'I need no reminding of that, thank you very much. Worst day of the year fer me.'

Maggie nodded, as if agreeing with him. Danny hadn't a clue what they were talking about. It was a nice day and he'd be able to play with Mavis next door until Dad and Maggie got back. Mavis was a bit older than him, but he liked her. Besides, her being a girl, she wouldn't be wanting to play with his new car.

People were going about their Saturday business, callously unaware of the Fishs' tragic anniversary. A game of cricket was starting up in the street as they left the house. Halfway down

Carrcroft Road they passed a horse-drawn roundabout surrounded by a crowd of eager children, all clutching their pennies. The children clambered on board, jostling for the much sought after place on top of the fire engine. The small, but wiry proprietor took their money then started to laboriously wind the wheel that would set the ride in motion.

'You shouldn't take it out on our Danny, you know,' said Maggie as they turned into Muscroft Street, heading for the tram stop.

'Oh, shouldn't I?' growled her dad. 'And who are you ter tell me what I should and shouldn't do?'

'I'm just saying, that's all. You're rotten to our Danny sometimes.'

'He only gets what he deserves. It's not easy yer know, being mam and dad ter the both of you.'

Maggie shut up. He was like this every year on the anniversary of mam's death. Correction, he got worse every year.

'Because of him, I were left with a six-year-old girl, a newborn baby and no wife.'

'It wasn't our Danny's fault,' argued Maggie stubbornly.

'I'm not saying it was,' he snapped. 'What I'm saying is that he was the cause of it . . . and it's not easy for me ter forget. Had it not been for Mrs Bradford helping ter look after yer both, I'd have had ter give up work. Then where would we have been?'

Maggie shrugged, she'd no idea where they would have been.

'Had it not been fer Danny,' he went on, sullenly. 'Your mother would've been with us now. I tell yer lass, if I had to choose between yer mother and Danny, I'd choose yer mother every time. That lad's been nowt but trouble since the day he were born.'

They walked along for a while until his anger at Danny subsided. Maggie squeezed his hand, prompting him to resume their conversation.

'I met her at a whist drive and dance,' he recalled. 'Did I ever tell yer that? She were a smashing dancer, but the worst card player I've ever come across.'

'Is that why you taught me how to play cards?' asked Maggie, curiously.

Johnnie shrugged. 'No idea, never thought about it that way.' He and Maggie had had many an entertaining evening playing

Rummy, Knockout Whist, Brag, Pontoon and Poker. For a ten year old she was amazingly proficient, especially at Poker.

'She trumped my ace,' he said.

'She didn't!' exclaimed Maggie, who knew what a cardinal breach of card etiquette this was.

Johnnie smiled. 'She partnered me at Whist, I put an ace down and she trumped it . . . I wouldn't care, but at the end of the night she won a prize. I couldn't believe it.'

'She was smashing wasn't she?' Maggie's question was rhetorical.

'Yes, love. Yer could say that. She were the best thing that happened to me.'

Maggie looked up at him. Tears appeared in his eyes, as if produced by her squeezing his hand. She relaxed her grip and looked away. Her dad crying in the street was one of the most embarrassing things she could think of. He did it a lot lately. In the street, at home in bed. She and Danny often heard him in the next room. It's to be hoped he didn't do it at work. Crikey, that would be embarrassing.

Danny looked up as Roy came charging through the gate into the back yard. He paused before he went into the house and farted lustily, grinning down at Danny and Mavis.

'Better out than in,' he announced.

'Pooh, yer mucky pig!' complained Mavis.

Danny laughed. He liked Roy. Mavis's big brother was always doing things that made Danny laugh. Mavis followed him into the house to complain about his bad manners. She knew such complaints would fall upon deaf ears, nevertheless, she felt she had to tell on him. Roy had left the wooden gate swinging open, contrary to his mam's instructions. Danny looked around to see if anyone was watching, then stepped through the gate into the street.

Brenda Venison was doing handstands up against the wall with her skirt tucked into her navy blue knickers and Alice Greenhough was skipping and singing out loud in time to the whirling rope.

The game of cricket was now in full swing at the bottom end, someone having lugged a dustbin out into the street to use as a wicket. As there was never more than one bat available for these matches, the lone batsman was often stranded at the wrong end of the cobbled pitch, having made an odd number of runs. His journey back to his crease would be under RST rules – 'Run to Save Time'. It was incumbent upon him to announce his intention, otherwise he left himself open to a run out.

Barry Knowles, the lone batsman, had made one run and was about to shout RST, when the escaping Danny collided with him, thus distracting him. Caught between wickets without claiming RST amnesty, a quick thinking opponent removed the dustbin lid while holding the ball.

'Howzat!' claimed half a dozen happy cricketers.

As there was no umpire to adjudicate, an argument ensued. Barry Knowles held Danny responsible and grabbed him by the scruff of his neck, almost choking him.

'That were your fault . . . yer little wazzock!'

'Lemme go!' shouted, Danny. 'I haven't done nowt.'

'Lerrim go, Knowlsie! It were nowt ter do with him. Yer out fair an' square,' yelled the gleeful opposition.

As Danny shook himself free, the ageing tennis ball, doubling as a cricket ball, came bouncing towards him, having been thrown back to the bowler by the wicket keeper. Danny, without thinking, took a wild kick at it, sending it soaring into Mr Brown's back yard. A bad place for a ball to go. Mr Brown never gave balls back.

A howl of anger came from the cricketers. All of them much bigger than Danny, who set off running as fast as his grimy little legs could carry him. Out of the street, into Carrcroft Road and as far as he could go before he was out of breath. He looked around but no one was pursuing him. Good, he'd keep on going. Bound to lead to somewhere. Maybe I'll try to whistle, Roy Bradford can whistle. He can belch as well. Danny grinned at the memory of Roy Bradford speaking as he belched. Danny hoped that when he got to Roy's age he'd be just as talented. A tram rattled past, Danny waved at the driver, who waved back. That's what I'll do, I'll wave at all the tram drivers and see if they'll wave back.

He now had plenty to do. What with whistling, belching and waving at tram drivers. The midday sun was warm on his legs. His knee-length trousers had their own shoulder straps, fastened to buttons on his trousers. But one button was missing, causing the trousers to hang lopsidedly, like a shopping bag with one of its straps broken. Tomorrow he'd be smarter. Tomorrow was

Whit Sunday. Maggie reckoned their dad had bought them new Whitsy outfits for Whit Sunday, whatever Whit Sunday was. It was obligatory that kids got new clothes at Whitsuntide, for rumour had it that if you didn't wear new clothes at Whitsuntide, 'The crows'll job on yer.'

Danny strode out happily, right to the end of Muscroft Street where it joined Seaforth Road, kicking at stones with his sandals. He wished he had his proper shoes on, they were better for kicking. He paused and read the word 'Jesus' on the sign outside the Methodist chapel. He couldn't make out all the other words. He recognised the word 'Jesus' from Sunday School, which he hated. He'd be starting big school soon, like Maggie, only she wouldn't be there, because she'd passed her skolship, whatever that was. He examined his reflection in a shoe shop window, pulling faces at himself. His mousy hair was shaved an inch above his ears, then left to its own devices, which, in Danny's case, meant sticking out at all angles. Satisfied with what he saw, he moved on. The coping on a low wall made an ideal road for his car. He ran it along, accompanied by loud revving and gear changing, until the wall stepped down, then it took off like a Spitfire (his favourite plane), looping the loop before landing on the lower coping. The wall ended and Danny turned right, as it didn't involve him crossing the main road. He knew he'd get in trouble if he crossed the main road on his own. After a few more turnings and darting across a road almost devoid of traffic, he found himself going down a steep hill with iron railings at the side of the footpath. Danny had picked up a stick earlier on in his journey in readiness for such an eventuality and ran it along the railings as he walked, producing a most satisfactory sound. His birthday was turning out all right, he'd even managed a whistle of sorts. By the time he got home, he'd be able to do it properly. Mavis Bradford couldn't whistle yet, and she was loads older than him. Two older boys approached, and blocked his path. Not as old as Maggie, but a lot older than him.

'Them's our railings. Who told you yer could rattle our railings?' The belligerent questioner was the smaller of the two. Danny looked at them uncertainly.

'Nobody,' replied Danny.

'What's yer name, kid?' demanded one.

'Danny Fish.'

'How old are yer?'

'Four. It's me birthday today.'

'Liar!'

Danny didn't know how to respond to this. He remained glued to the spot, trying not to look up at the scowling faces of the two boys.

'Have yer got any money?'

'No.'

'Liar!'

'If we search yer and we find any money we're gonna do yer in!' threatened one.

'I'll tell our kid. He'll come an' bray yer both,' lied Danny, uncertainly.

One of them pushed him backwards. 'Yer what? . . . I bet yer haven't got a brother. Anyway, if he comes near us we'll bray him!'

The smaller, more belligerent boy, spotted the Dinky toy protruding from his pocket.

'What that in yer pocket?'

'Nowt.'

They had him on the ground in a flash, kneeling on his back and removing the toy car from his pocket.

Danny struggled free and set off running again, down the hill as fast he could. The boys ran after him, hard on his heels. A door was open, he ran inside. The boys stopped outside, jeering at him from the doorstep.

'What's all this?'

A large woman appeared from the next room. And ran past Danny to the door, shaking a fat fist.

'Clear off yer little bleeders, afore I rattle yer bleedin' ear'oles!'

The boys ran off, laughing and hooting. Danny tried to dash out, but was stopped in his tracks by a hand grabbing his collar.

'Not so fast, young feller me lad! What were yer doin' in my house hey? Bloody thievin'? I'll tan yer little arse for yer.' She raised her hand. Danny burst into tears, softening the woman's resolve. The hand came back down and ruffled his hair.

'Yer mam wants her head seeing to, letting yer roam the streets wi' them two. They're both wrong uns yer know.'

Danny nodded because it seemed the right thing to do.

21

'What was it yer were after?'

'I weren't after nowt, missis.'

'Bloody typical o' them two, sending you in ter do their thievin' for 'em.'

'I weren't pinchin' nowt, missis. They were after me.'

She looked down at him and shook her head. 'Tell yer what,' she decided. 'You promise me you'll have nowt no more ter do with 'em and I'll not report yer ter t' bobbies. How's that?'

Danny nodded. Having nowt no more to do with them sounded a good deal to him. He looked at the open door warily.

'Would yer like some pop?'

'Yes please, missis.'

'At least yer've got manners, I'll say that for yer.' She took a bottle of lemonade from a cupboard and poured some into a mug with a picture of the king and queen on it.

'Sit yourself down lad. Yer look as if yer don't belong ter no one. What's yer name?'

Danny sat in an old and worn leather armchair, with a crocheted antimacassar over the back and matching arm covers, one with a built-in brass ashtray. He took the cup of lemonade from her. 'Danny Fish,' he replied. 'It's me birthday today, missis.'

'Well drink yer lemonade, Danny Fish, then bugger off home . . . and happy birthday.'

Danny looked around him. A wire mesh fire guard stood in front of the empty fireplace. In the hearth was a brass fireside companion, complete with a poker, brush, shovel and tongs, all highly polished. Much more impressive than the steel poker and wooden brush in the hearth at home. A brown Bakelite radio stood silently on a much bigger dresser than the one in Danny's front room. Carefully arranged around the radio were more framed photographs than Danny had ever seen in his life before. Mostly of soldiers in uniform. One of a man and woman in wedding clothes and one of a small boy about Danny's age. She saw him looking and picked up the photo of the boy, bringing it to show him.

'This is my Jackie when he were a lad.'

Danny studied the serious sepia face on the photograph, wondering how the boy got to be sitting on a stool in his best clothes, right in the middle of some mountains. He chose not to ask this question.

'Is he grown up now, missis?'

'He were killed in the war, lad. Him and me husband, both. He were only eighteen were our Jackie.'

'Oh,' said Danny, who didn't know what else to say. It would never have occurred to him to say sorry. He knew that people who went to war often got killed. So it was nothing to make a fuss about.

The woman sat down in the other chair, gazing at the photograph. Eventually she closed her eyes, as if the memory was too painful for her.

Danny finished his drink and went to the door, peering round it cautiously. They were still there, on the corner. Running at a gas lamp and trying to kick it into life. Danny went back and sat in the chair. The woman was snoring now, which amused him. He closed his own eyes and was soon fast asleep.

The search was already under way when Maggie and her dad got back. 'Honest, Johnnie, I hadn't turned me back two minutes and he were gone,' said Vera, lamely. 'We've looked all over, but we can't find him nowhere. Denis is still out looking for him.'

Johnnie nodded, accepting her apology. 'He can be a little sod, can our Danny. He'll turn up.'

He was more annoyed than upset. He'd have to go out and look for the little pest now. What a day to disappear – as if he didn't have enough to think about on such a day.

'It's our Roy's fault,' grumbled Vera. Roy had made the strategic mistake of standing beside his mother as she absolved herself of blame. She swiped him across the head, knocking him off the back step.

'I told you umpteen bloody times not ter leave that gate open,' she ranted.

Maggie stood beside her dad, her worry at her brother's disappearance lessened by his apparent lack of concern.

'Will he be all right, Dad?'

'Not when I get me hands on him, he won't! I'll take me damn belt to him when he gets home.'

Denis walked in through the gate and stood beside his wife.

'He's not turned up then?' he inquired.

Vera shook her head.

'Beats me where he's got to,' he said despairingly.

23

'I'll beat *him* when I get me hands on him,' snapped Johnnie. 'Putting people to all this trouble.'

'I reckon it's his birthday today,' Denis remarked, conversationally.

'Among other things,' said Johnnie.

'Did yer get him a nice present then?' continued Denis, innocently. He knew what he was doing.

'He doesn't deserve no presents, runnin' off like that,' replied Johnnie gruffly.

'I'd have bought him summat meself if I'd known you weren't goin' ter buy him nowt.'

'You mind yer own business before I mind it for yer,' snapped Johnnie.

Maggie was scared and shocked. She'd never known her dad be so rude before. Johnnie grabbed her hand and dragged her out of the yard. Vera pushed Denis back into the house and slammed the door. Roy stood there, amazed at what he'd just witnessed. His dad and Mr Fish falling out. By the time he'd suitably dressed up the story, blows would have been exchanged.

Danny woke up and blinked his eyes at his unexpected surroundings. It took him a few seconds to realise where he was. The woman was still asleep, snoring loudly. Danny went to the door and looked outside, the boys had gone, good. He looked back at the woman and wondered if he ought to wait until she woke up, before he left. What was the right thing to do? He heard a tram going past at the bottom of the street. That was it. He'd get on a tram and go home. At least them kids wouldn't dare try and get him on a tram. The conductor wouldn't let them. He'd need some tram fare though, at least a penny, maybe more. Sometimes they charged you twopence. There was a small vase on the mantelpiece. If it was anything like the vase on the mantelpiece at home, the rent money would be in it. It was too high for him to reach, so he pulled a chair across to stand on. Even so he had to get up on his tiptoes to reach it. He got his fingers to it and eased it to the edge of the shelf, trying to catch it as it fell. But he was never any good at catching. It smashed in the hearth, making a terrible racket.

His eyes were glued on the woman, willing her not to wake up. She jumped at the noise, snorted a few times, blinked her eyes, then went back to sleep. Danny breathed again and looked down. There was a ten shilling note and some change. A tanner, a three-penny bit and two pennies. The note was grown up money and therefore valueless to him. He picked up the coins and quietly left the woman snoring in her chair.

The street was empty of children. Most of them would be at the Saturday matinée by now, cheering Hopalong Cassidy and laughing at The Three Stooges. They were Danny's favourites, better than Laurel and Hardy. A couple of women were talking to each other across a back-yard gate. Headscarfed heads nodding and fleshy arms folded across pristine pinnies. They glanced disapprovingly at Danny. He was a small boy and therefore up to no good. He turned his gaze groundwards and slouched past them, remembering another game. You had to avoid the cracks and joints in the flags. Tread on a crack, marry a rat, tread on a line, marry a swine. A little further on someone had chalked out hopscotch squares. Danny picked up a stone and threw it on to the end square. He successfully hopped to the end and picked up the stone while standing on one foot but, as usual, didn't manage to jump around without falling over. He tossed the stone up in the air and volleyed it with his foot right across the road into someone's yard, clanging on a dustbin. The feeling of triumph he experienced at such a kick far outweighed the pain in his foot. Never volley stones in sandals, a valuable lesson learned.

The smell of fish and chips reminded him that breakfast was a long time ago. Dalton's Cornflakes and sterilised milk. He hated sterilised milk. Roy Bradford said it tasted like monkey sick. Danny followed his nose to a fish shop.

'Can I 'ave some chips please, missis?'

The top of his head was beneath the level of the counter and the woman had to lean over to see where the voice was coming from.

'Scraps?'

'Yes please, missis.'

'Salt an' vinegar?' she asked.

'Yes please.'

'That'll be twopence, love.'

He laid all his money on the counter for her to take what she wanted. She took the two pennies and made him stick the other ninepence in his pocket.

'Take that straight back ter yer mam,' she advised.

With a mouthful of chips he skipped all the way to the LCT tram stop, and stood beside an old man, to wait for the tram home. The man looked down at him. Danny smiled benignly back and wondered if he should say anything, perhaps offer the man a chip. Maybe not, anyway, he'd nearly eaten them all now.

The tram arrived and three women got off, all weighed down with shopping bags. Danny darted in front of the old man and ran upstairs, hoping to get a front seat. The upper deck was deserted, apart from a young couple on the back seat with their arms around each other, jerking apart at the unwelcome appearance of Danny. He ignored them and made his way to the front. Sitting on the wooden, slatted seat and peering excitedly through the window. The tram set off and the conductor came upstairs and looked around to locate his new passenger, tutting when he realised he'd have to walk the full length of the tram just to collect a half fare.

'Terminus?' he inquired. It was a good guess at Danny's destination as the tram route terminated in a couple of stops. Danny didn't know quite where Terminus was, but he'd heard of it before so it must be near home. He nodded and held out his sixpence.

'Have yer nowt less, young 'un? It's only an a'penny.'

Danny dug into his pocket and brought out the threepenny bit. The conductor took it, clicked out a green halfpenny ticket and gave Danny twopence ha'penny change. Danny examined this with delight. It looked a lot more substantial than the coin he'd swapped it for . . . and he'd got a tram ride into the bargain. Five minutes later, the tram arrived at the terminus outside the Chapelhill cinema. Danny looked through the window, but didn't recognise anything. He walked up and down the empty tram, looking through all the windows. A horse and cart clopped by beneath him, driven by an unkempt looking man shouting 'Ragbone' in a funny way that didn't actually sound like 'Ragbone'. He could see right into the window of a fishmonger's shop, with row after row of fish with open mouths and staring eyes. Danny didn't much like that. The sweet shop next door was better, sherbet and liquorice were his favourites. He liked bubble gum as well, but Maggie said he wasn't allowed to have any because if he swallowed it, he'd choke and die. The sun, magnified through the window, raised beads of sweat on his nose. He sat back in his front seat, uncertain what to do.

26

A new conductor clattered up the stairs and squatted beside him, opening up the destination box and winding a handle round as he looked down through the window at the driver standing in the road in front of the tram and calling up to him.

'Bit more, bit more . . . right, that's it.'

The conductor nodded at Danny, then hurried back downstairs. In the road below, he could see the driver holding a long pole up to the tram roof. Moving the pick-up the other way round, in readiness for a reverse in direction. A few other passengers came up, most of them immediately lighting up cigarettes. A man came and sat behind him, lighting up a pipe and blowing a cloud of smoke Danny's way, making him cough. The tram moved off once again, backwards this time. Danny thought he enjoyed this as much as going forwards. In fact it was better, seeing the road moving away from him. Roy Bradford once told him he'd put a six-inch nail across the tram lines and the tram had come off the lines and crashed into a shop and killed loads of people. He'd made Danny promise not to tell anyone or he'd be hung for murder. Danny began to worry that Roy might have placed some six inch nails across the lines today. Then his worry subsided as he realised it was Saturday and Roy would be at the pictures and probably wouldn't have time for putting six-inch nails on tram lines. So that was okay.

'Fares please.'

The new conductor was hovering above him. Danny held out his sixpence once again, hoping for another handful of coins.

'Where to young un?'

Danny was stumped, then he had an inspiration. 'Terminus please mister.'

'Half fare . . . twopence ha'penny.'

The conductor clicked out a red ticket and a green ticket and gave Danny three pennies and a halfpenny change. Danny dropped the change in his pocket along with his twopence ha'penny and rattled it all, enjoying the sound it made. The tram clattered towards the centre of Leeds and on towards the southern outskirts. Danny was having a great birthday.

The police had been reluctantly notified by Johnnie and had a car searching the streets for his son. Johnnie had decided to wait at home to see if Danny turned up there. He drew the curtains to keep out the pervasive sunshine. Today wasn't a day for sunshine. God help that little brat when he turned up. He looked at the clock on the mantelpiece. Four-thirty. Danny had been gone for four hours now, he smiled grimly to himself. Should be back any minute now. His empty belly'll see to that.

Maggie wasn't so sure. A remark made by one of the adult searchers had driven an arrow of dread into her.

'He's been gone a long time now. I reckon somebody's taken him.'

The man who said it, saw Maggie looking at him, and turned away, wishing he'd kept his thoughts to himself. The police said they'd put it out on the six o'clock news if he hadn't turned up by then. Maggie, Roy, Brenda Venison and Kevin Walsh had extended their search into Chapelhill. None of the kids in the street had gone to the pictures that Saturday afternoon. Searching for Danny was a much more exciting thing to do. Except for Maggie. A lump of lead was beginning to form in her stomach. It was her baby brother's birthday and her dad hadn't even bought him so much as a card. On her tenth birthday she'd had a party, with everyone bringing presents.

Danny got off at the terminus. It was adjacent to a recreation ground with swings and a slide and a long boat and pork pie roundabout. One of the swings came free and Danny raced for it, narrowly beating a mother and son who'd apparently been waiting for quite a while. The mother berated him as he worked it into action, forcing her to step away and drag her son to another vacated swing. His was the only swing not being pushed by an adult and the other kids were well aware of this and jealous of his independence. Danny added to their jealousy by swinging higher than any of them.

'He'll come off, just you mark my words!' was the hopeful prophecy of one mother.

'Shouldn't be allowed out on his own at his age. He's not the size of two penn'orth o' bleedin' copper.'

Danny heard none of this, he was in heaven. After half an hour he could see the long boat filling up with a gang of older kids. One of them, a tall, spotty lad of around fourteen, with a Vaselined quiff and a snake belt holding up a pair of trousers that his mother assumed he'd one day grow into, temporarily vacated the much sought after back seat to display his finery to a girl, as the rest of the places filled up. Danny leapt off the swing, ran across the cinders to the long boat and jumped on to the empty back seat while the boy wasn't looking. The ride moved into action. The older boy turned round, ready to impress the girl by jumping on when it was moving, only to find Danny in his place.

'Hey! That's my place,' he yelled angrily. 'I'll do yer when yer gerroff, young 'un.'

But it was Danny's birthday and he was oblivious to all threats. He was pressing and pulling with the best of them. He'd been on one before, but not with such big kids. They were all shouting with excitement, urging each other to more daring heights. At the other end from Danny, a fat-legged girl of around fifteen was standing up, holding on to the bars, working the ride with her feet and yelling encouragement to the twelve or so riders. They all responded with synchronised pushing and pulling and singing, 'Yo ho heave ho'. Higher and higher it went, faster and faster. Louder and louder went the screams of excitement. People were gathering round to watch. They'd never seen the long boat going as high as this before. 'Yo ho heave ho'. It was the best time of Danny's life. He didn't care if his dad hadn't bought him a birthday present, or if he'd smacked him for spilling the milk and made him cry. And them kids could keep his car if they wanted. Anyway, Maggie would get it back for him when he told her. She wasn't scared of no one wasn't Maggie. He wished Maggie was here to see him now. She'd be standing up like the girl at the other end, shouting louder than anyone. His dad would be proud of him as well, probably wished he hadn't smacked him if he could see him now. Playing with the big kids. Suddenly a boy in front of Danny lost his grip and fell backwards, knocking Danny out of his seat. He bounced on the ground, still laughing and got to his feet just as the ride came back and hit him on his head with tremendous force. Danny was dead before the ambulance arrived.

Chapter Four

April 1956

Grace Kelly married Prince Rainier on Maggie's fifteenth birthday, which conveniently fell in the Easter holidays. This entitled her to leave Leeds Central High School for Girls. Her leaving was premature and would have horrified her teachers had they known of her intent. Bright girls like Maggie were few and far between and everyone had high hopes for her. Except her dad.

The five years since Danny's death had taken their toll. His job as an instrument mechanic at Openshawe's was the first casualty. Demoted from popular chargehand soon after Jean's death, his work became slapdash, his timekeeping atrocious and his attitude towards his workmates sullen. When he was called into the office and handed his 'cards and coppers' for one misdemeanour too many, no one mourned his departure. Various jobs followed. Window cleaner ('Yer'll get no brass until yer come back and do me corners'), bus conductor (sacked for nipping into the pub at the terminus), builder's labourer ('Nice of yer to turn up . . . we could have done with you at eight o'clock when everyone else started').

Jobs abounded in Leeds in the mid-fifties. There was no excuse for anyone to be out of work. South of the river Aire in Hunslet and Stourton and surrounding districts, close to the railways and canals, lay the industrial pulse of Leeds. Pounding with the sound of iron and steelworks, copperworks, light and heavy engineering, foundries, precast concrete works, brickworks, printing, brewing and manufacturing of all kinds. And just over the river to the north were the factories producing food, clothing, footwear, electrical goods, optical instruments, ice-cream and jam, etcetera. Everyone was working but Johnnie Fish.

Maggie's morning and evening paper rounds had supplemented the meagre family income which, more often than not, was dole money. But it was on the cards that she'd have to leave school at the earliest opportunity to earn a proper wage.

If anything, Johnnie's own self-knowledge made things worse. Ignorance of one's own deficiencies, if not an attractive trait, is often a great preserver of sanity, but Johnnie knew exactly what he was. The void left by Jean, and the guilt and self loathing in the aftermath of Danny's death left him a shell of a man. What would Jean have thought of him – treating her son in that way?

Maggie kept him on the verge of sanity. Kept him alive when he'd contemplated the ultimate get out. But that would have been too easy, he knew he didn't deserve the easy way out after what he'd done. He had to stay alive. Take his punishment for the death of his son. Unfortunately, his self-loathing didn't fire him with any great desire to earn a decent living, and consequently didn't preclude him from allowing Maggie to leave school to help support him. Johnnie's rehabilitation into society had a long way to go.

'Is that it then?' he inquired as she plonked her school satchel down on the table at the end of the Easter term. He looked at her, as if for reassurance that all was well with her, and that she didn't regret her decision to leave school.

'I'll be okay, Dad,' she said. 'There's some jobs going at Burton's. Janet Jardine started there at Christmas, she's bringing home nearly three pounds a week.'

She was hoping he'd give her a fierce argument and work out a plan to enable her to stay on at school and take her O Levels.

''Course yer will love. Good firm Burton's. Yer don't want to be hanging round a school playground at your age.'

'I won't be able to sing in the school choir though. I was looking forward to that. It's the Harrogate Choir Festival next month. I'm supposed to be singing a solo.'

'Aye lass, shame that. Still, we can't have everything can we?'

'I suppose not.'

He saw the disappointment on her face and wasn't sure what to do. He couldn't remember the last time he'd hugged her, or even had a conversation as long as this with her.

31

'Come here lass,' he held out his arms. She went to him readily and held him tightly.

'I'm a useless sod, aren't I?' he said, perhaps expecting an argument.

'Yes Dad, you are.' She saw no point in glossing over the truth.

'It's just that it doesn't seem ter get any better. I might have got over yer mam by now, but I can't get over what happened to our Danny.'

'It wasn't your fault, Dad.' She'd told him this a thousand times.

'There's no point telling me that lass. He was my lad, mine and yer mother's ... and he died on his own ... on his birthday. And I treated him like shit. Sorry lass.' He was apologising for swearing, not for the way he'd treated her brother.

'Our Danny was no angel, Dad,' consoled Maggie. 'And from what I can make out he had quite a good time on his last day.'

Unknown to Johnnie, she, Roy, Kevin and Brenda had taken it upon themselves to trace Danny's movements on his last day on Earth. Starting with the two bullies, who responded to a reward notice on Chapelhill Primary School wall, they then tracked him down to the woman in the house and repaid the eleven pence he'd stolen. The woman had responded somewhat morbidly by giving them her Coronation mug, the last thing Danny had ever drunk from. On balance, Maggie decided that a Coronation mug wasn't the sort of thing she wanted to remember Danny by, so she offered it to the other two, who both wanted nothing to do with such a macabre item. Maggie threw it in a dustbin.

On hearing the woman's account of events, Roy and Kevin went back to the bullies and demanded return of the shilling reward money. The bullies paid up with great reluctance, even returning the stolen Dinky toy which, when handed over to Maggie, reduced her to tears for the umpteenth time. They'd even tracked down the gang on the long boat, who gave a glowing account of Danny's bravado. Little Danny Fish had gone out with a laugh and a bang. More than most ever did.

Maggie had never told her dad any of this. Perhaps she felt he didn't deserve it.

'I never told you did I,' she said.

'Told me what?'

'About what our Danny got up to on his last day.'

'Oh aye? And what do you know about it?'

'I know he was laughing when he died.'

She told him all she knew and drew a smile of admiration from her dad.

'I don't know whether that makes me feel better or worse. Fancy me having a son like that. He was a grand little lad, wasn't he?'

'He was Dad. And I'll tell you what. He thought the world of you.'

'That's not helping, Maggie.'

'Sorry.'

Chapter Five

She guessed it was her dad's way of spoiling her. She didn't
particularly want to go, but then again she didn't want to
disappoint him.

Friday night at Hope Street Working Men's Club was the best
night of the week. A comic had been booked and you needed to
get there early to get a table. Johnnie and Maggie, Vera and Denis
Bradford and Roy and Mavis, managed to commandeer a table
near the stage and not far from the hatch where pie and peas would
be served. The concert room had been recently refurbished with
plastic-tiled floors, apart from a square dance floor of wooden
parquet tiles in front of the stage. All the tables were in modern-
looking formica with plastic-backed chairs, easy for wiping down.
On the eau-de-nil wall, a photograph of Aneurin Bevan glared
across at the young queen on the primrose yellow wall opposite.
Beside the stage stood the concert secretary's box, from where he
presided over the events of the evening, like a parson in a pulpit.
Beginning with the announcement of any births, marriages and
deaths. Of course, any deaths would always be announced
immediately prior to the comic coming on, just to add an extra
challenge and to ensure that a collection box would be rattling
round the club during his act. He would issue dire warnings to
deaf ears and threats of banishment for repeated misbehaviour
from club miscreants, of which there were many. He would call
out the Bingo numbers, introduce the turns and, as a member of
the committee, would be eligible for a share of the all financial
fiddles, which were looked upon as fair remuneration for its
unpaid labour.

On top of the concert secretary's box stood a Dansette record player, wired into the two stageside speakers. The concert secretary had delegated the provision of background music to his assistant and heir apparent, a chubby young man, heavily Brylcreemed and festooned with acne, who stood by, waiting for Eddie Calvert's 'Oh Mein Papa' to finish, before replacing it with something more up to date. Ruby Murray singing 'Softly, Softly'.

'Our Maggie can sing better than her,' boasted Johnnie.

'Shurrup Dad,' complained an embarrassed Maggie.

'I'm only saying what's true. *You've* had proper lessons. She sounds as if she needs ter blow her nose all t' time.'

Everyone laughed and Maggie thought this a small price to pay for the re-emergence of her dad into society. Maybe after tonight, he'd think again about her leaving school.

The voices around her were working class like hers. The field of conversation restricted by a narrow breadth of knowledge. The humour coarse and obvious. Maggie felt she'd never fit in. Or to be more truthful, she didn't want to fit in. The fact that this might make her some kind of intellectual snob didn't bother her. There was a hardness about some of the women, not all of them, but most. Certainly with the older ones, a coarseness even. The bloom and vigour of youth hadn't lasted long. Maybe some had been fired with ambition once, but they'd all too quickly allowed their spirit to be crushed and resigned themselves to the lifestyle they'd been allotted. Maggie didn't want to end up like this. But if she left school now what chance did she have? Burton's trouser room? Married to some local lad; house full of snotty-nosed kids . . . and the highlight of her life, Ashburton Working Men's Club on a Friday night. Sod that!

Charlie Chipperfield, the young pianist, arrived on stage, plonked his pint down on top of the piano and began to tinkle out a medley he played every Friday night. A few people began singing, but tailed off when they realised it wasn't going to catch on. Cyril took up station behind his drums and Len, supposed to be doubling on sax and clarinet, thought he'd begin the evening by taking his teeth out and singing 'There'll Be Bluebirds Over the White Cliffs Of Dover'.

'Put a sock in it Len! Yer mekkin' me beer go flat' and other remarks prompted him to abandon this and complain, 'Yer don't appreciate good singers you lot.'

A howl of derision had him hurriedly replacing his teeth and picking up his clarinet. And Friday evening was under way.

Jimmy Diamond, the comedian, did his first set and went off to desultory applause. He'd worked in the club before, on several occasions, and hadn't bothered to change his routine. No one seemed to mind, he delivered his well-worn gags above a rising babble of voices, before dashing off to get to the front of the pea and pie queue. Bingo was in its infancy and as yet people hadn't acquired the expertise to cope with more than one card at a time. One card per person was allotted and Billy Bainbridge, the concert secretary, had the Bingo Lingo off pat. He rarely called out the actual numbers, the audience did this for him.

'Two little ducks.'

'Twenty two . . . quack, quack, quack.'

'Was she worth it?'

'Seven and six, seventy-six.'

'When you were sweet.'

'Sixteen.'

'Old age pension.'

'Sixty-five.'

'House!'

Vera Bradford's triumphant shout drew moans from those with just one number left to cancel. The card was checked and the main prize of four pounds seven and six duly handed over. She gave the seven and six to Denis, enough for two rounds of drinks including lemonade and crisps for the kids. The drink was having its effect on Johnnie, who was beginning to talk loudly, and it made Maggie feel uncomfortable. He went over to the ancient concert secretary and had a whispered conversation with him. Both heads turning occasionally in Maggie's direction. Johnnie came back with a conspiratorial smile on his face.

'What have you been up to, Johnnie Fish?' asked Vera suspiciously.

He tapped the side of his nose by way of telling her to mind her own business. The band arrived back on stage and the concert secretary climbed laboriously into his box.

'Lay an' gennermen. Best of order PLEASE!'

The noise subsided to a hum.

'Lay an' gennermen. We have in the audience a young lady with the voice of an angel. At least that's what her dad reckons.

Mind you, he's had a bit ter drink, so he'll tell me owt.' He looked around, grinning, as though demanding a deserved ripple of laughter. Which he didn't get.

Maggie was beginning to feel really uncomfortable. She was looking daggers at her dad, who had adopted an innocent expression.

'So, what do yer say, lay an' gennermen? Do we want to hear this young lady sing?'

'Yesss!' came the reply from a dozen or so voices, whose owners hadn't a clue who he was talking about, but anything was better than hearing Jimmy Diamond's jokes for the umpteenth time.

Billy Bainbridge looked across at Maggie, confirming her worst fears.

'Lay an' gennermen, put yer hands together for Maggie Fish!'

Maggie sat rooted to her seat. Wild horses weren't going to drag her on to that stage. She loathed and detested her dad for doing this to her. Embarrassing her in front of all these people. Johnnie stood up and took Maggie's hand. She resisted ferociously, forcing him to let go. He looked round and shrugged at the concert secretary, who picked up his microphone.

'Lay an' gennermen. She's a bit shy is the lass, she's only fifteen, so let's give her a bit of encouragement.'

Shouts of 'Come on, Maggie lass,' persuaded her to her feet at last. She climbed uncertainly on to the stage to loud applause and walked over to Charlie, the sympathetic pianist. A hurried discussion followed, before Maggie walked slowly over to a waiting microphone in the centre of the stage and looked nervously down at the hundred or so expectant faces gazing back at this shy schoolgirl. Her chestnut hair was held away from her face by a hairslide. She wore a dark green cardigan over a white blouse and grey pleated skirt. Part of her school uniform and the smartest clothes she had. In the relative anonymity of the audience it wasn't so bad, but not up here on the stage.

The audience saw her differently. To the women she was no threat. A mousy schoolgirl who might be able to sing a bit. The men noticed her bust pushing through her blouse, her pretty face, devoid of makeup, nice legs, what they could see of them, and the rest of her, tall for her age and slim where it mattered.

Charlie played an introduction, she opened her mouth to sing, but missed her cue. She turned and gave Charlie an apologetic shrug, he winked and nodded her in to her opening song: 'You Belong To Me'.

She sang of Pyramids along the Nile and tropic islands and the market place in Old Algiers. Reminding her boyfriend to remember who he belonged to when he was looking at all these sights. The Jo Stafford song had long been a favourite of wives and girlfriends of National Servicemen posted overseas, many of whom were in the audience. The hum of noise disappeared when it became obvious that not only could Maggie sing, but she had something special. They'd heard enough club singers to spot this. She was drawing tears from the old and admiration from the young, who wished they could sing like that. Johnnie sat back and bathed in the reflected glory. He knew Maggie wouldn't stop at one song, she never did at home.

She took her bow to thunderous applause. Even if she wanted to, the audience weren't going to let her go. Another discussion with Charlie and she returned to sing a medley of three, 'Arrivederci Darling', 'Pickin' a Chicken' and 'O Mein Papa', which had the desired effect on Johnnie, who had now been forgiven by his daughter, who was having the time of her life.

Having now sung every song she knew all the way through, she stood hesitantly on the stage not knowing how to leave. Then she turned to Charlie for help. A whispered word in his ear had him approaching the microphone.

'Maggie only knows one more song, so once she's done that she's finished – all right?'

The agreement from the audience was grudging. The comic, unhappy at having to follow this with another well-worn routine, was negotiating with Billy Bainbridge to let him off his second spot. Maggie looked at her dad uncertainly, not sure of his reaction to this, her favourite song, 'Danny Boy', which she never sang at home.

The opening notes rang out with a quality that reduced the audience to tears. Most of the audience knew about her young brother, Johnnie's son, and were struck by the poignancy of it. This was to have been her solo at the Harrogate Festival. After the intro, Charlie instinctively faded his playing to nothing, the drummer and clarinetist followed suit. Leaving her to sing *a cappella*. She half turned to the band and and lowered her eyebrows, questioning. Charlie smiled and folded his arms. He just wanted to listen. So did everyone.

Many eyes were on Johnnie, whose own eyes were glued to his daughter. The quality and clarity and ease with which she sang overwhelmed him. He'd no idea she was as good as this. Then the emotion of the song itself hit him, and memories of Danny flooded back. He cupped his head between his hands to hide the tears that would never go away.

As the final lyrics died away, there was a hypnotic silence, broken by thunderous applause. Everyone on their feet, clapping, stamping, banging on tables. Johnnie sat amongst it all, overcome with joy and grief and Tetley's Bitter. A dangerous combination for a man who drinks fighting beer.

Maggie returned to her seat and the congratulations of everyone around her. Johnnie smiled, his eyes dry now, but their redness still betraying what had gone before.

'Okay, Dad?' she asked.

'Never better, love. I've never heard nowt like that in me life.' He turned to Denis and Vera. 'I told yer she were better than Ruby Murray.'

'Yer bloody right an' all, Johnnie,' agreed Vera.

'Language, Vera, in front of the kids,' admonished Denis. He grinned at Maggie. 'Yer don't want to be botherin' wi' Burton's wi' a voice like yours, Maggie love. Yer can make a week's wages in one night.'

Maggie nodded. The prospect sounded attractive. She'd certainly enjoyed her quarter of an hour of glory and to be paid for it would be a real bonus. The comedian came and sat down uninvited.

'Are yer not doing another spot, Jimmy?' asked Denis.

'In a bit. I want 'em ter get over t'excitement o' this young lady first. I'd have got out of it if I could, but Billy Bainbridge wants his pound o' flesh. He'll dock half me money if I don't do another spot.' He looked at Maggie, the excitement still glowing in her eyes.

'Great, innit?' his question was rhetorical.

Maggie nodded, she knew what he meant. Being a professional meant that he must have been considered an outstanding talent as an amateur at some time. Although in Jimmy's case, it was a long time ago.

'If you want ter go pro, I can point you in the right direction,' he offered.

Johnnie resented this intrusion. 'She needs no help thank you,' he said loudly.

'Dad!' protested Maggie. 'He's only trying to help.'

'Nobody helps nobody in this world, without there bein' summat in it for them,' replied her dad, cynically.

Jimmy held up his hands and stood up. 'Okay, I get the message. I was only going to give her the name of a good agent, that's all.'

'That's all eh? Well, that's plenty,' snapped Johnnie.

Jimmy looked at him angrily, was about to say something, thought better of it and walked away.

There were half a dozen already in the Gents when Johnnie walked in. He stood impatiently back, waiting for a gap to appear at the urinal trough. The men in front of him were unaware of his presence.

'By hell, she's got a right voice on her 'as that lass,' commented one. Johnnie felt a surge of pride.

'She's got a right pair o' tits on her for a fifteen year old,' observed another. 'Not a bad looker neither.'

'Would yer give her one then?'

'Well, I wouldn't climb over her ter get ter my missis, I'll tell yer that.'

The red mist descended over Johnnie, who spun the man round just as he was shaking off the drops.

'That's my daughter yer talkin' about, yer dirty bastard!'

The man scarcely had time to understand why he was being hit. Johnnie's fists beat a vicious tattoo on the man's face. Unable to defend himself, as his hands were otherwise engaged, the man fell back against the urinal, blood pouring from his nose, his head banging on the tiled wall. Johnnie looked down at his handiwork, then went calmly into a cubicle to do what he came in for.

An ambulance took the man off to St James's Hospital and a police car took Johnnie to Chapelhill Police Station, where he spent the rest of the night in a cell, feeling sorry for himself.

Chapter Six

Her father was giving a slice of bread and marmalade a hostile glare as Maggie came down the following morning. He looked up and forced a guilty smile.

'Mornin' love.'

Maggie nodded her acknowledgement of his existence, went into the scullery and put the kettle on.

'I think I'll go up ter bed, love. I, er . . . I didn't get much sleep last night,' he called out.

'Really.'

'You were very good last night.'

'Right.'

She was staring at the kettle, waiting for it to boil; implying that the kettle was a more interesting thing to look at than her dad. Last night could have been a brilliant night for her, but he had to go and spoil it.

'I think you should stop drinking,' she commented, without taking her eyes off the kettle.

'What?'

She didn't repeat herself, he'd heard her all right.

'Come on, lass. If yer'd heard what that bloke were saying about yer . . .'

'You'd no need to hit him.' She appeared at the scullery door. 'When are you in court?'

'Monday morning. Don't worry. It'll only be a fine. Nowt I can't handle.'

'You wouldn't be able to handle it if I stayed on at school though, would you?'

'What? How'd you mean, love?'

41

'I mean I'd rather stay on at school and get some qualifications, than go out to work to earn money to pay your blasted fines!' Maggie had never spoken to her dad like this before. She'd always kept the adolescent rebel within her under control. But she saw no reason for this now. He wasn't worth it.

'Look, Maggie love. It's not that I don't want you ter stay on at school. It's just that I can't afford it.'

'Well, you'll have to afford it, Dad. Because I'm not leaving. Even if I have to get a part time job.'

'Part time? That's no good ter me,' grumbled Johnnie.

'What's good for you?' she mimicked. 'I'm not interested in what's good for you, Dad, only what's good for me . . . and if you want to know where I got that attitude from, just look in a mirror.'

She went back into the scullery and quite deliberately made just one cup of tea.

Her dad was in bed when a knock came on the door a couple of hours later. Her face lit up when she saw Charlie, the club pianist, on the step.

'Hello Charlie.'

He grinned. 'Morning Maggie.' He tried to look past her into the house. 'I've not come at a bad time have I?'

'Not at all . . . Rocky Marciano's in bed. Best place for him.'

Charlie laughed. 'So they let him out then?'

'Unfortunately, yes. Would you like a cup of tea or something?' she asked.

'Well, thanks, that'd be very nice.'

Maggie stood back and allowed Charlie into the back room as she put the kettle on again.

'I gather your dad sent Jimmy Diamond away with a flea in his ear,' remarked Charlie, as he sat down on one of the four dining chairs.

'You could say that. He was very rude to him was Dad.'

'Maybe it was the beer talking,' suggested Charlie.

'Maybe, maybe not.'

'I think Jimmy was only trying to help. Anyway, that's why I'm here.' He paused, not quite knowing what to say next. Maggie looked at him, waiting for him to continue.

'What is?' she inquired.

'Well, to help . . . what I'm trying to say is that if you want to sing professionally you need to get an act together.'

'I'm not sure what you mean,' she said. 'What makes you so sure I want to sing professionally?'

'Because it'd be a sin and a shame if you didn't . . . and it'd give me a kick to help get you started.'

Maggie poured the boiling water into the teapot and pondered over what he was saying as she waited for it to mash.

'So . . . you think I'm good enough do you?'

'It doesn't take a genius to see that, Maggie. Most of the club singers I've come across would give their right arm to have what you've got.'

'Oh yes, and what's that?' she handed him a cup of tea. Taking it for granted he took milk and sugar.

'Well, it's hard to explain. Some people call it a hook,' said Charlie. 'It's . . . it's something about your voice that attracts people's attention. Don't get me wrong, you've got a lovely voice and you know how to use it. But so have thousands of other singers. What they haven't got is, er . . . a hook.'

'I'm not sure what you mean. Tell me someone else who's got the hook?'

'No one round here – Peggy Lee, Eve Boswell.'

'What about Ruby Murray?' asked Maggie, curiously.

'Yes, now she's a good example. She's not a great singer, but she's got the hook. I know plenty of girls who can sing the socks off Ruby Murray.'

'But they haven't got this . . . hook.'

'Right,' he agreed.

Maggie sat opposite him at the table. He was older than her, but of the same generation. Maybe twenty, twenty-one. His face was cheerful and open, intelligent even. Handsome? Possibly, from a distance. He wore his fair hair unfashionably long, but on him it looked attractive. Tall and slim with the most beautiful hands she'd ever seen on a man.

'And you think I've got what they've got?'

'I know you have,' he replied.

'I think you're crackers.'

'I know that as well,' he grinned.

She laughed at this. Most boys she knew would have gone all defensive at such an insult, not turned it to their advantage.

'What do you suggest I do?' she asked.

'I suggest you come down to the club with me this afternoon

and run through a few songs. It's a free and easy night tonight. I'll ask Billy Bainbridge to let you have a half hour spot to yourself and I'll ring a couple of agents up to come and have a look at you.'

'Why would you do this for me?' she asked curiously.

'Pure selfishness,' he grinned. 'I want to come along for the ride. You give me your word you won't ditch me when things start to take off for you, and I'll get you started.'

Maggie sipped her tea and thought hard. Until last night she'd never even contemplated a career on the stage, but the shouts and cheers of the audience were still ringing in her ears. Few careers offered such rewards. Such job satisfaction.

She held out her hand. 'You've got a deal Mr Piano Player.'

Charlie gave a delighted grin and shook her hand vigorously.

'Just one thing,' she cautioned. 'I'm a schoolgirl. I'm staying on at school until I take my O Levels next year.'

'It's a deal,' agreed Charlie. 'It might take that long to knock you into shape.'

'And another thing,' Maggie thought she'd take advantage of the situation, being on a roll. 'I need something to wear on stage and being a poverty stricken schoolgirl, I can't afford anything.'

'A pair of jeans will do.'

'What? And cover up my gorgeous legs?'

Charlie looked down at her legs and gave an appreciative nod. 'You may have a point. I'll take you to Marks and Sparks for a skirt. I'll deduct it from our first payment.'

'And stockings and shoes.'

'Maggie, I'm a piano player. Piano players don't earn much.'

'They do when they team up with Maggie Fish . . . apparently.'

That afternoon she added 'Secret Love', 'Poppa Piccolino' and 'Sugartime' to her repertoire. Charlie took it upon himself to do all the introductions, including what he hoped were a few funny lines.

As Charlie closed the piano he smiled to himself. 'I've just thought of a name for our act,' he said, swinging round to look at Maggie.

'Go on.'

'Well, me being called Charlie Chipperfield, it's not hard to work out what my nickname is.'

'Chippy?' guessed Maggie.

'Chips,' said Charlie.

44

'We're not going to be called Fish and Chips?'

'Why not? It's a catchy name,' protested Charlie.

'I prefer Fish and Chipperfield . . . it's got, it's got a hook.'

Charlie laughed. 'Fish and Chipperfield it is then. Watch out world, here we come.'

Albert Drake swung round in his chair as Jimmy Diamond entered his office to pay Albert his agent's commission from the previous night's gig.

'How'd did it go?' asked Albert, more to make conversation than out of interest.

'Well, I were me usual brilliant self, the audience were crap though,' reported Jimmy.

'Did yer get paid?' Albert was interested now.

Jimmy handed over a pound note, Albert's ten per cent. The agent pocketed the money and entered the sum in a ledger.

'Getting paid's all that counts at our time o' life, Jimmy lad.' He sat back in his chair and contemplated the wizened old comic. 'How d'you fancy a three month tour wi' Tony Martini?'

'What? Moss Empires, up and down the country?'

'Thirteen weeks, thirteen theatres. Two ten minute spots a show, six nights a week, matinée on Saturday.'

'What about travel?'

'All paid for?'

'Board and lodging?'

'Don't push it, Jimmy. I can get you forty a week, yer can get decent digs for six. My commission's four quid, that leaves you thirty.'

It was good money, ten quid a week was good money in those days.

'I'll take it,' said Jimmy.

'I should think so. Make it when yer can, Jimmy lad, that's my motto. Five years from now, Variety'll be dead. Television's the next thing, but you and me are too old fer that.'

'When does it start?'

'Fortnight, Leeds Empire.'

'Blimey! It's a bit late in the day ter be getting yer acts together.'

Albert looked slightly embarrassed. 'I know. I've been let down. Chas Ball's been taken badly.'

'Oh, so I'm second choice am I?'

'Yer no worse, nor no better, as far as I'm concerned. I've a dozen comics on the books I can ask.'

'No need. I want ter do it.'

'You don't know a decent girl singer, do you? I had Edna Malone down, but she's gone and got herself pregnant again. Every singer I've got's booked up wi' summer seasons.'

'Yer mean, do I know a good girl singer that's out o' work?' asked Jimmy, almost sarcastically. 'All the good uns have got plenty of work.'

'Tell me summat I don't know.'

Jimmy scratched his chin. 'Tell yer what, Albert. There was a young lass got up last night at Hope Street Club . . . better than any you've got on your books.'

'Well? Is she working?'

'No,' Jimmy grinned. 'She's still at school.'

'How old?'

'Fifteen.'

Jimmy's recommendation was good enough for Albert. He picked up the phone and rang Hope Street Working Men's Club.

'Hello, Billy? . . . Albert Drake . . . Touch o' lumbago, but apart from that, I can't complain. Look Billy, I understand you had a young girl up last night who could sing a bit. Aye, Jimmy told me. No, he didn't tell me that . . . he told me he was brilliant but the audience were crap.' Albert laughed at something Billy was saying. Jimmy was craning his ears to hear the insult. 'What? Tonight?' inquired Albert. 'Good, I'll be there.'

'You're not going in that club without me,' said Johnnie firmly. 'Not after what they were saying about you last night.'

Maggie had returned from her rehearsals at the club and told her dad her plans to go back and sing that night. Ordinarily she'd have asked him, but not any more.

'That was only one man, Dad. Anyway, why don't you come with me?'

'I can't, not tonight anyway,' he said sheepishly.

'You mean you're barred?'

'What if I am? There's other clubs,' said her dad defensively.

'Well, you'd better unbar yourself, because I'm going,' she said firmly.

Her dad had the sense to realise the time had come not to argue. Had he been anything of a role model for her, he might have been able to lay the law down with some authority.

'I'll come,' he conceded. 'But you back me up if Billy Bainbridge turns funny.'

'We'll both back you up, Dad.'

'Who's both?'

'Me and Charlie Chipperfield. He's my partner.'

He looked at her with a certain sadness. His girl was slipping away from him. How he wished he could have done right by her. Maybe now was the time.

'Whatever you want ter do's all right by me. I'm with you all the way, Maggie love.'

'Thanks, Dad.' She walked towards him and hugged him. For all his faults he'd never hit her or ever said a wrong word to her.

Billy Bainbridge climbed into his box, wiped a dribble of gravy from his mouth, picked up the microphone and looked across to where Johnnie was sitting with a glass of orange juice in his hand. Denis and Vera had come with him, having promised Billy to keep an eye on him. Charlie had been accompanying an assortment of volunteer singers before the pie and pea break but now he waited with Maggie in the tiny communal dressing room for their introduction. He was as nervous as she was. Albert Drake eyed another agent, who'd just walked in, with suspicion and turned his back so his rival wouldn't spot him. If the girl was any good, he wanted her for three months. He couldn't afford anyone else taking a piece of her.

'Has this agent arrived?' asked Maggie nervously. Secretly hoping he might not be there to watch her make a fool of herself.

'Yeah . . . Albert Drake's here as well. I wonder who told him?' he aswered his own question as soon as he'd asked it. 'Jimmy,' he grinned. 'He was very impressed with you was Jimmy Diamond.'

'I liked Jimmy,' smiled Maggie. 'I thought he was funny. I couldn't understand why the audience didn't laugh.'

'They've heard him before, more than once . . . so have I.'

An amplified tapping came from the concert room. 'Best of order please!' called out Billy Bainbridge. 'Lay an' gennermen, we've a special treat for yer now. Last night, as some of yer know, we had a young lady called Maggie Fish get up and sing. And I'm bound ter tell yer, she were a good 'un. Anyroad, our pianner player, Charlie Chipperfield, has had her rehearsin' a few numbers this afternoon and between 'em they've formed a new double act. An' there's a free drink for anyone who can guess what they called theirsens.'

There was a hubbub of discussion as the audience racked their collective brains and came up with nothing.

'I'll give yer a clue. Her name's Fish and his name's Chipperfield.'

Albert winced, hoping his guess was wrong.

'Fish an' Chips,' shouted a man from the front.

'Wrong,' said Billy.

Albert breathed a sigh of relief.

'Fish and Chippy?'

'Wrong.'

'Fish and Chipperfield?'

'Correct . . . give that woman a free drink. Lay an' gennermen. Put your hands together and let's have a warm Hope Street welcome for our own . . . FISH AND CHIPPERFIELD.'

Maggie and Charlie walked on to great applause. To a certain extent their reputation now went before them. Charlie sat down at the piano and, as Maggie opened her mouth to sing a cold shiver went up Albert's spine. This had only happened to him once before, with Tony Martini. Was this how the football scout, who first saw young Stanley Matthews kicking a ball around, felt? The audience were mesmerised. Maggie was singing with more confidence than the night before, having rehearsed all her numbers. Charlie was slick with the links, even making the audience laugh and harmonising with Maggie on some of the songs. Albert could see the sense in them being a double act, for the time being at least. Maggie looked radiant and fresh in her new red skirt, with a matching ribbon tying her glossy hair back in a flowing pony tail. Charlie was wearing a bowler hat, loud waistcoat and broad grin. He'd been waiting for someone like Maggie to come along so he could exploit his own potential. He'd always thought of himself as more of an entertainer than a piano player. Albert looked at the other agent, whose face was transfixed on Maggie. Albert stood up and walked from the room, unnoticed.

As Fish and Chipperfield's act drew to a close to tumultuous applause, the phone behind the bar rang. The barman called across to Albert's rival agent.

'Dave! Telephone.'

Dave Greenwood finished his drink and walked to the phone as Albert slipped across the stage and into the dressing room.

Ten minutes later, Maggie had given up the idea of going back to school and was signing a contract as Dave knocked on the dressing-room door. His face dropped when Albert opened it.

'You sneaky bugger, Albert! It was you who made that phone call wasn't it?'

'I've just signed them up for three months at seventy quid a week. Can yer match that?'

'No, but I've got a gig for them next Friday.'

'Feel free to book them. It'll be good experience fer their tour.'

'Thanks Albert, you're all heart,' said Dave sarcastically.

'If yer want my advice I suggest twenty quid a night,' said Albert mischievously to Maggie and Charlie. 'You'll be worth a lot more than that when this tour's finished.'

'We'll do it for what's on offer,' said Charlie. 'Sorry Dave,' he said contritely. 'But a three month tour's just what we need to get us off the ground.'

'The gig's worth a tenner,' said Dave. 'And if you want my advice, Charlie, you'll sign a partnership deal with Maggie, before Albert tries to break you up.'

'He doesn't need to,' said Maggie. 'I gave Charlie my word.'

Albert gave Dave a cynical glance that Charlie and Maggie didn't catch.

'In that case,' said Dave. 'I hope you're one of the few people in this business who keeps their word. You're special on your own Maggie but with Charlie, you're extra special. I don't think Albert spotted that.'

Maggie wasn't sure what he meant, but she was happy to go along with him. Charlie was becoming special to her too.

'Yer never did say thank you,' said Johnnie, as he watched her getting ready for her first professional engagement at the Unsworth Labour Club.

'Thanks for what?' asked Maggie, ungraciously.

Johnnie didn't answer at first. It was up to her to work it out. She turned from the mirror she was using to apply the lightest of colouring to her lips. Charlie had advised against heavy make up. Just colouring to lips and cheeks, to counteract the fierce lights. She'd do her cheeks when she got there. Johnnie smiled at his daughter's questioning face.

'I've me own way of doing things, Maggie lass, that might seem clumsy ter you. Just answer me this. If I'd left it up ter you, would you have got up on that stage without me pushing yer?'

Maggie shrugged, she was still unhappy at the way that evening had ended.

'Let's face it. Yer didn't even want to go to the club,' he added.

'Are you trying to tell me you planned it all?' she asked, sharply.

''Course I did, yer barmpot. An' if yer don't believe me, ask Billy Bainbridge.'

'So . . . you thought you'd get me to leave school and earn lots of money in the clubs so that you didn't have to work again,' she said, cynically.

Her dad stood and shook his head. 'No, I didn't think that at all. I wasn't thinking beyond yer getting up and showing 'em what yer can do. All the rest was yer own idea. An' it seems to be turning you into something I don't like. Mebbe I should never have pushed you into it.'

As her dad stomped upstairs, with anger in every step, Maggie stared at her reflection. Her dad had rarely spoken to her like this. If nothing else, there'd always been a consistency about his love for her. An attribute that should have outweighed all his many faults. She followed him upstairs.

He was sitting on the edge of his bed, elbows on knees, head resting in his hands, staring at a photo of Jean on the dressing table. Several photos of Danny were jammed in the frame of the mirror. Maggie sat beside him and put her arm around him.

'Thanks,' she said.

He grinned, forgiving her easily, as she knew he would, and hugged her to him, not taking his eyes off the photograph. 'Yer get to look more and more like her every day.'

'You loved her a lot, didn't you?'

'Yes, I did,' he said simply. 'I spent over two years wandering round France and Belgium and I don't think a waking hour went by without me thinking about her. She loved me as well yer know.'

'I know she did, Dad.'

'Why? Did she tell you?' He was fishing for anything.

'She was always telling me. I got sick of hearing it.' Maggie realised she was laying it on thick. She remembered no such thing, but it didn't mean it wasn't true. Her dad stood up.

'By the way,' he said. 'Any money yer earn while yer away, yer keep for yourself. Yer can start paying board when yer get home.'

'Oh, yes, and how are you going to manage?'

'I've managed all right up to now,' he said sharply. Still unused to his daughter's new independence. 'Anyway,' he added with a wink. 'I'm starting back at Openshawe's next week. They've got a new manager who's never heard of me.'

'That's great, Dad, I'm really pleased. You're still coming tonight, aren't you?'

'Well, I was going to come with Denis and Vera, but Denis is on nights for the next few weeks, so I expect I'll come on my own.'

'I bet Vera would come,' said Maggie.

'I don't know what Denis would make of that,' grinned Johnnie. 'Me taking Voluptuous Vera out on the town.'

'Unsworth Labour Club's not exactly "out on the town",' argued Maggie.

Fish and Chipperfield played their first professional gig at Unsworth Labour Club to a rapturous reception. It was mainly due to Maggie's magical voice, but Charlie played his part.

No one applauded louder than Johnnie and Vera. She'd come along at Denis's insistence. Maggie was flushed with excitement when she came over to their table at the end of the evening.

'I think we're going to be okay, don't you Dad?'

'I've never doubted it, love,' smiled Johnnie. 'I just hope it's what you want.'

''Course it's what I want – and I won't be going back to school. I want to give this everything I've got.'

Johnnie nodded. 'No regrets at leaving – no blaming me?'

'Not any more, Dad. If I wanted to stop on, I would.'

'Fair enough, love.'

Charlie came over. 'Brilliant isn't she,' he grinned.

'You make a good team,' said Johnnie, honestly. 'I just want you ter remember though, that she's only fifteen and I've

51

got a lousy temper. Yer know what I'm talking about don't you?'

'I'll make sure she comes to no harm, Mr Fish.'

'I hope yer do, lad.' There was a benign threat in his voice, which Charlie knew would quickly turn malignant if any harm came to Maggie.

'I've got my van outside,' said Charlie. 'If anyone wants a lift.'

'Well I don't fancy curling up in the back of a van. I think Mrs Bradford and me can walk home. What do yer say, Vera?'

'Suits me,' agreed Vera. 'It's a nice night and not that far.'

Charlie pulled his Morris 8 van up outside her house and took out the two fivers he'd received for their fee.

'Fifty-fifty?' he suggested.

It had never occurred to Maggie that their money should be split anything other than fifty-fifty. In fact she wondered if she was worth as much as Charlie. After all, he was the musician. The one with the experience, the contacts, and the know how.

'Yes, if that's okay with you,' she said.

'Tell you what,' decided Charlie. 'Seeing as it's your first gig, I'll pay your agent's commission for you.'

He handed her a five pound note. The first she'd ever owned. 'I owe you for the dress and stuff,' she reminded him.

'Call it a getting started present. This time next week we'll both be on thirty-five quid a week. I reckon I can afford it.'

Thirty-five pounds a week for three months would be as much as Maggie could expect to earn in two years in Burton's trouser room. She leaned over and kissed Charlie fully on his lips.

'Steady on girl,' he murmured. 'You heard what your dad said.'

'He said you had to look after me. He didn't say how. G'night Charlie.'

'Goodnight Maggie.'

Charlie pressed the starter with mixed feelings. He didn't want a romantic entanglement to get in the way of a professional relationship. He didn't want anything to get in the way of their success. If she made a play for him, he'd nip it in the bud. At least he'd try.

Johnnie and Vera walked along, humming one of the songs Maggie had been singing. As they passed the gates of Paradine Park, Johnnie grinned.

'Fancy a go on the boats?'

'What, at this time o' night?'

'Best time. They let you on for nowt at this time. They did when I was a kid anyway.'

'How do we get in?

'Over the railings, higher up the road. It's easy.'

'Go on then,' she giggled.

The beer and gin had taken their toll. She stood on Johnnie's shoulders and sat on the iron railings. Jumping to the ground at the other side with a loud yell of fear and triumph.

'Sshhh!' said Johnnie. 'The Parky might get us.'

'Bugger the Parky.'

'Watch your language, you naughty woman,' admonished Johnnie, climbing over with experienced ease.

'You've done this before,' she giggled.

'Many many times, but not recently,' said Johnnie.

'Denis would never have done nowt like this. He wouldn't even fart in the street wouldn't my Denis.'

This amused Johnnie. 'Good bloke Denis,' he grinned. 'Straight as a die.'

'Straight as a die,' agreed Vera. 'Boring bugger though.'

They walked across the springy turf beneath a clear moon. Under other circumstances, two other people might have found it romantic. Johnnie kept such thoughts to himself. Not so Vera.

'Give us a kiss, Johnnie Fish,' she asked, boldly.

Johnnie stopped and looked at her. She wasn't a bad-looking woman. The war had hardened her, as it had many women - with the exception of Jean. Vera was in her thirties now, the bloom of youth long gone, but she wasn't without her good points.

'Yer a married woman, Mrs Bradford,' he said pointedly.

'I'm only talking about a kiss. Where's the harm in a kiss?'

It had been years since Johnnie had kissed Jean. He thought he'd never want to kiss anyone ever again, but the drink had relaxed him. He leaned forward and kissed her full on her mouth.

'See,' she said, taking his hand. 'It didn't hurt did it? Now where's that lake?'

Hand in hand they walked through the moonlit park. Vera's hand squeezing his. No one about but the two of them and a few scurrying animals and fluttering birds, angry at having their sleep disturbed by folk who'd no right to be there. It was a mild, still night. No breeze to bring the leaves to life. The only noise came from their feet clicking along the tarmac path that led down to the water's edge.

Clanking through an unlocked iron turnstile, they came out on to a cracked concrete jetty, where a dozen or more rowing boats were moored to metal rings set in the concrete. All with names such as *Freda* and *Mary Ellen* and *Bunty*. Johnnie freed a boat called *Wild Alice*, by deftly untying the mooring rope. He grinned and shook his head.

'We used ter do this when I were a kid. Yer think they'd have learned by now.'

He held Vera's hand as she stepped unsteadily into the boat, wobbling precariously on her high heels, giggling and cursing nervously. She sat down facing Johnnie and positioned herself dead central on her seat for the sake of good balance as Johnnie pushed it away from the jetty with one of the oars, then rowed out to the middle of the lake. Shipping the oars he leaned back on the seat.

'My God, this takes me back,' he said, looking up at the moon in the crystal clear night sky. 'I used ter do this wi' Skinner Atkins and a few others. Skinner could tell us the names of all the stars. That were his hobby, astronomy.'

'I'm a Taurus,' said Vera.

'That's astrology.'

'Is it? Oh, well I know the Plough,' she said, then pointed upwards. 'There it is, and the last two stars point to the North Star.'

'He's dead now,' said Johnnie, distantly.

'Who is?'

'Skinner Atkins. Killed in Normandy, he were my best pal.'

'I bet yer miss him.'

'Miss him? I never think of him. I've never thought of him once since Jean died.'

He held out a steadying hand as she positioned herself beside him, then put an arm around her shoulder. They gazed up at the stars together. Johnnie was as contented as he'd been for a long time.

'How long is it since yer've been with a woman?' asked Vera suddenly.

If Johnnie was taken aback he didn't show it. Maybe he sensed what might be on offer.

'Not since Jean,' he replied. 'I was just coming round a bit when . . .' he stopped.

'Yer still feel guilty about Danny, don't you?' she said, gently.

'I'll always feel guilty about Danny. I was weak and I took it out on the kid.'

'Yer were going through a bad time,' said Vera. 'Everybody knew what Jean meant to you.'

'We were close,' admitted Johnnie. 'And I blamed a newborn baby for her death. I once told him I didn't love him. He was only three years old. Poor little bugger burst into tears. Maggie gave me a right dressing down. Made me go and tell him I was sorry and I didn't mean it.'

'I didn't say much at the time, but it hit me as well yer know,' commented Vera. 'I pretty much brought him up from being a baby.'

Johnnie thought for a while about this new slant on things. 'Well, that's me isn't it,' he said. 'I never thought about you. Never thought about our Maggie, she'll have missed him as well. Just me, that's all I thought about. I asked her ter leave school so she could get a job you know. Bright girl like our Maggie. She could go on ter university could our Maggie.'

'From what I've heard tonight, I reckon your Maggie could do very well for herself without going to any university,' commented Vera.

She snuggled closer to him, enjoying this little heart to heart. She and Denis never shared moments like this. 'She looked after him like a mother did your Maggie. He thought the world of her. He thought the world o' you as well, if I'm any judge.'

An inquisitive duck glided past, perhaps hoping for a midnight feast. Where there was a boat there were usually breadcrumbs. But not tonight. With a disappointed quack he turned his back to them and disappeared across the glittering black lake. Johnnie watched it go then surprised Vera with his next remark.

'The worst part about it is that I'm supposed ter be a war hero.'

'Hero?' inquired Vera. 'What did yer do that was heroic? Was it you what helped Errol Flynn save Burma?'

'I got the Military Medal.'

'Military Medal?' repeated Vera. 'That's a big'un, isn't it?'

'Big enough for a useless prat like me.'

'How come yer never mentioned it?'

'Because I didn't deserve it that's why.'

'Did Jean know?'

Johnnie smiled. 'She didn't know much about medals didn't my Jeannie. She thought it were just another campaign medal, bless her. I didn't make her any wiser. I'm glad I didn't now, after the lousy way I treated Danny. I don't deserve to have anyone thinking of me as a hero.'

'I want ter know what happened. Did you get one o' them citation things with it?' she asked.

'Oh yeah ... biggest load of bollocks you ever read. I daren't show *that* to anybody.' He shuffled in his seat to make himself more comfortable, Vera snuggled closer. This was the best time she'd had for ages.

'It was early 1945,' he began, 'an' we were pushing across Europe. France, Belgium ... and into Holland. We found a billet just outside this village in Holland and one of the locals came round and told us about a house half a mile down the road with a cellar full of wine. We had this young captain ... Captain Briggs, posh as hell, mad as a March hare ... He asked for a volunteer driver to help him go and liberate this wine, so I stuck me hand up. First time I'd volunteered for anything. It seemed like a good skive and I'd end up with a few bottles of plonk.'

Vera gave a quiet laugh and lit two cigarettes, passing one to Johnnie.

'Anyway, I drove this lorry,' he continued, 'ter where this old chap had directed us, just me and Captain Briggs, and we went into the cellar. I couldn't believe it. There must have been thousands of bottles of wine, all dusty as hell and stored in racks. Briggsy started looking at the labels, he seemed ter know a lot about wine. According to him, we'd stumbled on a gold mine. He told me ter bring the lorry up ter the back door and we'd start ter load up.'

Johnnie took a deep drag on his cigarette as the memory of the incident took him back in time.

'Go on,' prompted Vera.

'I'd just got into the cab when shells started falling all around. All bloody hell let loose! I shot under that truck like a rat up a drainpipe. Christ, I was scared. After about two or three minutes it stopped. I looked out, and the house was a pile of rubble. They were clouds of dust, fires burning all over the place ... and yet there was no noise ... weird. I had a bit of a scout round, but I couldn't see any Jerries. I reckon one of their OPs must have spotted our lorry and directed some shellfire at us ter liven us up a bit. Anyway I managed to get back into the cellar and Briggsy were lying there, underneath all this brick and timber. He'd got two broken legs and God knows what else. Blood all over the place. He looked a right sorry sight. I managed to get him back ter the lorry, which was pretty much all in one piece. He kept telling me not ter say nowt when we got back and he'd do all the talking. If anyone asked me anything, I was just ter say I'd been obeying orders. It were him what recommended me for the gong. Well, he could hardly tell 'em the truth, could he? Risking a valuable corporal's life for a few bottles of plonk. So he made up this cock and bull story about how I'd volunteered ter go with him on this dangerous recce mission behind enemy lines and rescued him, without regard ter personal safety, under heavy enemy fire. That's what it said in me citation.'

'Did yer know yer were behind enemy lines?' queried Vera.

'I bloody did not! Apparently he did though, the mad bastard.'

'Yer brought him back in one piece, maybe yer do deserve a medal.'

'Well, he'd have bled ter death if I'd left the barmy bugger there ... no doubt about that. But there were far braver things went on over there, without anyone even being given so much as a pat on the back. I've always felt a bit guilty about that.'

A long silence followed, broken eventually by Vera. 'Do yer know what I feel guilty about, Johnnie?'

'What?'

'Not loving Denis.'

'He's a good bloke is Denis.'

'I know. I've never loved him though. I married him because I had to. Bugger that, isn't it? One daft fling can ruin yer whole life.'

'I thought you were okay together.'

'We are. He's the salt o' the earth is Denis. He bores me ter buggery though. The sad thing is, I've never actually *loved* anybody. No blokes I mean. I suppose I loved me mam and dad and I love me kids ... but that's not the same is it?' She slid her arm through his and rested her head on his shoulder. 'I used to get really jealous of you and Jean. You and her had something that I never had. In fact I reckon most people never have.'

Johnnie nodded. He knew she was right. Most people didn't have what he and Jean had. It had been an extra special love. Maybe if they'd had the ordinary love that most people have, her death wouldn't have been quite so hard to take.

'Most couples just sort of, yer know ... fancy each other,' continued Vera. 'And they end up getting married so they can legally shag the arse off each other. This wears off after about a fortnight, then they start thinking, "What the hell have I done?" Mind you, even that's a fortnight longer than me and Denis.' She turned her face up to him. 'I can see what Jean saw in you, Johnnie. Mebbe I could get ter love someone like you meself.'

'Me?' Johnnie laughed. 'I'd drive yer mad, Vera. Yer better off with Denis, believe you me.'

'I think before people are allowed to get married,' said Vera, 'they should be made to shag the arse off each other fer a fortnight, just ter see how they feel. What do you think?'

'I think you've got a wonderful way wi' words, Vera.'

Placing her cigarette in her mouth, Vera's free hand moved slowly up his inside leg, gently squeezing his crotch, sending out the clearest of messages.

They turned to face each other. Flicking their half-smoked cigarettes, like fireflies, into the dark water. Slowly moving into a kiss. Gentle at first, then a long forgotten passion overtook Johnnie and he began roughly unbuttoning her coat, with no resistance from Vera. No words were spoken now. Each unsure of how far they were prepared to go, but not wanting to stop. Vera's blouse came off, her breasts bulging over a bra that was too small for her. Pushing away Johnnie's fumbling hands, she deftly unhooked it. He sat back from her as she wriggled out of her skirt. Laying it in the bottom of the boat on top of the rest of her clothes.

'Your turn,' she challenged.

Johnnie carefully moved to the seat opposite and looked back at Vera, now wearing only knickers and stockings which she was unhooking from a suspender belt. He undid his belt. A year or two older than Johnnie, she looked younger in the moonlight. Her breasts large but still firm, belly bulging slightly, her legs sturdy but shapely. They removed the rest of their clothes in unison, hungry eyes on each other, until they sat completely naked, facing one another. Their bodies white, reflecting the moonlight, catching the eye of the park keeper, doing his midnight patrol.

'How are we going ter do this?' inquired Vera.

'Maybe we'd better get ter dry land,' suggested Johnnie, sensibly.

'No, let's do it here,' insisted Vera. 'I want ter remember this.'

She slid forward and lay on her back in the bottom of the boat, legs akimbo, knees slightly raised. She could see at an appreciative glance that he was ready for her. The sight of a naked woman for the first time in years had seen to that. Johnnie removed the plank seat he was sitting on, threw it into the back, then knelt between her thighs. He held a hand on either side of the boat to stop it rocking, then guided himself into her. A delicate manoeuvre, but once achieved, the rewards were abundant. Vera held on to him desperately as they writhed passionately about in the bottom of the boat. Understandably not noticing how dangerously it was rolling from side to side. Ignoring an angry shout from the lakeside and a powerful torch beam illuminating Johnnie's bobbing backside.

Vera's cries of ecstasy were matching the shouts of anger from the shore. She felt herself heading towards a rare orgasm. For one wild minute they both forgot where they were as they climaxed simultaneously, just as the boat tipped them out into the freezing lake. *Wild Alice* sank, along with their clothes and their passion. The park keeper panicked, believing he may have caused the accident by his shouting, and ran off to dial 999 for the police, the fire brigade and an ambulance.

Vera surfaced and looked round for Johnnie. Panic at his non-appearance coupled with selfish thoughts flashing through her mind. How would she get home with no clothes on? How would she explain this to Denis? There was a coughing and spluttering behind her as Johnnie eventually surfaced. In obvious distress. She swam towards him as he flailed about.

'Are you okay, Johnnie?' a daft question under the circumstances.

'Not really,' coughed Johnnie in between splashes. 'I can't bloody swim.'

Vera grabbed his flailing arms, spun him around and towed him towards the shore as she'd been taught in life-saving classes down at Cookridge Street Baths before the war. Surprising herself as to how well she was doing. Johnnie helping by kicking his legs as best he could, his head supported between Vera's buoyant bosoms. An enjoyable pastime under other circumstances. Eventually they made the opposite side, away from whoever had been shouting at them, and took cover in a clump of rhododendrons. Both stark naked and wondering what to do next.

'Yer the only fish I've ever come across what can't bleedin' swim,' remarked Vera, eternally grateful that Johnnie hadn't drowned, thereby placing her in a difficult situation with Denis. That and another, less selfish, reason.

'Thanks, Vera love,' said Johnnie, inadequately, eternally grateful that Vera had saved his life, and vowing to learn how to swim at the earliest opportunity. 'I were getting a bit worried out there.'

'Yer sure know how to give a girl a good time, Johnnie Fish.' shivered Vera. 'What delights have yer got planned for me now?'

'Finding some clothes is at the top of me list,' decided Johnnie. 'There's some gardens backing on ter the park through these woods. Maybe we can find a clothes line or something.'

'I suppose it's worth a try,' agreed Vera. 'I've never left clothes out on a line overnight meself but, there again, I've never had no garden.'

With Vera following Johnnie's gleaming white backside, they made their way through the woods. Trying to protect their naked private parts from scratching branches. Vera having much more to protect than Johnnie. After a painful few minutes they came to a line of rusty railings, beyond which was a row of gardens.

'Over there,' said Johnnie.

In one of the gardens was a clothes line, hung limply with bedlinen and ladies' underwear. Johnnie climbed very gingerly over the fence. Doing his best to protect his private parts from damage. Vera helping out with a cupped hand between him and the top railing.

'Thanks,' he said, gratefully.

'Any time,' she replied, cheekily.

He returned a minute later with two pairs of knickers and two bedsheets.

'Best I could manage,' he reported.

They dried themselves on the sheets before wrapping themselves up like a pair of Roman senators. First donning the knickers. This caused much giggling from Vera as Johnnie squirmed into his pair, then posed in front of her. They followed the line of railings to where it ran alongside a road. Darting back into the bushes as an ambulance clanged past, quickly followed by a police car and a fire engine.

'I wonder what all that's about,' queried Vera.

'No idea,' said Johnnie. 'If anyone says owt, we've been to a fancy dress party,' he advised, as they climbed over, into the now empty street.

'I hope my kids are fast asleep when I get in,' said Vera.

'Damn! Maggie's bound ter be up. She'll be wanting ter talk ter me about tonight's show.'

They arrived at the end of Hope Street in the early hours, after dodging through the shadows like a couple of fugitives. Hiding in the Co-op doorway as a police car passed, giggling and molesting each other until their sheets dropped to the ground, causing a distracted late night cyclist to fall off his bike at the sight of a bare breasted woman and a man in lady's knickers.

'Come into my house,' suggested Vera. 'I'll fix you up with summat of Denis's. Yer about the same size.'

'What? Everywhere?'

'Well, maybe not everywhere. There's less to him than meets the eye.'

Thankfully Roy and Mavis were sleeping soundly when they let themselves in with a key attached to a piece of string just inside the letterbox. Johnnie followed Vera up the stairs into her and Denis's bedroom. He removed his sheet and stood there in a pair of lady's knickers. Vera took off her sheet and stood in front of him, silently convulsed with laughter at the sight of him. Tiny squeaks escaping as she tried to subdue her mirth. Her breasts bouncing unashamedly up and down. Johnnie pulled her towards him. Within seconds they were on the bed, taking their time now. Johnnie gently kissing her neck, her lips, her nipples as she pulled down his stolen knickers and massaged him into life with both hands. Bringing him inside her, gently thrusting upwards to meet him coming down. Again and again. This time there was no cold, dousing end to it all. They took their time, enjoying each other's bodies until they could hold back no longer. Ecstatic release came in a frantic, muffled climax, followed by a deep, exhausted sleep.

Vera had become accustomed to the back door rattling open and banging shut at ten past six in the morning as Denis arrived home. She shot out of bed, shaking Johnnie into consciousness.

'Denis is back!' she whispered urgently.

'Bloody hell!' panicked Johnnie. 'What time is it?'

'Ten past six,' replied Vera. 'Oh shit! He's coming upstairs. He never comes straight upstairs, he usually makes himself a cup o' tea first.'

Still in the nude, she shot to the bedroom door and poked her head around it, as Johnnie unsuccessfully tried to squeeze under the bed. Cursing the fact that he'd woken up with a most inconvenient erection.

'Oh, it's you!' she said, as Denis arrived on the landing.

''Course it's me, who did you think it was?' asked Denis, jovially.

'I thought er . . . I thought one of the kids were up . . . just check they're okay will yer, while I put summat on.'

'Don't put owt on on my account. Anyway, since when did yer start sleeping wi' nowt on?' inquired Denis, attempting to open the door to get a better look at her. She smiled coyly and resisted, her shoulder against the door, revealing just enough of herself to tantalise him.

'Never you mind, just do as yer asked and I'll nip down and put the kettle on . . . and make you a bite to eat before you and me come back to bed.' She breathed the last few words as seductively as she could, under trying circumstances.

'Oh, right, fair enough,' said Denis, who wasn't used to such consideration from his wife. He usually crept in beside her sleeping body and stayed there until lunchtime when, if he was lucky, she'd rustle up a meal for him. This could be a welcome break from his normal routine. It seemed he might be in for 'a bit of nuptial naughtiness', as he liked to call it, before he went to sleep. A bit of nuptial naughtiness would certainly go down well.

Johnnie, in the meantime, had given up the idea of hiding under the bed and had found a pair of Denis's trousers and a shirt in the wardrobe. With the shirt flapping round his waist he slid up the window and shinned down the drainpipe outside.

Within seconds he was pulling the key to his own house back through the letterbox on the inevitable piece of string. Had there been anything worth stealing in Hope Street, a burglar would have had a field day. But Johnnie was home and safe, Maggie was fast asleep and, apart from Ruby Moffitt, peering through her bedroom window at the other side of the street, no one was any wiser.

Chapter Seven

Fish and Chipperfield were the first act on after the Empire Angels, a six-girl dance act that opened every Leeds Empire variety show. Maggie and Charlie waited nervously in the wings as the girls went expertly through their three-minute routine, coming off to loud applause and whistles, clattering happily past the nervous newcomers. Maggie's heart was beating like a steam hammer. It was the first show Monday night but the theatre was full. Tony Martini, the star of the show, always played to full houses.

Joe Modley, the manager and announcer sat by the sound man just out of sight, stage left. He spoke into the table-top microphone as the stagehand ushered Maggie and Charlie into position behind the plush red curtains.

'Ladies and gentlemen. We have great pleasure in bringing to you a brand new act that looks like taking the world of showbusiness by storm. Would you please put your hands together and welcome on stage . . . FISH AND CHIPPERFIELD!'

The curtains swished open; the band played the opening bars of 'You Belong To Me' to reveal Charlie sitting at the piano in a red bowler hat and gaudy waistcoat and Maggie, in a glittering sequinned stage dress, looking much older than her fifteen years. Johnnie was sitting dry mouthed in the front stalls with Denis and Vera. He could scarcely believe this radiant young woman was his baby girl.

She leaned against the piano, waited for the opening applause to die down then smiled uncertainly into the dazzling spotlights, blinding all but the front three rows from her vision. She began to sing, as if to Charlie. Once again, as soon as she opened her mouth, the audience were mesmerised. A voice of immense power and quality, and an indefinable something else. They all knew they were watching a star in the making. Charlie's harmonising voice was no match for hers, but he had humour. A useful quality in a musical double act. As the first number ended to delighted applause he picked up a glass of what looked like beer from the top of the piano and swung round on his stool to face the audience.

'Thanks ever so much ladies and gentlemen,' he said, taking a sip. 'Do you know, I've read so much about the evils of drink lately, that I've decided to give up reading.'

The laughter gave Maggie time to position herself centre stage, two single spots picking them both out. Charlie tinkled out the intro to the next number and spoke into his mike.

'Standing centre stage is my delightful partner, Maggie Fish. Fifteen years old, ladies and gentlemen, can you believe that.'

A murmur of amazement went around the theatre as Charlie continued: 'My name's Charlie Chipperfield. When I was Maggie's age I was just a snotty, obnoxious little kid, still learning to play the piano.'

'And all this success hasn't changed him a bit,' added Maggie, to the delight of the audience who had taken Fish and Chipperfield to their hearts.

Patrizio Franciosa, aka Tony Martini, looked up from his evening paper as Maggie's voice came singing through his dressing room speaker. If anyone could recognise a natural singing voice it was him.

Patrizio Franciosa, Paddy to his friends, was born in London of an Italian father and a Welsh mother. Impeccable forebears for a singer, but being half Italian during the war gave him a slanted viewpoint on life. His father spending much of the war in a British POW camp. When young Paddy's school broke the news to his family that their son had an exceptional voice, his father had insisted on him being classically trained. Twice a week, from the age of fifteen, he walked the two miles from his home in Jamaica Road, Bermondsey, over Tower Bridge, to the house of Winston Worthington in Spitalfields to learn how to use his 'God-given voice'. There were better singing teachers in London, but none so dedicated or cheap as Winston Worthington, who saw in Paddy a passport to reflected glory. Henrico Franciosa worked extra hours as a meat porter in Smithfield Market to pay for his son's lessons.

Hoping that Paddy would realise all the dreams that he himself once had.

One day, just after his seventeenth birthday, Paddy arrived early at the Worthington house and was lured into the bed of Mrs Worthington, who had lusted after his maturing dark good looks for some time. During the next few months, Paddy impregnated both Winston's wife and his nineteen year old daughter. A confused Winston decided that Paddy should do the decent thing and marry at least one of them, the only available one being his despoiled daughter. Henrico Franciosa, being a man of honour, reluctantly went along with this, but Paddy, feeling he had been unfairly seduced by the mother and daughter, was less than enthusiastic at the prospect. Her Majesty came to the rescue by calling Paddy up for his National Service and two years later, he walked out of Catterick Camp in Yorkshire and caught a bus to the great metropolis of Leeds where he planned to settle down, far away from complicated paternal obligations.

Making full use of his army training, he earned a good living as a burglar at first, but a three month spell in Armley Jail cured him of that. It was in jail that he met a drummer, who was serving a short sentence for disorderly behaviour. The drummer told him how he could make a fortune on the clubs with a wonderful tenor voice like his, and the day he came out of jail, on the drummer's recommendation, Paddy went to see Albert Drake, who promptly renamed him Tony Martini and put him to work in the northern clubs.

He made his way now into the wings to watch, tripping over pieces of magician's paraphernalia and ignoring a few choice curses from the angry illusionist, who was waiting to go on next. Tony made up his mind there and then to entice Maggie into his bed, or wherever else might suit his carnal purposes.

Fish and Chipperfield finished their act to a thunderous reception, helped along by whistles and clapping from Tony, who for all his shortcomings, was never less than generous in his appreciation of his fellow artistes, especially if they were young, female and pretty.

Two other acts followed before the interval, including Jimmy Diamond, who displayed his real talent for comedy in front of a proper audience, as opposed to a club audience, more interested in pie and peas and Bingo than being entertained.

66

'I'll gerrem in,' volunteered Johnnie nudging his way to the stalls bar.

'No, no, it's my treat,' insisted Denis. 'You got the tickets, besides, I owe yer one for taking Vera out the other week.'

Two pairs of guilty eyes met behind Denis's back. Guilt momentarily melting into amusement, then back to guilt, because the amusement was at Denis's expense, and he didn't deserve that. They were both wearing brand new outfits to replace the ones lost in the lake. Vera having had little problem explaining her loss away. To most men, a woman's wardrobe is one of life's many mysteries and Denis was more gullible than most.

'Actually, Maggie got me the tickets for tonight,' said Johnnie, 'and Vera paid her corner in the club.'

'That's right, we both splashed out, didn't we Johnnie?' winked Vera. Johnnie tried to suppress a grin, he hated having fun at Denis's expense. But Vera wasn't making it easy for him.

'Well, that makes a change,' grinned Denis, ordering the drinks. 'I were thinking about yer both when I were at work. Wondering what yer were up to.'

'Well, she kept me out of trouble if that's what yer thinking,' said Johnnie, defensively. Then changing the subject, 'What do yer think of my Maggie then?'

'Honestly?' teased Denis.

''Course, honestly,' said Johnnie. 'Why, what's wrong with her?'

'Nowt that I can see,' answered Denis with a smile. 'I honestly think she's brilliant. They're both brilliant. Everyone was well entertained. Bottom of the bill or not, they're the best act so far. That Tony Martini'll have his work cut out ter best 'em.'

A murmur of agreement came from other customers at the bar, who had no idea who Johnnie was.

By the time the tour arrived at Newcastle Empire for the final week, Fish and Chipperfield had crept up the bill and were closing the first half, having swapped places with Jimmy Diamond, who took his demotion philosophically. He could hardly grumble, after all, he was the one who discovered them. During the tour, Maggie had been much more impressed with Tony Martini's singing than with his attempts to charm her under-age knickers off.

'If my dad knew what he was up to he'd wring his greasy neck.'

'He'd have to join the queue,' replied Charlie, unhappy at the way Tony was openly flirting with his partner.

'If I had a boyfriend it might cramp his style,' suggested Maggie, pointedly.

Charlie had grown on her during the last three months. He was funny, he was talented and he was quite handsome, from a distance anyway. And, best of all, he cared for her. But he stopped short of becoming romantically involved, much to Maggie's frustration.

Charlie held up his hands. 'Maggie, you're only fifteen. I'm twenty-one next week . . . and I'm the one who promised your dad I'd look after you. Anyway, after this week he won't be a problem.'

'Any idea what we're doing after this?' asked Maggie.

'Not sure, Albert's coming up mid week to let us know.'

Albert was waiting in Charlie's dressing room as they came off the stage after Thursday night's show. He stood up and called through the door for Maggie to join them. She gave Albert a dazzling smile of greeting, causing him to catch his breath at the transformation in her this last three months. Despite her tender years she was now a fully blown young woman. Tall, shapely and quite beautiful. Albert made up his mind to go ahead with his plan.

'Right,' he said, after they'd both sat down. 'I think you should have a fortnight's rest, after which I've got provisional bookings for you both right up to Christmas. The revues you've been getting have made my job easy.'

'Provisional?' queried Charlie. 'What does that mean?'

'It means I haven't committed you to anything,' explained Albert. 'I want ter keep our options open for a while. In the meantime,' he looked at Maggie. 'I wonder if I could borrow you just for one night ter do a charity show at the Grand in Leeds.'

'Why not both of us?' asked Maggie.

'Because you'll be singing with a big band and with the best will in the world I couldn't persuade their pianist ter let Charlie take over from him. Anyway, I've got Charlie a good gig on the same night in Rotherham and I don't suppose you'll want to deprive him of twenty quid.'

'Twenty quid?' Charlie whistled. 'Just for one night?'

'That's right,' grinned Albert. 'That's how popular you are.

Mind you, I had ter twist their arms. You'll need to sort yourself out two half hour spots.'

'No problem,' said Charlie. 'I've been building up the comedy over these last few weeks.'

'So I understand,' said Albert. 'Now, obviously I can't be in two places at once so I'll be going with Maggie. It'll do neither of you any harm to have a solo string to your bows. It should strengthen yer act if anything.'

Charlie came off the stage in Rotherham to mixed applause. For a first attempt, his comedy had gone down reasonably well. Some things needed honing, others needed chopping out altogether. It's the only way with comedy, grit your teeth and hope for the laughs to come. Fortunately he had his music to fall back on, and between the two he gave the audience a couple of pleasant half-hour sets. But they knew he wasn't the star he'd been made out to be by the posters. The missing half of the act must be really good.

Maggie waited in the wings, sipping a glass of water as her cue came up. Breathe deeply, get the smile ready, nerves are good for you, gets the adrenalin rushing, gives you the edge you need. Albert was standing beside her, an avuncular hand on her shoulder, sensing the tension in his protégé and knowing it was good for her.

Laurie O'Neill, clarinet in hand, stood patiently in front of the microphone as he waited for the applause to die down in appreciation of his band's rendition of 'In the Mood'. The theatre was packed for the National Children's Charity Night. It was usually held in London but, just for once the organisers had brought it out to the provinces. Everyone who was anyone was there. If Maggie made a good impression here, there were plenty of important people who'd be only too happy to give her a hefty leg up the ladder. And Albert Drake knew this only too well.

Johnnie, Vera and Denis were in the the audience. Vera in the middle, her hand surreptitiously squeezing Johnnie's thigh, a little too high up for comfort.

'She's on next,' he whispered to his two friends, giving Vera a meaningful nudge. He didn't want her hand grasping his leg whilst his daughter was singing. It just wouldn't be right.

Maggie had spent the afternoon band call productively. Her

three numbers, 'Softly, Softly', 'Secret Love' and 'You Belong To Me', were already indelibly fixed in her brain from dozens of performances on the tour. But to sing them in front of a twenty-six piece band was a joy. She knew that this was where she belonged. Albert was banking on it.

'Ladies and gentlemen,' announced Laurie. 'We have a special treat for you this evening. A young lady from this very city, who's been receiving rave reviews on her recent tour.'

He made no mention of Charlie, but Maggie's mind was too preoccupied to notice this.

'Ladies and gentlemen, would you welcome on stage ... Maggie Fisher!'

Maggie knew nothing about her new name, but she liked what she heard, it sounded so much classier than Fish. Albert smiled at her. 'New life, new name ... go get 'em Maggie!'

Her nerves dropped away like an unwanted coat as she strode confidently on to the stage towards Laurie, now placing his instrument to his lips with one hand and waving his band into 'Secret Love' with his other. The house and stage lights went down, cloaking the band. A single spot picked out her full length pale blue dress, glittering with tiny sequins. Her dark chestnut, glossy hair flowing across her pale, smooth shoulders. Her young face, beautiful from any distance. A star in the making. If she could sing.

All doubts in this direction were dispelled as soon as she began. Her voice clear, with a bell-like resonance, and something else, something indefinable. The elusive hook. She looked down at her dad and smiled her recognition. Johnnie's heart almost burst with pride, his eyes moist as her voice rose and fell with effortless ease. From power to pianissimo. Her movements practised and professional now. Her emotions real. Her audience captivated. Her agent rubbing his fat hands, in anticipation of the money that would soon be flowing through them. Other acts were drawn into the wings to watch this young phenomenon. Les Crane the pianist; the Conway Twins, currently with a record in the Top Twenty; Marcus Hoffman the magician and Dolly O'Hare, one of the Old Time Music Hall Greats.

Tony Martini stayed in his dressing room, listening to her on the speaker. One day he'd have her. She'd resisted his advances for three months. No girl had ever done that to him. One day he'd catch her with her guard down but it wouldn't be tonight. Tonight would be her big night, everyone who knew her had anticipated that. Alone in his dressing room, he applauded her as she came to the end of her first number. Few people knew how it felt to be that good. But he did.

Charlie read the review in the *Yorkshire Evening Post* the following evening and knew he'd lost her. He also knew that Albert had done this on purpose. This left Charlie in a dilemma. Should he tell one of the best agents in the business to get stuffed? Or should he swallow his pride and accept the inevitable? He and Maggie were never destined to be a double act, she was far too good for that. He'd always known it, but wouldn't admit it to himself. Still, he'd had a good run and she'd done him a favour by kick-starting him into a solo career that would pay more wages than a mere piano player earns. He'd that to thank her for.

It was fitting that early autumn rain was dampening Hope Street as he walked down towards Maggie's house. It matched his mood. The street's single lamp, recently converted from gas to electricity, flickered into life, as if to herald a new, more opulent age. For Maggie, certainly. A halo of lamplight was illuminating the raindrops passing through it before they dropped on to a scruffy dog peeing against the lamp-post below. It then nuzzled up to his leg, as if to tell him he was next. The world was conspiring to make him more miserable. Sod Maggie Fish! He never liked her anyway. Good bloody riddance! He'd be better off on his own. He turned into the yard and knocked on the paint-peeling back door, petulantly wondering how big a star she'd need to get before she bothered to have her door painted. Somehow he was surprised to see her answering his knock. A big star like her opening her own back door. He could see the mixed emotions in her eyes and knew his assessment of the situation had been right. In a darkened corner of his mind he'd held out some hope that he'd read the situation wrongly and she didn't want to split with him. But it was a forlorn hope. He knew that now. Make the best of a bad job, Charlie. Don't make things any harder than they need to be. He could see she was glad to see him, but worried how she was going to break the news to him. He thought too much about her to torture her like this.

'I've had a bit of an idea,' he said, as he walked through the

71

door. 'Hello Mr Fish,' he waved a hand of greeting at Johnnie, who was sitting half asleep, with his feet up on the table. He stirred into movement.

'Don't get up on my account,' said Charlie. 'I've just come to have a quick word with Maggie.'

'Go through ter t'room,' suggested Johnnie. Charlie and Maggie did as they were told.

'What I thought,' said Charlie, thinking on his feet. 'Was that we should maybe have a go at branching out as separate solo acts, just to see how we go on. I mean, I did okay last night and I reckon you did.' He saw the relief in her eyes. His subterfuge was worth it. He couldn't stand the thought of causing any pain to this lovely girl. 'What do you think?' he asked innocently.

Maggie wasn't sure what to say. Despite her tender years, she wasn't stupid, she knew exactly what he was doing. She'd been planning what to say to him all afternoon, but he'd come up with a much better version of the same story. Placing her hands on his shoulders, she kissed him gently on his mouth. Charlie remembered the last, and only other time, she'd kissed him. He felt a shudder of longing run up his spine, his arms went around her waist and he held her to him. The kiss turned into something special and he knew he'd always been in love with her. But now he was about to lose her to fame and fortune. 'Cut your losses now, Charlie,' he told himself. 'If you let this get out of control it could do a lot of damage to both of you.' He stepped back and forced a smile.

'I'd er . . . I'd b . . . better go,' he stammered, turning away from her sad, liquid eyes. Another second looking into them and his would be a lost cause. He walked through into the back room. Maggie behind him.

'Bye, Mr Fish,' he said, startling Johnnie into consciousness once again. His feet jerking off the table and banging down onto the floor.

'Oh! Right . . . see yer Charlie,' he said.

Maggie followed him into the back yard. 'Charlie,' she said quietly. 'I'll miss you terribly . . . but if you think it's for the best.'

'Believe me,' replied Charlie. 'It's for the best all right. Bye Maggie Fisher.'

Maggie turned and ran upstairs, flinging herself on to her bed, weeping noiselessly into the pillow. Charlie walked sadly to his van, as Johnnie daydreamed about Vera and wondered whether it was worth all the potential hassle he'd get if Denis ever found out what was going on. Perhaps one more time, then call it a day. After all, Denis was a good bloke.

Albert Drake contemplated his future. Last night, in the midst of her euphoria, he'd signed Maggie up as a managed act. An interesting contract that she'd have been well advised to have checked over by an expert before she signed it. The audience, including bigger names than him, had gone wild. He knew he had to act fast, but he wanted to make sure she could actually sing with a big band before he signed her up. He now had two big names on his books, Maggie Fisher and Tony Martini. Charlie Chipperfield had apparently gone down quite well and it had been well worth the extra tenner he'd bunged the concert secretary to give to Charlie, with the instructions, 'Don't mention it's from me, let him think it's all part of his wages.' The concert secretary had long since given up trying to understand the workings of an agent's mind and did as he was asked. It had ensured that Charlie went along to the gig on his own, without kicking up too much of a fuss. In Albert's hand was a recording contract for Maggie from Delius Records. He was wondering how much commission he could get away with. Tony Martini wouldn't let him get away with anything, but Tony Martini wasn't a fifteen-year-old girl who trusted him. Foolish girl, he grinned inwardly, fancy trusting an agent.

Chapter Eight

Ruby Moffitt had kept the the Fish and Bradford households under constant surveillance for two years. Noting with outward distaste and inner glee the clandestine comings and goings, growing in frequency as time went by.

It had been a memorable two years for the Fish family. Maggie's emergence on to the pop scene had been carefully nurtured by Albert Drake, who didn't want her to be a one-hit wonder. Maggie was to be his pension. After her success at the Grand Theatre and her split with Charlie, she did a month in Blackpool, during which time she recorded her first hit record, 'Teenage Days and Lonely Nights', which shot straight to number three in the Top Twenty.

The year 1956 was not the ideal time for a British ballad singer to be breaking into showbusiness. The early fifties had been the time for singers such as Dickie Valentine, Alma Cogan, Ronnie Hilton and Ruby Murray. Rock and Roll had been a fad from the other side of the Atlantic, not destined to make any lasting impression here. Everyone knew that Rock and Roll would be here today and gone tomorrow.

As 1956 turned into 1957, a new word was being banded about among Britain's teenagers. Skiffle. Britain didn't have any notable Rock and Roll bands, but Lonnie Donegan, Charles McDevitt, and the Vipers were bridging a gap. Filling a need created by Bill Haley, Elvis Presley and Buddy Holly. From the thousands of skiffle groups throughout the country, a few made their way to the 2 Is coffee bar at 59 Old Compton Street, Soho. A spawning ground for British Rock and Roll. Musical entrepreneurs, such as Larry Parnes (Mr Parnes

Shillings and Pence), went there to turn the embryo stars into real ones.

A young man from Bermondsey went there as Tommy Hicks and emerged as Tommy Steele, Harry Webb became Cliff Richard and Terry Nelhams became Adam Faith. Two Geordie guitarists, Brian Rankin and Bruce Cripps, became Hank Marvin and Bruce Welch, meeting up with Terence (Jet) Harris and Tony Meehan to form the Drifters which subsequently turned into the Shadows. And Vincent Joseph Robinson became Vince Christian, Maggie's first lover. In March 1958, Elvis Presley joined the army and by the time he came out he'd be sharing the charts with a host of British artists.

Albert took care of all Maggie's contracts. She was given money to spend and a chaperone to keep a watchful eye on her. Promiscuity was all right for young male pop stars, but should word get out that a teenage girl singer was putting it about, it would be a black mark on her career which, in Albert's old-fashioned eyes, would be difficult to erase. The agent's fears were kept at bay in this respect. Maggie was kept too busy for boyfriends. On top of which, the split from Charlie had left a hole in her heart she had difficulty repairing. Maggie was seventeen before she had her first serious romantic encounter.

Despite competition from the Rock and Roll phenomena, her next two records had made the lower reaches of the Top Twenty and the money was flowing in. She trusted Albert implicitly with all her finances. He always made money available whenever she wanted it. It was the autumn of 1958. Maggie was a seventeen-year-old veteran, touring with Vince Christian, a twenty-two-year-old heart throb, with four consecutive Top Ten hits to his credit. She'd fallen for his good looks even before she met him in person. He wasn't like the rest of them. Many of the young male stars were coarse tongued and brainless. Overwhelmed, overpaid and unprepared for their overnight success, much of which was down to record producers and promoters, rather than to talent. Vince was gentle, unassuming and kind and Maggie gladly went along with his plan to elude her chaperone after the show one night and go off to a club with him. Eluding her chaperone was scarcely a problem. Eileen Patterson was more of a friend and mentor, who had learned to trust Maggie. She read Maggie's note, explaining she'd be a bit late back, with few misgivings. Maggie was a teenager and entitled to her own time.

Vince had his own car, a Ford Zodiac convertible, in which he and Maggie drove to the Starlight Roof Club in Liverpool, hoping the dim lighting would prevent them from being recognised. A local band was on stage, doing their own version of 'Shake Me Down', one of Vince's hit records.

'People are looking at us,' observed Maggie nervously as she stuck to Vince like glue.

A young girl walked right up to him and stared hard into his face. He stuck his tongue out at her, causing her to shake her head and walk away to report to her friends that no way was this rude bloke Vince Christian. He looked around at other staring faces and whispered from the side of his mouth.

'Make your way to the door, quick.'

An announcement from the stage hastened their departure. A message had been passed to the lead singer, who didn't like having his glory stolen by the presence of a more famous act. He'd been enjoying the undivided attention of a semi-circle of groupies, and was making up his mind as to which one he would bestow his carnal favours on that night. Vince Christian's mere presence in the club would easily eclipse his limelight. But he knew how to get rid of him. He made his announcement in broad Scouse.

'Ladies and gentlemen, I understand we've a couple of celebrities in the club tonight. Vince Christian and Maggie Fisher!'

Pandemonium broke loose. Screaming girls scoured the club for a glimpse of their idol, boys likewise, but without the screams. Maggie had become an object of fantasy, her picture adorning many a pubescent boy's bedroom wall. It was her first experience of the difficulties of celebrity life.

She and Vince made their escape as the announcement was being made. Vince had been in this situation before and knew the problems facing them. They were both laughing as he screeched away from the fans pouring out of the club, hard on their heels. Tearful girls, beseeching their idol to come back. Frustrated boys, turning and trudging back to their girlfriends, ordinary by comparison. Back to the real world.

Vince was staying in the same hotel as Maggie and Eileen. He took her hand as they entered the lift and pressed the button for his floor.

'I've got a couple of bottles of wine in my room, if you fancy a nightcap,' he suggested. 'You might as well, the evening's been a washout so far.' He'd come over to England as a twelve year old. A lot of his Donegal accent had been ironed out, leaving behind a gentle, attractive lilt.

'I don't suppose one glass of wine will do me any harm,' she smiled. He kissed her lightly on her lips as the lift doors closed. She thought he was physically the most attractive person she'd ever known. A shade under six feet tall, with a permanently serious expression on his handsome face, belying his sense of fun. Luxuriant jet black hair, swept back in the style of Elvis, and dazzling white teeth, the result of expensive dentistry. She ran her fingers around the back of his neck and pulled him to her. It was about time she started acting like a normal teenager, not some sort of singing nun.

An elderly resident did a double take of the feverishly embracing couple when the lift door slid open on the fifth floor. He'd seen them both somewhere before, but he wasn't certain where, perhaps it was at breakfast. He cleared his throat loudly, to alert them of his presence. Vince looked up at the floor indicator.

'This is us,' he said to Maggie, without a hint of embarrassment. Maggie became aware of the old man and blushed slightly, keeping her eyes on the floor as they stepped past him, out into the corridor.

'He saw us!' she exclaimed, as the lift took the man downwards.

'So what? We were only necking,' protested Vince.

'It's not so much what we were doing, as who we are. It'll be all over the hotel in the morning.'

'Relax, Maggie. You'll have to learn to live with this sort of thing. Anyway, I doubt if your man knew who we were.'

'Do you really think so?'

'I really do,' soothed Vince, convincingly.

He opened the door to his room and checked the corridor behind them, before following her in.

Maggie eyed his double bed suspiciously. He caught her looking at it.

'I'm an active sleeper,' he explained. 'Stick me in a single bed and I'll fall out of it.'

Maggie laughed, watching him as he took a bottle of wine from the fridge. A luxury not afforded her.

'I asked for the fridge especially,' he said. 'And a constant supply of booze. Let's face it, the money we make, we can afford it.'

Maggie was uncertain how much money she actually made, so she didn't pursue the subject. She took the glass of wine and sipped it.

'Very nice,' she said appreciatively. She knew nothing about wine. The nearest she ever got was the occasional bottle of Babycham. Vince took off his jacket and hung it carefully on a coat hanger. Then he loosened his tie and took Maggie's free hand.

'You're very beautiful, Maggie Fisher,' he told her.

'So are you.'

She put down her glass and entwined her arms around him. How natural it seemed, despite her inexperience in such matters. Girls up and down the country would have given anything to be where she was right now. Vince was thinking much the same thing, only about Maggie's male following.

His lips had felt the softness of many a pliant girl, but none so sweet as Maggie's. They fell onto the bed locked together, his hand moving to her breast. She shivered with excitement and eased herself away to allow him freedom of movement. Vince sensed her compliance and undid her silk blouse, running his hand inside, up and down her stomach, then both hands around her back, expertly unfastening her bra.

'I do believe you've done that before,' she scolded gently. Vince smiled and said nothing.

Her young breasts were full and firm, the nipples hardening to his touch. She began to unbutton his shirt, knowing full well where this was going to end and having made up her mind to make her first time as memorable as possible. A couple of feverish minutes later they were both naked. She felt him hard against her stomach and moved her hand down to hold him. His hands moving slowly all over her. His finger tracing a slow and sensuous line down her spine across her bottom, around her thighs and brushing tantalisingly through her pubic hair. His hand between her legs now, feeling her softness turning damp. He eased himself on top of her. She felt an exquisite pain as he entered her, gently, slowly. She grasped his buttocks, her fingernails digging deeply into him. Urging him into action. Vince responded vigorously and soon she felt him surging inside her and it was all over for him, but much too soon for Maggie. She was still thrusting upwards, wanting him to continue and not just lie there like a dead fish. He pulled himself together and matched her movements until she climaxed noisily beneath him. His duty done, Vince rolled off her and closed his eyes. They lay there together, not speaking. Maggie wondering whether she should be happy or guilty or disappointed at the speed of it all. She certainly hoped there'd be more to it. After a while she propped herself up on one elbow.

'Now that you've relieved me of my virginity, aren't you supposed to offer me a cigarette?' she asked.

'I thought you didn't smoke.'

'Well, I don't. But I can't think of a better time to start, can you?'

Vince laughed and reached out for his Senior Service, sitting up and lighting one for each of them.

'Here,' he said, handing her one. 'And don't blame me if it knackers your voice.'

Maggie took a deep drag and exploded into fits of coughing. Vince moved to take it from her, but she held up her hand as if to say, 'Leave me alone, I'll master this if it kills me.' A couple more drags and she gave in, stubbing it out in a bedside ashtray. Vince followed suit, out of politeness. Maggie regarded him quizzically.

'I read somewhere that you were a devout Catholic.'

Vince smiled. 'Altar boy, choir boy. That's how I got started with the singing.'

'But haven't you just committed a sin?'

'Original sin, no less.'

'There wasn't anything original about it.'

'Oh yes, and how would you know?' he laughed.

Maggie lay back and stared up at the ceiling, a worrying thought springing to her mind.

'Does this mean you'll have to confess what we've just done?'

'In my book,' said Vince, stretching out beside her. 'A sin is something that harms someone. Now who on God's Earth have I harmed?' He leaned over her, kissed one of her nipples and then her lips. 'I'm a great believer,' he whispered, 'in the word of St Augustine, who said, "Lord give me chastity – but not just yet".'

There was a radio beside the bed. He twiddled with the knobs and tuned into 208 metres Medium Wave, Radio Luxembourg, with its customary poor reception. Buddy Holly was singing 'Maybe Baby'. On the bedside table was a packet of Garibaldi biscuits. He broke a couple of pieces off and offered one to a surprised Maggie.

'Sex, booze and Garibaldis,' he said. 'My idea of heaven.'

They lay back on the bed crunching Garibaldis and drinking wine.

'I suppose you realise it wasn't my first time,' he said.

'I'm not daft Vince, 'course I realise.'

'It was the first time I've ever . . . you know.' He was struggling to express himself.

'Deflowered a virgin?' suggested Maggie, helpfully.

'Right.'

'Bit of a coincidence that.'

'Coincidence? How d'you mean?'

'I've never been deflowered before.'

Vince smiled. 'Well?' he asked.

'Well what?'

'What did you think?' His male ego was asking the question.

She didn't answer straight away. Having nothing to compare it with, she couldn't make a fair judgement.

'I . . . well, I thought it might last a bit longer,' she said at last.

'Ah! That was my fault,' he admitted. 'You got me over-excited. I'm supposed to exercise a bit more self-control. With you it's not easy.'

'Should I feel flattered?' she asked.

'Very.'

Buddy Holly finished and Maggie Fisher came on, singing 'Young Dreams and Broken Hearts' through the crackling reception. Maggie, who was sipping wine, burped loudly with surprise. Her records were rarely played on Radio Luxembourg. She was more of a Light Programme artiste. Vince grinned as she excused herself.

'Just think. All the fellers listening to this'll be wanting to be the one to come to the rescue of heartbroken and innocent Maggie

Fisher. And here you are, lying on my bed, stark naked, slurping wine, belching and smoking a fag.'

'So you think this is bad for my image?' she inquired.

'There's nothing wrong with your image from where I am.' Vince leaned over and kissed her once again.

'I thought we might try and get our timing right this time,' he decided.

'What if we don't?' asked Maggie

'Then we'll just have to keep trying until we do.'

'Ah well, that's showbusiness,' conceded Maggie, sitting astride him, as her own sweet voice serenaded them from the Bakelite box beside the bed.

Chapter Nine

The exclusivity of Johnnie's sex life was beginning to cause him some anxiety. It was exclusive to Vera and she was talking about leaving Denis to live with him. To Johnnie, this seemed an incredibly bad idea. Even if he agreed, where would they live? She could hardly move in with him next door. Vera was allowing herself to get careless, as if she wanted Denis to find out. For this reason Johnnie decided to call it a day with her. She took this very badly.

Johnnie had been made up to chargehand at Openshawe's once again. He was still a relatively young man, the right side of forty, and with no ties. The world was his oyster. Having it off with Vera was just pure laziness on his part. There were dance halls in the city, full of young women eager to meet the more mature man. So every Saturday night, Johnnie, under Vera's jealous gaze, would walk through his back gate, clad in best bib and tucker, with a smile of anticipation playing on his lips, and head towards the Majestic Ballroom, City Square.

Her curtains would twitch upon his return, having caught the late night bus. Then the night came when he didn't come home alone. Tears of rage and jealousy flooded Vera's eyes.

'Come ter bed, Vera, love,' grumbled Denis, who couldn't understand why she bothered to look out of the window at that time of night. She was getting as bad as Ruby Moffitt. He heard Johnnie's door bang shut.

'Is that Johnnie coming in?' he asked, grinning to himself.

'What? Oh, yes.'

'Has he got himself a woman yet.'

'It bloody well looks like it,' she said quickly.

'Good for him. It's about time he got himself fixed up.'

Vera exploded. 'Fixed up! Yer call bringing a whore home at this time of night, fixed up?'

'Steady on,' objected Denis. 'What're yer getting so upset about? He's entitled to his pleasures, same as anybody. Good luck to him, that's what I say.'

Vera flounced across the room and threw herself into bed, turning her back to Denis. He made no overtures to her. They hadn't made love for months. At least Johnnie was getting his share. Nice to know someone was.

If Malcolm Moffitt, Ruby's youngest, hadn't broken Vera Bradford's scullery window with a football, life in the Fish and Bradford households might well have returned to normal. With no one any the wiser, apart from Ruby Moffitt.

Vera, having just seen Johnnie's overnight visitor wobble off down the street on her high heels, was in no mood for having her window broken. She hurtled into the street, caught the fleeing Malcolm by the scruff of the neck and fetched him a resounding clout around his grimy ears. His howl of pain brought Ruby out, with a sweeping brush in her hands. She charged angrily towards Vera, knocking her to the ground, producing a shout from Vera that brought Denis into the street. He pulled off the angry Mrs Moffitt, only to find himself being half strangled by her husband Larry, who'd walked out to find his wife being assaulted by Denis. The four of them became embroiled in a violent fist fight, most of the violence coming from the women. The men weren't quite sure what they were fighting about and eventually broke off their own hostilities to separate their respective wives. By this time the street had filled up with an assortment of fight fans, Johnnie among them.

'Yer want ter keep that lad of yours under bleedin' control,' seethed Vera. 'He's just broke our bloody winder!'

'It'll have been an accident, Vera,' soothed Larry Moffitt. 'I don't suppose our Malcolm did it on purpose, did yer lad?' He turned to his son, who was standing in his own back yard on top of the dustbin, watching the proceedings over the wall. Amazed at all the trouble he'd caused.

'Who's gonna pay for it, that's what I want ter know?' demanded Vera.

'Young Malcolm'll pay for it out of his pocket money like our

Roy had to,' said Denis, winking at Larry, who nodded his agreement.

'Over my dead bloody body!' shouted Ruby angrily. 'After what she did ter Malcolm, I've a good mind ter call t' police!'

'Yer can call the bloody army for all I care,' retorted Vera, unwisely. 'You owe us for a new winder, yer loud-mouthed slag!'

'Slag?' screeched Ruby. 'Who the bloody hell are you calling a slag! Yer bleedin' whore!'

Johnnie was hoping against hope that Ruby couldn't back up what she was saying with any facts. To the delight of the spectators, Vera went for her again, punching Ruby full in the mouth before Denis hauled her off, kicking and screaming.

'Don't you call me a bleedin' whore, yer fucking slag!'

The F word sent the row on to a higher plane. 'I'll call yer a bleedin' whore any time I like,' screamed Ruby. ''Cos that's what you are!'

Denis was having trouble holding on to Vera. Larry had a restraining hand on his wife, ready to grab her the minute she sprang at her venomous adversary.

'And I'll call you a fuckin' slag any time yer like . . . 'cos that's what you are!' yelled Vera, who was running out of insults. Ruby played her trump card.

'At least I'm not shaggin' me next door neighbour!'

A shocked silence descended on the crowd. All eyes on Vera, then on Denis, to see what his reaction was . . . and then on Johnnie, the only possible culprit. Vera's other next door neighbour was Mrs Smithson, a seventy-year-old widow.

'You've nowt ter say now, have yer?' gloated Ruby. 'I've seen him comin' in an' out of your house at all hours, when your Denis were on nights.' She turned to the crowd. 'He once climbed down her drainpipe, after her Denis walked in through t' door.'

Denis's world fell apart. He knew from the look on Vera's face that it was true. The absence of any denial from Johnnie reinforced this.

'Is this true, Vera?' he asked, hoarsely.

She spun round on him, her anger not yet abated. ''Course it's bloody true . . . I'm surprised it took yer so long ter find out!' She suddenly looked shocked at having made such a public admission. Roy and Mavis were staring at her, wondering what it was all about. A shocked and confused Denis looked across at Johnnie's guilty face.

'You!' he said.

Johnnie shrugged apologetically and hung his head. He felt two feet tall. Denis walked slowly towards him, fists clenched.

'Give 'im a crack, Denis,' urged the crowd, smelling blood.

Denis was no fighter, but he needed an outlet to purge his rage and devastation. Johnnie made no attempt to defend himself against the flailing blows Denis was raining on him, he knew he had it coming. He could easily have got the better of the fight, but Denis didn't deserve this. Johnnie fell to the ground and curled up as Denis kicked him. Shouts of 'Get up and fight like a man, yer bloody coward!' came from the men in the crowd. Johnnie just lay there until Denis stepped away, his eyes brimming with tears, and walked back into his yard. The crowd began to disperse as Johnnie sat up painfully, nursing his wounds. A child's voice shouted 'Yeller belly!' He stayed where he was for a minute until the street had cleared, then stood up to go. Vera stepped into his path. Their eyes met. Hers worried, his remorseful.

'What am I going to do, Johnnie?' she asked.

Johnnie held her in his gaze, wiping blood from his mouth with his sleeve and checking to see if his jaw was still intact. He knew exactly what she had to do.

'Go in and tell him yer sorry. Start being a proper wife to him. At least if something good comes of it, he might see his way clear ter forgiving you.'

'Forgive me?' she excaimed. 'Johnnie, I don't want him ter forgive me. I want you.'

'Vera,' sighed Johnnie. 'Go back ter Denis. What we had started out as a bit of fun, then it got out of hand. It's over now. I told yer that, weeks ago.'

'Yer a bastard, Johnnie Fish.'

'It doesn't matter what I am. What matters is you picking up the pieces before yer lose your family. Loving Denis would have been a nice bonus, but what yer've got's better than most.' He patted his shirt pocket to locate his cigarettes and frowned when he found the packet had been flattened by Denis, as had the contents. Selecting the best of the bunch, he rolled it back into shape between his fingers and lit it. Pointedly not offering Vera one.

She stared at him, not wanting to hear his words, even if they did make sense. She heard herself blurt out the words, 'Johnnie, I love you.'

'Maybe yer do Vera, maybe yer don't,' said Johnnie wearily. 'But yer'll never take the place of Jean ... no one could ever do that. It's something I'm stuck with.'

Vera stood there with tears edging down her pale cheeks. Out of sight in his back yard, stood Denis. His fingers unconsciously crossed, willing his wife to do as Johnnie asked and come back to him. He went into the house to await the outcome.

'Denis loves yer, Vera,' said Johnnie. 'When love's one sided, that's the best way round. Loving someone who doesn't love you, that's the hard bit.'

'How would you know?' inquired Vera petulantly. 'Jean worshipped the ground you walked on.'

'Maybe,' said Johnnie. 'But that was then. I need ter know she'd still love me now, after what I did ter Danny. I've got it in me mind that Jean's out there somewhere, loathing me, bloody despising me ... and the worst part of it is that I'll never be able ter make it up to her.'

Vera knew she was beaten. 'I could never be part of your life could I?'

'No one could, Vera. Take what yer can. Having a husband who loves yer makes yer better off than most. Don't throw that away. Denis can give yer much more than I ever could.'

Denis was sitting with his back to the door as Vera walked in. Trying to sense her mood without turning round, determined not to be a lap dog. He'd heard enough to know Johnnie didn't want her. What he wanted now was some sign that she was back for good, that she was sorry for hurting him. He'd always known she didn't love him, but he never thought she'd ever hurt him in such a way.

'Denis, I'm sorry,' her voice came from behind him, almost inaudible. Denis didn't know how to handle it, he just sat there. She walked round and stood in front of him. The tears she'd shed for Johnnie still streaming down her face.

'Who are yer crying for Vera?' asked Denis. 'Johnnie? Or yerself?'

'A bit of both,' answered Vera truthfully.

'What about me? Don't I deserve any o' them tears?'

'You deserve all of 'em Denis, love.' She knelt in front of him and rested her head on his lap. 'It's just that I've never been able ter give yer what yer deserve.'

His hand hovered over her head, desperately wanting to run his fingers comfortingly through her hair. Telling her it was all right. But he knew this was the easy way out. He pushed her away gently and stood up.

'I love yer, Vera lass ... but I can't just ignore what yer've done to me. Not just ter me, but ter the kids. They were out there, listening ter what were being said. I'm sorry, but what yer did were ... well, it were bloody unforgivable.'

Vera was still kneeling down. Suddenly frightened that Denis might not be able to forgive her. Frightened she might lose him. Lose this good man who loved her intensely. Frightened that she'd pushed him beyond the limit. She slowly got to her feet and turned to him.

'I don't want ter lose yer, Denis,' she said simply, and headed for the stairs. She called to Roy and Mavis, who were in the front room, discussing this odd turn of events, to go out and not come back for an hour or so. Denis gave them both a wry smile as they passed, then followed his wife upstairs, stepping over her discarded blouse in the bedroom doorway. Maybe Johnnie had done him a good turn after all.

Chapter Ten

Eileen Patterson put down the phone and shrugged philosophically. All good things come to an end. She didn't blame Maggie for the bad news, although she had every reason to.

'Who was that?' inquired Maggie, towelling her hair as she came in from the ensuite bathroom.

'Mr Drake,' answered Eileen.

'Albert? What did he want?'

Eileen looked at Maggie, smiled and shook her head. 'Apparently my services are no longer needed,' she explained.

'You mean he sacked you?'

'That's another way of putting it.'

'Why?'

Eileen picked the *Daily Mirror* up from the bed and handed it to Maggie. Thirty-six hours had gone by since her brief fling with Vince, during which time the press had been busy. The pop group in the Starlight Roof Club had cashed in on their story about Vince and Maggie. The reporter had tracked Vince back to the hotel and either Vince had told everything, or the reporter had put two and two together, and unfortunately had managed to make four. The two of them were headlines in the showbusiness page:

'Vince and Maggie's Night Of Passion'.

The reporter had stopped short of describing what exactly went on behind Vince's bedroom door, but he'd fired the reader's imagination in such a way as to leave little doubt.

'Shit!' cursed Maggie, uncharacteristically.

'My sentiments entirely,' agreed Eileen. She regarded Maggie sympathetically, wondering whether or not to break all the news at once.

'You'd better read page two,' she advised.

Maggie looked quizzically at Eileen, then thumbed back through the pages:

'Maggie Fisher's Dad Beaten Up By Wronged Husband'.

The reporter told in sensational detail how Maggie's dad had cowered beneath the violent onslaught of the cuckolded husband of his lover and next door neighbour, Mrs Vera Bradford (42). And how he'd once been seen climbing down a drainpipe just after Denis had gone in through the front door after his night shift. It also tied the story up with Maggie's affair with Vince Christian. Posing the question 'Did Maggie Fisher inherit her rampant libido from her love cheat dad?'

Maggie flopped down on the bed. How could her dad do this to Denis? And with Vera Bradford! It didn't bear thinking about. She lay back and closed her eyes, contemplating the implications of it all. Eventually she opened them and looked up at Eileen.

'How will this affect my career?' she asked, curiously.

'A damn sight less than it has mine!' retorted Eileen, a little taken aback by Maggie's selfishness.

Maggie frowned at her friend's abrasiveness, then realised how thoughtless she'd been.

'Oh hell! Sorry Eileen. I've lost you your job and all I'm thinking about is myself.'

'That's okay,' smiled Eileen. 'It was always on the cards that a pretty girl like you would slip the leash. I must say, I admire your choice in fellers.'

'Not if it was him who spilled the beans,' grumbled Maggie.

'I doubt if he knows anything about it. It's not as though he's a nobody trying to make a name for himself. It could have been anyone who saw you together.'

'There were plenty of them,' admitted Maggie. 'A whole clubful.'

'Well then, there you are. Why blame Vince?'

'Oh, I don't know, it's all new to me. Anyway, you didn't answer my question.'

'How will it affect your career?' Eileen pondered this one for a moment. 'I think it'll make you appear more human,' she decided. 'More vulnerable, more accessible even. Up to now you've been pure and innocent. Maggie Fisher, the Singing Virgin. Not much of an image for the Rock and Roll era. I don't think you've done yourself any harm.'

Maggie nodded. Eileen made sense. 'Is this what Albert thinks then?' she asked.

Eileen shook her head. 'Albert wants you to stay as you were. He's an old fogey, stuck in the past. Rock and Roll's an innovation. At Albert's age, innovations are beyond him.'

'Well, he's pretty safe with me,' said Maggie. 'I'm no rock singer.'

'I get the impression that Rock and Roll's not just about singing,' countered Eileen. 'It's an attitude of mind. It's about rebellion, danger, not going along with convention. What's in the papers today might make the kids sit up and take notice of you. Up to now, your audience has been the over-thirties.'

'What are you suggesting? That I try my hand at becoming a rock singer?'

'Not at all. You'd make a lousy rock singer. I'd be interested to hear you sing something with slightly more raunchy lyrics though. That'd make people sit up.'

'How raunchy?' asked Maggie, slightly shocked at seeing a side of Eileen she didn't know existed.

'Ideally, something the BBC would ban from the airwaves,' suggested Eileen. 'Imagine how the kids would flock to buy a record with that sort of reputation.'

Maggie stared at Eileen for quite a while, causing her friend to fidget uncomfortably, then she picked up the phone and dialled Albert.

'Morning Albert . . . yes, I've read them . . . isn't it brilliant? All this great publicity for nothing. By the way, do Eileen's wages come out of my money or your commission? I thought so . . . so she works for me then? In that case I'll decide for myself who gets sacked, thank you very much . . . and I want my friend Eileen to stay.' She held the phone away from her ear, as Albert's reaction rose in volume, then plonked the receiver back down.

'Silly old sod,' she said cheerfully. 'When he's calmed down I'll tell him to give you a rise. Now, who do we know, who can write raunchy songs?'

'Your dad?' suggested Eileen. Maggie howled with laughter. The phone rang, then went dead just after Eileen picked it up.

Johnnie could hear his daughter laughing in the background. Maybe this was why he put the phone back down, he didn't want to spoil whatever fun she was having. He didn't know how to explain things to her. She must think him the lowest of the low to do what he did. Perhaps he'd try again some other time.

Chapter Eleven

February 1959

On 3 February a small plane crashed just outside Mason City, Iowa, depriving the music world of three of its top artistes. Buddy Holly, the Big Bopper and Richie Valens. Because of this tragedy, Mike Cuthbertson, head of of Delius Records, delayed the release of 'Love Me Any Way You Want' until the spring, not wishing to dilute the impact of what promised to be a controversial record. He wasn't entirely convinced it was a suitable song for Maggie, but it was certainly a great tune with unforgettable lyrics by Brian and Harry Foster and he knew that once Maggie had added her own ingredient to it, the result would be unique. A small but select group of session musicians were put together and the record cut in one afternoon at Delius's Gattonfield Studios. The B side was less controversial, a more usual Maggie Fisher song entitled 'My September Sunset'.

'Love Me Any Way You Want' was first heard on *Housewives' Choice*, whose unsuspecting producer had included the record without actually listening to the lyrics. The station was bombarded with complaints from irate listeners. The record was immediately banned by the BBC and talked about in all the papers. Luxembourg played it endlessly and within two weeks it was at number one in the Top Twenty and Maggie was at her peak. A tour of one nighters was arranged with her and Tony Martini, who now needed to cash in on her fame to fill the theatres.

Charlie only took the job because he'd heard Maggie would be staying there. She was playing the Leeds Empire and staying at the Great Northern Hotel. One of the best hotels in Leeds. Of course she could have stayed at home with her dad but, as Albert pointed out, the accommodation was part of her wages, so why not take full advantage.

He and Albert had parted company, Charlie having served his purpose. He was still doing the clubs and earning more money than he used to as a club pianist, but he wasn't booked up every week. That was why he was filling in for the hotel lounge pianist for a week.

Maggie's success pleased and saddened him. It was no more than her talent merited, but it also put her out of his reach. With him dragging her back, she'd never have reached the heights she had, and yet he missed her desperately. An awkward situation in view of the fact that he was about to become engaged to a pretty girl Maggie's age, who apparently loved him to bits and whose love he returned as the next best thing to his love for Maggie. Perhaps, if he could have a heart to heart with Maggie, he could sort himself out once and for all. If Maggie wasn't available, he'd propose to Brenda and put Maggie right out of his mind for good.

A middle-aged woman had had her eye on him all evening. Before long she'd be making a discreet, but indecent, request. She wouldn't be the first. Harry (Fingers) Radford, the pianist for whom he was standing in, had warned him about such women. 'They're only after one thing and fortunately for them, I'm very obliging in that department. So, if you happen to fancy your chances, Charlie boy, just remember I've got a reputation to maintain. I don't want to come back and find I've lost all my clients due to you failing to give due satisfaction. And whatever you do, don't let the manager find out. He's got this thing about not wanting his hotel to become a knocking shop.'

Charlie intended smiling and saying he had to get back to his wife, which would be enough to put the woman off. Harry would no doubt have taken advantage, in return for a welcome wad of notes. But to follow in Harry's footsteps would make him a gigolo. Actually, it didn't sound so bad; it had a sort of racy ring to it. Gigolo. It was a much nicer word than prostitute. He was running the pros and cons of becoming a gigolo through his mind as he banged out 'Side Saddle', pretty much in the style of Russ Conway. The woman advanced, he sensed her approach and got his response ready.

'Is Harry not here this evening?' she asked, her voice more syrupy than seductive.

Considering Harry's obvious absence, it was a pointless question. Charlie was tempted to say that Harry was under the piano working the pedals, but he suspected the woman wouldn't see the funny side. She looked the type who might even glance under the piano to see how Harry was managing.

'No, he's on holiday for a week, I'm sitting in for him,' was Charlie's eventual response.

'Harry's quite masterful with his ... instrument,' she cooed, in a manner that told Charlie that she wasn't talking about Harry's piano.

The woman drew closer, leaning against the piano in what she hoped was a seductive manner. Her braless nipples pressing against her tight, satin dress, a mite too low, but shapely enough. Her nyloned legs exposed to view, revealing the beginnings of a pair of substantial thighs. Not bad looking, late forties, running to fat, but extremely well preserved, glittering with jewellery and reeking of perfume. Harry (Fingers) Radford would have had no hesitation.

Just at that moment, Maggie walked in on the arm of an unusually handsome man. Laughing and giggling as they walked to the lift. Her escort obviously took great care of his appearance; every gleaming black hair in place, immaculate cream suit, lightly bronzed skin and flashing white teeth. Charlie felt scruffy just looking at him. He glanced up at the clock, eleven pm, she must have come straight here from the theatre. He was hoping she might have stopped in the bar for a drink, where he'd planned to join her and engage her in a long and cosy chat. Perhaps worm his way back into her affections. Things never work out the way you want. They were kissing now, not passionately, thank God. Just pecking each other on the lips. But what would they get up to in the privacy of her room? The lift door opened and closed behind them, whisking them up to who knows what? Charlie got to his feet as the woman pressed her room key into his hand. An unreasonable need for revenge overcame him. He looked down at the key and then up at the woman. Nodding his acceptance of her mute proposal, he led her to the lift. She followed, surprised but delighted at the swift success of her seduction. Glancing in passing at a mirror and giving herself the seal of approval. She still had it.

Maggie stepped out of the lift and looked around the lounge, wondering where Charlie was. She was sure it was him at the piano, even though she'd only seen him from the back. She'd know her Charlie anywhere. Roddy, the choreographer, who'd come back to the hotel with her, had declined her invitation to go back down for a nightcap once they'd changed. Maggie had smiled her understanding. Roddy's sexual preferences lay else-where. Namely in the form of a lithe young male dancer who stepped into the lift as she stepped out.

'Where's the piano player,' she asked a passing waiter. 'Is he on a break, or has he finished?'

The waiter grinned. 'You mean Charlie? He's just gone upstairs, Miss Fisher, with one of the guests, to give her a private performance. I think you might say he's finished – he will be if the manager finds out.'

Maggie stared, disbelievingly, at the vacant piano stool. How could Charlie treat sex so casually? She was no angel herself, but she'd never sink to this. Saddened, she went back to her room.

Maggie was topping the bill. A dressmaker had made her a collec-tion of outfits, her favourite being a backless little red number, slit up the side and low at the front. Simple in style, but devastating to look at, especially on Maggie. The session musicians from the recording studio had, bar one, all been hired to accompany her. The exception being the drummer, who had to be replaced at the last minute due to marital difficulties. His wife having found out where he was going. The show was halfway through a sixteen venue tour and had arrived at the Free Trades Hall in Manchester. Maggie had made her TV debut the week before in Birmingham on a show called *Thank Your Lucky Stars* and the Manchester show was a sell out.

It was one of those periods in life when everything seems to be going just too right, causing Maggie to search for little imperfec-tions to restore a bit of normality. She just wished Charlie was here to share it with her. But she knew she was doing things she couldn't have done with him as part of the act, although she some-times thought she'd swap what she had to have him back again. She always felt safe with Charlie around. What he'd done in Leeds seemed so much out of character. Maybe the waiter had got it wrong and she was doing Charlie an injustice. Eileen was funny and nice and easy to talk to, but she was no Charlie. All such thoughts were swept from her mind as the curtain swung back and the wall of rapturous applause brought a broad smile to her lips. Such sensations are restricted to the very talented and can't be bought, sold or even described. The applause subsided and rose again momentarily as her band played the opening bars of her first song 'Don't Give Me Roses'.

She saved 'Love Me Any Way You Want' until the end, having been taught a sensuous dance routine by the show's choreographer. Every night it brought the house down, she'd learnt to do 'false tabs' – walking off the stage and waiting in the wings until the shouts of 'More, more', brought her back on to sing it again. She took four curtain calls before signalling to the stage hand not to lift them again, despite the continuing applause. Life for Maggie couldn't get any better. Unfortunately, Tony Martini thought he knew differently.

He was waiting in her dressing room when she came off stage. She wasn't unhappy to see him, they'd got on okay up until then. No hint of jealousy at the reversal of fortunes, Tony had had his time and he accepted that. He was opening a bottle of champagne when she walked in. Accepting a glass she sat down heavily.

'I'm knackered,' she grinned.

'You don't look knackered, you look radiant,' said Tony, with a charm that melted his audiences nightly. He was disgustingly handsome, she thought. More so than Vince or either of the other two young men she'd taken to her bed since that first time.

'Why are you here?' she asked, curiously. Perhaps slightly suspicious that he'd chosen the one night when Eileen was not in the theatre.

He held up two hands of innocence. 'No particular reason, I just felt like it. You're a beautiful young lady and they're my favourite companions.' She noticed an empty bottle of champagne on the floor.

'Have you drunk that one already?' she asked.

He looked down and picked up the empty bottle, holding it to his mouth and drinking the dregs. 'I have now,' he smiled.

She felt a growing sense of unease, knowing he must be drunk.

'Look,' she said, finishing her glass. 'I have to get changed . . .'

He interrupted by holding out the bottle. 'No, no, no,' he insisted. 'Have some more. We must finish off the bottle.'

'Tony, I don't want any more,' she said, firmly. 'I want to get changed, so if you'll excuse me.'

'I'll help you,' he offered.

'What?'

'I'll help you get changed. I'm an expert at removing women's clothing.'

'I've no doubt you are ... but not this woman's clothing.' She went to the door and opened it, standing there as he got unsteadily to his feet and walked towards her. With a laugh he edged behind her, slamming the door, turning the key in the lock and slipping it into his pocket.

'Tony! ... What the hell are you doing?' she snapped. 'Give me the key and get out of my dressing room.'

'Not before you've given me a kiss.'

'Don't act so stupid!'

'Stupid?' he protested. 'I ask for a kiss and I'm stupid. What does that make all the others?'

'All what others?' She was frightened now.

'All the ones you allow to screw you,' he said angrily.

'Get out Tony!'

He put his arms around her and pulled her to him, forcing her to struggle, pulling at the front of her dress with one hand and knocking her to the floor with the other. He wanted her desperately. She'd shown no interest in him whatsoever, which made him want her even more. She'd become an obsession with him. Tonight he'd have her, no matter what the cost. The drink had relieved him of all common sense. He was kneeling over her, his hands were at her throat, shutting off her screams, choking her into unconsciousness. She stopped struggling. Perfect. Alive but unconscious. He pulled her dress off roughly. Underneath it she wore nothing, all part of her allure. Kissing her roughly he loosened his trousers and pushed her legs apart, squeezing her breasts and forcing himself inside her. Thrusting drunkenly and frantically. Maggie's breath was coming in choking gasps that he fooled himself into thinking were gasps of ecstasy.

He climaxed as she regained consciousness, his body relaxing in a dead weight on hers. She tried to cry out but couldn't. No sound came from her at all, bar a faint croaking noise. With a supreme effort she pushed him off her and staggered to the door, only to find it was locked. She banged on it in frustration then remembered that Tony had the key in his pocket. As she turned round, he looked up at her with a stupid grin on his face, as if it had all been one big joke. Tears of rage and fear and self-loathing streamed down her face as she picked up the half full champagne bottle and smashed it down on his head. He fell back, unconscious, no further threat to her.

There was blood on the floor now, Tony's blood. She stared at him, consumed with revulsion, then felt inside his pocket for the key. Her nudity forgotten in the heat of the moment, she stumbled out of the dressing room and collapsed, in tears, in the arms of one of the dancers.

Half an hour later, still in her dressing room, she sat with Albert, Eileen, who had dashed to the theatre as soon as she heard the news, and a police inspector.

Albert had been shocked to the roots by her accusation of rape. Not from any particular sympathy for Maggie, but out of concern for the show. Before the police arrived he'd tried to dissuade her from making such an accusation.

'Are you sure it wasn't a just a bit of horseplay gone wrong?' he'd pleaded.

Maggie had pointed to her throat and shook her head. Mouthing the words, 'He raped me!'

'Why did you let him in your dressing room?' Albert had asked pointedly. Maggie shook her head. Eileen answered for her.

'She didn't let him in, Albert. He let himself in.'

'Jesus Christ,' moaned Albert holding his head in his hands. 'This show's had it.'

'Thanks for your sympathy,' mouthed Maggie.

'What did she say?' asked Albert. But before Eileen could translate, the police arrived. Tony having already left in one ambulance, a second was waiting to take Maggie away.

'You'd better send someone off to the hospital,' advised Eileen. 'That's where they've taken the bloke who raped her.'

'Rape?' queried the officer.

'Tony Martini raped her in here half an hour ago.'

The policeman looked at Maggie, who was shivering with shock. 'You'd better tell me what happened,' he said.

'She can't,' interrupted Eileen. 'The bastard choked her. She's lost her voice.'

An ambulanceman was hovering in the doorway. The inspector turned to him, saying, 'You'd better take her.' Then to Maggie, 'We'll take a written statement when you're feeling up to it. In the meantime you'll need to be examined by a police doctor.'

Maggie nodded. All she wanted was to get out of this place with its awful memories.

It was her word against his. Tony was denying rape. 'Why should I rape anyone? I can get any girl I want.'

He was being interviewed in his hospital bed by the police inspector. His skull was fractured, but it was a thick skull and whatever lay inside it was intact.

'In that case, why did you choke her half to death, Mr Franciosa?' inquired the inspector, whose brusque bedside manner was causing concern to a hovering nurse, who wondered why on earth anyone would want to talk to her idol in such a fashion. Especially in his state.

'It was horseplay that got out of hand,' protested Tony. His words surprisingly close to those of Albert, who'd had a quiet word with him before the police arrived. 'You know how it is with us showbusiness types, inspector,' he joked lamely. 'We tend to go over the top sometimes.'

'You nearly went right over the top, Mr Franciosa. You nearly killed her.'

'Nearly killed her? What about what she did to me? . . . Why aren't you arresting her?'

'Because you choked her first. She was acting in self defence.' The inspector didn't like Tony. He never had liked bloody Italians. They were like Germans, only browner. However he didn't like the idea of trying to convict him on Maggie's word alone. He was a famous man was Franciosa/Martini, with plenty of money to spend on lawyers.

Tony Martini was charged with rape and instantly released on bail. The papers made a meal of it. Albert had to cancel the tour and Maggie's voice showed little sign of improving. On the day she came out of hospital, a car had been booked to bring her from Manchester back to Leeds. She asked the driver to call in at Albert's office. Her reception was less than sympathetic.

99

'Well, I don't know how you've the cheek ter come in here after all the trouble yer've put me to,' snapped Albert.

Maggie couldn't believe her ears. She'd gone round expecting tea and sympathy. An apology even, for putting her in a show with a potential rapist. She'd made up her mind to absolve Albert from all blame. How could he possibly have anticipated what Tony was going to do? What Maggie didn't anticipate was Albert blaming her. She wasn't ready for this.

'What are you saying, Albert?' she said. Her voice little more than a whisper.

'I'm saying these things happen and when they do happen, we deal with them ourselves. We don't go running ter the police. You've ruined the whole tour.'

Maggie sat down, trying to collect her thoughts. She hadn't looked at it from Albert's point of view. Was he right? Should she have kept it from the police? How could she? The theatre staff had rung the police, what was she supposed to have done? Tell them it was all a big misunderstanding? She sat there, running things through her agile, but confused mind for some time. No! In no way was she going to feel guilty. She looked up at Albert, with hurt in her eyes. He was showing himself up in his true colours.

'I was raped, Albert. I don't expect you to understand what that does to a woman. But your attitude makes you no better than him.'

'I don't know what yer talking about,' protested Albert, who didn't like being classed alongside an alleged rapist. He took a hundred and twenty pounds out of a drawer and handed it to her. 'Here,' he said. 'This is yer next month's spending money.'

Maggie took it and stuffed it in her pocket. 'I'll be wanting *all* my money as soon as you can make it up, Albert. All the money that's in my account.'

Albert shuffled in his seat, uneasily. 'It's not as easy as that. As yer agent I agreed to invest yer money wisely, ter get decent amounts of interest. I can't just draw it all out like that.'

Maggie ignored his protests and came straight to the point. 'There's no point in you being my agent any more. You've obviously taken Martini's side.'

'I haven't taken anyone's side.'

The situation was becoming clearer to Maggie by the second.

'You've taken Martini's side, because he's the one who hasn't lost his voice, which makes him worth money to you.'

Albert looked uncomfortable at this. He tried to push the conversation in another direction. 'So, yer want ter break yer contract, is that it?'

'I'd have thought that's what you want,' said Maggie. 'What use am I without a voice?'

'Yer'll get it back,' he argued.

Maggie felt her anger rising. 'Oh, so you're a doctor now are you? How come you know more than anyone else? I've been told by experts that it might be permanent. At best, my voice is unlikely to go back to what it was. My career's over. I just want all my money sorting out. Will I need an accountant or can I trust you?'

'It'll take a while ter sort out, there've been a lot of expenses,' grumbled Albert. 'And I'll have ter pay a massive bloody penalty because I cancelled the tour. The insurance didn't cover one artist claiming the other one raped her.'

'I do hope you're not thinking about taking any of that out of my money,' protested Maggie, frustrated at not being able to shout at him.

'The person ter blame should pay for it,' said Albert. 'Only, until it goes ter court, we don't know who's ter blame.'

'Albert, you idiot! Why do you think he almost choked me to death?'

'How would I know?'

'Because you're supposed to have half a bloody brain that's why.' She spun on her heels with tears in her eyes. Her confidence sagging. She needed support, not this. 'Just ... just have all my money ready for me in three days, with proper accounts that I can present to my accountant, and if he's not satisfied, I want him given full access to your books. I understand I have the right.'

Maggie didn't understand anything of the sort. She was blurting out the first thing that came into her head. Albert didn't know either. He wasn't happy with the prospect of his books being examined by a strange accountant. Not one little bit.

Maggie sobbed all the way home. She had no idea whether her voice would get back to normal or not. She just wanted to be rid of Albert. His attitude was appalling. In contrast, her dad had been to see her in hospital and had to be restrained from paying a violent visit to Tony's guarded bed. Charlie's visit had been a great comfort at first, until he told her he was engaged. She congratulated him, her damaged voice concealing the sadness she felt at such news. Maggie's happy world had turned upside down in the space of a couple of days.

Chapter Twelve

September 1959

Johnnie had led the life of a recluse since the showdown in the street. The neighbours had felt obliged to take sides and Johnnie had been cast as the villain of the piece. His only respite came at work. His workmates ribbed him at first about his sexual exploits, but this had soon worn thin and no mention was made of it now. A chance meeting with Denis in the Crimea Tavern had helped ease his confused conscience. But only a little. Johnnie had many things playing havoc with his conscience, his affair with Vera was one of the minor players.

The Crimea Tavern stood on the corner of Inkerman Road and Florence Nightingale Street. Built in the late eighteen fifties, just after the end of its namesake war, it sold Bentley's beer, which made it unique amongst the array of Tetley's and John Smith's houses. There was an old saying among the drinking fraternity of Leeds, 'There are three types of beer, good, bad and Bentleys', but the beer in the Crimea belied this, and proved that a well-kept cellar was the best way to bring in the customers. The cellar at the Crimea was kept as well as any in Leeds.

The conversation-killing juke box was slowly progressing northwards, having made its noisy migration across the Atlantic. Fortunately, it hadn't reached the Crimea, where darts, dominoes and dirty jokes were more than enough to keep the drinkers amused.

Over the years, in keeping with the pub's military background, the taproom had witnessed its own share of battles, all presided over by a faded print of *The Charge of the Light Brigade*. Ornate

Victorian tiles still decorated the bar which sported the original hand pumps. The marble topped tables were supported by heavy, wrought iron legs and would challenge even the most determined thief, of which there were many amongst the Crimea's colourful customers. An ornamental cuspidor had recently been removed by the landlord when one of the more intellectual of the customers explained to his fellow drinkers what a cuspidor was and they promptly put it to its original use.

Johnnie had just walked in and ordered his customary pint on his way home from work. It would be the first of several. He wasn't yet used to living on his own and a few drinks helped ease the loneliness. Then fish and chips or maybe he'd open a tin of spam. Not the ideal diet. Thankfully Openshawe's had an excellent canteen, of which Johnnie took full advantage. His affair with Vera had scared him off women. There'd never be anyone to replace Jean, so why bother trying? He had his hand in his pocket, pulling out a handful of coins when a shout came from behind him.

'I'll get that.'

Johnnie recognised the voice instantly. He turned round uncertainly as Denis got up from his seat and walked across to him, carrying an empty pint glass. The last time Denis had spoken to him had been as a prelude to smacking him in the mouth. Johnnie was understandably cautious.

'Put another one in there while yer at it,' said Denis, cheerfully, to the barman. Johnnie felt himself frowning. Denis held out his hand.

'How're yer doin' Johnnie?'

Johnnie took his neighbour's hand, wondering what the catch was. 'Okay thanks.'

An awkward silence followed, broken by Denis. 'I come in here now and again when I'm on split shifts. Good pint isn't it?'

Johnnie took a long drink then put his glass down on the bar. 'I come in every night, practically,' he said.

'I know,' replied Denis. 'I bet yer knackered. Fancy a sit down?'

He turned, not waiting for an answer, and returned to his table. Johnnie stood there for a second before joining him. Another awkward silence followed. Johnnie wondered whether this was a good idea. Some of his pals would be in shortly, looking for a game of darts. He knew full well that Denis didn't play. Denis did very little apart from decorate his house and go to the pictures. Johnnie was quite surprised to see him in a pub.

'Actually,' admitted Denis. 'I've never been in here before.'

'I didn't think so,' said Johnnie, wondering what this was leading up to.

Denis's face crumpled to the verge of tears. He looked across at Johnnie. 'She's at it again,' he sighed.

Johnnie allowed himself a second or two to figure out what Denis was talking about.

'Vera?' he inquired.

Denis nodded. 'Oh, don't get me wrong. I know it's not you . . . not this time.' He gulped at his beer, spilling some down the front of his jacket. 'One of the blokes at work reckoned he saw her out with someone.'

Johnnie shrugged, at a loss to understand what all this was to do with him. 'Any one yer know?' he asked, not really interested in the answer.

Denis shook his head. 'Just some feller. It's all round at work. I can feel 'em talkin' about me behind me back. That business with you were bad enough.'

'Sorry about that,' said Johnnie inadequately.

Denis smiled. 'I could've bloody killed yer that day!'

'Yer very nearly did.'

'Funny thing was, though, she came crawlin' back ter me and it were brilliant afterwards. She were a proper wife . . . if yer get me meaning.'

Johnnie grinned awkwardly. 'Why are yer telling me all this, Denis?' he asked.

Denis had the look of a defeated man. In his forties, he looked twenty years older. The war had done that to him. He didn't seem to have an answer to Johnnie's question.

'I'm scared ter death of losing her,' he admitted, at last.

Johnnie didn't know what to say. He tried a stab in the dark.

'Yer'll only lose her if yer kick her out,' he advised. Not entirely convinced of his own wisdom. 'There's things she needs ter get out of her system. Tell her yer know about her feller and threaten ter go round and sort him out if she doesn't stop seeing him. She saw how yer sorted me out.'

105

'If I find out who he is I damn well will sort him out!' snapped Denis.

There was another long silence as they both finished their drinks. Then Denis dropped a bombshell.

'Mavis isn't mine yer know.'

Johnnie was on his feet as Denis said this, about to order more drinks. He sat down again.

'Bloody hell, Denis! Are you sure?'

'Damn sure. She were born eight months after I got home. Everybody thought she were a bit premature.'

'I remember Jean saying something about that,' recalled Johnnie.

Denis gave a wry smile. 'That's what we agreed ter let folk think. When I got back from Burma I were in no fit state. I couldn't have fathered a flamin' frog.'

Denis's unconscious alliteration brought a brief smile to Johnnie's lips.

'That war knackered me up no end,' went on Denis. Apparently not wishing to dwell on Mavis's parentage. 'I wished they'd have dropped that bloody atom bomb a few years earlier. Saved a lot o' people a lot o' grief that would.'

'It knackered us all up, Denis,' agreed Johnnie. A certain unwanted memory making one of its frequent excursions into his thoughts. He went to the bar and returned with two foaming pints, having decided at last to tell someone about it. It had troubled him for years. Jean hadn't been the person to tell and Vera had been a bit too shallow for him to share such an experience with. For all his shortcomings, there was nothing shallow about Denis. He placed the drinks down on the table, took his seat, then picked up his own pint, bringing the frothy head to his lips and sipping away the first inch or two, Denis followed suit.

'It knackered me up for a start,' said Johnnie, continuing the conversation as though there'd been no break. 'Not the actual fighting. I could handle that . . . just, but I could handle it . . . It was afterwards, when they kept us back to sort out all them displaced persons.'

'What happened?' inquired Denis. Guessing from Johnnie's demeanour that there was a particular incident that had upset him. Denis had experienced many upsetting incidents.

Johnnie took another reassuring drink of his beer before continuing.

106

'We were in Belgium, just outside Nijmegen trying ter get ter this place called Hertogenbosch. I was driving a three tonner with three blokes in the back and me and Alfie Greatorex in the front. We'd been drinking all day and I hadn't a bloody clue where I was. Shouldn't have been driving really. All the road signs had been taken down, for all I know I could've been in Timbucbloodytu.' He took another drink as the memory came back to him. 'Anyway,' he continued, 'we passed this young girl standing at the side of the road thumbing a lift. Nobody else saw her, only me. I stopped and asked if she knew where Hertogenbosch was, only I didn't pronounce it right and she gave me the most brilliant smile you ever saw. She was about as old as Maggie is now and just as pretty. Didn't understand a word I was talking about, apart from the name of this town, which was a bloody miracle. She pointed down the road and spoke in Dutch. I hadn't a clue what she was saying. Anyway, some of the lads had got out and asked if she wanted a lift. It seemed a good idea ter me, because if I got lost she could always help me out. Trouble was, she got in the back with the three lads ... four lads,' he corrected himself. 'Alfie decided he wanted ter ride in the back.'

Johnnie took a deep breath and another drink. A frown creasing his forehead.

'After about twenty minutes I came ter this fork in the road, so I stopped and yelled through the window for the lads to ask the girl ter come round ter the front. There was all this laughing and carrying on in the back and they obviously couldn't hear me so I got out and went ter see what was going on.'

Johnnie stopped for a while as he gathered the strength to put into words what he saw.

'They had her stripped naked. Alfie was going at her like a steam train. He was the last. They'd all been at her, all four of them.' Johnnie's eyes moistened. 'The girl was crying. Not saying anything. I've never seen anyone so frightened and shocked. I climbed into the back as Alfie finished. They all started pushing me down on her.'

Denis looked shocked. 'Johnnie, you didn't.'

Johnnie took a deep breath and held Denis in his gaze, shaking his head slightly. 'No, I didn't. I'd done enough. I bent down to help her, but she shuffled away from me like a frightened rabbit. She was terrified. The lads were still laughing and goading me on. I should have said something to them, done something. I was the corporal. I was in charge. I just picked up her clothes and threw them at her, telling her ter get dressed. She pulled her stuff all around her ter cover herself up, but she wouldn't do anything while we were watching. She didn't trust us. I made the lads get out of the truck and stood with me back to her as she got dressed. I think at this stage the lads realised what they'd done. They stood around all quiet, not talking to each other. Christ! They'd raped a young girl. As she got out she turned and spat at me. As far as she was concerned it was all my fault. She were bloody right an' all.'

There was a silence between them, Denis wondering how to react and Johnnie wondering if he'd done the right thing telling him.

'What happened then?' asked Denis, eventually.

'Nothing,' said Johnnie. 'If the army had found out about it, we'd have all got ten years. What was I supposed ter do? The girl ran away. Even if she'd reported it, which she probably didn't, there were hundreds of army lorries all over the place and we were where we shouldn't have been. They could never have traced us. A week later we were sent ter France. It's the worst thing I've ever seen. Rape's the worst crime of the lot and I'm responsible for what happened ter that girl.'

'What about the other blokes?' asked Denis. 'How did they feel when they sobered up?'

'Them?' Johnnie almost spat in his beer. 'They were too shit scared of what might happen ter them to have any sympathy for the girl. I played them along for ages, telling them it was me duty ter report it. Anyway, when we got ter France, we split up. I never saw them again. They're probably still waiting for a knock on the door. Serve 'em bloody right.' He took out his cigarettes and offered Denis one. 'Odd thing was,' he added. 'That you'd never have thought them capable of it. They were just ordinary blokes.'

'It'll have been the bloody war,' commented Denis, accepting a cigarette and flicking his lighter into life. 'It brutalises yer. Turns ordinary fellers into animals.'

Johnnie didn't consider this to be much of an excuse, but he didn't say so, Denis had had a much harder war than him. Denis took Johnnie's glass and went off to get two more pints. Johnnie

sat there feeling drained, having dredged up a memory he hoped
would go away. But he knew it never would. Denis returned with
his own problem still on his mind.

'So, you think I shouldn't be too hard on Vera then?'

'I never said that,' argued Johnnie. 'Go home, give her a right
bollocking. Tell her yer want ter know the name of this bloke
she's having it off with, so yer can go round and sort him out. If he
finds out about it, he'll drop her like a hot brick.'

Denis seemed to be running Johnnie's instructions through his
mind, nodding as he did so. Johnnie's advice made perfect sense
to Denis, a lot more sense than it made to Johnnie, who wasn't all
that interested in his neighbour's marital problems.

As luck would have it, Johnnie's advice worked, earning him
Denis's eternal gratitude. Something he could have really done
without.

Less than a week later, Maggie hit the headlines for all the wrong
reasons. Johnnie had immediately dashed over to Manchester to
visit his daughter in hospital, and had been frustrated in his
attempts to vent his anger on Tony Martini. He was now looking
forward to her coming home. It was Saturday morning and he
made his umpteenth visit to the window to check the street outside
for an approaching car. A few weeks at home with him and she'd
be as right as rain. That Eyetie singer'll get his come uppance. A
few years in clink and he'll be singing a different tune. He felt a
rage surge inside him at the very thought of Tony Martini. At last
a car drew up outside. It could only be Maggie. Cars were still few
and far between in Hope Street. As he opened the door she threw
herself into his arms, weeping noisily. The driver, standing behind
her, shrugged his lack of understanding and waved a farewell
hand, which Johnnie returned automatically.

Taking her into the front room, he sat her down. The look on
her face disturbingly reminiscent of a certain young lady's face
from the past. A ghost not yet laid.

'I'll make you a nice cup of tea,' he decided, inadequately.

'Thanks, Dad.'

Her entourage of sycophants had faded into the background,
leaving only, as far as she knew, her dad. Whose love she knew
she could rely on. She listened to him whistling away, perhaps to
introduce a cheerful atmosphere. It helped. He brought back two

cups of tea. Hers made exactly as she liked. 'Never mash tea with the water off the boil' was his tea making motto. 'Always take the pot ter the kettle.'

Her tears were still dropping into her cup.

'Yer'll make yer tea go cold, crying into it like that,' he joked, gently.

She smiled and wiped her eyes. Johnnie didn't press her on anything. It would all come out in her own good time.

'You must think I'm a real softy,' she said.

'I think yer a lot of things, love,' replied her dad, 'but softy's not one of them.'

'I've just been in to see Albert,' she explained. 'I've just told him I don't want him any more.'

'You'll have had your reasons,' accepted Johnnie, wondering what the reasons were.

'Bloody good reasons,' said Maggie, giving her dad a guilty look for swearing in front of him. He hadn't noticed. 'He reckons I'm as much to blame as Tony Martini,' she explained without thinking. Unaware of the strong feelings her dad had on the subject. He didn't say anything.

'He's had to cancel the tour and reckons I should pay my share of his losses.'

Johnnie felt his anger rising to boiling point.

'He reckons me being raped was just a bit of horseplay that got out of hand and I shouldn't have told the police.'

This was too much for Johnnie. If Maggie had realised what she was doing, she'd have kept her mouth shut. Johnnie opened and shut his fists, trying to control himself.

'Look, Maggie,' his voice was shaking with emotion. 'I need to go out for a bit . . . will yer be okay on yer own?'

She took his hand and squeezed it.

'Course I will, Dad . . . oh, and Dad.'

Johnnie turned.

'Thanks,' she said.

'Thanks for what?'

'For being a smashing dad.'

This was the biggest compliment he'd ever been paid, and it was with mixed emotions that he strode out in the direction of the Albert Drake Entertainment Agency.

*

110

Tony Martini waited in his car until Maggie left. The press had been hounding him all week, but this morning he'd given them the slip. Surprisingly, no one was watching Albert's door. Maybe the rape was old news now, he certainly hoped it was. His solicitor, to whom Tony had professed his innocence, had told him he'd probably get away with it. His word against Maggie's, the jury wouldn't know who to believe. Maggie would be well advised to drop charges.

He waited for a minute or two after Maggie's car had disappeared, before going into Albert's office. He was another one who had a vested interest in believing Tony's version of events.

He greeted his manager cum agent with a cheery, 'Morning Albert.'

'Morning Tony . . . I suppose you saw her leaving?'

'I did,' confirmed Tony. 'I thought it better to keep my distance.'

'Very wise . . . she's an unbalanced young lady at the moment. She's just told me she doesn't want me ter manage her any more. Mind you, with her voice gone, there's not much left ter manage.'

'I blame myself for that,' said Tony, with contrived contrition. 'Our game got a bit rough. I got a bit over-excited.'

'Who can blame you?' excused Albert. 'She's a beautiful young lady. Still, there's no excuse for her to accuse you of rape. Did you get on ter that solicitor I told you about?'

'Yes I did. He figures there's not much of a case against me.'

Albert nodded and lit a cigarette. 'I'm always suspicious of women who reckon they've been raped,' he commented. 'There's an old saying, woman with skirt up, runs faster than man with trousers down. Lot of truth in that y'know. Drink?'

Johnnie's mind was ablaze as he stormed through the streets towards Albert Drake's office. There was no fixed plan in mind. He just wanted to confront the man who thought his daughter was partially to blame for being raped. He wanted Drake to tell him this to his face, if he dared.

He felt an unreasonable sense of guilt for not having been there when she needed him. Story of his life. Never there when people need him. He should have been with Danny on the day he died. His birthday of all days. Died on his own on his birthday. If he'd made sure the girl in Holland had got into the front of the truck with him, she wouldn't have been raped. Why him? He was no worse than the next man, so why him all the time? His mind was becoming a confusion of self pity and self-flagellation as his pace quickened to match his racing thoughts.

They were halfway through a bottle of Scotch when Johnnie burst in. The sight of both of them together turned his confusion into blind rage. Without saying a word, he threw a punch at Tony that knocked the singer right across the room and on to the floor. Johnnie was on him in an instant, pummelling him into unconsciousness, trying to purge his anger, but not succeeding. Albert, in an attempt to save Tony's life, smashed a chair over Johnnie's head, then stepped back in dismay as Johnnie stood up and turned on him. No words had been spoken up to this point, Johnnie changed all that.

'You lousy bastard!' he hissed. The venom in his voice making Albert's blood run cold. 'You think my daughter asked for it did yer?'

Albert shook his head. 'Now then ... I never said that, Johnnie!' he protested wildly. Johnnie had picked up the chair Albert had hit him with and was advancing on the terrified agent. Johnnie could feel himself going dizzy, blood was pouring down his face from a wound caused by Albert's attack on him. Only his intense rage kept him conscious. He feinted with the chair, causing Albert to cringe, turning away and protecting his head from the inevitable attack. Johnnie smashed the chair down on him with all the force he could muster. Albert dropped to the floor and Johnnie hit him again and continued to hit him until he himself passed out, knocking over a paraffin heater, the fuel spilling over the floor and bursting into flames. But Johnnie was oblivious to this, as were Albert and Tony Martini.

The office was on the first floor, above a bank, which was closed on Saturday and the flames had taken hold before anyone noticed them. The three bodies were charred beyond recognition. It was a fair assumption that one was Albert. Tony Martini was identified by the inscription on the gold medallion around his neck, still readable, despite almost melting in the intense heat.

It was early evening, when Maggie heard about the fire. She'd fallen asleep on the settee and switched on the news when she woke up. Instinct and common sense told her who the unidentified body probably was. She knocked on Vera's door, needing moral support. Denis answered. He'd heard the news, but hadn't associated it with Johnnie. Maggie's garbled, panicking outburst made a little too much sense, especially as he knew Johnnie's views on rape. He was a time bomb waiting to explode.

Between the two of them they identified Johnnie, from his shoes and his watch. Proper identification of all three bodies would have to be made by a pathologist. Maggie threw up in the mortuary. She'd be doing a lot of that in the coming months.

Chapter Thirteen

Maggie's heart lurched when she saw Charlie at the back door. The one person in the world who could make things right for her. The person she'd ditched in favour of the glittering prizes and after promising him she'd never do such a thing. And now she was down and practically out. What right did she have to ask him to join her in her misery? None at all. As she opened the door he thrust a bunch of flowers at her.

'Hiya Maggie.'

She wanted to fling her arms around his neck, but she knew she mustn't. He was engaged now and who was she to spoil it? She accepted the flowers graciously.

'They're lovely, thanks ... and er ... nice to see you,' her manner was deliberately formal.

'I'm ... I was sorry to hear about your dad,' he stammered, not wishing to regurgitate her recent sorrows.

'Thanks, come in.'

He hesitated a second before stepping inside. Not trusting himself not to break his vow of self-restraint and make a grab for her.

'I thought you might have brought Brenda ... I'm dying to meet her,' lied Maggie, convincingly.

'Oh, you'll like her. She's really nice.'

'I bet you love her very much,' Maggie's eyes were searching his for the truth behind his answer. But he avoided her gaze.

'Yes,' he said. 'Very much.' He looked at her, sadly. 'Look,

114

Maggie, we're still good mates, me and you. If there's anything you want, any way I can help, you've only to . . .'

'I know, Charlie . . . and thanks.'

He stood there awkwardly for a second, knowing he couldn't stand much more of this.

'Right,' he said. 'I'll be off.'

'Yes . . . thanks for coming.' Maggie didn't want him to go, any more than he wanted to. A breakdown in understanding. He left quietly and Maggie sat down at the kitchen table and wept.

She sat across the table from Vera, not knowing what to say. She'd tried to get hold of Eileen, without success. No one was answering the phone, perhaps she was away, chaperoning some other young hopeful.

Charlie had been round to see her again, this time with his new fiancée. Maggie could have done without that. Once again she'd cried hopeless tears when they left. Brenda was fairly ordinary, worked as some sort of secretary. No chance she'd ever desert Charlie for fame and fortune. After her dad died, Charlie was Maggie's one hope of salvation. Her one chance of salvaging some happiness from the tragedy surrounding her. But Sod's Law prevailed with a vengeance. She'd wished Charlie and his mousy bloody girlfriend every happiness and wondered afterwards if she should go into acting after such a performance.

Vera was the nearest she had to a confidante. It was a damp Monday morning and her neighbour had been contemplating whether or not to make a start on the washing. A job she hated. Vera's washing machine, although at the cutting edge of technology by Hope Street standards, was barely one step up from a peggy tub and posser. A metal tub which heated the water and did little else. Agitation of the washing was manual, as was the attached mangle. Today's bad weather meant a clothes horse steaming in front of an open fire. Maggie's visit had given her the excuse she needed. Blow the washing – it'll still be here tomorrow.

She reached across and took Maggie's hand, anticipating what she was about to hear, having been in the same boat herself once. Although at the time, she'd confided in no one. Under her particular circumstances, it had been better that way. She decided to ease Maggie's discomfort.

'When's it due, love?' she asked, gently.

Maggie looked slightly shocked at first that Vera should have read the situation so accurately. If she knew, who else did?

'How did . . .?' she began.

'An educated guess,' smiled Vera. 'Don't worry, it's not obvious.'

'End of May, apparently,' said Maggie, answering Vera's original question. 'That's if I have it.'

'Oh!' Vera's face registered no shock, just understanding. 'Need I ask who the father is?'

'I think you've guessed.'

'Tony Martini.'

Maggie nodded, then dissolved into tears. 'God, Mrs Bradford . . . what am I going to do?'

'Right now, nothing love. You've got a bit of time to think about it.'

'I've thought of nothing else for the last week.'

'Who else knows?' inquired Vera.

'No one.'

Vera stood up and walked around the table. Leaning over her and encasing Maggie in her arms. 'Look love,' she consoled. 'Don't ask me how, but I know what it feels like to keep something like that to yourself. It's the loneliest feeling in the world. And it must be ten times worse for you, just having lost your dad.'

'I sometimes think I'm going mad, Mrs Bradford. It's as though someone planted a bomb underneath me and blew my world up. A few weeks ago, I had everything and now it's all gone.'

'I know love,' said Vera. 'Still, you must have quite a few quid kicking about somewhere. That's some consolation.'

'Kicking about somewhere, just about sums it up,' replied Maggie, disconsolately. 'I've been to see an accountant. He did a bit of checking for me, and all my money's tied up in one of Albert Drake's investment accounts. His finances are so complicated it might take years to sort it all out. Even then the taxman gets first bite. Then the accountants and lawyers. I'm owed thousands, but I might not see any of it.'

'Oh dear,' said Vera.

'So,' summed up Maggie. 'In the space of a week, I was raped, lost my voice, my money and my dad.'

'It were just one o' them weeks, love,' sympathised Vera.

Maggie looked at her, astonished at such a grossly inadequate summing up of her situation. Vera realised what she'd said and clasped a hand to her mouth. Their faces began to twitch as they looked at each other. Maggie let out a sharp titter, closely followed by Vera. Soon they were helpless, their laughter bordering on hysteria. The type of laughter where you don't know what you're laughing about. Similar to bursting into tears, insofar as it helps to alleviate the pain.

As the laughter subsided, Vera steered the conversation away to more practical things, like how Maggie was going to live.

'I've got seventy quid between me and the workhouse,' announced Maggie.

This was a lot more than Vera had in the house, but Vera had Denis bringing in fifteen pounds a week.

'It'll not last long,' said Vera.

'If I'm frugal, I can last ... I don't know ... a couple of months,' calculated Maggie.

Something outside caught Vera's eye. Through the kitchen window, beyond Maggie's back-yard wall, she could see a trilby-hatted man pacing up and down. His coat collar turned up against the fine drizzle. Maggie followed her gaze then shook her head, annoyed. Recognising what was underneath the hat.

'It's a reporter.'

'I'll get rid of him if yer like,' offered Vera.

'I wouldn't mind. I've had it up to here with them.' Maggie held a flattened hand up to her forehead.

Vera stood up, went into the scullery and picked up a bucket of dirty water she'd been mopping the floor with. Heaving it out into the yard, she waited until the trilby hat had moved within range, then threw the contents over the wall. A howl of anguish went up from the man. Vera rushed out into the street.

'Oh dear! I'm ever so sorry love. I didn't see yer there,' she lied cheerfully. 'Good God! Yer soaked ter the bloody bone. Were it Maggie yer wanted to see? Only she's gone off for a few weeks to stay with her auntie in Bridlington.'

Maggie was forced to smile as the sodden trilby hat moved off down the street. Vera came back with a triumphant grin on her face.

'He's gone,' she announced. 'Doubt if he'll be back.'

'Thanks Mrs Bradford,' said Maggie, feeling a bit less sorry for herself. A passing neighbour attracted her eye. Mrs Venison, casting a curious glance at Maggie's house. That's what Maggie had become, an object of curiosity. Her record was still at number three and she was back at number seventeen Hope Street. Hard to understand that.

'Do you know what I wish,' she said suddenly.

'What's that love?' asked Vera.

Maggie looked up at her. 'I don't want you to take this the wrong way, Mrs Bradford.'

'Oh, dear!' said Vera, not wanting to be involved in Maggie's wishes.

'I just wish people had thought a bit more about my dad. I gather they all turned against him when er . . . you and him . . .'

'All right love, you don't have ter spell it out. When me and yer dad had a bit of a fling?'

'Something like that.'

Vera shrugged. 'I thought a lot about yer dad. It just happened. As far as I were concerned it were more than just a fling.'

'You mean, you loved him?'

Vera's eyes dropped, her face colouring up. 'I don't know love, maybe I did.'

'You either did or you didn't,' said Maggie, who was young and therefore everything was black or white.

'All right then, I did,' admitted Vera. 'I couldn't help it . . . it just happened.'

Maggie felt a wave of compassion for her neighbour. 'Then . . . you must feel awful about him dying.'

'I do love . . . you've no idea. I'd have run off with him at the drop of a hat.'

'Why didn't you?'

'Yer dad wouldn't have it.'

'Didn't he love you?'

Vera pondered this question. 'I like ter think he did. I like ter think he made me go back ter Denis for me own good and for the kids.'

'Everybody in the street thinks he was a coward for not standing up to Denis, when Denis beat him up,' said Maggie.

Vera laughed. 'I reckon yer dad could've knocked seven bells outa my Denis if he'd wanted. Yer dad just took his punishment like he felt he had to. He were that sort of feller.'

'Thanks,' said Maggie. 'I wouldn't like to think of my dad as a coward.'

Vera looked at Maggie. An idea forming in her head. An idea to boost the posthumous reputation of the man they had both loved in their different ways.

'Yer dad's got a box of medals somewhere, hasn't he love?' inquired Vera.

'Yes,' answered Maggie, puzzled. 'They're in his wardrobe in a shoe box. I once asked him about them, but he reckons they're just the medals everyone got. Campaign medals I think they're called.'

'Never mind what you think, just you nip round and get 'em while I put the kettle on,' ordered Vera, kindly.

She was pouring the steaming water into the teapot when Maggie returned with a John White's shoe box. She placed it on the kitchen table for Vera to open. In it were her father's dog tags, three medals, two round, one star shaped – the France and Germany Star and a small box containing a fourth medal. She showed it to Maggie. 'Have you any idea what this is?' she asked.

In the box was a round, silver medal attached to a red, white and blue striped ribbon. Maggie took it out and examined it carefully. It was inscribed 'For Bravery in the Field'.

'Is it something special?'

'You might say that. It's the Military Medal. Short of the Victoria Cross it's about the best bloody medal they awarded to the common soldier. They only give them to real heroes.'

She found the citation in an envelope at the bottom of the box and handed it to Maggie, who read it with tears in her eyes. The words, 'bravery under fire' and 'without regard to personal safety' jumping from the page.

'Oh my God,' she whispered. 'Daddy, you were a real hero, and you didn't tell us.' She hadn't called him Daddy since she was a girl.

'He didn't tell anyone,' said Vera. 'Yer mam knew, naturally,' she lied. Thinking that Maggie might question why her mother hadn't been let into the secret.

'And you knew,' said Maggie, reproachfully. 'Did he tell you why he kept it to himself?'

'He did,' replied Vera, her mind racing. Maggie looked at her. Her face asking the question.

119

'He wasn't boasting about it when he told me. He just needed someone to talk to. That's how me and him started. One night he just poured his heart out to me and . . . well, I just fell for him.'

'I can imagine that happening,' sympathised Maggie. 'He had a lot of charisma, didn't he?'

'Well, I'm not sure what that means, but it sounds like what he had,' replied Vera. 'He lost a lot of good pals in the war, and saw a lot of awful things. If it got out that he was a hero, it would have been all people talked to him about and he just wanted to forget it.'

'He could have told me,' said Maggie, slightly hurt.

'He would have, in his own good time. But after what happened to Danny, he didn't feel much like a hero. So he forgot about it. But he was definitely going to tell you,' she lied.

'I should hope so,' said Maggie. Her own troubles temporarily forgotten. Tears of self-pity replaced by tears of pride she felt for her hero dad. Vera smiled as Maggie held the medal to her chest and looked at herself in the mirror. Some lies were well worth telling.

Chapter Fourteen

November 1959

Maggie watched the cloud of steam rising from the bath and wondered at what stage she should start drinking. It wasn't as if there was anyone to whom she could turn for advice. Inducing a miscarriage was a very private and secretive business. Those who knew about such things didn't go around broadcasting it. She wished she'd had a bit more practice at drinking. The last alcohol that had passed her lips had been courtesy of Tony Martini, enough to put anyone off booze and Italian tenors for life. She'd bought some bubble bath to make things a bit more pleasant. Kneeling down beside the bath, she dipped her hand in to swirl the water round, then pulled it out quickly before she was scalded.

She looked around the tiny, steam-filled room. At least she'd got this out of her singing career. A new bathroom. Her old double bedroom was now a single, having forfeited half its area to provide space for the bathroom. Just a bath, a toilet and a small wash basin, but a world away from the trip down the yard to the outside lav or a tin bath in front of the fire. The landlord had been quite happy for his tenants to do the conversion at their own expense. At the end of the tour she had intended splashing out on a new house. A three bedroomed semi in Roundhay or Alwoodley. Somewhere nice, away from Hope Street and all its mixed memories.

She turned on the cold tap, then poured herself out a large measure of gin. Uugh! It burned the back of her throat. She diluted it with orange juice, fifty-fifty, filling a tumbler with the mixture then gulping it straight down. Not so bad. A few deep breaths to ventilate her burning throat then she repeated the exercise. Half a pint of gin should be plenty for a non-drinker, she assessed. Better get undressed and into the bath before the alcohol hits the spot.

Placing her clothes neatly on the floor, she dipped a tentative toe in the water, then withdrew it. The water wasn't quite boiling, but it was really hot. She'd have to get used to it. The stories she'd heard all mentioned a really hot bath and a bellyful of gin. She was feeling dizzy now. Dipping a foot right to the bottom of the bath, she gritted her teeth until the pain became bearable, then put her other foot in. Five painful minutes later, she was sitting in the bath. A red mark around her body just below her breasts. Gradually she sank down until the water was up to her neck. Her mind in a fog now. The half-empty gin bottle was on the floor beside the bath. It occurred to her that now she was in position, it would do no harm to have a final swig. If you're going to do a job, do it right. Who said that? No idea, but it's a good saying. She reached for the bottle, and without bothering to dilute it, steeled herself and took a series of large gulps that took care of half the remainder. The raw liquid scorched her throat, she dropped the bottle in the bath, allowing the contents to mix with the bath water. Closing her eyes, she tried to fight the swimming sensation in her head. It wasn't so unpleasant once you got used to it. But what now? she asked herself. How did it happen? Would a tiny baby come out and float to the surface? Oh my God! Surely not? She raised her knees in the air and slid further down into the water. Overcome with drowsiness, then sleep. A drunken, uncomfortable, dizzy sleep.

Then she was awake. The light outside the frosted glass window had turned to darkness. But she had no awareness of time, only of feeling violently ill. Her limbs were leaden and unresponsive to the confused commands of her befuddled brain. With a great effort of will she managed to sit up. The water was cold now. She ought to get out, but the violent nausea within her took priority over everything. With a great retching heave, she vomited into the bath water, time and time again until she was retching on an empty stomach. Exhausted she sank back. The water now polluted with her own vomit, but she didn't care. Closing her eyes, she fell mercifully asleep again.

Hours later, a loud banging on the door woke her for a second.

But her brain switched off the disturbance and she dropped off again. This time sinking dangerously deeper into the water.

Vera was concerned. She knew Maggie was in a state with herself, so just before she went to bed that night she'd called round to check up on her. But Maggie wasn't answering the door. She was definitely in. At lunchtime Vera had heard her running the water for a bath. She definitely hadn't gone out since, or Vera would have noticed.

Both front and back doors were locked. Roy came noseying round to see what was going on and suggested a solution.

'Go on then,' agreed his mother.

Roy went back into their house and reappeared with a hammer, with which he gave the window a sharp tap just below the catch. Within seconds he was inside, opening the door for his mother.

'Maggie!' shouted Vera.

No answer.

'Are you okay Maggie?'

A cursory look into the back room and the scullery confirmed she wasn't downstairs, so Vera, with a degree of trepidation, made her way up the stairs, Roy hard on her heels. There was a choking sound coming from the bathroom, but the door was locked.

'Maggie! Are you okay?'

Silence.

Roy stepped back and kicked at the door with the bottom of his foot. The flimsy bolt gave way almost instantly and Vera pushed past him, looking down in shock at the sight of Maggie, submerged beneath a bath of floating sick. Together they pulled her out and heaved her on to the floor. To Vera's relief, Maggie coughed up a lungful of water straight away.

'There's an airing cupboard on the landing, fetch me some warm towels, Roy,' instructed Vera quickly.

Roy gazed dumbly down on the distressed, naked form of the girl who'd figured in many of his sexual fantasies.

'NOW!' shouted his mother.

Roy reluctantly left the bathroom, returning a minute later to hand the towels to his mother, before being instructed to go downstairs, put the kettle on, and stay down there.

For the second time, Vera's life-saving skills saved the life of a Fish. Applying old fashioned artificial respiration, she soon had

Maggie breathing normally. Although it took a warm fire and several cups of black coffee to restore her to some kind of real normality. Roy had been thanked and banished back to his own house.

'What time is it?' asked Maggie, still disorientated.

'Nearly midnight. I were just about ter turn in when I decided ter check up on yer.'

'Thanks,' said Maggie. 'I'm glad you did.'

'Yer must have been in that bath for nigh on twelve hours, what were yer thinking of?'

Maggie gave her a you-know-very-well look.

'Daft question, weren't it?' conceded Vera.

'Didn't work though,' said Maggie mournfully. 'I went through all that for nothing.'

'Yer not the first an' yer won't be the last,' consoled Vera. 'Mother's ruin only works when it wants.'

Maggie nodded. Her head banging with the worst headache she'd ever had.

'My head's killing me. I need to go to bed, Vera,' she said.

'Best place for yer lass. I'll get yer some aspirins.'

'In the cupboard,' directed Maggie.

Vera stopped to think before she handed Maggie the aspirin. 'Look love,' she said, 'if you really want ter go through with it. I know a woman who'll do a proper job.'

Maggie looked up at her and nodded.

'Right,' said Vera. 'We'll talk about it tomorrow.'

'Mrs Bradford.'

'What, love?'

'Thanks, you're a real pal. I won't forget this.'

'Anytime love.'

Death by Misadventure was the verdict returned on all three victims of the fire. The bodies were too badly charred to reveal any evidence of the fight, thus saving Johnnie's reputation. Henrico Franciosa caught Maggie's eye as she was leaving the coroner's court. He made his way towards her and came straight to the point.

'You could help restore my family's good name.'

Maggie was taken aback. A couple of reporters were taking an interest and she didn't want to become involved.

'How could I do that? Mr Marti . . . Mr Franciosa?'

'I think you know.'

Maggie shook her head, genuinely puzzled.

'You could tell the press that you were mistaken in accusing him of . . . that thing.' He couldn't bring himself to say the word. Maggie helped him out.

'Rape? You want me to say I falsely accused him of rape?'

'All you have to do is say it was a misunderstanding and you were about to drop the charges.' He was aware of the reporters and was keeping his voice low.

'Look, I'm sorry you lost your son, Mr Franciosa. But I lost my dad and I'd be letting him down if I started telling lies just to save your son's reputation. I don't know what went on in that fire, but I know my father wouldn't even have been there had it not been for your son.'

Henrico's voice took on a tone of derision. 'How can you compare your father with my son. My son was a great singer, a famous man. Your father was a coward.'

'I beg your pardon?' Maggie was outraged. The reporters moved in closer.

'I read about your father,' continued Henrico. 'About how he cowered in the street like a frightened puppy when his lover's husband beat him up. How can a man like this compare to my son?'

Maggie addressed herself to the reporters while jabbing a finger at Henrico. 'Did you hear that?' she yelled. 'A bloody Italian accusing my father of being a coward. Do you know who my father was?'

The reporters kept scribbling and said nothing, hoping Maggie might enlighten them.

'My father was John Fish MM. Do you know what MM means?' She turned on Henrico and addressed the same question to him. 'Do you know what MM means, Mr Franciosa? It means Military Medal. My dad won the Military Medal during the war. The only thing better than that is the Victoria Cross. My dad was a proper hero. Your son was a rapist.'

Maggie spun on her heels and stormed away, followed by the more intrepid of the two reporters, who calmed her down enough to get himself an invitation to look at Johnnie's citation. The following morning, the newspapers made Johnnie an official war hero. Vera read the reports with some satisfaction. If nothing else, it would be one in the eye for the neighbours.

Maggie and Vera hadn't spoken a word all the way there. A bus ride to the West Yorkshire bus station and another out to Birstall. It was a dismal journey. Dismal in purpose, dismal weather and dismal outlook. The scruffier end of Leeds. The trading end. Factories and terraced streets and nothing green to speak of, apart from the bits between the graves in the Jewish cemetery. The most cheerful part of the scenery.

As they stepped off the second bus, Maggie felt her heart in her mouth. Fear of the unknown, self loathing for what she was about to do. She and Vera had kept the secret well. News such as this would have been manna from heaven for the papers.

'Keep yer nerve, Maggie love,' said Vera, supportively. 'I know what yer going through.'

Just for a second, Maggie wondered how Vera knew, but only for a second. She was breathing deeply, convincing herself that she was doing the right thing. Of course she was. She didn't want the child of a rapist. How could she love such a child? What sort of future would she have? With no money to bring the child up it would have to be adopted or put in a home . . . and what would the future hold for Maggie Fish?

'Just up this street,' said Vera, who seemed to know her way. 'And you mustn't worry. Freda Joynson used to be a midwife, only she's sort of retired now. She'll do the job right. And don't mention the crackpot methods you've been using.'

It was a terrace house, a bit bigger than the ones in Hope Street and built in Yorkshire stone. The house even had a small front garden. Well tended, roses neatly cut back for the winter, the lawn nicely edged, with a stone bird bath at one end. A normal garden. Must belong to normal people. Reassuring that. On the stone gatepost was a rustic sign, the type sold in gift shops. ALFREDA, it read. A strong clue as to the names of the occupants, handy for the over-friendly door-to-door salesman. Maggie clutched the twenty pounds in her pocket. The last of her money, after this she'd have to rely on the dole. Vera knocked on the door.

A woman answered. This must be Freda. Maggie examined her face for any signs of madness or brutality or criminal tendencies of any sort. Any hint and Maggie had made up her mind to walk

126

away. Trust your own judgement Maggie. Don't let just anyone fiddle around with your body. You have to have absolute trust in them. Freda gave her a motherly smile which Maggie returned.

'You must be Maggie,' she said. She gave no hint as to whether she knew exactly who Maggie was. A famous pop singer with a record still in the Top Forty. Maggie handed her the twenty pounds as she walked in. Freda took it with a polite 'thank you' and showed Maggie into a neat lounge where a plump, middle-aged man was reading the *Telegraph and Argus*. He looked over the top of it and said 'Good morning' to the visitors.

'This is my husband, Alf,' said Freda. 'He'll be off to the club shortly.' She emphasised the end of the sentence by way of a hint to her husband. He folded up his paper and, with a polite, 'Good day ladies,' left the room.

They both returned his pleasantry and sat down on a three-seater settee. Freda brought a tray laden with tea and gypsy creams, to which they helped themselves with the politeness of visiting distant relatives. Maggie nibbled a biscuit and looked around. It was an ordinary room, quite pleasant even. A pleasant house lived in by pleasant people. Maggie was trying to reassure herself that she was in safe hands. Caring hands. Above the tiled fireplace was a print of *The Haywain*, the carpet was newish and soft underfoot. The settee was comfortable. It was a painless room. There was a fourteen inch television set in the corner, set in a large wooden cabinet. Maggie had been thinking of getting one for her dad before . . .

Freda broke into her thoughts. 'I'll take you upstairs shortly.'

She detected a worried expression descend on Maggie's pretty face. 'It'll be okay love,' Freda reassured her. 'I've done it plenty of times before.'

'Will it hurt?'

Freda didn't answer straight away, she looked to Vera for support.

'A bit,' said Vera. 'No more than having a tooth out.'

'I'm not allowed to use anaesthetic, you see,' explained Freda.

It crossed Maggie's mind to remind the woman that she wasn't allowed to carry out abortions, full stop. She kept her thoughts to herself.

A teenage boy, fifteen maybe, came bounding into the house. All noise and energy.

'Mum, can I have a shilling for some sweets, we're off to the shops.'

Freda dug into her pocket for some change as her son hovered impatiently.

'Hurry up, Mum, they're waiting for me.'

'My purse is upstairs,' said Freda at last.

'Whereabouts? I'll get it.'

'No you won't, my lad. I remember what happened last time.' She turned to her two visitors. 'Asked for a shilling, took half a crown.'

The youth grinned sheepishly at his mother's two visitors. He wore turned up jeans and a dirty round-necked jumper, beneath a podgy face. His impatient eyes settled on Maggie. The grin freezing on his face as he recognised her. Freda, realising this, led him into the kitchen before he could blurt out anything embarrassing. But his voice was loud enough for them to overhear.

'What's she doing here?' he asked, excitedly.

'They're old friends, come to visit me.'

'That's Maggie Fisher!'

'Paul, I know very well who she is, I'm not stupid.'

There was a silence as realisation dawned on him. 'Has she come for?'

'Never you mind what she's come for.'

'She has, hasn't she? I read about her in the papers.'

'Paul, if I hear you've been gossiping to your pals again about things that don't concern you, I'll ...'

This was enough for Maggie. She wasn't going to be gossiped about by the Pauls of this world. She stood up.

'Thanks for the tea, Freda,' she called out. 'We'd better be off now. 'Nice to have met you.'

Vera had no intention of giving Maggie an argument. The situation was delicate enough, without having teenage boys sniggering about it. She walked into the kitchen and smiled at Freda.

'Do you still want me to get you that ...' she finished her sentence with a knowing nod.

Freda looked baffled.

'It'll be twenty quid,' went on Vera.

'Oh, right.'

Freda took the money out of her pocket and gave it reluctantly to Vera, before returning her undivided attention to her son, who'd lost any chance of a shilling for sweets.

Chapter Fifteen

Christmas 1959 came and went without celebration at number seventeen Hope Street. Maggie's accountant had confirmed that her money was well and truly tied up in Albert's estate. Instead of placing her money in his clients' account he had, for reasons best known to himself, put it in his business account, leaving a web of confusion to disentangle. At best she was an unsecured creditor behind the taxman, the accountants and the solicitors. Between them they managed to lay claim to the exact amount owed to Maggie, leaving the cupboard bare and Maggie officially broke. The Bradfords had invited her round for a Yuletide glass of sherry, but Charlie had been conspicuous by his absence. Roy had been nice to her though. Having grown up together they almost regarded each other as siblings. At least that was how Maggie regarded Roy. His affection for her had little to do with brotherly love. Like Maggie, he was eighteen. Big, likeable and clumsy. On leaving school, Johnnie had got him a job at Openshawe's, where he was well thought of, but would never aspire to management. Just another shop floor worker. He referred to Maggie as 'Our Lass' as opposed to Mavis, who was 'Our Young Un'.

Maggie's erstwhile celebrity, oddly enough, kept many suitors at bay. Roy included. He assumed that Maggie had her sights set on someone better than him, so he never made a play for her, much as he would have liked to. He had to content himself with the memory of her lying naked and half drowned on the bathroom floor. Her body liberally smattered in vomit. Not a memory he'd have chosen as ideal, but beggars can't be choosers.

Having spent the last of her money, she would now have to place herself at the mercy of the state. A grim prospect for a pregnant, unmarried young girl in 1960. It wouldn't have been so bad if her voice could get back to normal. At least she'd have that to fall back on.

Having given up the idea of abortion, she'd now resigned herself to having to go through with the pregnancy. Adoption seemed the best course now.

The Employment Bureau had nothing to offer on such a short term basis for someone with no qualifications, no experience and four months' pregnant.

'I suggest you try Bridgefield House,' suggested the man behind the counter with ill-concealed disgust. 'They cater for people in your er . . . position.'

'Bridgefield House?' Maggie repeated the name with horror. She'd never seen the place. Up until then she wasn't even sure it actually existed outside dirty jokes and seedy remarks. Bridgefield House, home for fallen women, to give it one of its more respectable descriptions. The Pudding Club Hotel and The Beeston Bastard Baby Home, being more popular titles.

'Never in this world,' she said, getting up to leave. 'I'll throw myself under a bus first.'

'That's what they all say,' said the man, before adding ominously, 'at first.'

'Honestly love,' said Vera. 'I'd let yer stay here, but as yer can see there's just no room. Our Roy has to have his own room and our Mavis's room just isn't big enough for two young women and a baby. Anyroad, if t' landlord found out there'd be hell ter pay.'

Maggie knew she wasn't just making an excuse. She hadn't actually asked Vera, but she wouldn't have turned her down if she'd have offered. But it wouldn't have been practical. She'd made discreet inquiries about Bridgefield House and she wasn't impressed. Unfortunately, it looked like being her only hope.

Her landlord's agent had reluctantly given her notice to quit. 'If it were just up ter me, yer could stay on love, but I'm only the messenger boy.' All landlords were beginning to use agents to do their dirty work for them. Bridgefield House beckoned.

It was 1 February when she moved in. Her furniture and household goods in Hope Street had been bought by a house clearance man for £45 17s 6d – a price she wasn't in a position to refuse.

Vera, who knew about such things, advised her to say nothing to the warden at Bridgefield House about having any money.

'Stick it where they can't find it. A bit o' cash allus makes yer feel more secure, especially if no one knows about it.'

So Maggie put £40 in the Yorkshire Penny Bank, left her bank book with Vera and treated herself to a five shilling taxi ride to Bridgefield House.

All her stage clothes were stored in a trunk in Vera's attic. The rest of her stuff crammed into a leather suitcase, a reminder of better times. The clothes inside her suitcase spoke of an opulence far removed from the present reality of her life.

Bridgefield House was a charitable institution funded by various churches and subsidised by the state. It was to provide a haven for unmarried girls with unwanted pregnancies. Girls with nowhere else to go. A last resort. The babies would invariably be put up for adoption and the girls sent on their way with a flea in their ear and a sermon about the dangers of promiscuity.

There was no one to greet her. At first she thought this odd, having told them she was coming. She'd long since become used to people not fawning over her any more, but this was worse. This was a place where the residents were one step removed from jailbirds. There was a large hallway with brown lino on the floor and a noticeboard on the paint-peeling wall mainly informing residents of what they mustn't do:

No smoking in communal areas.

No alcohol allowed on the premises.

No loud radio or gramophone playing in residents' dormitories.

Doors locked at 9 pm opened 7 am. Entry or exit between these times only in an emergency. Residents wishing to enter or exit between these times must ring the warden's lodge.

No male visitors allowed without permission from the warden.

Anyone found committing a criminal act of any kind on the premises will be immediately handed over to the police.

Maggie was browsing through the list when she sensed someone behind her.

'You'll be our famous new resident then.'

Maggie turned round slowly. A young woman was standing there. Quite a lot older than Maggie, late twenties in the face and late forties around the eyes. Not as tall or as pretty as Maggie, but there was a certain cheekiness about her that would see her through the life she'd chosen for herself. She held out a hand. 'I'm Sylvia,' she grinned. 'No need ter tell me who you are.'

Maggie took her hand and nodded ruefully. 'Just don't expect me to go round singing all the time and we'll get on fine, me and you,' she said.

'Fair enough,' said Sylvia. She took out a cigarette and lit up with complete disregard to the regulation Maggie had just read. 'Have yer seen Cuddly Dudley yet?'

'Who?'

'Cuddly Dudley, that's what we call him. Mind you he's not so bloody cuddly.'

'You mean Mr Dudley, the warden?'

'Yeah, he's in his office now. Shall I show yer?'

'Please.'

She followed Sylvia up a flight of stairs, at the top of which was a door marked Manager.

'He don't like being called warden,' explained Sylvia. He reckons manager sounds posher. Snobby bugger.'

'What's he like?' asked Maggie.

'Have you ever seen an arsehole wearing a wig?'

'No.'

'You will in a minute.'

Maggie knocked on the door and waited. No answer.

'He's definitely in,' said Sylvia.

Maggie knocked again. This time the door swung open and she was confronted by a large, angry-looking man. Sylvia had gone.

'I heard you first time,' the man thundered. 'No need to try and knock the door down.'

His deep-set eyes glared at her from either side of a long sharp nose. His head was curiously adorned with a wig, which he'd obviously bought some time before his straggly beard turned grey. Dudley was in his late fifties and looked a good ten years older.

'I assume you're Margaret Fisher, the singer,' he went on.

'Maggie Fish, the ex-singer,' corrected Maggie, taking an instant dislike to the man.

'You'd better come in and let me have a few particulars,' he grunted.

She followed him through and sat in a high-backed chair to face

133

him across a small desk adorned with just a telephone, a half empty cup of tea and and the *Daily Mirror*. He must have been too busy reading that to bother with her first knock, deduced Maggie. At least she knew where she stood with him.

'Question number one,' he asked. 'Better get this out of the way. How much money do you have?'

'About five pounds.' She saw no reason to tell him of the small sum she had left in her bank.

'So, what happened to it all?' he asked, rudely. 'I thought you pop singers were all millionaires.'

'Whatever money I have is all tied up in my dead agent's estate.'

His face brightened at this. 'Ah! So you do have money then?'

'None that I can lay my hands on. Why are you asking me about money, Mr Dudley? I don't wish to be rude, but if I had money I'd hardly be here would I?'

'I'm asking, Miss Fish, because Bridgefield House isn't a free ride. You either pay or you work. The board and lodging here costs six pounds a week. If you work, we pay three shillings an hour, so we expect forty hours' work a week out of our non-paying residents. It's spread out over seven days, so it's not as bad as it seems.'

'What sort of work, Mr Dudley?'

He lifted his tea to his mouth and took a noisy slurp. 'Cooking, and cleaning mainly. We take in outside laundry to supplement our grant, you'll be expected to do your share of that as well.'

Maggie nodded. Hard work might help take her mind off things for now.

'What about medical care?' she asked, politely.

He nearly choked on his tea. 'Medical care? How do you mean, medical care?'

Maggie stood her ground. 'I mean do we get pre-natal care? Does an obstetrician come round at all? Things like that.'

'You're taken proper care of, young lady. And may I remind you that you're in no position to get bolshy with me. The state you're in is of your own making. You've no one to blame but yourself.'

'I'm in this state because I was raped, Mr Dudley,' she said coldly. 'And may I remind you that the last person who said I brought it on myself is dead and buried for his trouble.'

She knew she should have held her tongue. He fixed her with an icy glare. 'This interview is over, Miss Fish. You're in room six. Good day.'

Room six contained four single beds, two of which were currently occupied. Rooms 1–6 were all pre-natal. The post-natal rooms, 7, 8 and 9, were all on the ground floor as was the maternity room, where the babies were delivered, unless there were complications, in which case Hyde Terrace Maternity Hospital was only a five-minute ambulance ride away. There were thirteen mothers-to-be in residence, all thirteen paying their way by working right up until the last week of pregnancy. They would all be allowed one week's free post-natal residence and as few of the young mothers would be in a position to bring up their babies on their own, the infants would normally be sent away for adoption or fostering. Officially, mothers would only be allowed to keep their babies if they could prove they could give them the care they needed. As this often presented difficulties, some of the new mothers would disappear with their babies, knowing that no effort would be made to find them.

Maggie lugged her suitcase along the corridor, past two girls lethargically scrubbing the floor. She stepped carefully, trying to avoid messing up the area they'd just cleaned. A harsh voice boomed from behind her.

'We're paying you ter work, not piss about. Put some beef into it.'

Maggie turned round. The voice belonged to a long thin woman, with mean eyes and a white coat. She turned her attention to Maggie.

'Are you Maggie Fisher?'

'Yes.'

'Will yer be working or shirking?'

Maggie hadn't a clue what she was talking about, so she kept her mouth shut. The woman spoke again.

'While yer here, will yer be workin' like these two are pretending to, or will yer be paying yer way?'

'Oh,' Maggie understood now. 'I'll be working.'

'By heck! I bet the papers'd love that if they find out.'

'I've no doubt they would,' replied Maggie. 'But you'd lose your job if the trustees found out it was you who told them.'

135

Maggie had few friends left, but a local councillor pal of Johnnie's, who just happened to be a trustee of Bridgefield House, had been round to call on Maggie when he heard the rumour that she'd applied to go into the place.

'I'd love to be able to pull a few strings for you, love, and get you in somewhere better. But the truth is, there is nowhere better, unless you're prepared to pay. All I can do is give the place the hard word to keep their mouths shut about you being in there. If they value their jobs they'll do as I say. The same goes for all the girls as well.'

'I'm going to be popular when I get there,' Maggie had said.

'So long as you haven't got reporters buzzing around you all day long, that's all that matters.'

The mean-eyed woman grunted something and walked off, too far away to hear the cursed insults of one of the two girls scrubbing the floor. Sylvia was standing at the door to Room 6 as Maggie arrived.

'Take no notice of her,' she advised. 'The snotty cow were in here herself once. Thinks she's a cut above everyone now.'

'Who is she?' asked Maggie.

'Lorna Boothroyd, her offical title's care supervisor, though yer wouldn't know it. She doesn't care a toss, doesn't our Lorna. She's got three care assistants under her, they all work shifts, there's only ever one here at a time.'

'Only one,' remarked Maggie. 'And how many, you know, girls are there?'

'Thirteen with, three without,' said Sylvia, informatively. 'The three without are all giving their sprogs up for adoption. Best thing for 'em. I gave me last one up.'

'So, this is your second?'

'Hazard of the industry, Maggie lass. Not all of me clients are gentlemen. This is it though, for me. From now on, no more bare back riding.'

Maggie didn't need her to spell out what her profession was. She couldn't help feeling a wave of disgust at Sylvia's blasé attitude towards it all.

'What about the other girls? Are they . . .?' she was searching for the words.

'Prozzies?' said Sylvia, helpfully. 'Nah, a couple of 'em are. But most were just caught out.' She studied Maggie keenly. 'How come you're in here?' she asked suddenly. 'Why didn't you have it sorted out?'

'Abortion you mean? I tried, but couldn't go through with it.'

Sylvia nodded her understanding. 'I know, messy business. Bloody dangerous as well. I had a pal died a couple of years back, having an abortion.'

Maggie didn't want to talk about this; she changed the subject. 'Are you a worker or a shirker?' she inquired, using Lorna's terminology.

'Me?' laughed Sylvia. 'I'm a worker. We all bleedin' work. I expect you've got enough stashed away not to have ter bother, haven't yer?'

'I've got five quid stashed away. Most of the rest is where I can't get at it. Probably never will.'

Sylvia didn't understand this and made no attempt to try. 'Tell yer what. I'll tell Cuddly that you and me want ter work together as a team. We should have a few laughs if nowt else. What d'yer say?'

'Will he allow it?'

'He will if I ask him.'

Maggie decided not to ask Sylvia what sway she held over Cuddly Dudley. 'It's okay by me,' she agreed.

One of the corridor cleaners came into the room, her stomach swelled to imminent birth proportions.

'This is Marie,' introduced Sylvia.

'Hello Marie,' said Maggie, holding out her hand.

Marie took it in a featherlike grasp. 'Hello,' she muttered, head bowed. Maggie detected a hint of an accent.

'Marie's a Catholic,' explained Sylvia. 'She's from Ireland. Two weeks on English soil and she's up the duff. Her loving mammy and daddy kicked her out and the loving father's nowhere to be found. Apparently he were a Bradford lad. You'd expect no better from a Bradford lad.'

Marie looked about fourteen, curly red hair and heavily freckled face. She looked as though she should still be at school.

'She's only sixteen,' went on Sylvia. 'Lorna treats her like shit, so us girls make up for it by mothering her along a bit.' She smiled at Marie. 'Don't we, darlin'?'

Marie gave a wispy smile and nodded.

'I'll leave you two ter talk, while I have a word with Cuddly about our roster,' said Sylvia, cheerfully.

Maggie looked around the room that was to be her home for the next few months. There were four single beds, a chest of drawers beside each and four clothes rails along the walls. Two of which were partially hung with clothes. It was obvious at a glance which was Marie's and which was Sylvia's. Marie's was sparse, just a drab dress, a skirt and a pair of slacks. Sylvia's was crammed with an assortment of gaudy attire, spilling over on to one of the empty rails.

The floor was covered with a threadbare carpet square bordered by lino. There were two windows, each with venetian blinds, one broken and hanging at an oblique angle, half closed. The pictures pinned on the wall indicated a variety of musical tastes from Elvis to Frank Sinatra. Maggie shivered and walked over to the radiator, it was cold.

'Don't they have any heating in the place?' she asked.

'They switch it on in the evening,' answered Marie, 'from six until eight. By nine o'clock it's freezing so you have ter go ter bed.'

'Bastards!' commented Maggie, wondering what her trustee friend would have to say if he knew. Marie said nothing. Maggie began to unpack her case.

'You don't look as if you've long to go,' she said, conversationally.

'I'm due next week.'

'And they're still making you work?'

'Dey reckon it does no harm,' said Marie, without a hint of self-pity.

'I don't suppose it does much good,' said Maggie, thankful she had some money in the bank. It would be enough to ensure that she could give up working and pay her way for a few weeks when she got nearer her time.

She finished her unpacking in silence, Marie not being much of a conversationalist. Sylvia came bursting back in.

'Right, Maggie love, that's settled. Me and you are doing morning cleaning, afternoon laundry. Two days on, one day off.'

'You must be on good terms with Dudley,' commented Maggie with badly disguised suspicion.

Sylvia laughed out loud. 'Dudley has a wife who thinks the sun shines out of his arse. I keep threatening to ask her what she thinks about the mole at the end of his dick. Oddest looking thing, like a bowler hat.'

Maggie was shocked. 'You mean he . . . with the girls?'

Sylvia laughed, mainly at the expression on Maggie's face. 'Don't get yer knickers in a twist, Maggie love. He used ter be one of me clients, well sort of. Yer should've seen his face when I turned up here. He takes his business ter Bradford usually, so he doesn't get recognised. Only I was there one night, visiting a mate. She said I could try out her patch for a couple of hours, which I thought was very nice of her. Anyway, this clapped-out old Austin rolls up and this hairy face pokes out of the winder. I knew whose face it was straight away . . . like a rat peeping out of a yak's arsehole.'

'Dudley?' guessed Maggie, recognising the description.

'Correct,' said Sylvia. 'He asks how much for a straight shag, just like that. No finesse or nowt. He didn't recognise me at first. Well, I were in me working gear, yer know, tits practically hanging out, skirt up round me arse.' She took out her cigarettes and offered one to Maggie, who refused, not having touched one since that night with Vince Christian. Sylvia blew out a cloud of smoke and sat on the edge of her bed.

'Well, we both got in the back of his car and I asked him ter get his dick out so I could make a start. I were late for me bus see, I only had twenty minutes. He seemed a bit embarrassed so I got it out for him. Honestly, I thought he'd got a chocolate raisin stuck to it. He saw me staring at it, which I suppose was a bit rude on my part. But I couldn't help it. End on it looked just like Stan Laurel. Well, I just couldn't help meself. I just cracked out laughing. I know it weren't very professional, but honestly Maggie, you'd have done the same.'

Maggie was laughing anyway. Marie, who'd heard the story before, smiled a little. Sylvia continued.

'As soon as he heard me laughing, he remembered who I was and told me ter piss off and what was I doing in Bradford? As if he owned the place. Anyway, we did no business but I got a good look at his dick.' She laughed at a sudden recollection. 'I once asked his wife if Stan Laurel made her laugh. He nearly had a fit.'

'So,' said Maggie. 'You've got a bit of a hold over him. Handy that.'

'All three of us have got a hold over him, Maggie. But yer must remember, knowledge is power.'

Maggie was impressed by Sylvia's grasp of philosophy.

'One of me clients is a university professor,' explained Sylvia. 'He likes to educate me while we're doin' business. Each to his own, I say. It's one way o' learning. Never took much notice at school. Funny how yer never forget things what's taught to yer while yer havin' a shag. Have you noticed that?' She seemed genuinely curious. Maggie and Marie shook their heads. Marie had only had the one and Bradford lads tend not to philosophise much while copulating.

'What I'm trying ter say,' expounded Sylvia. 'Is ter keep this thing about Cuddly between the three of us. It stops bein' useful once his wife knows. And I don't trust some of them other lasses not ter blurt it out at the first opportunity.'

Chapter Sixteen

Had it not been for Sylvia, life at Bridgefield House would have been unbearable. The work was tedious and arduous. Especially the laundry room. Marie had a baby girl the week after Maggie moved in and the child was instantly snapped up for adoption. Marie, looking drained and emaciated, called in to say her goodbye. Maggie got the impression that she and Sylvia were the only friends the girl had in this country. She was being sent back to Ireland, presumably to restart her life. Her unplanned motherhood a well-kept secret. She'd marry some lusty Catholic lad who'd give her a brood of children and a drunken crack round the head on a Saturday night. But she'd be happier than most.

March came in like the proverbial lion, blowing slates off the roof and causing the rain to come into Maggie and Sylvia's room. They weren't the only ones to suffer, but Sylvia miraculously persuaded Dudley into having theirs repaired first. No one else came to replace Marie during Maggie's stay, which was handy, as both she and Sylvia took up more than their share of space on the clothes rails. Maggie half expected Charlie to turn up. A visit from him would be nice. She had to switch him from her thoughts, lest she became too depressed. March turned into April and Sylvia was now full term and carrying all before her.

'They ought to issue us wi' bleedin' wheelbarrows to carry the buggers about in,' she commented as they sat together on the wooden garden bench in front of Bridgefield House, watching the buses go by. Maggie had a question to ask and was trying to consider her wording carefully.

'What's it like, giving your baby away?' was all she could come up with.

Sylvia was still for a moment before replying quietly. 'It easier if yer don't bugger about.'

'How do you mean?'

'I mean,' said Sylvia, flicking her cigarette stub over the wall with practised ease. 'You let 'em take it away as soon as it's born. Don't ask ter look at it. If they ask you if you want ter breast feed, tell 'em "No". They'll bring some papers for you to sign. Registration of birth, adoption papers and stuff. Don't even read 'em. Just sign. It's the only way.'

'Sounds a bit . . .'

'A bit what?' asked Sylvia, challengingly.

'I don't know . . . callous,' suggested Maggie.

'Maybe it is . . . but it's the only way. The more you have ter do with the kid, the harder it is. Yer can't have it both ways. You either give it away or yer keep it. Me an' you are giving 'em away. A few weeks from now, it'll all be forgotten about.'

Maggie could see the sense in this, but it still seemed a callous thing to do. Looking up at the early spring sky, she let the warm sun bathe her face. A skylark was hovering, way above her, twittering its cheerful song. She wondered if she'd ever sing on stage again. The memories were still fresh. The immense shiver that ran through her body as she walked on stage, nerves transforming into energy. The band playing the opening bars, the audience applauding in anticipation. Her voice filling the auditorium with perfect pitch and power and sweetness of tone and . . . she thought once again of Charlie . . . the hook. Would she ever get it back? The skylark stopped its song and flew away, releasing Maggie from her thoughts. She looked at Sylvia, lighting yet another cigarette.

'You smoke too much,' she observed.

'You're not wrong, Maggie love.'

'What will you do when you leave?'

Sylvia shrugged. 'Back on the game I suppose. It's all I know.'

This depressed Maggie more than she cared to admit. 'You could get a proper job,' she suggested.

'I smoke too much, I ought to get a proper job, what is this? I thought you were me mate.'

'I am,' insisted Maggie. 'And I think you should get a proper job.'

'You just said that.'

'I know and I'll keep on saying it. You're better than that. You're sharp, you're clever, you're throwing your life away. What're you going to be doing in say twenty years?'

'I've heard all this before.'

'Not from a friend you haven't. Go on, what're you going to be doing? Pushing fifty, no husband, no kids who know who you are, what?'

'Why should I care?' argued Sylvia. ' I'll probably be dead.'

'Dead stupid, that's what you are!' said Maggie, angrily. Being raped had given her a whole new slant on life: men who forced girls to give up their bodies, either by force or by bribery, were abhorrent to her.

'I can't do nowt,' protested Sylvia. Taken aback by Maggie's vehemence. 'I've been on the streets since I were seventeen. Me stepdad kicked me out and me mam were too soft to stick up for me.'

'Didn't you have any other relatives you could go to?'

'I've got two older brothers, well, stepbrothers. Our Trevor were in Armley Jail on remand and Ronnie were in Strangeways doing five years for GBH. Mind you, they both think the world of me.'

'They both sound really nice.'

Sylvia laughed at this. 'They're a pair o' rascals all right.'

'What did you do before you were kicked out?'

Sylvia grimaced, almost embarrassed. 'Well, I were still on the streets, but not as a pro.'

Maggie was curious. 'What as then? Surely you weren't begging at that age?'

'Not quite,' grinned Sylvia. 'I were a busker. I had this banjo and I sang comic songs.'

'A busker?' Maggie was impressed at last. 'Why didn't you mention this before?'

'Give over. Me talk about me crappy busking ter somebody what's had records in the Top Ten. I do have some bleedin' pride.'

Maggie could have given her a good argument here, but she chose not to. 'Do you still play the banjo?' she asked instead.

'Nah, I ended up selling it ter buy food. That's how good I was. And that's how I ended up on the game.'

Maggie was inclined to press her for details of how she started, but she wasn't sure of her own motives, so she didn't.

'Actually I weren't all that bad,' mused Sylvia. 'At least I were good on the banjo. Me voice is a bit crap, but I could make 'em laugh.'

'I bet you could.'

'The muckier the song the more they laughed. I got moved on half a dozen times a day by the bobbies, but they never arrested me or nowt.'

'Being able to make people laugh's a much rarer commodity than having a good voice,' said Maggie.

'Give over,' argued Sylvia, faintly.

'I'm telling you,' pressed Maggie. 'Comics have to put up with a load of abuse if things go wrong. Us singers don't.'

Sylvia shook her head in disbelief. Maggie pressed her point home. 'Imagine Mario Lanza walking out on to the stage at the Covent Garden Opera House and saying, "I'm a gonna sing forra you, 'Nessun Dorma'." You never hear anybody shout out "We've heard it! Gerroff Fatso!"'

Maggie had heard Jimmy Diamond crack this one many times, but it had Sylvia laughing. She was still laughing when her waters broke.

Maggie coughed as she lay on her bed, then she cursed mildly, coughing wouldn't do her throat any good, and her voice was her only passport out of this mess. She had a temperature as well. Wonderful! What a time to get flu. Working in the laundry room didn't help, it was a breeding ground for germs.

Sylvia had gone, she was on her own. As planned, Sylvia had given up her baby son for adoption. There was a constant waiting list for healthy babies. Maggie wondered if Dudley was on some sort of a fiddle, selling babies for money. She never referred to him as Cuddly. To her, he was no better than a rapist. Sylvia said she'd keep in touch. Maggie had made her promise to give work a try and not go straight back on the streets. Sylvia had given her solemn word, but Maggie suspected her fingers may have well and truly crossed at the time. She was still determined to follow in Marie and Sylvia's footsteps and have her child adopted. No rapist's bastard for her. Vera had promised to put her up until she found somewhere of her own to stay. She tried her scales as she lay there, her sore throat forcing her to give up halfway through. Normally, her voice was good enough to impress the other girls, who often knocked on her door and asked if they could listen. But that little bit extra wasn't there. That thing which had set her apart from a thousand other club singers. The hook.

Dudley's deferential attitude towards her had hardened since Sylvia's departure. She was tempted to tell him what she knew about his unusual mole, but he was so loathsome that she found it impossible to broach such a personal matter with him. Besides she always sensed that he'd back down rather than risk a confrontation. He was essentially a lazy man, a former cook in the merchant navy, who looked upon the job as a form of semi-retirement. The revenue from the laundry was supposed to help towards the upkeep of the place, but most of it finished up in his pocket. Consequently, he was keen to take in more laundry than was necessary. Prising herself out of bed she made her way downstairs to look at the work roster.

Lorna Boothroyd had had her working in the steamy laundry nonstop for a week since Sylvia's departure. When Maggie looked at the roster for the following week and saw her name down for the laundry every day she rounded on Lorna.

'I'm eight and a half months' pregnant and you've got me sweating full time in that bloody laundry. What's your game, Boothroyd?'

'Don't be so insolent, Miss High and Mighty Fish,' snarled Lorna 'You'll do as you're told.'

'I thought you were supposed to be a care supervisor,' snapped Maggie. 'Has anyone explained to you what the word "care" means? Where did you work before this? Bloody Belsen?'

The rest of the girls were enjoying this exchange, some of them openly encouraging Maggie. Lorna spun on her heels and marched off to Dudley's office.

Maggie was drinking a cup of tea when Lorna returned.

'Mr Dudley wants to see you,' she sneered.

'Didn't you tell him where I was?' enquired Maggie, wearily, looking up. Her face a combination of ill health and bloody mindedness.

'What are you talking about?'

'If Mr Dudley wants to see me, I'm right here. Run along and tell him.'

Lorna's mouth opened and shut like a goldfish, she turned and retraced her steps. Some of the more timid girls left the room to go about their business. Just the curious and courageous remained. Dudley's heavy boots echoed on the parquet floor as he made his angry approach.

'When I ask to see you, I expect you to come to me,' he bellowed.

'What did you want to see me about, that's so important?' inquired Maggie lethargically.

'I understand you're refusing to do laundry duty as per your roster.'

'Correct, I'm eight and a half months' pregnant and I feel ill. You should know better than to expect me to do that. That's why I've decided to give up work and pay my way, from here on in.' She peered up at Dudley and added, 'By the way, your wig's on crooked.'

Dudley's face reddened and his hands went up to his hair, at a loss what to do. Maggie's embarrassing observation had put him at a disadvantage. They were all looking at his hair.

'Paying your way?' spluttered Dudley, turning on Lorna. 'You didn't mention this to me, Miss Boothroyd!'

'She never told me!' protested Lorna.

Maggie thrust six pounds into Dudley's hand. 'Here's my first week's board. I'm going back to bed. I don't feel at all well, I think I've got flu and I don't want to be disturbed.'

Her attitude did wonders for the morale of the watching girls. She left Dudley and Lorna arguing and, coughing fitfully, she climbed wearily back up to her room. Thankful to Vera for foreseeing such an eventuality. Her forty pounds should, she hoped, see her through her pregnancy and beyond. God knows how the likes of Sylvia and Marie had managed to work right up to the last moment. Bridgefield House's reputation was well deserved.

Chapter Seventeen

It wasn't the usual midwife who attended Maggie. Nurse Felix was on holiday in Bridlington and her place taken by Nurse Peggy Irvine, a kindly young Scot. Nurse Felix would have whisked Maggie's infant son into the next room as soon as it was born, but her stand-in didn't know the protocol of such births. To Nurse Irvine, nativity had just one protocol, and that was to place the newborn baby into the mother's arms.

On holding her baby for the first time, any animosity Maggie thought she might feel towards the unwanted child of a rapist didn't materialise. Just a warm feeling that she'd never experienced before. A deep love for this tiny helpless thing nestling in her arms, its eyes closed, its head sticky and skin slightly yellow.

'Is he okay?' she asked, slightly concerned at the colour.

'It's a touch of jaundice, love. Fairly common, nothing to worry your head about.' She looked closely at Maggie, a hint of concern in her eyes. 'How do you feel?' she asked.

'Exhausted,' smiled Maggie. 'Mind you I haven't felt too good for a while now. I think I've got flu or something. Maybe I shouldn't go too near my baby.'

'Babies tend to have a natural immunity to all sorts of things,' Peggy assured her. 'Still, there's no point taking unnecessary risks.' She took the baby from Maggie. 'Right, Mummy. I think we'd better give him his first wash, so he looks presentable for visitors.'

She took the child out of the room and immediately Maggie heard raised voices in the corridor. One of them, Peggy Irvine's. Maggie lay back and closed her eyes. Within seconds she was asleep. It was a couple of hours later when she woke to see Dudley standing over her, with a man she'd seen just once before. Mr Prestwick, the obstetrician. He gave her a broad smile.

'How are you feeling, Miss Fish? Or do I call you Miss Fisher,' his manner was slightly unctuous and made Maggie suspicious.

'I'm feeling a bit weak still . . . and my name's Maggie.' She looked round. 'Where's my baby?' she asked.

Dudley stepped forward. 'Under the circumstances,' he said. 'I thought it best to keep him in the next room.'

'Under what circumstances?' inquired Maggie.

'It's our experience,' said Dudley, attempting a smile, 'that girls who are putting their babies up for adoption shouldn't form a bond with the child. It makes things so much harder in the long run.'

'I want to see him,' insisted Maggie. 'I want to hold him.' The feeling she'd experienced when he'd been placed in her arms was still with her. Unforgettable. She wanted her baby back.

Dudley shuffled uncomfortably, glancing at Prestwick, as if for help. 'I must advise against it,' he said.

'Mr Dudley's right,' confirmed the obstetrician, folding his arms across his chest and looking down upon her with his head to one side. Patronisingly. 'It will only make things harder for you when the time comes to let him go.'

'I'm not letting him go,' decided Maggie, suddenly.

'What?' said both men in unison.

'I want to keep him. He's my baby and I want to keep him.' Maggie had never wanted anything more.

'But you can't!' blurted Dudley.

'Why can't I?' Maggie was frightened now. She had no energy to argue. A tear bubbled up in the corner of each eye.

'You're tired,' soothed Prestwick. 'Just get some rest and we'll talk about this later.'

They turned and left the room. Maggie could hear them talking outside the door, but couldn't make out what they were saying. They moved off down the corridor leaving her alone and desolate and wondering if she'd ever see her baby again.

She was intermittently crying and coughing when Nurse Irvine came in. A shocked look on her face at the sight of her forlorn patient. Taking Maggie's hand, she tried to comfort her. Maggie looked at her imploringly. 'Peggy, please can I see my baby?' she asked.

Nurse Irvine remained silent for a moment, wrestling with her conscience. Then, without saying a word, she stood up and left the room, returning a few seconds later with the baby in her arms. Maggie took her son and cradled him, protectively and gently. Singing to him softly: 'Danny Boy'. The young nurse was entranced. She sat beside Maggie for an hour, chatting. Her soft Edinburgh accent, soothing and comforting. Offering advice, agreeing wholeheartedly with the name Danny, especially when Maggie told her about her dead brother. The door opened and Dudley stood there, fuming.

'Nurse Irvine, what's going on here?'

Peggy turned round, surprised at his attitude. 'What do you mean, Mr Dudley?' she asked.

'I mean,' he snapped. 'Why has Miss Fish been allowed to hold her baby, when it's against my express wishes?'

Peggy Irvine's eyes flashed defiantly. This man had no authority over her. 'I'm afraid Miss Fish's express wishes take priority over yours, Mr. Dudley. We have no right to deny a mother access to her child. You should know that.'

'I'm not talking about right. I'm talking about what's best. It's now going to be so much harder for Miss Fish to give up the child for adoption, and I hold you responsible for that.'

'Adoption?' queried the nurse, taken aback. She looked at Maggie. 'But I thought you said . . .?'

Maggie nodded as she looked up at Dudley. 'I told Peggy I want to keep him. So she hasn't done anything wrong.'

Dudley's mouth opened and shut. Without saying any more, he turned and left the room. Peggy shrugged and grinned at Maggie. 'I seem to have ruffled his feathers. Anyway, I'm glad you're keeping him. He's a bonny wee thing.'

'He is, isn't he?' agreed Maggie, kissing Danny on his soft forehead.

Prestwick was waiting in Dudley's office when he got back.

'Well?' he asked. 'Has she seen sense?'

Dudley looked downcast. 'She wants to keep it. That idiot midwife brought him to her. She was clutching the little bastard in her arms when I walked in.'

'Shit!' exploded Prestwick. 'I promised a certain person that he could have the child.'

'There'll be others,' said Dudley. 'We've got one due any time now.'

'Not with this child's pedigree you haven't. Both parents are brilliant singers and good looking to boot. The child's bound to carry some of their genes. The er . . . certain person's wife had her heart set on this child ever since I told her about it. She has a face like a horse. The Fish child would add a much needed new strain to the family line.'

'Would this certain person be someone who could give your career a boost?' asked Dudley, who knew that Prestwick always had ulterior motives.

'More to the point is the fact that I could give your career a kick in the arse if I blew the whistle on some of your activities,' roared Prestwick, stamping his feet and drawing dust from Dudley's threadbare carpet. 'That should be enough to ensure I don't have any trouble over this. Sort it out, or start looking for another job.'

He pushed past Dudley and stormed out of the building. Dudley watched dismally through the window as Prestwick got into his car. He knew he meant what he said. The dole queue would be beckoning if he couldn't persuade Maggie to change her mind. Maybe even a spell at Her Majesty's Pleasure.

Baby Danny was sleeping peacefully in a cot at the side of Maggie's bed when Dudley came into the room the following morning. Peggy Irvine had gone, leaving Maggie in the dubious care of Lorna Boothroyd and her assistants.

Maggie shot a protective hand out in Danny's direction when she saw Dudley. He held up his hands.

'What on earth do you take me for?' he protested, 'some sort of child abductor? I was acting in your best interests, but if you want to keep the child, so be it. There's nothing I can do about that. Mind you, you might have a job convincing the powers that be that you're a fit person to look after it.'

'I'll cross that bridge when I come to it,' replied Maggie firmly. She still felt weak and didn't want to fight with him over Danny's custody. He looked closely at the tiny beads of perspiration on her brow. 'Are you sure you're okay?'

'I'm a little weak,' she admitted, coughing slightly. 'But there again, I've just had a baby.'

An idea came into Dudley's devious mind. 'I'd better get Mr Prestwick in to give you the once over. You're not looking too well.'

'Okay.'

Maggie didn't object to this. He was right. She'd been feeling ill for a couple of weeks now. She knew it was nothing to do with Danny. A expert diagnosis wouldn't do any harm. Dudley gave a half smile and left. After a while Maggie got up and sat on the edge of the bed. Maybe it was a distortion of her memory, but the baby in the cot looked the spitting image of her brother. She ran a gentle finger across his downy cheek, causing him to open his eyes.

'Hello Danny darling, I'm your mum. You're going to be seeing a lot of me, so the quicker we get to know each other the better.' She picked him out of the cot and carried him over to a chair by the window. Her legs were like jelly and it was with some relief that she managed to sit down. It was a warm May day. All she could see from her low vantage point were clouds and the tops of a few trees. It was a start. Danny couldn't learn about everything at once. After pointing out the limited scenery, she began to sing to him 'Brahms Lullaby'. Singing was the most natural thing in the world. It was what she did. She sat with him for hours. Chatting, singing, kissing him. A mum and her baby boy, enjoying being together. The best time of her life.

A knock on the door heralded Dudley's unwelcome return. He had Prestwick with him.

'Mr Dudley tells me you're not feeling well,' he said, with a concerned frown.

'Yes, Doctor,' she confirmed. Addressing him by a title he'd long since disposed of. 'I've been feeling like this for a few weeks now. No energy, sweating, coughing, headaches. I thought it was due to being pregnant.'

'I see,' he said, fixing a stethoscope to his ears, in that reassuring way that doctors have. 'Let's have a listen to you.'

As he listened, he made a concerned tutting noise. 'I'll just check your blood pressure and then, if you don't mind, I'd like to do a blood test.'

'Blood test? Why do you want to do a blood test?'

'Nothing to worry about, Miss Fish. It's just routine. There's something I want to eliminate from my diagnosis and I can't do it without testing your blood.'

'Eliminate?' queried Maggie. 'Eliminate what?'

'Probably nothing,' said Prestwick. 'So don't start worrying for nothing. Tell me. I know about the tragic circumstances surrounding your poor father's death, but is your mother still alive?'

'Mam? My mam died when I was six.'

'Oh,' said Prestwick. 'I'm sorry to hear that. Do you know how she died?'

'Yes.'

Maggie didn't really want to talk about it at such a time, but she felt she had to.

'She died in childbirth. I'm not sure why.'

'I see,' was all Prestwick said.

His checks complete, he gave her a bottle of aspirin and promised to come back the following day with his diagnosis. Maggie wasn't unduly worried. She knew what was wrong with her. If she had to put a name to it she'd call it BridgefieldHouseitis. Once she was away from there, she was sure she'd be on the mend. Because of her condition she'd been advised not to breastfeed and Danny was taken away at feeding times by one of the care assistants and brought back an hour later. Maggie didn't mind too much. It gave her a chance to get some much needed rest. The following day she felt weaker. Prestwick arrived just after lunchtime. His face was grave when he came into her room. He was alone.

'How are you feeling today Miss Fish?' he asked.

'Not so good,' replied Maggie.

He nodded.

'Have you found out what's wrong with me, Doctor?'

He nodded again.

She studied his grave face and panic set in.

'What?' she asked, frightened of the reply.

He held her hand. 'Maggie,' he began. 'I can call you Maggie can't I?'

She nodded, weakly.

'Maggie ... I'm afraid the diagnosis wasn't good,' he said, very gently. 'It confirmed my suspicions.'

'What suspicions?'

There was a long pause before he said, 'Have you heard of something called leukaemia?'

Her heart was pounding now. 'Leukaemia?' she said. 'It's something to do with your blood isn't it?'

'It's a form of cancer,' he explained. 'Some people call it Cancer of the Blood.'

'Are you telling me I've got . . . leukaemia, Doctor?'

He stared at her sadly. 'I'm afraid it's looking that way Maggie.'

She lay back and looked up at the ceiling. She'd got cancer. Her baby had just been born and she'd got cancer. He'd grow up with no mum, just like her. Only her Danny wouldn't have a father. Her eyes were veiled with silent tears now.

'Is there a cure, Doctor?' she managed to ask eventually.

'There's always hope, Maggie. Science is progressing by leaps and bounds.'

Science progressing wasn't exactly a hope. It was his way of telling her the worst. Maggie knew that.

'Could you leave me on my own, doctor, please?'

'Of course, Maggie. I'll be here for a couple of hours, call me if you need me.'

Maggie lay there with her heart thumping. Confused. Frightened. Wanting her dad, her mum, Charlie, Vera, Sylvia, anyone. My God! She was going to die. This is for real. Nineteen years old and she was going to die. It was so unfair, she didn't want to die. Danny began to cry. She lifted him from the cot and they wept together. One with tears of hunger, the other with tears of despair.

'It's only a question of time now,' announced Prestwick, with a self-satisfied grin on his face.

'What have you said to her?' inquired Dudley, relieved that his job was looking safer.

'I've given her a little fright that's all,' answered the obstetrician. 'Enough to make her hand her baby over.'

'What did you tell her?'

Prestwick hesitated, fixing Dudley with a piercing stare. 'I want you to back me up on this,' he demanded.

'Back you up on what?'

'I told her she's got leukaemia.'

153

'Leukaemia? Bloody hell! You mean she hasn't got it, but you told her she has?' He smiled. An ulterior motive behind his smile. Now he had something on Prestwick. No way would Prestwick ever blow the whistle on his dodgy dealings now. 'What if anyone finds out?' he asked. 'Won't you be in a lot of trouble?'

'Find out?' said Prestwick. 'Who's going to find out? I haven't given her anything in writing. If anyone says anything, I'll deny it. I'll simply say she was confused.'

'Right,' agreed Dudley. 'She's confused all right. One minute she's putting the kid up for adoption, next minute she changes her mind. We can't be putting up with that sort of carry on. I'll back you up all the way.'

And don't even think about blowing the whistle on me, Mr Prestwick, you unscrupulous bastard, he thought.

'By the way, what actually is wrong with her?' he asked.

'Well,' said Prestwick. 'I'm not absolutely sure, but I reckon she's got the flu.'

'Best not go too near her then,' said Dudley.

'Best not . . . I'll leave it a couple of hours, then I'll pop back in to see her while her mind's still not right. Have you got all the forms ready?'

'I'll get Bridget Smith over from the Register Office, she'll sort out the birth certificate. The adoption papers aren't a problem.'

Danny was asleep in Maggie's arms. Her mind seemed to have been racing for hours. What to do about Danny? How much time did she have? She was feeling dizzy now, better put him back in his cot. She kissed him and laid him gently down for the last time.

Prestwick entered quietly. A little apprehensive as to what state he might find her in.

'How are you, Maggie?' It seemed such a stupid question.

'Okay, Doctor,' was the best she could muster.

He sat beside her bed and took her hand. 'Maggie,' he began. 'It occurred to me that you might be worried about what might happen to your son.'

She was staring up at the ceiling. He assumed she was listening to him, so he continued. 'So I took the liberty of making some inquiries on your behalf, so to speak.'

'Inquiries about what?' she half turned to look at him. Danny's welfare being uppermost in her mind.

'Well, I know you didn't want him adopted, but this puts a different complexion on things.'

'Go on, Doctor.'

'I know of an excellent family. I can't divulge their name for obvious reasons, but they're a family of the highest calibre. And they're wanting to adopt a baby boy.'

Maggie returned her gaze to the ceiling. 'I don't want to think about this right now, Doctor.'

'I know, Maggie. I'm sorry. It was clumsy of me, forgive me.' He stood up to go.

'You say they're a good family?' she asked, still looking up at the ceiling.

'Lovely people.' He sat down again.

'How do I know they'll love him?'

'Because they're that sort of people, that's all I can tell you. He'd have a wonderful life, never want for anything, especially love.' Love was obviously Maggie's Achilles' heel, he decided to play the love angle for all it was worth.

'The trouble is,' he went on. 'Is that if we're to place him with them, we must act quickly. They're desperate to adopt.'

'Are you sure they're nice people?'

'They'll give young Danny all the love in the world, Maggie.'

It was the first time he'd referred to the child by his name. Maggie liked that, it seemed to sway her. At least his welfare would be off her mind. If she didn't take this opportunity she'd be doing Danny a grave disservice.

'What do you want me to do?' she asked.

'You're sure you want to do this?' he was taking a risk asking the question, but he thought it might reinforce her commitment.

'Of course I don't want to do it, Doctor, but what option do I have?'

'I'm sad to say that I don't think you have any option, Maggie.' He leaned over and kissed her on the cheek. A Judas kiss. 'I'll see if I can get all the necessary papers,' he said.

Danny awoke again. Not crying, just making baby sounds. Maggie made to pick him up.

'Might I make a suggestion?' asked Prestwick, then continued without waiting for an answer. 'Might I suggest you don't pick him up. Just say goodbye to him where he is. It's just a suggestion. I don't want things to be any harder for you than they already are.'

He left as quietly as he'd come.

Maggie looked down on Danny, smiling through her tears. She stared at him for several minutes. Memorising every detail of his face. The beginnings of his dark hair, his deep blue eyes. All babies had blue eyes. What colour eyes would Danny eventually have? She'd never know. He grasped her finger with his soft and tiny hand and she wished that moment could freeze in time. She wished that they could die together, go up to heaven . . . anywhere. Just so long as they were together. It was the purest love of all. Opening the bedside drawer, she took out her father's Military Medal and pinned it on to his pale blue matinée jacket. One of the two alternatives that Vera had knitted. Then she leaned over and kissed him. Her falling tears landing on his face and making him blink.

'Sorry my darling,' she whispered. 'But mummy has to say goodbye.' He gurgled and smiled up at her. Probably wind, but she remembered it as a smile. Prestwick came back into the room, this time with Dudley and the lady from the Register Office. Her heart almost stopped beating when Dudley quickly picked Danny up and carried him out of the room.

'No . . . don't!' she pleaded. But he was gone.

It was the worst time of times. A couple of scribbled, tear-stained signatures and she was on her own. All alone now. They were walking away down the corridor. With her baby. But what about her? They'd made no mention of what was going to happen to her. Were they just going to leave her here to die? Her cough returned, this time she saw specks of blood on the bedsheets. She was coughing up blood. Here she was, dying, coughing up blood, and in the hands of the most callous bastards on the face of the earth. She wasn't going to die here, among all these uncaring people. Forcing herself out of bed she stood on shaky legs and dressed herself. Checking that her purse still contained two five pound notes and some loose change. It was still there, good. At least they hadn't robbed her of that.

Just her baby.

Her suitcase was too heavy to carry, so she took just the clothes she needed. It looked a nice enough day outside. No one was about, apart from a new girl, scrubbing the hall floor. She looked up at Maggie, a smile of greeting turning into a look of concern.

'Bloody hell, love! Yer look terrible!'

'Thanks,' said Maggie, sitting down on the only chair. She fumbled in her purse, took out a couple of coins and held them out to the girl. 'I don't suppose you could ring a taxi for me could you? The phone's in the doorway.'

''Course I can, love.'

Two minutes later she was back. 'It'll be here in five minutes, they're just round the corner.'

'Thanks.'

The girl returned to her scrubbing, looking up at Maggie occasionally, as if to check that she was still conscious. A hoot outside alerted them to the taxi's arrival. The girl helped Maggie to her feet and outside into the waiting cab. A simple act of kindness, one of the few Maggie had received in that place.

Vera was amazed to see Maggie on her doorstep. 'Is it all over and done with, love?' was all she could think of to say.

Maggie collapsed in her arms. Denis came rushing, in response to Vera's yell. They carried her into the front room, where they laid her on the settee.

'Has she had the baby, do we know?' asked Denis.

'I think we can safely say she has,' deduced Vera, looking at Maggie's recently deflated stomach.

'Blimey! She's not looking so clever,' observed Denis. 'Shall I fetch the doctor?'

'I think yer better had, quick as yer can.'

The doctor took a cursory look at Maggie, did the usual checks, then sent Denis out to ring for an ambulance.

'What's wrong with her, Doctor?' asked a concerned Vera.

The doctor took her on to one side, out of Maggie's earshot. 'I'm not absolutely sure. But there's a strong possibility it could be tuberculosis.'

'TB!' exclaimed Vera. 'Bloody hell! Me dad died of TB just before t' war. Poor lass.'

'It's not as serious as it used to be. Not with modern anti-biotics. I'm fairly sure she'll be okay, provided we've caught it in time.'

'Oh my God, Doctor, I do hope so. She's just had a baby you know.'

'No, I didn't know. Where was it delivered? There's no way she should have been sent home like this.' The doctor was visibly angry.

'Bridgefield House,' said Vera. 'I don't know any more, she passed out when she arrived here.' She walked across to Maggie, whose eyes were flickering open. 'The doctor's here, love. You're going to hospital.'

Maggie gave her friend a thin smile. 'Hello, Mrs Bradford. I had a boy . . . I called him Danny, after . . .' her voice tailed off and she was asleep again.

The doctor's diagnosis was correct. Her life hung in the balance for two days, during which time she lapsed in and out of consciousness. Dreaming confused dreams of Danny the baby and Danny the brother. Of her dad and Charlie and standing on stage in front of two thousand applauding fans, then looking up at Tony Martini as he raped her.

Had Maggie caught TB as a child, and had she been one of the lucky ones who survived, she'd have been convalescing in a sanitorium for anything up to two years. But antibiotics had changed all that. Streptomycin, para-aminosalicylic acid and isoniazid. Long names to shorten the cure. As she regained her strength, her returning health was tempered by an increasing sense of loss. She wept for Danny every day. Charlie came to see her, with Brenda in tow.

'Sorry I haven't been to see you before. I'd have come when you were in . . .' he stopped short of saying the name.

'Bridgefield House,' said Brenda, who had no such reservations. 'He couldn't come because he had mumps, didn't you, Charlie?'

'I can speak for myself, Brenda,' said Charlie sharply. Maggie detected something of an atmosphere between them. Probably caused by Charlie's insistence on coming to see her. No way would Brenda have let him come alone. Their visit only made matters worse. No mention was made of her pregnancy. Some men tend to shut their minds to things like that. He looked uncomfortable, as well he might. Coming to visit the woman he loved, accompanied by the woman he intended marrying. Maggie tried to hint that if he wasn't doing anything during the day, while Brenda was at work, she would welcome a visit. But he didn't seem to take the hint. Maggie didn't see the kick Brenda gave him when she made the suggestion. Brenda could see there was still something between them, and knew they must be kept well apart.

Vince Christian had paid her a flying visit, much to the delight of the nurses. He left a card attached to a gigantic bunch of red roses: 'You weren't the first. But you were the best.' Maggie blushed with pleasure as she read it. High praise indeed coming from him. She hid the card in her drawer, the memory of that time with Vince coming back to her. A happy memory. She needed happy memories of that sort to diffuse the memory of her last sexual encounter. The very thought of sex had become an anathema to her. Good old Vince.

Word got back to Sylvia, who shot down to see her. Maggie told her what had happened. About being told she'd got leukaemia. How could Prestwick have got it so wrong?

'Maybe he got it wrong on purpose,' guessed Sylvia, cynically.

'How do you mean?' asked Maggie.

'Well, it made you sign them adoption papers double quick, didn't it?'

Sylvia made it her business to tell her interpretation of events to anyone in the hospital who cared to listen. She found a willing ally in Vera, with whom she got on famously.

'Don't tell her I were a prossie,' implored Sylvia, one day.

'Why should I? If you're not one any more,' asked Maggie, meaningfully. 'You're not are you?'

'No,' answered Sylvia, truthfully. She'd have been even more truthful if she'd added, 'Not yet.'

Mr Gilbert, a hospital administrator, came in to see her a few days before she was due to go home. Home being Vera's for the time being. He came up with the usual platitudes about how well she was doing and how they just caught it in time, then his face took on a serious expression.

'There's a nasty rumour going round the hospital, concerning Mr Prestwick, the consultant obstetrician.'

'If it's the rumour I'm thinking about, it's not a rumour, it's true.'

'Really? Oh dear.' Mr Gilbert didn't look too happy.

'He told me I'd got leukaemia,' said Maggie. 'And talked me

into having my baby adopted. As soon as I get out I'm going to get my baby back.'

'I see,' he said. 'Do you mind if I offer a piece of advice?'

'Not at all,' said Maggie. Assuming he was going to advise her on strategy.

'Mr Prestwick's a man with a lot of influence. He's talking about suing you for slander. So if you don't have absolute proof of what you're accusing him of, I suggest you and your friends stop spreading these rumours. You could land yourselves in a lot of trouble.'

'Proof?' protested Maggie. 'What sort of proof do I need? Why would I sign adoption papers unless I thought I was going to die?'

'Look, Miss Fish, I'm not a lawyer. I suggest you find one as soon as you get out. I've no doubt he'll give you the same advice as I just have.'

Maggie was collecting her belongings from her old room, accompanied by Vera, when Dudley appeared at the door. They'd stopped off at Bridgefield House on the way home from the hospital.

'I came back for my things,' explained Maggie.

'I hear you were ill,' he said, lamely.

'TB,' said Maggie. 'It wasn't leukaemia after all. Aren't I the lucky one? Fancy an eminent medical man like Mr Prestwick making such an obvious mistake. No doubt you'll be arranging for me to have my baby back, won't you, Mr Dudley?' Her voice had taken on a menace she didn't know she was capable of.

Dudley was flapping now; he tried to regain control. 'But ... you signed the adoption papers. There's no going back now. You should have thought about this before you signed.'

He'd assumed she wouldn't kick up a fuss. That she'd be glad the child had been taken off her hands, especially under the circumstances. It being the product of a rape ... or so she said.

'I was tricked into thinking I was dying, by your pal Prestwick,' said Maggie, her voice growing louder, out of control. 'He ... he told me I had leukaemia. If you think I'm going to leave it at that, then ... then you don't know me, Mr Dudley.'

'I'm afraid there's absolutely nothing I can do. I know nothing about this leukaemia nonsense.'

160

'That's bollocks!' roared Maggie, hurling herself at him. 'You're a lying bastard Dudley. You're in it up to your neck. I want my baby back!' She was thumping him on his chest, crying in frustration. He held his arms out to indicate he wasn't retaliating. Vera pulled her away and stood facing Dudley with her arm around her.

'I've never met you before, Mr Dudley,' she announced, icily. 'But if you and your mate think you can get away with summat like this, you're in deep shit.'

'Just get out, the pair of you,' he hissed.

'We're going,' sobbed Maggie. 'But we'll be back. Don't you worry about that.'

They passed Lorna Boothroyd in the doorway. 'We'll have you as well,' Maggie screamed into her face, with piercing venom. 'You're as bad as the rest of 'em! I won't rest until you're all bloody locked up.'

During the ten-minute wait for the bus, Maggie neither stopped talking nor crying. She was convincing herself that she had a watertight case if it went to court.

'I mean, it's obvious that I wasn't myself when I signed that form. Christ I was delirious! Even if he hadn't told me I'd got leukaemia, which he did, he'd no right to ask me to sign . . . and he didn't spot I'd got TB. Your doctor spotted it in a minute. Why didn't Prestwick? He's supposed to be a consultant . . .'

She was in full flow when the bus arrived and Vera helped her young friend on board. Not sharing Maggie's faith in British justice, but not telling her. Prestwick was a powerful and influencial man. It would take a lot more evidence than Maggie had to get Danny back. Evidence they didn't have.

Had they arrived back in Hope Street ten minutes earlier, they'd have seen the Chevrolet Impala drawing away, followed by a crowd of hooting kids.

'Hey! Mrs Bradford, Vince Christian's been in your house,' yelled an excited Malcolm Moffitt.

'Vince?' puzzled Maggie. 'What's he been doing round here?'

Denis was at the door to welcome them. Almost as excited as the kids. 'You've only just missed him,' he announced. 'He said he couldn't stop long, he'd got a plane ter catch. I thought yer'd be back before this. I made him a cup of tea,' he added proudly.

Vince was still a big star. One of the few who'd never be entirely eclipsed.

Maggie smiled at Denis's excitement. 'Did he ask if you'd got any Garibaldis?' she inquired.

'Hey! He did. How did you know he liked Garibaldis?'

'Because he's a friend of hers, yer big dope!' said Vera scornfully.

Denis accepted his rebuke, than added sadly. 'We didn't have none though. Best get some in, just in case.'

'What, did he say he was coming back?' asked Maggie.

'He just said he'd pop in when he could. Oh, he left yer some flowers.'

On the kitchen table was another huge bunch of roses with an unsealed envelope attached. Maggie snatched it before Vera could read it, then she looked at Denis suspiciously. He hadn't looked inside it. It wouldn't occur to him to pry like that. Inside the envelope were a couple of keys and a rent book for number seventeen. The note read:

If I wasn't such a tight sod, I'd have bought the house for you. You'll just have to settle for a few weeks' rent. Hope it helps.
Vince

The rent was paid for a full year. Hope it helps? If only he knew just how much. Maggie could feel the tears coming. She handed the note to Vera, who whistled her appreciation and passed it to Denis, who had an idea what the note said.

'Nice bloke,' he commented, 'wish we'd had some Garibaldis in.'

'Nice bloke? You always thought he was a flash bugger,' said Vera.

'Only on the telly,' protested Denis. 'In real life he's just an ordinary bloke like me.'

'I bloody wish you was like him,' snorted Vera. 'I'd have yer locked in that bedroom all day.'

'Don't be so crude, Vera Bradford,' said Denis.

'I've got no furniture,' said Maggie, suddenly.

'I er ... I think he thought of that as well,' grinned Denis. 'Yer'd best have a look inside.'

The house wanted for nothing. Even a washing machine, TV

162

and fridge. The most well appointed house in Hope Street. The landlord, unhappy at it being unoccupied for so long, had had it redecorated in an attempt to sell it. But the small house buyers of that era had an abundant supply of new bungalows to choose from, so the landlord gave up the idea. All Maggie needed now was a job . . . and her son back. Not necessarily in that order.

Chapter Eighteen

'So . . . you're saying your baby was adopted illegally,' said Mr Styren. Maggie had been fobbed off with a junior solicitor, Mr Styren. A nervous young man with sallow features and long, nicotine-stained fingers. He didn't inspire confidence. 'Not an easy thing to prove,' he said.

'What sort of proof would I need?' asked Maggie, already depressed at what she'd heard.

'Well . . .' he studied the ends of his fingers. 'If we could prove your signature was forged, or not properly witnessed. But that doesn't seem to be the case, does it?'

'No, it doesn't. My argument is that I was tricked into believing I was dying.'

'A serious accusation. Which would result in loss of job and probably a long custodial sentence.'

'That's what he deserves.'

'I agree, but you've no witnesses to support your claim.'

'No.'

'Just your word against his.'

'Yes. I was suffering from TB. I was vulnerable. He took advantage of me.'

He looked at her keenly. 'Miss Fish, I believe you. I honestly believe you. But to pursue this, we need a concrete case which we have a chance of winning, or the Legal Aid Board will turn you down flat.'

'Right.' Her mind was racing, trying to come up with something. It all seemed so straightforward, until she was confronted by the law. Open and shut. Now it wasn't even open.

'I think Dudley, he's the warden. I think he was on some

sort of fiddle. I don't know what, but I might be able to find out.'

'Anything you can dig up to discredit them will be of help,' he said, with as much enthusiasm as he could muster. He felt sorry for Maggie and genuinely wanted to help. Deep down, he knew the case was hopeless, but he couldn't bring himself to tell her. Besides, he wanted to see her again.

'I can produce a doctor who says I shouldn't have been allowed out in my condition,' she said, racking her brain for anything.

'Allowed out?' he mused. 'You mean they sent you home?'

'Not exactly. I sort of. You know . . . sneaked out. I couldn't stand being in the place a minute longer.'

'Sneaked out? We can't use it against them.'

'I don't suppose so. It's not looking good is it?'

He tried to put on a cheerful face. 'Nil desperandum, Miss Fish. See what you can find out about Mr Dudley's activities and we'll take it from there.' There was no harm in letting her down gently. Besides, she might turn up something useful. Miracles do happen. But rarely in the legal profession.

Vera, Sylvia and Maggie sat around Maggie's kitchen table. Sylvia was on her third job in as many weeks. Serving behind the counter in the Tomato Dip Café. Her language was as coarse as the lorry drivers she served and her tips came in direct proportion to the depth of her cleavage. Sylvia, it seemed, had found her niche in catering.

'Did yer notice the look on that woman's face when yer said she were in it as well,' remarked Vera.

'You mean Lorna Boothroyd?' queried Maggie.

'If that's her name. She looked shocked. I don't think she had anything to do with it.'

'Yer could be right,' agreed Sylvia. 'She's a hard-nosed bastard is Lorna, but that's just the way she copes wi' some of the types what go through that place. I don't think she's bent though.'

Maggie understood what Vera was getting at. 'Maybe we should work on her,' she suggested. 'Get her on our side. Find out what she knows.'

It was the evening of Maggie's visit to her solicitor. She knew she had no time to waste. Sylvia had popped in for a chat and Maggie had called Vera in to join them in a council of war.

'Well,' said Sylvia. 'Unless the rotas have been changed, she'll be on duty as we speak.'

'What are we waiting for then?' said Maggie.

'I'd love ter join yer girls, but I've got Denis's dinner on,' apologised Vera.

'I wouldn't want to come between you and Denis,' smiled Maggie. 'It doesn't run in the family.'

Sylvia joined them in grinning at their private joke, although she hadn't a clue what they were talking about.

The clock on the wall struck eight. It was a relic from the days when Bridgefield House was an hotel. One of the very few reminders. Lorna hovered outside Dudley's office, forming what she was going to say in her head. It had been three days since the Fish girl had said her piece. During which time her words had been festering in Lorna's brain. What had that bastard Dudley been up to now? She knew about his laundry scam, but kept quiet about it because she felt marginally indebted to him for giving her the job. She'd been a resident herself at one time. It seemed a long time ago now. Twelve years, a bad time. The father did a runner as soon as she told him. Her boy was at grammar school now. That was the one thing she'd done right. She couldn't imagine life without him. Every penny she earned went on her David. Not like the slags that went through this place. Having babies and sending them off for adoption as though it didn't matter. Of course it mattered. Babies were precious things, not to be given away to the next person in the queue. This is what she couldn't stand about these girls. But it seemed that Maggie Fish had had her baby adopted against her wishes. If this was true it was bad. A very bad thing for anyone to do. She knocked on Dudley's door.

'Come in.'

She walked in with a nervous determination. Dudley looked up from his evening paper. It was unusual for him to be on duty at this time. He looked at his watch.

'It'll have to be quick, Miss Boothroyd. My wife's picking me up in ten minutes. It's our wedding anniversary. We're off to the Crown and Mitre for a meal.'

'Very nice,' commented Lorna, totally uninterested in Dudley's wedding anniversary. 'I've er . . . I've come to ask you about the other day.'

'What other day?'

'When the Fish girl came round.'

Dudley's jaw tightened. 'I don't wish to talk about the Fish girl, Miss Boothroyd.'

She took a deep breath. 'I do,' she said. 'She seems to think I'm mixed up in something and I'd like to know what it is.'

'You mean you haven't heard? Good grief! You must be the only person in Leeds who hasn't.'

The rumour going around the hospital had been successfully nipped in the bud by the powers that be, before it went out of control. Dudley gave a forced laugh that didn't fool his care supervisor.

'She's trying to say that Mr Prestwick of all people, tricked her into having her baby adopted. Can you imagine the cheek of the girl? Anyway, he threatened to sue her for slander, which seems to have done the trick. I don't think we'll be hearing any more from her.'

The door burst open and Maggie and Sylvia walked in.

'Yer wife's just parking her car. By the way she's struggling, yer should have a few minutes to tell us the truth before she comes in,' announced Sylvia.

'If I'm to get my baby back I need you to tell the truth about what Prestwick did,' said Maggie. Her voice quivering.

'Get out of here!' roared Dudley. 'Before I call the police.'

'Your missis'll be in here in a minute,' said Sylvia, cheerfully. 'As soon as she comes through that door I'm going ter give her an accurate description of the mole on the end of your dick.'

'Would that be the one that looks like a bowler hat?' asked Maggie.

'The very same.'

'All the girls have seen that,' lied Maggie. She turned to Lorna. 'I bet even you've seen that, haven't you Lorna?'

Lorna went white, almost as white as Dudley.

'You can't say that in front of my wife,' he pleaded. 'Anyway, it's a lie.'

'If it's a lie, you've nothing ter worry about have you?' challenged Sylvia. 'You've either got a mole on the end of your dick or you haven't. You either pick up prostitutes in Bradford, or you don't. Let's see what your wife thinks.'

Mrs Dudley's footsteps were echoing along the corridor. The handle turned on the door.

'Okay ... okay,' said Dudley. His frightened expression contorted into a strange smile as his wife entered.

'I wonder if you could give us a minute dear,' he asked, then added, 'in private.'

She swirled round in a huff and went out without a word. Sylvia feigned a worried expression.

'Oh dear, she's seems to be in a bit of a mood, Mr Dudley. Perhaps it's a bad time for me to tell her my bit of information.'

'All right,' he snapped. 'What is it you want?'

'I want you to tell the truth about Prestwick telling me I'd got leukaemia,' said Maggie.

'I know nothing about any leukaemia,' he insisted.

'I'll get your wife,' said Sylvia, opening the door.

'All right, all right!' he said quickly. 'Maybe he did make a bad diagnosis. He's an obstetrician. Not a medical doctor.'

'He'll have trained as a medical doctor though,' said Lorna. The other two women turned in surprise at this unexpected ally.

'Mr Dudley,' demanded Lorna. 'I think I'd like to hear the truth.'

He sat down, defeat staring him in the face. If Lorna turned against him, he was sunk.

'It's one thing fiddling the laundry money, Mr Dudley,' went on Lorna. 'But selling someone's baby, that's bad, very bad.'

'We ... I mean he, didn't sell the child. It was legally adopted.'

'I'd like the police to decide about this,' said Maggie. She turned to Lorna. 'Would you tell the police what you know about him fiddling the laundry money?'

Lorna nodded. 'Everything,' she agreed. If there was something fishy going on about the adoptions, she didn't want to be involved. She could see Dudley losing his job over this and she would be next in line.

'I think you'd better tell your wife that the celebration's off for tonight, Mr Dudley,' said Lorna. 'You wouldn't want the police calling into the Crown and Mitre to arrest you, would you now?'

Dudley looked as if he was about to throw up. He walked to the door and closed it behind him.

'Thanks, Lorna,' said Maggie.

Lorna grunted.

'That means, don't mention it,' interpreted Sylvia.

Mr Styren tapped his fingers together. They told of excessive cigarette smoking and an innate nervousness. Maggie looked at him suspiciously.

'Now that Dudley's blown the whistle on Prestwick, I should be able to get my baby back, shouldn't I?' She added the last two words of her question forcibly, as if to jolt him into agreeing with her. He was hesitant.

'It's not quite as straightforward as that, Miss Fish.'

'How do you mean? Of course it's straightforward. We've got proof that Prestwick was lying.'

'I know, but we're not out of the woods yet. We have to play things very carefully. For a start, we don't know who the adoptive parents are. I suspect though, that they're powerful people. People with a lot of clout. As far as we know they haven't done anything illegal. The signing of the adoption papers was correctly witnessed by a registrar, no less. At the moment all we have is Dudley fiddling the laundry money and Prestwick deliberately giving you a false diagnosis. He may well get struck off for that but he's hardly going to be inclined to help you with your end of the problem. Dudley's already lost his job, so he's no use to us.'

'So all this has been a waste of time.'

'Not entirely. At least we have evidence that your baby being taken away was . . . well, unlawful.'

'Is that the same as illegal?' she asked.

'There's a subtle difference,' he replied. 'Hard to explain.'

'I know . . . one's breaking the law and the other's a poorly bird,' said Maggie, sourly. Another of Jimmy Diamond's gags. Styren didn't get the joke, so he didn't laugh, which was fortunate. Maggie wasn't really in a joking mood, it just came out.

'I'm not going to get him back, am I, Mr Styren?' she asked, pointedly.

He shuffled uncomfortably in his chair. 'I'd like to leave it up to the Legal Aid Board to assess your chances of success,' he said, fobbing the responsibility off on to someone else. 'It's always a good guide to things. As soon as I've heard from them, I'll let you know.'

169

He didn't need to spell it out for her. Forces greater than her were at work.

'Is that Mrs Dudley?'

'Yes.'

'You don't know me. I'm one of the girls what used to be in Bridgefield House.' Maggie had deliberately coarsened her accent so as to make her unrecognisable.

'What can I do for you?' asked Mrs Dudley guardedly.

'We need some advice from you. Me an' the other girls that is.'

'Really?'

'Well, me an' the other girls have all been a bit worried about that black mole on the end of yer husband's dick. Yer know, the one what looks like a bowler hat. We were wondering if he's got some sort of venereal disease what he could have passed on to us. I mean, if he has, it could affect quite a lot of us . . . Mrs Dudley? Are yer there.'

The line had gone dead. Maggie replaced the receiver, having gained a certain satisfaction from this cheap revenge. The Legal Aid Board had turned her down. Danny was lost to her now.

Chapter Nineteen

If Maggie was to come to terms with the loss of her son she had to do something to take her mind off him.

'Perhaps it was all for the best,' suggested Vera. 'Considering how he were conceived an' all that. It'd have been at the back of yer mind all the time.'

It was the first time Vera had dared to suggest anything like this. It was Saturday morning and she'd popped in to Maggie's, as she had almost daily, since they'd heard the bad news about Danny.

'I know all that, Mrs Bradford, and I fully intended giving him up for adoption. It's just that . . . when I held him in my arms, I'd never known anything like it before.'

Vera nodded in reluctant agreement. 'I know, love. I were the same with our Roy, an' look what a big daft bugger he turned out ter be.'

'He's a nice lad is your Roy. A girl could do a lot worse than him.'

'Don't let him hear yer say that, he might get the wrong impression.'

'How do you mean?' asked Maggie curiously.

'Nay, Maggie lass. Surely yer've seen the daft look in his eyes every time you're around. He dotes on you does our Roy. I tell yer what, if yer dad hadn't gone after that Martini feller, I reckon our Roy would.'

'I didn't realise.'

'There's none so blind as them what can't see,' chuckled Vera.

Maggie shrugged. She'd never understood this old saying. She had other things on her mind now, apart from Danny. She was due to start a new job in two days' time, a prospect she wasn't relishing. Her lack of O Levels had limited her choice and she'd had to settle for a job at Jameson's Boot Protectors. Trainee at first, then after a year she'd become a fully qualified seg maker. Supplying segs to her Majesty's forces and boot makers throughout the world. A secure job, with a future, poorly paid but you can't have everything.

An invitation to Charlie's wedding lay on her sideboard. RSVP it said. Maggie had yet to reply. She'd been invited to bring a friend, maybe Roy would like to come with her. There was no 'maybe' about it. Roy would jump at the chance. How would she cope with seeing the love of her life marry someone else? Would she break down and spoil it for everyone? Perhaps she shouldn't go. She knew deep down she would – be drawn like a moth to a light.

'Do you think your Roy would like to come to Charlie's wedding with me?' she asked.

'I'm sure he would, love. But yer'd best ask him yerself. He's in now. Just one thing young lady,' she said with mock severity. 'I don't want you putting ideas into his head that you can't back up ... if yer get my drift. He's a big daft lump is our Roy, but he's all mine.'

'I'm just asking him to come to a wedding, Mrs Bradford. Nothing more.'

'So long as yer make that plain to him then.'

Charlie sat in the Crimea Tavern, staring at the array of drinks in front of him and then up at the array of friends surrounding him.

'I defin ... definitely can't drink all them,' he decided. A reasonable assessment in view of what he'd already drunk. Any more would also sit very heavily on the Egg Foo Yung he'd had at the Kee Hong Chinese Restaurant.

'There's only one of each,' argued Cyril the drummer. 'Come on, sup up an' then we can all go to the Mecca.' He looked at his watch. 'And you'd best get a move on, they don't let anyone in after ten.'

'They'll have to let you in, you're the bleedin' drummer!' pointed out Roy Bradford, who'd been invited along.

'Come on Charlie! Sup up!' urged the other eight party-goers, out celebrating Charlie's last night of freedom.

Charlie took a deep breath and picked up the glass of whisky, drank it in one, then picked up the gin and repeated the exercise. Glasses of brandy, rum, vodka, green chartreuse, crème de menthe and advocaat followed. All washed down with a pint of bitter. For reasons best known to the participants, it's traditional to throw wisdom out of the window on stag nights.

It was most unwise of Charlie to lean over the balcony of the Mecca Locarno Ballroom to look down on the gyrating dancers below. Also gyrating was a large fan, suspended from the ceiling at a point a few feet below him. The dancers were at their enthusiastic best. Contestants in the National Rock 'n' Roll contest. The winners would go down to the televised finals in London, so there was much at stake.

Tony Stevenson was the hot favourite, with his partner, Thelma Prisk. They'd moved in front of the stage, on the compere's instruction, to perform their solo speciality. Charlie's bit of the balcony was immediately above. The fan was whirling briskly, as the evening was warm and the dancers sweating.

Charlie threw up with one great heave, the blades of the fan spraying all the contestants with a liberal coating of virulent vomit, especially the two favourites immediately below. Cyril, who'd taken over the drumming from his stand-in, knew immediately who the culprit was. He left his seat and dashed upstairs to find Charlie sitting at a table, smiling.

'I'm all right Cyril, I feel fine now,' announced Charlie, cheerfully.

There was a rush of feet up the stairs behind Cyril, instilling a sense of urgency in him. 'Make yerself scarce Charlie,' was all the advice he'd time to give.

Tony Stevenson was in the lead, his coat discarded, but still enough of Charlie's Chinese meal stuck to him to ensure he was given a wide berth. It was obvious who the culprit was.

'You dirty bastard!'

He flung himself at Charlie, other stained bodies followed, trying to get a blow in themselves. Charlie's pals tried to drag them off and the inevitable fight ensued. Charlie sat beneath a table as the mayhem broke out all around him. One young man falling over the balcony and breaking a leg. In the great tradition of Wild West saloon fights, the band kept on playing, albeit minus a drummer, trying to maintain a semblance of normality. The two bouncers were wisely keeping well clear, this was a job for the police.

Charlie remained beneath the table, watching with drunken fascination as arrested feet were dragged away by uniformed legs. Many obscene protests of innocence, then all was quiet. The band stopped playing, having done their brave duty. Charlie crawled out and made his way down the stairs. Tony Stevenson was at the bottom, struggling violently with a large constable. Anger lit his eyes when he saw Charlie strolling freely out of the door.

'That's him!' he yelled. 'He's the bastard what started it.'

'Watch your language son,' cautioned his captor, who then gave Charlie a suspicious look.

Charlie moved nonchalantly outside into the arcade beyond the door, then unwisely set off running. 'Stop that one!' came the shout from behind. Galloping feet quickly caught up with Charlie, whose heart sank as his arm was grabbed and thrust up into the small of his back.

'I'm getting married tomorrow,' he protested.

'Congratulations,' said the policeman, frog-marching him towards a waiting van.

Charlie was awakened by a call of nature urging him to the stainless steel toilet in the corner of the cell he was sharing with Roy. The realisation of his plight dawned on him as he relieved himself noisily into the pan.

'Roy!' he called, urgently.

Roy stirred and went back to sleep.

'Roy!'

He was shaking him now. Roy opened his eyes and blinked. 'Oh shit!' he said, as the realisation of his whereabouts struck home. 'What time is it?' he asked.

Charlie made to look at his watch. 'Christ, I must have lost my watch,' he moaned.

'They'll have taken it off you,' said Roy.

'Oh, right. Is that what they do?'

There was a silence as Charlie tried to arrange his thoughts. 'I'm in jail, my head's banging, I feel rotten and I'm getting married at half past eleven.'

He banged on the door until he heard footsteps outside.

'Hello,' he shouted.

A small panel in the door slid open revealing a pair of irritated eyes.

'Excuse me officer, but I'm getting married at half past eleven,' he said, trying to elicit sympathy.

'You should have thought of that before you started fighting.'

'Fighting? I didn't start fighting. I was poorly. Everyone else was fighting.'

'It's true,' shouted Roy from behind him. 'Charlie was the only one who wasn't fighting. He shouldn't even be in here.'

'That's right,' agreed Charlie. 'None of you lot can have seen me fighting so why am I in here?'

''Cos you started it, that's why, yer dirty bastard.' Charlie didn't recognise Tony Stevenson's voice coming from the cell opposite.

'Quiet,' roared the policeman. 'You'll be let out when we're good and ready and not before.'

The panel in the door slammed shut and footsteps were heard disappearing down the corridor. Another, more distant door opened and slammed shut, illustrating just how far away from freedom they were.

'Anyone who wants ter marry a dirty bastard like you can't be right in their bloody heads!' shouted Tony Stevenson.

'Piss off!' called out Roy, in defence of Charlie who was nursing his throbbing head.

'Who're you tellin' ter piss off? I'll kick yer bleedin' head in when we get out of here.'

'If yer fight like yer dance, I've nowt ter worry about, yer big daft girl!' retorted Roy.

'Leave it,' pleaded Charlie. The shouting was hurting his head.

Roy looked out through the tiny cell window. 'I reckon it must be about eight o'clock,' he surmised.

'How can you tell?' asked Charlie, mildly impressed.

'There's a clock on that church over there,' smirked Roy. He sat down beside Charlie. 'They're bound ter let you out in time for yer wedding,' he said reassuringly.

Charlie nodded, 'let's hope so.'

'Yer don't sound all that worried ter me.'

'Worried? 'Course I'm worried. Christ, it's all arranged. Church, reception, cars, photographer . . . the lot.'

Roy nodded. Charlie looked at him and shook his head. 'Do you know what's really worrying me?'

'What?' asked Roy, flattered that Charlie was confiding in him. No one ever confided in Roy.

'I'm not sure if I'm doing the right thing,' said Charlie.

'Isn't that what they call last minute nerves?'

'Yeah . . . I suppose so.' He sat quietly for a while before continuing. 'If it was someone like Maggie, I don't think I'd have any doubts.'

'Maggie? Maggie Fish? Yer fancy her, do yer?'

'I do, she's a great girl is Maggie. I'd marry her like a shot if she'd have me. You know her, what do you think of her?'

Roy reddened. He daren't disclose his own affection for Maggie. Not now that Charlie had confessed his.

'She's a good pal is Maggie,' he said.

Charlie nodded his agreement. 'She is, isn't she? Wouldn't it be great to have a wife who's your best pal? It'd be like that if me and Maggie got married.'

'Have you ever asked her?'

Charlie shook his head. 'No point,' he grumbled. 'I know what she'd say. Anyway there's no point embarrassing her into saying no, I think too much of her to do that.'

'So,' said Roy, baffled by what Charlie was about to do. 'Do yer love this Brenda?'

Charlie was quiet for a long time, contemplating his answer. 'Yes,' he decided at last. 'I do love her . . . but in a different way, if you know what I mean.'

'Oh,' said Roy, who hadn't a clue what he meant.

Brenda sat in front of her dressing table mirror carefully painting on her eyeliner.

'God, the first time I cry, I'll look like Coco the Clown,' she said to Alice, her chief bridesmaid, who was hovering behind her, trying to share the mirror to put her own makeup on.

'I can't see you crying today,' remarked Alice. 'You should be jumping for joy that you've managed to pull it off.'

'Don't be so cruel, Alice Galsworthy. He's doing well for himself is Charlie, getting someone like me.'

'I reckon he'd have still been sniffing round that Maggie Fish if you hadn't steered him clear of her,' commented Alice, somewhat tactlessly, considering the occasion.

'He's a lot better off with me than with her,' snapped Brenda. 'I've preserved my virginity for him, which is a lot more than that tart can say for herself. Men are all the same. They don't know what's good for them. They're always looking for something else. I'll clip his wings when I get him home, you mark my words.'

'Is he happy about living with your mum and dad? I'm not sure I'd be. When I get married I want us to have a place of our own.'

'Beggars can't be choosers,' replied Brenda. 'There's plenty of room at mum and dad's and we'll have a place of our own as soon as we save up for a deposit.'

'I wouldn't have thought saving up was Charlie's style. They're not ones for thrift, aren't musicians. Not from what I've heard anyway.'

'Well, that's just where you're wrong. He's got five O Levels has Charlie. He can get a good job with five O Levels and still play his piano in his spare time.'

'By heck, Brenda, you've got his life mapped out for him.'

'It's the only way with men. He'll thank me for it in the long run.'

'Does he know about all these plans of yours.'

'Not yet ... there'll be time enough to tell him after we're married.'

Charlie shook his head, trying to clear his mind for the ordeal ahead of him. Even if he had wanted to back out his spirit was severely weakened by the fiercest hangover he'd ever experienced. He and Roy had both been released without charge. A kindly policewoman had driven him home, where his mum and dad were beside themselves with worry. Cyril, his best man, had escaped arrest by claiming that as an employee of the ballroom, he was only trying to keep the peace. In truth, he'd been one of the worst culprits.

Maggie noticed the abundance of expensive hats down Brenda's side of the church and was glad she was on Charlie's side, where her hat was as good as anyone's. Generally speaking, in a hat competition, Charlie's side would have been beaten out of sight. He hadn't brought along as many supporters as Brenda.

177

He'd capitulated to the argument Brenda had put forward about there being a lot of people in her family who wouldn't look too kindly on being left off the guest list. It did occur to him to mention that he had just as many relatives as her, but decided it wasn't worth an argument.

'Marriage is all about compromise,' Brenda had sagely informed him. He wondered if she'd actually grasped the meaning of the word.

Roy sat beside Maggie, all too conscious of her proximity. Like Charlie, if he could marry someone it would be her. He was pondering ruefully what sort of man it would take to capture her. It would never occur to him to ask her himself. She leaned over and whispered mischievously into his ear.

'I gather you and Charlie spent the night together.'

He grinned awkwardly. 'Yer could say that.'

'What did you talk about?' she was genuinely curious. She wanted to know if her name had cropped up.

'Things,' said Roy, mysteriously.

Maggie sat back. The bride was late, as per tradition, the people in the church were growing restless, looking round to see where she was. Smiling at long lost faces and thinking how so and so's looking her age and is that her new husband? A child started crying and received a loud slap for its trouble, provoking disapproving murmurs from the non-smacking faction. The embarrassed mother picked up the howling child and carried it back up the aisle, its screams dying away in the distance. A young man in front of Maggie was surreptitiously smoking, wafting the incriminating fumes with his hand, until caught in the act by an older woman two places along, who appeared to hold some authority over him.

'Put that out, Peter, this minute. Have you no bloody respect?'

Maggie stared sadly at the back of Charlie's spinning head. 'I always fancied him myself, you know,' she said suddenly. Not having any idea why she was telling Roy this. He said nothing at first, but the implications of her remark were beginning to sink in.

'Fancied him?' he asked. 'You mean yer loved him?'

Maggie laughed at Roy's naivety. 'Fancying and loving are two entirely different things, Roy.' She sounded unintentionally patronising.

The wait for the bride continued, ten minutes late now. Charlie was looking uncomfortable. Leaning on Cyril for support. He just wanted to get it over with.

'Actually, yes,' said Maggie.

'Yes, what?' inquired Roy.

'Yes, I did love him,' admitted Maggie. 'But you don't always get what you want in this life.'

'No, yer don't,' agreed Roy, with some feeling. He was wishing everyone hadn't suddenly decided to confide in him. The wedding march struck up and a hundred expectant heads turned to see Brenda striding slowly down the aisle, in carefully rehearsed time to the organ music, on the arm of her father. Her bouffant hair crowned with a diamante tiara, holding in place the veil which hid the smug expression on her face. The train of her white satin dress held in Alice's pink gloved hands. Behind her a small, smiling bridesmaid carried a posy of flowers. A smaller page boy trudged disconsolately beside her, carrying the same and hoping no one from his school was there. The organist hit a wrong note, which everybody but Maggie noticed, but he wasn't the regular organist and what did they expect for two pounds ten? Maggie's mind was elsewhere.

Roy looked at her and saw the tears begin to well up. By the time Brenda had reached the altar, Maggie was in floods. A handkerchief held permanently against her eyes to stem the flow.

'Do you still love him?' asked Roy.

She nodded slightly, then shook her head despairingly. Mixed messages for Roy. Why should he care if Charlie married Brenda? It would leave the way clear for him and Maggie. Who was he fooling? Maggie would never love him. They were just mates. Always had been, always would be.

The wedding ceremony was well under way. Charlie and Brenda stood side by side. Cyril and Brenda's father had stepped away. The exchange of vows was imminent. The minister called out to the congregation. 'Therefore if any man can show any just cause why they may not lawfully be joined together, let him now speak, or else hereafter forever hold his peace . . .'

The usual silence prevailed, the minister, having waited the statutory three seconds, opened his mouth to continue.

'I do!' shouted Roy.

Vera, sitting immediately behind him, slapped him roundly across the back of his head.

'Ow!' he yelled.

'I'll give you "Ow", when I get you home, Roy Bradford,' she scolded.

The congregation were enjoying this. Any deviation from the boring norm was music to their ears. The minister held up a calming hand.

'May we proceed?' he asked, politely.

'Yes, of course you can,' said Vera.

'No, you can't,' objected Roy, loudly. 'He's marrying the wrong lass. You just ask him. He told me last night that he'd rather be marrying Maggie . . . and Maggie's just told me that she loves him as well . . . I'm sorry, but it just doesn't seem right ter me.' He turned, defiantly, to his mother. 'I've said me piece an' I'll say no more.'

'I think you've just said plenty, my lad,' said Vera.

Brenda looked at Charlie and then at the minister. 'Can we get on with it, please?' she demanded sharply. 'Or are you going to let this lunatic spoil my wedding?'

'He's not a lunatic!' The buzz from the congregation stopped, at these words from Charlie.

'I beg your pardon!' gasped Brenda.

Charlie looked at her sadly. 'I'm sorry, love, but he's right . . . I'd marry Maggie like a shot, if I thought she'd have me.'

'She told me she loved yer,' called out Roy.

Maggie, by this time, was in a state of shock. The whole wedding was collapsing because of something she'd just said to Roy. Everyone's eyes were on her. Waiting for a reaction, a decision. Brenda was running back down the aisle in tears, followed by her father and the rest of her family, many of whom fired out a variety of unchristian comments as they passed Maggie's pew. Charlie made his way towards her, taking her hand and leading her to the quiet of the vestry, where the minister tactfully left them alone.

'Well?' he asked.

'Well what?'

'You've heard me say I'd marry you like a shot if you'd have me.'

'Is this a proposal, Mr Chipperfield?'

'I suppose it is.'

'Then I accept.'

Charlie took her gently in his arms and kissed her. It was a sweet kiss and, despite them having known each other for many years, only their third.

Chapter Twenty

'She put the phone down on me.'

'I'm not surprised,' said Maggie to Charlie, as he returned to their table.

The car Charlie had hired to whisk him and Brenda off on honeymoon to Blackpool was parked outside the Coffin Makers Arms in Drighlington, several miles away from any potential trouble from Brenda's relatives.

'I tried to explain how it was for the best in the long run and all I got was a mouthful of abuse,' reported Charlie.

'No tears then?' inquired Maggie.

'No, that's not Brenda's style.'

'It might have been if she loved you.'

Charlie sat down behind the pint Maggie had bought him while he went to the telephone to make his apology to Brenda. He reached across the table and took her hand.

'We've both been a bit daft, haven't we?' he summed up.

'Well, I have,' agreed Maggie. 'Doing the dirty on you like I did, after promising not to break the act up.'

Charlie squeezed her hand and shook his head. 'It was on the cards, I'd have held you back. You weren't at the top for long, but at least you've been there. I'll never be able to say that.'

'As far as I'm concerned, Charlie Chipperfield, you are the top.'

As she gazed lovingly at Charlie, Maggie felt as fulfilled as she'd ever been. Just one thing stood between her and true fulfilment. Just one small person. But you can't have everything. Sadly, Maggie had never been able to accept this unfortunate fact of life.

'I've booked an hotel in Blackpool,' said Charlie, suddenly. 'A full week at the Cumberland, all paid up front. No point wasting it, why don't we go?'

Maggie shook her head. 'If it was booked for you and Brenda, I'd rather not. I don't want her turning up on the doorstep.'

'That's just it,' grinned Charlie. 'She didn't know where we were going, it was to be my big surprise. I reckon she thought we were going abroad somewhere, because she kept dropping hints about did she need a passport?'

'And what did you tell her?' asked Maggie.

'I told her she would,' laughed Charlie. 'Thought I'd throw her off the scent good and proper.'

'I'd love to have seen her face when you ended up in Blackpool when she thought she was going to Majorca,' laughed Maggie. 'It might have been worth going through with the wedding just for that.'

'Hey! I think I see what you mean,' chortled Charlie. 'Honest, I didn't think about that at the time.'

Maggie looked at this open and honest and funny young man. 'I'd have loved to come to Blackpool with you Charlie,' she said sadly. 'But I can't. I'm starting a new job on Monday.'

'New job? What new job?' asked Charlie.

'Jameson's Boot Protectors in Armley. It's not much, but it's a job.'

Charlie sat quietly for a time, disappointed. 'I don't want you to work at Jameson's Boot Protectors. Why not team up with me again? I've got a string of gigs booked for when I got back from honeymoon. Good money, we can split it down the middle like we used to.'

'As opposed to you having the lot,' said Maggie. 'Which you would if I wasn't tagging along.'

'With you tagging along I can get more money. Your name still carries a lot of weight in the business.'

Charlie lit up a cigarette and sent a smoke ring spinning past Maggie's ear. His face was alive with ideas. 'What's your voice like? I hear you got it back, after a fashion.'

'After a fashion's about right. It's not what it was. Martini damaged my throat when he tried to throttle me. Anyone else would think they were back to normal, but there's something missing and I think it's that thing that made my voice special.'

'The hook?'

Maggie smiled, 'That's right. I've only ever heard you call it that.'

'So, basically your voice is as strong as ever?' he inquired.

'More or less. I can still sing better than you,' she grinned.

'Then that's settled then,' he decided. 'Fish and Chipperfield are back on the road. London Palladium here we come.'

Maggie had never seen Charlie so happy. No way could she have said no. Jameson's Boot Protectors would just have to find another trainee.

The booking clerk at the Cumberland gave them a suspicious smile of greeting. He knew an unmarried couple when he saw one, these two looked much too happy. The rules had been relaxed in recent years, but he still liked his bit of fun.

'Two singles?' he suggested as they approached the desk.

Charlie was equal to his game. 'Two singles? That might be how you Lancashire lads spend your honeymoons, but us Yorkshire lads do it different. Honeymoon suite please.'

'I'm afraid the honeymoon suite's booked, sir,' responded the clerk, loftily.

A man in a dark suit appeared from a door behind the clerk. 'Everything all right, sir?' he addressed himself to Charlie.

'Never better . . . at least it would be if your lad got his finger out and gave me the keys to my room.'

'Your room? And that would be?'

'The honeymoon suite, as per my booking in the name of Mr and Mrs Chipperfield.'

The clerk's face dropped as the manager perused the book, then beamed up at them.

'Welcome to the Cumberland, Mr and Mrs Chipperfield. Keys please, Rodney, and we hope you enjoy your stay.'

A porter appeared and took their cases. Maggie had stopped off at home to pack hers hurriedly.

Maggie and Charlie followed, the name Mrs Chipperfield ringing in Maggie's ears.

'I still want to be Maggie Fisher,' she decided, after the porter had left, with a welcome five bob tip in his pocket.

'You can be who you like, as long as you're my wife.' Charlie looked at her for the hundredth time that day, scarcely able to believe how the day had turned out. A day to remember. He took off his jacket and tie and sat on the bed next to Maggie. 'Something's been worrying me all the way here,' he said.

Maggie linked her arm in his and squeezed. 'Something to do with me?'

'Well ... yes,' he said, awkwardly. 'It's something I read about girls who'd been ...'

'Raped?'

'Yes,' he said. 'I mean, I fully understand if it worries you. We can take things steady at first, see how you feel.'

'I assume we're talking about sex?' she asked, 'and has being raped put me off?'

'Er ... yes.'

'I don't know, Charlie, it's as simple as that. It would certainly put me off one night stands; but sex with the man I love, now that's a different thing altogether.'

She began to unbutton his shirt. 'I love you, Charlie Chipperfield. There's no way a dead dago can come between us.'

Charlie was mildly shocked at the term she used to describe Tony Martini. Perhaps it was her way of handling things. They kissed passionately as they undressed each other, their love, foolishly unrequited for so long, pushed aside all inhibitions. Maggie's experience with Martini forgotten, as was Charlie's near miss with Brenda. As Maggie lay naked on the bed, Charlie kneeled beside her and looked down on her for a while. In his biased opinion she was the most beautiful thing he'd ever seen.

'You're embarrassing me Charlie,' she said gently.

'I'm sorry ... it's just that I've waited a long time for this moment. Waited? What am I talking about? I'd given up all hope of this moment ever coming. It's like a dream. I've loved you since I first saw you in the Hope Street Working Men's Club.'

'You dirty old man, Charlie Chipperfield. I was only fifteen.'

'Never mind the dirty old man, you tried it on with me after our first gig at the Unsworth Labour Club. Christ, I was scared to death.'

'Scared? Of what?'

'Of what I might do if you tried to kiss me again.'

'Damn, I wish I had done.'

Charlie lay beside her, caressing her, and she him. Not wanting to rush this first time. Both wanting it to be something to remember. He moved on top of her, his passion getting the better of him. Maggie laughed gently at his eagerness and guided him inside her, then rolled over on top of him thrusting out her beautifully formed breasts.

'How do I compare with Brenda?' she asked cheekily.

'You mean Brenda the virgin?'

'Really?'

'She was saving herself for me,' said Charlie.

'So have I,' said Maggie. 'I just thought it as well to have a bit of practice, so I could get it right when the time came.'

'Good thinking, I hate working with novices.'

They made love all evening, all through the night and fell asleep at dawn; exhausted and happy and very much in love. They emerged at lunchtime, to be greeted by the manager.

'You must be hungry,' he said, tactfully. 'I've reserved a table for two by the window.'

The Cumberland Hotel overlooked the bay between the South and Central Piers. Gaily coloured holidaymakers, dressed more for the Costa Brava than for the drizzly Lancashire coast, were taking their constitutionals up and down the broad promenade. Determined to make the most of their week despite the miserable weather. The men shaking off hangovers in preparation for another session that evening. The women scolding their children for dropping candy floss or ice cream or hot dogs on the already littered ground. Half the adults with cigarettes in their mouths. The window was slightly open, allowing the breeze to blow in the unique smell of Blackpool. Salty air, hot dogs and horse droppings. The latter in abundant heaps along the road where the horses and traps plied their busy trade, in direct competition with the trams. The lead-coloured sea, livened up by a sharp north westerly, was thundering up on to the promenade, sending people dashing out of range, some not quite making it, providing amusement for the ones who managed to get clear. For they were on holiday and knew how to make the best of things.

'See how easy it is to make people laugh,' observed Charlie. 'Especially people on holiday. They're out for a good time. If there's a laugh to be had they'll go for it.'

He drank his coffee and looked across at Maggie. 'We're going to be brilliant, me and you.'

Maggie nodded. 'It's got to be easier making these people laugh than that po-faced lot back in the clubs. I've watched them when the comic comes on. You can almost hear them saying, "Come on, try and make me laugh."'

'I know where we can go to get work,' said Charlie. 'What do you say?'

'I thought we were on honeymoon?'

'We could make it a working honeymoon.'

'You're so romantic, Charlie Chipperfield.'

'Is that a yes?'

'I can't think of anything I'd like better.'

'Not anything?' asked Charlie, with a raised eyebrow.

'Well, nearly anything,' corrected Maggie.

Charlie yawned and stretched. 'I'm a bit tired, I think we ought to go to bed for the afternoon. We'll start tonight.'

The Commercial Club in Station Street was where most of the Blackpool agents showcased their acts. Any acts unlucky enough not to be working on Saturday night would turn up at the Commercial in the hope of picking up work for the following week. The place was packed out, mainly with locals and holiday-makers in the know. The Commercial was far better value for money than the shows on the piers or the town's theatres, with their inflated prices.

Bookers and agents aplenty would be there, accepting drinks from would be clients, some of whom might be rewarded with a booking, providing they shaped up on stage.

Maggie was recognised as soon as she went in through the door. She had been a headliner in Blackpool in the not too distant past and outside London, Blackpool was the showbusiness Mecca of the country.

'Making a comeback, Maggie?'

'Nice to see you . . . are you singing tonight?'

Maggie had been a talent and no one appreciated talent more than these people. She was ninety miles from Hope Street, but she couldn't have felt more at home. This was her world, not making segs at Jameson's Boot Protectors. Charlie booked them in for a fifteen-minute set at nine-thirty. A time when everyone was happy, but not yet drunk. On the stage was a band, varying in numbers from two to seven, depending on who fancied sitting in. The only employees were the drummer and the pianist. The pianist happily vacated his instrument to make way for Charlie.

There was a hushed anticipation as they stepped on to the stage straight out of the audience. An MC dressed in a well-worn dinner suit introduced them.

'Ladies and gentlemen. Half of our next act needs no introduction. Tonight, Maggie Fisher has once again teamed up with the man who gave her her stepping stone to stardom ... pianist and comic, Charlie Chipperfield. We all know what happened to her and she's told me to tell you that her voice never recovered, but she's going to give you what's left of it which, as far as I'm concerned, is plenty good enough for the Commercial on a Saturday night.'

It was as good an introduction as they could wish for, but it was a nervous pair who took up station on the stage. Charlie played the intro to 'Don't Give Me Roses' to a ripple of expectant applause. Maggie walked to the microphone and opened her mouth to sing. Charlie stopped playing and walked over to her.

'Do you want me to be funny?' he asked.

'No, just be yourself.'

There was a pause, then laughter from the audience. Charlie went back to the piano and played the intro again. Maggie hit the opening notes clear and true and as sweet as any singer who had ever graced that stage. But the old Maggie had never played there. She finished to warm applause, the bookers were ready to make their approach. Charlie introduced the next song with one of his comedy routines and they finished with an amusing duet.

She turned to Charlie at the end; whatever special magic she'd had was gone. But that smiling man at the piano more than made up for it. He winked at her and stood up to share the applause, holding her hand.

Part Two

Chapter Twenty-One

Maggie and Charlie were home for a rare weekend. Home being Hope Street. The fact that Vince Christian had paid a year's rent for the house was of little concern to Charlie. What did concern him was Maggie's voice. She never mentioned it, but he knew it got her down. She had black moods, when she was best left alone. Not very often, but it wasn't like the old Maggie. At first he thought it might have something to do with her son. He'd asked her about it, but she assured him that Danny was far better off where he was; and how could either of them possibly love a child conceived in such circumstances? He'd been sworn not to bring the subject up again, an oath he willingly upheld.

They'd had a quiet wedding at the Leeds Register office in Park Square with a small reception in an out of town hotel for just a few selected friends. A much more informal and friendly affair than the one he and Brenda had planned. Charlie felt a pang of guilt for all the money Brenda's father must have wasted on the abortive wedding and every morning for weeks he'd expected a large bill to drop through the letterbox.

Charlie had been on the phone as Maggie watched television. He walked through to the front room, now carpeted, with wall lights and a plush three-piece suite.

'Who was on the phone?' she asked, absently.

He sat on the arm of the settee and put his arm around her shoulders. 'Do you promise not to get mad?' he asked.

'No,' she said.

'I knew you'd say that.'

'For all I know,' she pointed out. 'It might be one of your many admirers wanting to whisk you off for a weekend of debauchery.'

'So, that's the sort of thing that'd make you mad, is it?' he inquired.

'Come on, Chipperfield, spit it out. You're up to something.'

He took a deep breath. 'You know that Ear, Nose and Throat bloke down at the Dispensary?'

'Him that we met when we played at the Christmas party last week?'

'That's right. I told him about your voice and how it wasn't quite right.'

'And he said there was nothing he could do.'

'I've just been speaking to him,' said Charlie. 'I asked him if there was anything anyone else could do, and he said he'd make inquiries.'

'And . . .?'

'There's apparently a bloke in Chicago, who specialises in that sort of thing.'

'Chicago? Charlie, that's in America!'

'Is it? Blast! I thought it was just outside Doncaster.'

Maggie thumped him, good naturedly. 'Did he tell you how much it would cost?'

'Ah, yes, he did. Now don't fly off the handle, we can manage it if we save up.'

'How much?'

'Fifteen hundred pounds.'

'How much?'

'That would be for everything. Flight, hospital stay, operation, everything.'

'Would you be there?'

'Er, no, I'd have to pay extra.'

'It's not worth it, Charlie, we're all right as we are.'

Charlie sat down beside her and kissed her. 'I'd like to give it a go, Maggie. I'd like to hear your old voice again.'

'My old voice split us up last time.'

'We weren't married last time.'

'It'd take a long time to save up.'

'Not when we put our mind to it.'

Maggie couldn't refuse Charlie anything. It might be nice to have her old voice back, but it wasn't the be all and end all of everything. It wouldn't stop her thinking about Danny. It wouldn't stop her black moods.

December 1961

Charlie examined the Halifax Building Society book carefully. Accountancy of any sort had never been his strong suit. His brother kept him on the straight and narrow as far as tax was concerned, otherwise he may well have followed many of his fellow musicians into the bankruptcy courts.

'£971 15s 4d,' he announced. 'Not bad after just a year.'

'By the time we save up the fifteen hundred, the price will have gone up,' remarked Maggie, pessimistically. Saving for the operation had never been foremost in her thoughts. Her black days came and went, but she hid her true feelings from Charlie. Or so she thought. Danny would be walking now, saying his first words. Saying 'Mummy' to this woman who wasn't. Each stage in his development was mapped out in her mind. His first day at school, his childhood ailments, chicken pox, measles, mumps. Learning to read on his mother's knee just as she had. Stop it, Maggie, you'll drive yourself mad . . .

Another child was the answer. This was Vera's solution. It had apparently worked for her, no explanation offered or asked for. Maggie couldn't help but study the implications in her head. But another child wasn't practicable. They were far too busy. Her life with Charlie was in many ways idyllic. They weren't headliners, but nor were they bottom of the bill. The boom in holiday camp entertainment had kept them busy throughout the summer. A month on the club circuit, then over to Blackpool for the Lights season.

Sundays, Mondays and Tuesdays were spent back in Hope Street, as they only worked four nights a week, which, including Saturday matinée, was plenty. They could have picked up hotel work during their nights off, but Charlie was adamant. Working every night leaves you stale, it shows in the act. Maggie didn't disagree with this. All decisions regarding the act, she left to him. So far, things were going well. A child might ruin it all. Up to now, Charlie had agreed, and would continue to agree until they had enough money for her operation. Maggie had certain apprehensions as to what might happen after that. As far as she was concerned, the longer it took to save up, the better. She sat back and looked around the house she'd lived in since she was born. With all its memories, good and bad. The pre-war Bush radio on the dresser, contrasting with the fourteen-inch black and white Baird television in the corner. They had colour television in America, she'd rather have one of them than an operation. Pictures of her mam and dad stood on the mantelpiece alongside the one and only photograph of her brother Danny, taken by Denis Bradford on Danny's third birthday. He grinned out at her, forcing a smile to her lips. His photo was the most important thing in the house.

'It's daft paying rent for this house,' she said. 'The landlord tried to sell it when I moved out. I bet he'd sell it to us if we offered him a fair price.'

The prospect of being tied down in such a manner frightened Charlie who, in many ways, was much more of a free spirit than Maggie.

'One thing at a time, love. Let's get your voice sorted out first. You never know, we might be able to afford a mansion with the money you'll be earning ... and I can take a well-earned retirement.'

She knew he wasn't serious. The stage was in his blood, just as much as it was in hers. So why was he jeopardising their act? She couldn't understand it. If she did get her voice back, the only way to promote it was for her to go solo. Splitting their act up. But Charlie's mind was set on it, he loved her so much that she hadn't the heart to disappoint him. She felt a black mood coming on. The picture of her brother hadn't helped. The association of the two Dannys was a hard one to separate. Without a word, she ran upstairs. Charlie said nothing, these bouts were becoming more and more frequent, every time the subject of her voice came up. Hardly a coincidence. No doubt she thought she would never get her voice back, and that Charlie was living a pipe dream. Maybe so, but Maggie deserved that one last chance to get back the magic that so few were blessed with.

The Waters Twins had been a top act throughout the fifties. Now topping the bill on Blackpool Central Pier in the run up to Christmas, ably supported by Fish and Chipperfield, Bobbie McPherson the comic, Eldo the Magician and the Seaside Strollers.

Paul and Jimmy Waters had a suite in the Cumberland, to which they'd invited the rest of the cast for Saturday night, after show drinks. Eldo, as usual, had been excluded from the usual game of brag between the the the four men and Maggie. The dancers chose not to risk the pittance they were paid on the card table. On occasions, Maggie and Charlie would back out if the drinks took command of the stakes, leaving Paul, Jimmy and Bobbie to risk their week's money on the turn of a card. An interesting spectator sport. All right for the three men, who had no ties to speak of. At least one of the dancers would make herself available at the end of the night. A share of the winnings would make a welcome supplement to her wages. Maggie had often scolded them for prostituting themselves in such a manner, but the argument she was given was that they were all attractive men, so why not make the most of a situation? There was a logic in there somewhere that she felt unqualified to dispute.

For the umpteenth time, Maggie threw the cards she'd been dealt back in disgust. To start with, the maximum stake was a shilling seen, sixpence blind. Even modest amounts such as that could add up to a sizeable kitty.

'Let's play something else,' she suggested.

'Such as?' inquired Paul Waters. 'Strip Poker?' he grinned and eyed Maggie up and down, Charlie clenched his fists. Paul had a way of getting people's backs up. One of the dancers pricked her ears up, expectantly, at the mention of a game she could join in at last.

'Poker,' suggested Maggie.

Charlie frowned, unaware of Maggie's expertise at the game.

'Poker?' he said. 'Have you ever played Poker before?'

'Well,' she hesitated. 'Not for money, but it's the same idea as brag, you just get more cards that's all. At least I'd have a chance of a hand. The cards I've had tonight have all been rubbish.'

'Typical female logic,' said Paul, scornfully. He also had a tendency towards male chauvinism. 'Anyway, it suits me. I haven't played Poker in ages. Deal 'em, dealer.'

Maggie and Charlie had a pre-agreed losing limit of five pounds each. Their combined week's wages of fifty pounds was divided up in their respective pockets. Over the many times they'd played, their winnings balanced out their losses, so all in all it was an enjoyable and cheap form of entertainment, smattered with jokes and impromptu songs. Some extremely dirty, but beautifully sung.

The drinks were flowing freely and the noise grew louder. A knock on the door from the manager quietened them down for a few minutes. Charlie stood up, unsteadily, to go.

'My wife and I,' he began, 'must be pissing off home to the palace, before the corgis crap all over the coconut matting.' He gave a regal wave and fell down unconscious.

'One last hand,' decided Jimmy Waters. 'Then we'll get a taxi for his majesty.' He dealt out the last hand.

Maggie examined her cards. She was relatively sober, a trick she'd learned from her dad. There were only two ways to deal with a hand like that this. Play safe or take a gamble.

'None for me,' she said, when offered cards.

'Hello, hello? Pat hand!' remarked Jimmy. Maggie smiled at him and shrugged.

'Dealer takes three,' said Jimmy.

Bobbie and Paul took one and two cards respectively and Paul opened the betting with a shilling, which the rest of them matched, then Maggie said. 'Let's make it no limit, just for the last game.'

'Hello, Diamond Lil's got a royal flush,' said Paul. 'I'm in for five bob.'

'There's my five bob and I'll raise you five bob,' said Bobbie, throwing a ten shilling note in the middle.

'There's my ten bob and I'll raise ten bob,' said Maggie.

'I'm out,' declared Jimmy.

Paul studied Maggie intently and put a pound note and a ten shilling note in the middle. 'That's the fifteen bob I owe and I raise it another fifteen.'

Charlie sat up, stared at the table and slurred, 'I hope you're not gambling away your voice, Maggie Fisher,' before lying back and falling asleep again.

Bobbie and Maggie raised the stake in turn, each convinced that Paul was holding nothing. The dancers stared at the kitty with some envy. Paul looked at his full house, kings over jacks. No way could Maggie beat this. He was tired and wanted to go to bed so he decided to end the game quickly and dramatically.

'Is my credit good?' he asked. 'Unlike you lot, we get paid by cheque.'

'As the Bank of England,' said Bobbie, who'd already decided to throw his hand in if Paul continued. Paul looked at Maggie, questioningly.

'Good enough for me,' she said. 'Providing mine's good as well.' Paul obviously had a good hand, or had he? She'd known him bluff before.

He put two pounds in the middle to match the bet, then reached across to a drawer and took out a pen and notepaper on which he scribbled his IOU. Grinning at Maggie, he announced, 'I'll raise you two hundred and fifty pounds.'

'One of these days you'll do that and somebody'll take you to the cleaners,' grumbled Jimmy, who hated his brother's flash ways.

Charlie woke up again, uncomfortable where he was. 'What's happening?' he asked.

'It's Maggie's bet. Paul's just raised it to two hundred and fifty quid,' said Bobbie.

Maggie treated Paul to her vacant smile, fully intending to throw her cards in.

'Let's have a look at our cards,' demanded Charlie, with a wide, drunken grin on his face.

'Is it okay if I show my financial adviser my cards?' asked Maggie of Paul.

'Be my guest,' said Paul.

She flashed her hand quickly in front of Charlie's eyes.

'Jesus!' he shouted. 'Is that what I think it is?'

'Shurrup Charlie,' scolded Maggie.

Charlie passed out again. Maggie turned her vacant smile back on Paul, wanting to drag out the tension. He had that patronising smile on his face. She hated that.

'Pass me the paper,' she said.

Paul grinned, uncertainly. At this stage, all she wanted to do was to teach the supercilious sod a lesson.

'Bloody hell!' ejaculated Bobbie.

'I hope you know what you're doing, Maggie,' warned Jimmy. 'Our Paul'll hold you to it.'

'I hope he does, I intend holding him to it. There are some hands you just can't throw in, Jimmy. You know that.' She quite liked Jimmy. He was as different from his brother as chalk from cheese.

'She won't go through with it, she hasn't got the nerve,' sneered Paul.

Up to that stage, Maggie had no intention of going through with it, but she wasn't through with Paul. She proceeded to calmly write out an IOU for five hundred pounds and held it over the kitty. Was she about to snatch it away at the last minute? Paul was secretly hoping she would, the silly bitch, what was she playing at? The sneer was no longer on his face. But she knew it would return if she backed out.

'I'll match your two fifty,' she said, 'and raise you two fifty.'

Five hundred quid! Christ. What had she done? Paul's face was set like stone. With a great effort of will, she took a sip of wine and returned his penetrating gaze with her own vacant smile. The smile that had so infuriated her dad when she'd played with him. Paul drummed his fingers, nervously, on the table, then took a deep breath. To her dismay, he picked up the paper again and wrote out another IOU, also for five hundred.

'That's your two fifty, and another two fifty.'

She looked down at Charlie, sleeping like a baby. This could well put an end to all the nonsense about her having an operation.

'I do hope you're not gambling with money you haven't got,' sneered Paul, uncertainly. Unhappy with the situation he found himself in, but determined not to come out the loser.

'Me and Charlie have got enough money saved up to cover this many times over,' she lied. If she told Paul exactly how much they had, he'd have known she barely had the money for one more bet, and would force her out of the game.

'Always make them think you've got plenty of money,' her father had often drilled into her. Oh, sod it! In for a penny, as they say.

She wrote out another IOU. Paul's face was twitching nervously, she liked that. This time, without any hesitation, she threw in the note as though the action was merely a formality, a prelude to her scooping up the kitty. If you must lose, lose with style. That's what her dad always said. She was beginning to wish her dad had kept his mouth shut. It was the end of the line as far as she was concerned, still, she might as well end the game with as much panache as she could muster. All Paul needed to do was raise the stakes and she was out. No way was she going to bet with money she didn't have. What she was doing was foolish enough. She gave Paul a broad wink.

'There's your two fifty and another two fifty,' she declared.

Paul picked up his cards and studied them intently. Kings over jacks was a great hand, a good full house. Could be beaten by aces over anything though. Could be beaten by any four of a kind, any straight flush – the number of hands that could beat his hand piled up in his mind. He looked up at Maggie's annoyingly vacant smile. Then it struck him, clear as day, the smug bitch. She'd got four of a kind. It was written all over her. How could he be so stupid as to think a novice like her would bet everything she owned unless she was pretty certain her hand was unbeatable? It wouldn't surprise him if she had a straight flush, probably ace high. Whatever it was, it would beat his full house. No point in just seeing her – that would be a stupid waste of another two hundred and fifty quid. It crossed his mind to up the stakes and try to force her out. But they were playing with IOUs, bits of paper, she could match him every step of the way. If she had an unbeatable hand it was like money in the bank to her.

'Bollocks to this!' he snapped. 'I'm out.' He flung his cards on the table, kicked his chair over, and stormed into the bathroom.

Maggie's heart was pounding. She picked up the notes and loose change, then studied Paul's two IOUs totalling seven hundred and fifty pounds.

'He's good for it,' Jimmy assured her. 'You have my word on that.'

'I'm sure he is . . . I don't know whether I should hold him to it though. It's a lot of money.'

'He'd have held you to it, Maggie,' said Bobbie. 'And he wouldn't want the word to get out that he was a welsher.'

'Well, when you put it like that, I suppose I'll be doing him a favour,' grinned Maggie.

Both Bobbie and Jimmy were looking at her with expectant looks on their faces. She'd no obligation to show them her cards and she fully intended to put them back in the pack unseen, as any good gambler would.

'Go on,' said Paul, petulantly, from the bathroom door. 'Show 'em your four of a kind.'

Maggie hesitated for a second, then gave her cards to Bobbie, who looked at them and burst out laughing.

'I don't believe it! Nothing, not even a pair. Bloody queen high! That's all she'd got. You mad bugger, Maggie. Wait till Charlie wakes up and finds out what you've been up to.'

'Finds out what?' asked Charlie, momentarily conscious once again.

'Nothing,' said Maggie, 'go back to sleep, Charlie.'

They were changing trains at Preston the following morning, before the enormity of what Maggie had done struck home to Charlie. Up until then his hangover had taken priority. He'd been concentrating on not throwing up for the whole of the twenty-five minute journey.

'You bet a thousand quid on a queen high, and you reckon you've played before.'

'It's supposed to be a game of bluff. I was better at it than Paul because I had a good teacher.'

'Teacher?'

'My dad.'

'But it was our money. I wouldn't have done that to you.'

'Done what?' asked Maggie. 'I didn't do anything to you.'

'You gambled all our savings on a queen high,' said Charlie, evenly. 'You're a worry.'

Maggie looked suitably contrite. 'I didn't intend to gamble our money. All I set out to do was wipe the supercilious smile off Paul's face. It just got out of hand that's all. Anyway I won, so what're you worrying about? We can stop saving up now.'

'You're missing the point.'

'What point?'

Charlie shook his head. 'Never mind,' he conceded. He could see an argument brewing, and arguing with impossible people such as Maggie was a waste of energy.

They were sitting in the station café, waiting for the connection to Leeds. It was late Monday morning, and all the early commuters were safely ensconced at work, leaving the station comfortably empty. Maggie and Charlie never travelled at rush hour if they could help it, one of the perks for those who work unsociable hours. A man in an Alpine hat looked hard at her then shook his head as if to say 'No, it couldn't be'. Maggie knew she'd been recognised, there was a certain satisfaction still to be had from this. Charlie looked at the man and smiled at Maggie.

'You'll have to put up with a lot more of that, when you get your voice back, which won't be long now. I reckon we've got enough money now for me to come with you to Chicago.'

200

She held his hand. 'It scares me, Charlie,' she said.

He tried to reassure her. 'It's not a life threatening operation, Maggie. If I thought there was any danger, I wouldn't let you go.'

Maggie shook her head. 'It's not the operation I'm scared of. It's losing what we've got. I'm happy the way things are with you and me.'

'Maggie, you'll never get rid of me. I just want my lovely Maggie to get her lovely voice back, that's all.'

He leaned over and kissed her and she knew he'd beaten her again. A tap on her shoulder had her turning round. It was the man in the Alpine hat.

'I wonder if I might have your autograph, Miss Fisher,' he asked politely. 'I'm a great fan of yours.'

Charlie was beaming all over his face, as Maggie obliged the man, who'd unwittingly aided and abetted her husband in his quest to get Maggie her voice back. She was surprised he hadn't asked the man his opinion on the matter.

Chapter Twenty-Two

January 1962

Styren was pleased to see her. Beautiful people such as Maggie rarely sat in the chair opposite him. She looked a world away from the careworn young lady he'd last seen sitting there. Showbusiness imbued its own air of glamour. Her clothes were more daring than the norm, without being tasteless. Her blue silk blouse showed her rich chestnut hair off to its full advantage, as well as a tantalising amount of cleavage. A well-tailored lilac skirt had accentuated the curve of her hips as she entered his office, even the way she carried her coat over her arm spoke of grace and poise.

'What can I do for you, Miss Fi . . . oops, it's Mrs Chipperfield now, so I understand. I'd like to offer my belated congratulations.'

Maggie smiled at his awkwardness. She was used to men being slightly awkward in her presence. Generally speaking, people in showbusiness are acutely aware of their physical attributes, and Maggie was no exception.

'Professionally I'm still Maggie Fisher, but as far as we're concerned, I'm Mrs Chipperfield . . . and proud of it.'

'Well, I've never met Mr Chipperfield, but he's a very lucky man,' oozed Styren.

The formalities over, Maggie leaned forward, 'I don't need Legal Aid any more. I have my own money for getting Danny back.'

Styren nodded. He'd been studying her file for an hour before she arrived. He took it off the top of a pile next to him and opened it, as Maggie continued.

'First of all,' she said. 'Now that Prestwick's been struck off, we should be able to find out who the adoptive parents are, so at least we know where he is. Then let them know exactly what they're up against. That way, they might just give him up like that. Once they realise how I was cheated out of my own baby by a crook like Prestwick. I can't see any decent people . . .'

Styren held up his hand, stopping her in mid-sentence. 'Before you go any further,' he said politely. 'Let me tell you what the situation is, as I see it.'

'Right,' she accepted, impatiently. She'd planned her strategy down to the last detail. Charlie knew nothing about it as yet. He'd be let in on the plan as soon as she'd got Styren's blessing.

'Firstly, it's impossible to find out who the adoptive parents are without a court order and we can't get one of those without good reason.'

'But surely,' she argued, 'we've got a good reason, my baby was stolen from me.'

'You know that, and I know that, Maggie. I can call you Maggie can't I?'

'Yes, yes . . . get on with it.'

'In this case, the court would need a criminal act to have taken place before they give us an order.'

'But a criminal act has taken place. Christ, Prestwick was struck off for what he did.'

'I'm aware of that. The BMA took a dim view of his actions, but the police were unhappy about pressing charges. Mainly because they were struggling to find a charge that would stick. On top of this, he's disappeared.'

'Disappeared? Oh no!' The impossibility of the situation was dawning on Maggie. All her carefully thought out plans, her kitchen table discussions with Vera, were coming to nothing.

'The odds are that he's skipped the country,' said Styren. 'Gone somewhere not quite so fussy about his past histo . . .'

He stopped at the sight of Maggie's tears. Not quite knowing what to do. She wasn't the first woman who'd burst into tears in his office, just the first he'd had any genuine sympathy for. He'd learned to switch his sympathy on and off like a tap with most people, but not with Maggie.

'Look, I'm sorry . . . I've obviously been completely tactless.' He fumbled in a drawer. 'I've got some tissues here somewhere.'

Something fell out of the drawer on to the floor. 'Damn!' he exclaimed. 'Oh, sorry, here they are.' He held out a packet of paper handkerchiefs, but Maggie was already wiping her eyes on one of her own.

'I was . . . I was so sure in my mind that I'd get him back,' she sobbed.

'I don't know what to say, Maggie. I can only tell you the facts. I've checked with my seniors. They all agree with me.'

She held out her hand. 'Thank you for your help. I won't be troubling you any more.'

'It was no trouble, Maggie. I just wish I could have been of more help.'

In a daze, Maggie strode up The Headrow, heading for the taxi rank on Briggate. Taxis instead of buses were a little perk she allowed herself. After all, Charlie had a car. She'd been taking driving lessons herself, but had failed two tests to date, leaving her exasperated with the over-fussy examiners. Her tears dried in the crisp, morning air. Pull yourself together, Maggie. She hadn't expected failure so abruptly. The least she expected was a fight in the courts with all the attendant publicity, perhaps enlisting public sympathy on her behalf. But she'd cried many tears over Danny, maybe it was time to accept the inevitable. An estate agent's sign caught her eye. They were also the rental agents for her landlord. The people to whom they sent rent every month. Purely on a whim, she went inside.

Chapter Twenty-Three

Charlie just knew this would cheer her up. For the past two weeks she'd not been herself. She'd switched on the personality every time she walked on stage, it was an automatic thing to do. But off stage she'd been morose, moody even. Snapping at him for the smallest thing. Not like Maggie at all.

They'd been living full time in Hope Street since Christmas. Playing the northern clubs. Come spring they'd be off again, doing the rounds of the holiday camps. Dave Greenwood, now their agent, could get them all the work they needed. They were his most valuable act.

Charlie passed an airmail letter he'd received that morning over to Maggie as she ate her breakfast cornflakes.

'What's that?' she asked, without looking at it.

'It's from that surgeon in Chicago, Mike Willard. Or rather from his office. They want you to go across before the end of the month. If we reply straight away with a deposit, they'll fit you in on the 27th. Brilliant that, isn't it? They reckon you'll be able to talk normally within six weeks and your voice will be completely back to normal in three months. Just think, by May you'll have your old voice back.'

'I don't want my old voice back.'

Charlie laughed at first, then the smile froze on his face. 'Don't be daft, how can you not want your old voice back?'

'I'm happy as I am.'

'You could have fooled me.'

It was the first time he'd ever spoken to her with anything of an edge to his voice.

'What's that supposed to mean?' she demanded, sharply.

'It means you've had a face like a busted clog for the last few weeks, and it's about time you did something about it.'

'I see. And a trip to Chicago will sort me out, will it?'

'Well, as a matter of fact, yes. I think it will.' He stood up, uncertain as to why they were arguing. He thought she'd be over the moon. 'Look Maggie,' he said, placatingly. 'Your voice is at the bottom of all your moods, can't you see? I'm doing this for you. At least, I thought I was.'

Maggie sipped her coffee, angry at Charlie's lack of under-standing. An anger qualified by the knowledge that she'd kept him in the dark about the reasons for her moods, allowing him to jump to wrong conclusions. Still, if he had any real love for her, he'd have an instinct about these things. She shouldn't have to spell it out for him. She knew she was being unfair, but she needed to get angry with him to tell him what had happened, without going to pieces.

'We can't afford it,' she announced.

'Don't be daft. With the money you won off Paul, we can easily afford it.'

Maggie gritted her teeth. Charlie was the most affable man she'd ever met and he loved her to distraction. But how would he take this? Might as well tell him the whole story in one go.

'I spent the money. I bought this house.'

There was a silence as Charlie stared down at her. 'I do hope you're joking, Maggie.'

'No joke, I signed the conveyance yesterday, it's ours, bought and paid for.'

'You're not kidding, are you?' Charlie's face had gone white with anger. 'You've spent our money buying this bloody dump when we were saving it up specifically for you to have an operation?'

'In a nutshell,' agreed Maggie.

'Why . . . why didn't you ask me?'

'Because you wouldn't . . .' her voice tailed off. She wasn't exactly commanding the moral high ground in this argument. 'Look I just did it . . . all right?' she snapped.

Charlie's voice was shaking, his fists clenching and

unclenching. 'No, Maggie, it's not all right. You should have told me . . . you should have asked me.'

'I know. I'm sorry, what do you want me to say?' she shouted the words, not sounding in the least sorry.

'You're a liar, Maggie . . . a selfish, self-centred bloody liar! Just like you lied to me when you promised not to split our act up . . . you lied to me then. If it hadn't been for me starting you off, you'd have been a bloody nobody!'

'Well, you'd know all about being a nobody wouldn't you? Because that's all you ever were.'

'Maybe I was, but I'm not a liar. You lied to me when you promised not to gamble more than five pounds.'

'Stop calling me a liar,' she screamed. 'It's all your fault. You've no idea have you? You've no idea what's been wrong with me?'

'I'll tell you what's been wrong with you, shall I?' he retorted angrily. 'You've been feeling sorry for yourself, that's what's been wrong with you.'

'I've lost my baby,' she screamed. 'That's what's been wrong with me!'

There was real venom in her voice now. Next door, Vera was pricking up her ears in dismay. She'd never heard a wrong word between them, up until now, much less a violent slanging match like this. Charlie had heard enough. It was a cheap shot, bringing the baby in, when she knew very well it was nothing to do with any baby.

'If you ask me, your baby's better off where he is. At least he's with someone he'll be able to trust.'

'How can you say that to me?' she sobbed. 'You lousy bastard!'

'I'm saying it because it's true,' he yelled.

Charlie was as much out of control as Maggie. All the pent-up frustrations of the past few weeks were pouring out. All the hours sitting out her moods, without a word of apology from her.

Maggie flew at him, her fists pounding into his face, blood pouring from his nose. He broke free and dashed out of the house into his car parked outside. She followed him, banging on the roof as he drove away, then dropped to her knees, sobbing hysterically, until Vera appeared and led her back inside, away from prying eyes.

*

Charlie drove until his anger subsided, the injustice of her actions appalling him. How could she have done such a thing? Have said such cruel things? It was February and he had no jacket, no money on him and no breakfast inside him. He headed for his parents' house. It took his mother less than a minute to assess the situation.

'You've had a row, haven't you?'

'Sort of.'

'Sit down, I'll get you something to eat.' His mother wouldn't sit in judgement, she liked Maggie a lot more than she'd ever liked Brenda. 'Your dad's at work. Are you working tonight?'

'We're supposed to be. I'd better ring Dave Greenwood and tell him I'm sick or something.'

'Come off it,' said his mother encouragingly, 'you'll have probably made it up before then.'

'I don't think so,' said Charlie, gloomily. It would need someone to apologise and of course he had nothing to apologise for. He couldn't remember Maggie ever apologising for anything.

It was lunchtime before Maggie began to think rationally. Charlie's cheap jibe about Danny had cut her deeply. Too deeply for her to ever forgive him. Was there a man anywhere whom she could trust never to hurt her? Charlie had seemed perfect. How could he have said such a thing? Vera had tried to placate her.

'It was the heat of the moment, love. You always say things you don't mean in the heat of the moment. I've no doubt he'll be licking his wounds somewhere, wishing to God he hadn't said such a nasty thing.'

'But it must have been in his mind for him to have said it in the first place,' argued Maggie. 'Somewhere, deep down inside him, he must have thought it.'

'Stop trying ter read too much into things, love,' Vera advised. 'You have ter learn ter forgive and forget. If yer brood over things, you might as well give up before yer start. That's what marriage is all about. So long as he's not knocking you about, nor running round with other women, you've nowt ter worry about. All the rest is the normal crap what goes with a marriage.'

'I don't know, Mrs Bradford. He shook me when he said that.'

Vera smiled. There was no hatred in Maggie's eyes, just a mixture of shock and self-pity. It would be a long time before they had another row like that.

'You love him a lot, don't you?' she said.

'I don't know what I'd do without him, Mrs Bradford.'

It was early evening when Charlie drove past the end of Hope Street for the third time, wondering if she might have calmed down long enough to let him in through the door. His nose was swollen to twice its normal size. He'd rung Dave Greenwood and told him he'd had an accident and couldn't do tonight's gig. It was the first time he'd let Dave down, so his excuse had been believed. 'Sod it,' he decided. 'I'll have a pint in the Crimea and then march straight in. I'll tell her straight, I'll say ... what will I say? God knows, but me and Maggie arguing is stupid. That's not what we're about.'

One pint turned into several as the evening wore on. He was invited to the dartboard and stayed on for an hour, no one could knock him off. Hand-eye co-ordination is all that's required for a darts player, same as playing the piano, but without the beer belly. He was explaining this to one of his opponents when a shout from behind him made him turn round.

'Pianner player? I know you. You're the one what plays wi' Maggie Fisher.' He was a large young man with a floppy mouth and unpleasant grin.

'That's right,' grinned Charlie. 'Where've you seen us?'

'Hey! I wouldn't mind playing with her meself. I've heard she shags like a rattlesnake,' he leered.

'Leave it Bazza,' cautioned one of his companions.

Bazza ignored this advice. He'd been soundly beaten at darts by Charlie a couple of times and now he knew who Charlie was, he could see a way of exacting revenge.

'Wasn't it her what got raped by Tony Whatsisname? Yer know, that Eyetie what got killed by her dad?'

Charlie's rage had returned. He put down the darts and advanced on the man.

'Raped?' went on Bazza. 'I bet it were the other way round.' He turned round to address the rest of the customers who were watching apprehensively. 'Maggie Fisher ... Hey!' he sniggered. 'I bet she's had more pricks in her than this dartboard.' Charlie went for him. A mismatch if ever there was one. Charlie was long and thin and had never had a fight in his life and Bazza, who outweighed him by several stones, couldn't do anything else. He pushed Charlie away with an outsize hand as he finished off his pint with the other. Charlie staggered back, fists flailing. Bazza wiped the froth from his mouth, grabbed Charlie by his shirt collar and punched him hard in the face, several times. Charlie dropped to the floor, barely conscious as Bazza turned his back to him, took the fresh pint handed to him by one of his pals, then held out his arms in innocence.

'You're all witnesses. He started it ... it were only self-defence.'

Charlie reached out a hand and pulled at one of Bazza's ankles, bringing him down on top of him, the beer from Bazza's fresh drink spilling all over him, the glass smashing as it fell to the floor. Bazza, now in a rage, picked up the bottom half of the glass and jabbed it at Charlie's face, Charlie saw it coming and tried to avoid it, but the broken glass cut deep into his neck. A horrified gasp came from the crowd. Bazza looked up, challengingly.

'What're you lot bloody staring at? It were self-defence ... he started it ... awright?'

Blood poured out of Charlie's neck, causing screams from the women and panic from the men. Someone rang for an ambulance as Bazza made a hasty exit, leaving behind a threat to anyone who squealed on him to the police.

Maggie was beginning to watch the clock go round. All the anger had left her and the soul searching had begun. How could Charlie possibly have known how desperate she was at losing Danny? She'd hidden her true feelings at every turn. He thought her moods were due to her losing her voice, a misunderstanding she had encouraged at every opportunity. Dave Greenwood had rung, asking if Charlie would be fit for tomorrow night's gig. Maggie hadn't a clue what he was talking about at first and had to think on her feet a bit.

'He banged his nose,' she explained. 'I imagine he'll be okay for tomorrow.' She made a joke about Charlie coming on as a red-nosed comic and promised to ring Dave back first thing in the morning, which in agent's language meant ten am.

Coronation Street came on at half past seven, the first time Maggie had ever seen this much talked about programme. Now into its second year, some newspaper critics were predicting it could run for another five or six years, such was its popularity. It reminded her of Hope Street. Elsie Tanner could have been Vera, Denis Tanner was about as bright as Roy. She amused herself with these associations, then her anxiety took over. She switched off and went to the window, vainly hoping to see Charlie's head bobbing along beyond the yard wall, turning in the gate, as her dad's head had once done. She'd sit and wait for her dad every night after school. At first he was rarely late, six-fifteen on the dot. Then he began stopping off for a drink and his arrivals grew later. Sometimes Vera would invite her in for tea. If Denis was there, he rarely hid his disgust at the slack way Johnnie looked after Maggie. But by and large he'd been a loving father. Never raised his hand to her. He just allowed his moods to get the better of him. Like father like daughter. She smiled to herself ruefully at this similarity, picked up the phone and dialled Charlie's parents.

'Hello . . . it's Maggie.'

Charlie's mother had answered. To save Maggie any embarrassing explanations she took over the conversation. 'I suppose you want misery guts. For heaven's sake, kiss and make up before he drives me mad.'

Maggie laughed. 'I'll do my best, Mrs Chipperfield.'

'When are you going to start calling me Ethel?'

Maggie had an innate respect for her elders and found it difficult to call them by their first names. Ethel paused for a reply, but none was forthcoming, so she continued. 'He's gone out to drown his sorrows. If he comes back here I'll send him back to you, but I reckon he's looking for a bit of Dutch courage so he can face you.'

'He won't need Dutch courage to face me Mrs . . . Ethel.'

'I'm glad to hear it. Give me a ring if you see him first.'

'I will, thanks . . . Ethel.' It just didn't sound right.

The short conversation had taken a weight off her mind. At least she knew that Charlie was as miserable as she was. There was some consolation in that. She went upstairs to do her hair and fix her makeup. Perhaps slip into something more comfortable, as they say. In Maggie's case it was a silk dressing gown, with nothing on underneath but Chanel No. 5. She and Charlie had a lot of making up to do.

There was blood all over the pub floor by the time the ambulance arrived. An erstwhile St John's Ambulance cadet had tried to stem the flow by applying as much pressure as she dare, without choking Charlie to death, while her boyfriend nipped the sides of the wound together with his fingers. A crude, but effective attempt at First Aid.

Maggie frowned at the loud banging on the door. This wasn't a neighbourly knock, more of an official knock. She looked at the clock, ten past ten. What sort of official would bang on her door at this time of night? She glanced through the curtains, her frown deepening at the sight of a policeman and policewoman on her doorstep. She still didn't associate their presence with Charlie. As she opened the door the policewoman took half a step forward.

'Mrs Chipperfield?' she asked

'Yes.'

'I'm WPC Holmes and this is PC Wallington from Chapelhill Police, may we come in?'

The reason for their presence suddenly dawned on Maggie. A cold fear clutched at her body.

'What is it? Is it Charlie?' She stepped back from the door to let the two constables through.

'There's been an incident, Mrs Chipperfield,' said the WPC, as gently as she could. 'Look, perhaps you'd like to sit down.'

Maggie sat down on the settee, the WPC sat beside her and the policeman remained standing, shuffling his feet uncomfortably.

'Your husband's in the LGI ... he was attacked earlier this evening,' the WPC informed her.

'Attacked?' blurted out Maggie. 'How d'you mean, attacked? Is he all right?'

The eyes of the two constables met. 'He's still alive. Mrs Chipperfield ...' said WPC Holmes, without giving much away.

'I want to go and see him.'

'Yes, well we can take you straight there,' said the policeman, who looked even younger than Maggie.

'How is he? I mean how bad?'

'We don't know, Mrs Chipperfield ... it's Maggie, isn't it?' The WPC seemed to know exactly who she was. Maggie nodded as the WPC continued. 'Someone attacked him with a broken glass, that's as much as we know.'

'Oh, my God!' gasped Maggie. 'I'll get dressed, could you give me a moment?'

'Of course we can.'

Accompanied by the two constables, Maggie weaved her way through the late night customers of the Leeds General Infirmary. A smell of stale beer hung over the waiting area. The staff purposely dealing with the genuine cases first, at the expense of the injured drunks who, in any case, were anaesthetised with alcohol. Some of the language was coarse and insulting and scarcely designed to elicit preferential treatment from the harassed doctors and nurses who were well used to such behaviour.

A nurse led the trio past the waiting area, stepping gingerly over a stream of urine, meandering across the polished floor from the direction of a snoring, incontinent drunk, along a corridor and into a smaller waiting area beside a door marked Theatre. She motioned them to take a seat. 'They're operating on him now,' said the nurse, 'I'll see what I can find out.'

Maggie was numb with fear. The lack of information she was being given had begun to sound ominous. No one had tried to reassure her that he would be all right. Everyone was being just a bit too non-committal.

'Would you like me to bring you a cup of tea?' asked the young constable, who dreaded what lay in store and hoped he might be absent when the nurse came out with bad news.

'Yes please,' muttered Maggie automatically.

The constable started to ask how she liked it, but was forestalled by his colleague looking at him and shaking her head. He went away, knowing that Maggie probably wouldn't be drinking it anyway. He'd just vanished round a corner when the nurse returned. Maggie searched her face for good news, but saw none.

'Your husband sustained a very serious wound to his neck, Mrs Chipperfield. He's lost a lot of blood and we're having trouble stabilising him.'

Maggie got to her feet and for some reason looked back at the WPC for reassurance. 'Stabilising him? What does that mean?' The WPC nodded towards the nurse, directing Maggie's attention to the person who could answer.

The nurse took a deep breath. 'Well . . . they've just managed to stop the bleeding. As I said, he did lose a lot of blood, but he's undergoing transfusion right now.'

Maggie wanted to know what his chances were, but she

213

couldn't bring herself to ask. The nurse thought it prudent to answer her unspoken question for her. In her experience, when giving someone bad news it was better to cushion the blow first.

'I have to tell you, Mrs Chipperfield, your husband's chances aren't very good, but we're doing all we can.'

Maggie collapsed into WPC Holmes' arms.

It was midnight when Charlie's mother and father arrived, the news having reached them only after Maggie had had the presence of mind to have it passed on to them. She was sitting, ashen-faced with fear when they arrived. Her appearance sufficient to tell Mr and Mrs Chipperfield the worst. Maggie couldn't answer their questions.

'He's still critical,' said WPC Holmes. Her colleague had left with her blessing. 'Worse than bloody useless,' she'd muttered under her breath as he gratefully departed.

Charlie's parents just nodded dumbly and sat down in the only other two seats.

'Do we know how it happened?' asked Tom Chipperfield.

'Some drunk attacked him in a pub. It wasn't your son's fault, Mr Chipperfield,' the policewoman assured him.

'I could've told you that, miss,' sighed Tom. 'He never were much for fighting, weren't our Charlie. Music, that's all he ever thought about. I wanted him to follow me into the building trade, but it were like talking to a brick wall.'

WPC Holmes felt herself smiling at the unintended pun, but straightened her face before anyone noticed.

'Have you got the feller what did it?' asked Tom.

The policewoman shook her head. 'We've got a name. If it turns out to be the right man, he'll be looking at a long sentence this time. He's already got a record for violence.'

'I hope they throw the bloody key away,' cursed Tom.

'That's not going to do our Charlie any good though, is it?' said his wife.

Maggie sat with her hands clasped together, praying silent prayers, deaf to the voices of her companions. Please God, let my Charlie be all right. Don't take everyone away from me. You've got my mum and dad ... and our Danny ... and my own Danny for all the good he is to me. Please let me have my Charlie.

There was a flurry of activity with a nurse running out of the theatre, away down the corridor, to return a minute later with another nurse and a doctor in tow. Tom Chipperfield stood up and peered through the small round window in the theatre door.

'Bugger it! Can't see nowt,' he cursed, stamping impatiently back to his seat. 'It wouldn't be so bad if we knew what were going on.'

Ten minutes later a doctor came out and made off up the corridor, Tom strode after him. 'Doctor!' he called 'I'm his dad.'

The doctor turned round, impatiently, his expression softening when Tom's identity sunk in. 'He's still with us,' he said. 'We nearly lost him, but he's still with us. God knows how, but he is.'

'Do you mean he's going to be all right?' asked Tom, hopefully.

The doctor's expression changed, angry at himself for raising their hopes. To him, the fact that Charlie was still alive was good news, but he still didn't give much for his chances. Maggie, Charlie's mum and dad and WPC Holmes were all staring at him, waiting for him reply.

'The next couple of hours are going to be critical,' was the best he could do. Erasing the hope from all four faces.

The next hour was spent in silence, everyone absorbed in their own thoughts. Each time the theatre door banged open, and someone walked out, four hearts stopped beating, WPC Holmes having, unprofessionally, become involved. She'd never even met Charlie, but she sometimes found it hard to stay detached under such circumstances. Tom looked at his watch, one-fifteen.

'Another hour . . . if we don't hear anything for another hour he should be in the clear.'

Even as he spoke a weary-looking surgeon emerged from the theatre, seemingly unaware of their presence. A nurse followed in his wake and spoke quickly in his ear, inclining her head in the direction of the waiting foursome. He turned to them. This was it, Tom got to his feet. WPC Holmes put her arm around Maggie and held her tight as the surgeon approached.

Barry Beedon, Bazza to his pals, who were few and far between, knocked on his brother's door. A bolt was drawn and the door unlocked by his sister-in-law, whom he barged straight past. Gary Beedon was sitting in the front room watching a tiny black and white television.

'I'm in bother, I need to stay here for a couple o' days,' panted Bazza.

Marjory Beedon's face dropped. From behind her brother-in-law she shook her head vigorously.

'Why?' asked Gary. 'Watcha done now?'

'Me? I haven't done nowt,' protested Bazza. 'This pillock in the Crimea went for me, so I decked him. It'll be my fault when the cops find out . . . it always is.'

'I wonder why,' commented Marjory, cynically. 'Anyway, you can't stay here, we've got visitors coming ter stay tomorrow.'

'I'll say whether he can stay or not,' snapped Gary, annoyed at this threat to his male pride. 'Stay as long as yer want, our kid. You'd do the same for me.'

'When you say, "decked him", what exactly do you mean?' asked Marjory. Bazza looked nervous.

'He means what he . . .' began Gary.

Majory held up a hand to stop him continuing. 'I'd like Bazza to tell me. Why would the police come looking for you if you only decked him?'

Bazza was reluctant to answer. 'Come on Bazza,' insisted Marjory. 'If you're going to stay here, we want to know what the score is. At least I do.'

'I glassed him,' admitted Bazza. 'It were his fault, he pulled me down. I did it without thinking.'

'Glassed him?' inquired Gary. 'In his face?'

'I caught him in his neck . . . it were accidental like.'

'Oh my God!' gasped Marjory. 'How is he?'

'How do I know? I didn't stay around to find out.'

'And you think the police won't find you here, do you?' said Marjory scathingly. 'Christ, Bazza! After your house it's the first place they'll look.'

Bazza was visibly shaking now. 'Jesus, if he snuffs it, they'll hang me, with my record.'

Gary and Marjory looked at each other, they didn't need this. Gary had been going more or less straight since coming out of jail three years previously. Even harbouring Bazza could send him back inside.

'You think he might peg it?' asked Gary.

'He didn't look too good.'

Gary thought long and hard. 'If it were a fight, it could

have been his fault and you were just sticking up for yourself.'

'Yeah . . . that's right,' agreed Bazza, eager to clutch at straws. 'He went for me, all I did was crack him one.'

'And stick a broken glass in his neck,' added Marjory.

'It doesn't look good, does it,' admitted Bazza.

'Depends,' decided Gary. 'We might have to have a quiet word with the witnesses. I suppose all your daft mates saw it?'

'Oh yeah . . . they'll back me up. The wouldn't dare do nowt else.'

'And if anyone else pokes their nose in, we can have a quiet word,' said Gary.

'You mean *you* can have a quiet word,' pointed out Marjory. 'Bazza won't be having a quiet word with anyone where he's going.'

'How do you mean?' asked Bazza.

'I mean,' explained Marjory. 'That you've got to go straight to the police and tell them your story. You'll be held on remand till your case comes up, but you'll have to accept that.'

Bazza looked at his brother, who shrugged his agreement to Marjory's assessment of the situation. 'She's right, our kid. It'll go in yer favour if yer give yerself up.'

Bazza looked immensely disappointed at their solution to his problem. 'Supposing he doesn't snuff it, and it's my word against his.'

'Depends on who he is,' said Marjory.

'His name's Charlie Chipperfield.'

'What?' said Marjory. 'Charlie Chipperfield as in . . .?'

'Fish and Chipperfield,' Bazza said it for her.

'Not your normal thug then,' said Gary. 'If he doesn't snuff it, we'll have to put the hard word on his missus. He won't like that. If he refuses to testify against you, you're home and dry . . . you might not even get remanded.'

Bazza's face brightened for a second, then clouded over again. 'Mind you,' he said. 'I reckon he'll snuff it.'

Marjory left the room in disgust. If it was up to her, Bazza would be locked up for life . . . or worse. Still, if he handed himself in, at least she wouldn't be lumbered with him.

The surgeon stopped in front of them, examined his hands, then looked up at the desperately nervous group of people in front of him. He was a good surgeon, but useless at talking to people.

'Mrs Chipperfield?' he inquired.

Both Maggie and Charlie's mum said, 'Yes.'

The surgeon expelled a lungful of breath. 'It'll be a while before he's playing the piano again,' he announced. 'But he's over the worst.'

Maggie and the policewoman clung to each other tearfully, as did Tom and his wife. The surgeon smiled, they'd never know how brilliant he'd been, why should they? But he knew that it was only thanks to his consummate skill that the world hadn't lost a piano player. The surgeon had always admired piano players, being a failed concert pianist himself. He walked off to the canteen, wondering if this admiration had given him the extra edge he seemed to have had that night. He gave a wry smile. If this was the case, it was a bit unfair on any non-piano players who came under his knife.

Chapter Twenty-Four

Sylvia felt slightly awkward sitting alone with Charlie. It was obvious what Maggie saw in him. He was a little pale after his ordeal, but nice to look at. Handsome in an Anthony Perkins kind of way, only his face was a lot more cheerful, despite the swathes of bandages around his neck. Maggie had nipped out to the shops, leaving her unexpected visitor to look after her recuperating husband.

A week in hospital had seen much of his strength return, although he was nowhere near fit enough to go back to work. Apparently, Maggie hadn't spent all of their money on buying the house, so they wouldn't starve.

'They got the bastard what did it then?'

Sylvia's question was rhetorical. Bazza's arrest had made headlines in the *Yorkshire Evening Post*. Maggie was still worth a column or two, it'd do no harm at all to their act. Dave Greenwood had rung to tell them of a summer season in Scarborough, this had cheered Charlie up. He'd given up on the idea of Maggie's operation. If she wanted it, she'd go for it herself, no point him trying to persuade her into anything she didn't want to do. He'd learned that lesson the hard way.

Charlie nodded, 'Bazza Beedon . . . I'm not looking forward to going to court.'

'Don't blame yer,' sympathised Sylvia. 'They're bastards are them Beedons.'

'What? You know them then?'

'I don't, me brothers do.'

Charlie chose not to question her further on this. 'Would you like a cup of tea?' he asked.

Sylvia sprang to her feet. 'It's me what should be making you one. If Maggie finds out I've had you running round after me, she'll play hell.'

Charlie laughed, 'You've got that right, Sylvia.'

As she busied herself in the scullery, she called through to him. 'I brought me banjo.'

'I noticed. Maggie tells me you've gone back to busking.'

'Yeah,' Sylvia's voice had a note of apprehension in it. How much had Maggie told him about her?

'Must be a lot more satisfying than your old job,' he called out.

'Yeah.' She was inwardly cursing Maggie for not minding her own business. He was a nice bloke was Charlie, what must he think of her?

'Mind you ...' continued Charlie. 'I used to go in the Tomato Dip myself you know, best bacon sandwiches in Leeds.'

Sylvia breathed a sigh of relief as she waited for the kettle to boil. Good old Maggie.

'Would yer like to hear me play?' she ventured. This being the reason she'd brought the instrument. She had some vague idea that Charlie might be able to get her work in the clubs.

'I'd love to,' replied Charlie, cleverly hiding his lack of enthusiasm.

Sylvia brought his cup of tea through and sat opposite him, sipping hers.

'I'm not a proper musician like you ... I mean I can't read music or nowt.' She was making excuses for her own ineptitude before she'd even started.

Charlie studied her over his cup. Neither plain nor pretty. A few years older than him, but a face that had been around the block a few times. A mass of dark curls framing her dark complexion gave her a gypsy look. Her face broke into an embarrassed grin, displaying two rows of even white teeth; an attractive smile that wouldn't look out of place on stage. He'd a good idea why she'd brought her banjo: she'd come for an audition.

She took her instrument from its case and plucked the four strings one by one, looking up at Charlie for his agreement that it was in tune. He'd no idea.

'Sounds all right to me,' he said, eager to get this over with.

She introduced her first number. 'This one's about a bloke what were born without an 'ole in his arse,' she said, quite seriously.

'So he weren't able ter fart . . . and me song's all about him finding out how ter fart. It's one of me most popular numbers . . . It's called "Fanshawe the Farting Phantom".'

She broke into a raucous song about the unusual affliction of a certain Freddie Fanshawe. Charlie's expression went from amazement to shock to howling with laughter at the end, when the unfortunate Freddie dies with his first anal outburst and is doomed to haunt the pub where his flatulent debut took place.

'Brilliant!' cried Charlie, when she finished. 'Have you got any more?'

Sylvia, pleased at his reaction, sang him another of her songs about a young woman with breasts on her back, who was the most popular girl at the dance. He was still laughing at this when a loud knock came at the door.

Charlie was halfway to his feet when the door was kicked open and three large men came in. The one in the lead had a vaguely familiar face. It was a menacing face, a face not to be argued with. His hair was cropped unfashionably short, adding emphasis to his bulging neck. He wore a dark suit that his body seemed to be pushing its way out of, and black leather gloves. It was these gloves that set off the alarm in Charlie's panicking brain.

Gary Beedon stared at Sylvia. 'You're not Maggie Fisher!' he snarled.

'My wife's out,' said Charlie, as evenly as he could. 'Who are you? What do you want?'

Gary gave a broken-toothed grin. As evil a grin as Charlie had ever seen. 'I've come ter tell yer that if yer give evidence against Bazza Beedon, yer can forget ever going on stage again . . . and so can that tart of a wife of yours.' He took a step towards Sylvia and punched her full in the face, knocking her clean across the room, where she landed in a heap beneath the dining table.

'That's the sort o' thing I'm talking about . . . only we won't stop there when it comes ter your missis. We'll cut her up so's nobody'll want ter look at her.' He walked across to the television set and kicked at the screen, shattering it with a crash that Vera heard next door, but ignored, thinking it was just one less piece of crockery in the Chipperfield household. Charlie sprang to his feet, fists clenched, Gary sneered at him.

'Wotcha gonna do? Hit me with yer powder puff? Hey! And don't try telling the coppers, because we're not here, are we lads?'

He turned to his two cronies for support; they shook their grinning heads.

'We're all playing snooker down at Napoleon's ... that's where we are right now. Still ...' he wrapped his huge hands around Charlie's damaged neck, causing him to shout out with pain. 'You've got more sense than ter call the police, haven't yer, Charlie boy? Yer wouldn't want your Maggie marked for life, would yer?'

His face was an inch away from Charlie's now, Charlie shook his head very slightly, every movement agony.

'Good boy, Charlie,' he turned to his cronies again. 'See, I told yer he'd see sense.' He returned his menacing glare to Charlie. 'So ... I can tell Bazza Beedon he's nowt ter worry about then, can I?'

Charlie nodded, hating himself for doing so, but wisely preferring self-preservation to foolish heroism.

Gary took half a step back. 'Good lad, Charlie,' he said, then fired a short, powerful jab into Charlie's mouth, knocking him unconscious.

Sylvia was kneeling beside him when he came round. She was holding a towel to her face, trying to stem the flow of blood from her nose. Charlie coughed and spat out a broken tooth. The door opened and Maggie walked in, a bulging shopping bag in her hand, which she dropped at the sight that greeted her.

'What?' she began.

Charlie opened his mouth to speak, but only managed a croak. Sylvia took over the explanation.'We've just had a visit from Bazza Beedon's mates. They don't want Charlie to testify against him.'

'I'll ring the police,' said Maggie, angrily.

Charlie held up a hand. 'Not yet,' he croaked.

'Charlie, how do you mean?' protested Maggie. 'Look what they've done to you? First the bastard nearly killed you, then this. I'm ringing the police.'

'It won't do any good, Maggie,' said Charlie. 'We don't know who they were. I think one was probably his brother.'

'Good, I'll ring the police.'

'No!' shouted Charlie hoarsely. 'We won't be able to prove anything. I'd rather leave it ... for now.'

'Leave it until the trial, you mean?' asked Maggie.

'Something like that,' said Charlie, uncertainly. He looked up at his wife's concerned face. 'He threatened to scar you for life, Maggie.'

There was a silent reaction to this, broken by Sylvia. 'They would as well. They're bad bastards them Beedons.'

'We can't ignore a threat like that, Maggie,' said Charlie, quietly.

Bazza made his way to the visitors' room with a broad grin on his face. This will have been his brother's second visit of the week, his first will have been to that pillock Chipperfield. Bazza's grin broadened at the thought of Charlie Chipperfield being paid a visit by their kid. Tougher men than Charlie had shit themselves at the sight of Gary in full flow. As he entered the crowded room, he looked around for his brother. A baffled frown creasing his narrow forehead at the sight of Marjory sitting at a table, nervously smoking. No smile for him as he approached.

'Where's Gary?' he asked.

She blew a belligerent cloud of smoke in his face, causing him to waft it away with his hand. 'He can't come,' she replied.

'Can't come? Why can't he come?'

There were tears in Marjory's eyes. More tears of anger than of sorrow.

'Did he say if he'd been round ter see Chipperfield?' asked Bazza, anxiously.

'Oh, yes, he warned Charlie Chipperfield off all right. Knocked him about a bit. Do yer know who else he knocked about?'

'What? His wife? Do no harm ter give her a slap.'

'No, not Maggie Fisher.' Marjory stubbed her cigarette out and immediately lit another, without offering one to Bazza. 'It wouldn't have been so bad if it had been Maggie Fisher. Maggie Fisher were out . . . but her mate wasn't.'

'Her mate? Who's her mate?' inquired Bazza, impatiently.

'Sylvia Tattersall.'

'Never heard of her.'

'I bet yer've heard of her brothers.'

'Tattersall?' A look of shocked realisation came over Bazza's face. 'Ronnie and Trevor Tattersall?'

Marjory nodded, grimly.

'Our kid beat their sister up ... oh shit!' he exploded. 'The stupid pillock!'

'Nice of you to ask after Gary,' said Marjory, scathingly.

But Bazza was too full of self-pity to worry about the welfare of his stupid brother.

'They asked him which hand he used to hit her with,' wept Marjory, tears streaming remorselessly down her cheeks. 'Then they chopped it off with an axe.'

The blood drained from Bazza's face as his eyes met hers. The people they'd come up against were in a different league from them.

'They sent you a message,' said Marjory.

'What's that?'

'Plead guilty and stop harassing their mates.'

With no word of goodbye, she stood up and left him there, shaking at the prospect of ten or more years inside.

Part Three

Chapter Twenty-Five

Christmas 1975

The Reverend Norris Pike glanced across at his wife as the young man's voice echoed round St John's Church. It was the Christmas Carol Service and tradition dictated that Lambourne Wells School provided the choir.

The young man was singing 'Adeste Fidelis', that most traditional of all Christmas hymns, and singing it in the most traditional of manners, a cappella – in the style of the church. The redundant organist had turned on his stool and was also watching the young man. And, like Mrs Pike, the thoughts running through his mind could hardly be described as 'in the style of the church'.

Reverend Pike was in his fifties, almost thirty years his wife's senior. He was aware she'd married him for prestige and security. Physically, he wasn't much of a catch for a pretty young girl like her.

Daniel Aylesbury-Took's voice drew tears from sentimental eyes, admiration from others and jealousy from Reverend Took, who was sure there was something going on between the boy and his wife. A most unchristian desire for revenge welled within him.

The headmaster glared at Daniel from behind a pair of pince-nez, which he removed with a theatrical flourish to deliver his admonition. It was the first day of the spring term and Daniel had been summoned before the head, immediately after assembly.

'I had a most disturbing telephone call from Reverend Pike,' he said. 'Concerning your behaviour.'

'Oh?' inquired Daniel. 'In what way, sir?'

'I believe you know what way, boy.'

'I'm afraid I'm at a loss to understand what all this is about, sir.'

'It's about theft, boy ... stealing church property. A most heinous crime.'

'I agree, sir. I do hope I'm not being accused of such a crime.'

'Reverend Pike tells me that he has it on good authority that you stole a quantity of communion wine from the vestry during Christmas choir practice.'

'I'm afraid the Reverend is mistaken, sir. If I were the type to steal wine, sir, it most certainly wouldn't be the Reverend Pike's communion wine.'

The headmaster felt himself agreeing with Daniel's defence of himself, but didn't show it. Discipline was a byword in his school.

'Nevertheless, I have to take the Reverend's word for this.'

'I understand, sir ... but the Reverend is mistaken.'

'You will be confined within the school grounds for a period of two weeks.'

'Yes sir, thank you sir.'

'What was all that about?' asked Henry Prentice, who had been waiting for his friend outside the head's study.

'I've been gated for a fortnight,' said Daniel.'The village vicar reckons I've been nicking his communion wine.'

'Why would you want to nick communion wine?' asked Henry.

'You tell me. I'd rather nick the village vicar's wife.'

Daniel accepted this miscarriage of justice with the equanimity of the young. There'd been plenty of far worse crimes he'd got away with. Overall, the scales of justice were still balanced well in his favour. However, it wouldn't do to let such a malignant accusation go unpunished. The Reverend Pike had no reason to bear a grudge against Daniel, and must therefore be given one. Inevitably it was Henry who came up with the best idea.

It took almost a month to assemble the instrument of their revenge. It was constructed by the two of them, with Henry, the artist, being responsible for its design. On the second Saturday in February, the Reverend Pike had to attend an ecumenical seminar in Scarborough, leaving his wife behind. The time was ripe for Daniel's revenge.

The church was propped by a series of flying buttresses of a stepped construction, which allowed Daniel to climb easily on to the roof. Around his waist was a rope, tied at the other end to

Henry's work of art. The climb to the top of the steeple taxed all the youth's strength and climbing expertise. Occasional footholds in the steeple's ribbed construction helped marginally, but it still took a climber of considerable skill to reach the spire.

'Okay!' he called back down to Henry in an audible whisper and started to pull on the rope until Henry's masterpiece was in his grasp. Daniel untied the rope, slid the object over the top of the lightning conductor projecting from the spire and shinned back down on to the roof. He could hear Henry laughing out loud, he looked back up at his handiwork and burst out laughing himself.

'Hey! Watcha doin' in there?'

A torch shone across the graveyard surrounding the church, right on to Henry, who set off at a gallop, bounding over gravestones, an irate policeman in hot pursuit. Daniel watched them go and silently thanked Henry for providing a distraction. The policeman would need to be a swift runner to catch his old friend, who could run like the wind. Especially away from trouble. As Daniel was clambering back down one of the buttresses, the church clock above him struck ten o'clock, causing him to miss his foothold. He fell the last six feet on to the hard ground below.

He tried to get up but couldn't, his ankle was twisted. Cursing volubly, he tried to hop towards the wall, wondering how on earth he was going to get over it. The alternative was the main gate, but this seemed too much of a risk as they'd already been spotted.

'All right! What have you been up to?'

Daniel froze. Blast, he'd have got clear had it not been for his damned ankle. He turned and saw Mrs Pike, illuminated in the pale moonlight. A coat across her shoulders to keep out the February chill.

'I er . . . nothing,' he answered awkwardly.

She took a step towards him. 'You're young Daniel Took aren't you?'

Oh God – she knows who I am. This is desperate, expulsion loomed. He didn't say anything.

'Daniel Took, the singer,' she repeated. 'Here, rest on my shoulder, we'd better take a look at that ankle.'

With an arm around her shoulder, he hobbled to the vicarage, where she lay him on a soft, chintz settee and took off his shoe. The swelling was quite pronounced.

'Rest it on these cushions,' she ordered. 'I'll see if I can find some ice or something to bring the swelling down.'

Daniel lay there feeling most awkward. Looking despairingly down on him was a picture of Jesus with his hand held up, palm outwards, forgiving. Daniel felt inwardly that this forgiveness wasn't directed at him. He could hear the lovely Mrs Pike humming to herself from the kitchen. He quite fancied her, as did most of the Lambourne Wells boys. She figured in most of their sexual fantasies.

Would she be as sympathetic if she knew what he'd just done? How the hell was he going to get out of this one?

She returned with a pack of frozen peas. 'It's the best I could do,' she said apologetically.

'You're very kind, Mrs Pike,' he said. Wondering just how long her kindness would last. She packed the peas around his ankle and sat with him in silence for a while. The silence eventually broken by her. 'You know, you're actually quite dirty. Good Lord! Just look at you . . . you're filthy.'

Daniel looked down at himself. The climb up the steeple had left his clothes in a filthy state.

'You'd better take them off,' she decided.

'Pardon?'

'Well, you can hardly go back to school looking like that,' she explained.

'Oh, right.' He sat up and removed his sweater and shirt, revealing a muscular young body on which she rested her gaze for a couple of seconds.

'I'd better help with your trousers,' she decided. It wasn't absolutely necessary, but he thought it better not to argue. She was someone he needed to keep on the right side of.

Her hands brushed against his legs as she pulled them down, at the same time the front of her blouse hung open and it was more than obvious that she wasn't wearing a bra. It was over the back of a chair in the kitchen where she'd just left it after swiftly unhooking it and pulling it through her sleeve, the way that women can.

This was Daniel's first glimpse of naked breasts. He'd touched Cecilia Hovingham's once or twice, but she never let him take her bra off. Besides, having now seen the fullness of Mrs. Pike's bosom, Daniel decided that Cecilia Hovingham's breasts

230

would scarcely have counted anyway. Mrs Pike's breasts were all the more tantalising because he wasn't supposed to see them, or so he naively thought. They were full and firm and the object of Daniel's undivided attention as she tugged at his trousers. She looked back at him, then down at herself.

'Why, you naughty boy! What are you looking at?'

Daniel blushed. 'Nothing,' he lied.

'Oh! So that's what you think of them is it . . . nothing?'

'I er . . . I didn't mean that,' protested Daniel, now lying there, dressed in only his underpants, inside which there was an obvious movement that hadn't gone unnoticed by Mrs Pike.

She took Daniel's clothes into the kitchen, from where he heard the sound of a washing machine starting up. Presently she came back into the room and stood over him, her eyes fixed on the disturbance in his underpants.

'You could do with a shower before you put your clothes back on. There's a bathroom downstairs, perhaps you can hop in there.' For some reason she'd undone another couple of buttons on her blouse. Daniel was beginning to see where this might be leading and he didn't feel in any position to argue.

'Thank you,' he said, swinging his good leg on to the floor and pushing himself to his feet. She put her arm around him to help, the movement stretching the front of her blouse open, leaving little to Daniel's imagination.

'You're looking at me again,' she accused.

'Sorry.'

She stepped away from him, leaving him balanced precariously on one leg. 'I know how curious young men can be about women's bodies,' she smiled. 'You might as well take a look, they're only breasts.'

She undid the rest of her blouse buttons and slowly took it off. Daniel almost lost his balance.

'Well?' she inquired. 'What do you think?'

'I think you've got beautiful breasts, Mrs Pike.'

'Oh please, call me Fiona. You can hardly look at my breasts and not be on first name terms. Perhaps you'd like to touch them? Have you ever touched a lady's bosom before?'

She walked towards him and took his hand, placing it on her breast. Then she put her arm around his neck and kissed him like he'd never been kissed before. Certainly not by Cecilia

231

Hovingham, nor any of the other girls in the Lower Sixth.

The bathroom was off a short corridor leading from the living room. She led him there and turned on the shower.

'You don't mind if I join you, do you Daniel?'

'Er . . . not at all.'

He watched in awe as she proceeded to strip in front of him. Eventually standing there in just her panties. He'd seen plenty of naked women in the many magazines smuggled into school, but Fiona was real and just as beautiful. Her long dark hair was becoming limp in the bathroom heat, clinging to her shoulders. She smiled at him, her teeth white and even behind dark red lips.

'I think we've reached the "you show me yours and I'll show you mine stage,"' she giggled, hooking her fingers into the side of her knickers and slowly pulling them down.

Daniel did the same with his underpants. Each pair of eyes were fixed firmly on what the other had to reveal. And neither of them was disappointed, especially Fiona. She moved towards him and rubbed her body against his erection. He kissed her with the passion of youth and went eagerly with her as she brought him to the floor. With a little guidance, he entered her and thrust away wildly, she knew there was little she could do to curb his passion. This was his first time, let him do it his way. They had the whole night ahead of them. With a noisy grunt of ecstasy, Danny exploded inside her, then slumped to one side. She kissed him on his forehead and waited for a while before easing herself out from under him.

'Time for that shower, my darling,' she whispered, helping him to his feet and taking him into the shower with her.

They clung to each other under the warm spray, kissing and caressing. Fiona took a tablet of soap from the tray and worked up a lather on him. Daniel took it from her and did the same, making the most of this first time experience. Not knowing that it would never be quite like this again. She felt him come to life again and took him inside her, both of them in the bottom of the shower, with water bouncing off their naked bodies as they enjoyed each other, much more slowly this time. Fiona reaching the first climax of her married life.

Daniel awoke in the vicar's bed, wondering just for a second, where on earth he was. Then he saw Fiona slumbering peacefully beside him, her hair almost hiding her pretty face. He pushed it to one side and kissed her on her nose. She woke up and smiled, kissing him back, and moving on top of him.

'One more time for luck,' she whispered, knowing she might never get such an opportunity again. Her husband was due back that afternoon and the occasional sex she had with him was more of a duty than a pleasure. Outside, the church bells struck up, calling the faithful to worship.

Daniel thrust away joyfully in time to the bells, with Fiona responding enthusiastically above him. She glanced up through the bedroom window at the church tower. Her movements froze, causing Daniel to follow suit. He moved his head slightly to follow her gaze and realised what she was looking at. His eyes returned to her, unable to gauge her reaction. She was frowning slightly, trying to make sense of what she saw. This wasn't good news. At some stage he would have to apologise to this naked beauty. Would she want him to finish what he was doing first? He sincerely hoped so.

Suddenly her face broke into a grin. 'You bugger!' she cried, 'that's supposed to be Norris, isn't it? That's my husband!'

At the top of the steeple was a seven foot papier mâché penis. The business end of which formed the unmistakable face of the vicar, complete with toothy smile and sticky-out ears. A work of art in many respects, but totally unbecoming a church steeple. Especially on the sabbath. It was becoming the object of much animated discussion by the crowd gathered below.

Perhaps the sight of such a gigantic organ excited her, but Fiona returned to the business in hand with renewed enthusiasm, making Daniel forget his intended apology. For the time being at least.

As they lay in each other's arms for the last time, Fiona started giggling again. Her husband's penial image was framed in the high window to the side of the bed.

'I'm sorry if I've caused any embarrassment,' said Daniel. 'But he wrongly accused me of stealing the communion wine. I know it was a bit childish, but . . .'

He was cut short by Fiona, her giggling was now verging on hysterics. 'Let me get this right,' she was almost choking, trying to get her words out. 'My husband accuses you of nicking the communion wine, so for revenge you paint his face on a giant nob, stick it on the church steeple, then shag the arse off his wife . . .

and you call that childish? I'd hate to cross you when you grow up.'

It was three days before the fire brigade found time, reluctantly, to remove it. During which time a downmarket tabloid newspaper had published a half-page photograph under the heading the 'new mascot of the Church of St John Thomas'.

Chapter Twenty-Six

September 1976

The first Saturday in September was a memorable day for Fish and Chipperfield, support act to Daisy Shadrac the American country and western singer, who pulled out at the last minute because of flu. She'd arrived at the Mount Preston Variety Club in Bradford, only to pass out in her dressing room. Maggie and Charlie were about to go on stage when the manager popped his head around the door.

'Daisy's fainted ... she can't go on. You'll have to carry the show.'

'Carry the show?' repeated Charlie. 'You mean do an extra hour over and above our own half hour?'

The manager wagged his head as if checking Charlie's figures.

'Actually, I need an extra hour and a half,' he said. 'Can you do it?'

'We'll do our act, then give us a fifteen-minute break to sort something out with the band,' decided Charlie. 'What do you think, Maggie?'

'It's a lot to ask,' cautioned Maggie. 'Do you mind if we bring in someone to help out?'

'Do what you like ... I'll break the news to the punters,' said the manager, unhappily.

Few people took up the manager's offer of a refund. They'd come for a night out and a night out they'd have. Besides, Fish and Chipperfield had a good reputation. They were welcomed on stage a little more warmly than usual, perhaps a patriotic rebellion against these soft American stars, who gave in too easily. Maggie and Charlie were home grown and made of sterner stuff.

Charlie sat down at his piano and leaned over to his mike. 'My dad used to say, "Laugh, and the world laughs with you. Cry, and I'll give yer summat ter bloody cry about!"'

Sylvia Tattersall had been sitting at home, contemplating her lifetime's achievements when the phone rang. Behind her was a failed marriage, a failed career as a prostitute and two children, both adopted. Oddly enough, she didn't miss the children. In fact she felt some sense of worth at having had them both adopted, thus giving them a chance of a decent life. There were plenty of kids who'd have jumped at such an opportunity. Her for one.

Her unmarried mother had married Lennie Tattersall when Sylvia was six years old. Why anyone should want to marry a vicious drunk remained a mystery to Sylvia. Her mother and her two stepbrothers all suffered under his drunken fists. The boys emerging from this with an inbred violent streak in them, which had seen them both locked up at an early age. Thankfully, neither of them were incarcerated when their father had picked on her that Saturday night. She was just sixteen and her mother had gone to bed early in an attempt to avoid her husband's flailing fists and, despite her mother's instruction to the contrary, Sylvia was up late, watching television when he arrived home.

'What're you doing? Still up at this time o'night?' he spat the words out, sending a shiver of fear up Sylvia's spine.

'I was just going up, dad.'

'Dad? Who're you calling dad? I'm not your dad, yer stupid little bitch!'

He scowled at her, swaying unsteadily. 'You ... you're someone's bastard, that's who you are. I don't know who you are, but yer bugger all ter do wi' me.'

He blocked the way to the stairs as Sylvia tried to get past.

'Can I get past yer please?' she asked. Her fear of him now coupled with annoyance at his outburst.

'Can I get past yer please?' he mimicked, pushing her backwards and stepping after her.

She tried to dodge round him once again, but he caught her with a fist which slammed into the side of her head, knocking her to the ground.

'Yer'll go ter bed when I say so, and not before!' he snarled. 'Yer little bastard.'

He emphasised this with a heavy kick in her ribs which knocked all the wind out of her. She was still trying to catch her breath when all hell broke loose around her.

Trevor and Ronnie had arrived home. Respectively two and three years older than Sylvia, they looked upon themselves as her guardians. And here she was being assaulted by the very man who'd made their lives such a misery. The man whose fault it was that they'd both spent a large part of the last three years in various penal institutions. They'd come to this conclusion over several drinks in the Barraclough Arms and here was a heaven-sent opportunity to exact their revenge on this man.

Ronnie, the older and bigger of the two, went in first. Stepping over his sister's prostrate figure to land a bone-crunching blow on his father's nose. They then dragged him outside into the small back garden and proceeded to vent all their anger and frustration and revenge on him. Leaving him broken and bleeding and unconscious.

Sylvia had watched all this through the back door, as had her mother through the bedroom window. Her mother took instant charge of the situation. She appeared beside Sylvia and gazed down at the unconscious figure lying in the middle of the unkempt garden.

'Sylvia . . . upstairs to bed. You know nothing about this. Keep out of the way, I don't want anyone asking questions about that bruise on your face.' She then turned to her two stepsons. Respect showing on their faces as she addressed them.

'You two, make yourselves scarce. You weren't here tonight. Someone beat your dad up and this is how he arrived home. I'm ringing for an ambulance.'

'What if he tells the cops who did it?' asked Trevor, still breathing heavily after his exertions.

'If word gets out that he's shopped his own sons to the cops, he'll never dare show his ugly face around here again. He might be stupid, but he's not that stupid.'

The young men nodded and walked towards the door, Ronnie giving his father a complimentary kick in the ribs as he passed. He leaned over and kissed his stepmother.

'Thanks, Mam,' he said. 'And tell him that this was only a

warning. If he lays a finger on you or our lass ever again, we'll kill him.'

Within a year, both boys were in jail for crimes of violence and their father took this as an opportunity to kick Sylvia out of the house. Fear of his sons' retribution had kept his violence towards his wife to a minimum, but Sylvia's caustic tongue was too much for him to bear. She took to the streets, busking with her banjo. Unfortunately, busking was not very profitable at that time and she was eventually drawn by poverty into prostitution.

Sylvia allowed the phone to ring several times before picking it up. Phones had always seemed to bring her bad news. She'd heard of her mother's death over the phone. Her stepfather's message had been typically abrupt and unfeeling. 'I thought yer might want ter know that yer mam died last night.' Not a mention of how or why or where. It had brought Sylvia immense sadness. Her only blood relative was dead. She picked up the phone apprehensively.

'Hello?'

'Sylvia?'

Sylvia's animated face broke into a grin as she recognised the voice. 'Maggie? Is that you?'

''Course it's me . . . Sylvia, are you doing anything right now?'

'Yes.'

'What?'

'I'm talking to this strange woman on the phone.'

Maggie laughed. 'Can you get across to the Mount Preston Club straight away. I've got a gig for you.'

'How do you mean, straight away?' inquired Sylvia.

'I mean we're due on stage in two minutes and you're following us. I'll send a taxi to pick you up.'

'I'll be there.'

Sylvia had made her home in Bradford, after establishing herself as a club performer. Charlie's recommendation to Dave Greenwood had given her an initial boost, but her own talent had taken over from there. Unfortunately, the tone of her act dictated the type of venue. Hers was an act of pronounced vulgarity, popular to the extent of almost giving her cult status in some quarters, especially at university venues. But a lot of the male-dominated working men's clubs found it unacceptable to have a vulgar woman performing on their stages. Obscene men yes, but vulgar women were too much to stomach.

Hen nights were very much her speciality. She often teamed up with Nude Nigel and his talking cock. Nigel was a Ventriloquist who performed nude apart from a rubber cockerel, which preserved his modesty while being very cheeky to its owner. An act that appealed to the baser humour, found just as much in women as in men.

If not more so.

At the end of their regular set, Maggie and Charlie left the stage, having promised the audience a surprise guest in the next part of the show. Sylvia had arrived and was waiting backstage, talking to a worried club manager.

'I'm not sure the audience will go for your type of act, Miss er . . .?'

'Tattersall,' said Maggie, interrupting. 'And the audience will love her.'

'I've got the club's reputation to think about,' argued the manager.

'It's all right . . . I'll go home,' said Sylvia. 'I wouldn't want to ruin the club's reputation.'

'We'll give you a lift,' said Charlie, annoyed at the manager's attitude.

'But,' protested the manager, 'you can't leave me in the lurch like this.'

'Why not?' argued Maggie. 'We've done our act. Why not give Billy Farthing a ring . . . he went down a bomb here the other week, despite all his effing and blinding.'

'That's different . . . the punters know what to expect when they come to see Billy.'

Maggie, Charlie and Sylvia were walking away from him, back to the dressing rooms. The manager shouted after them. 'All right, you bloody well win. I just hope you haven't lost me my job.'

'You won't regret it,' said Sylvia unconvincingly. 'I'm a society entertainer me.'

'She once did a Christmas party for the Leeds and Holbeck Building Society,' explained Charlie. Maggie turned to her old friend. 'Just fill in for half an hour while we cobble a routine together for the last hour.'

The manager cum MC switched on a broad smile and walked

out onto the stage to announce the next act. There was a gasp of surprise from those in the audience who knew about Sylvia, and she walked on to a raucous round of applause.

'I've rushed straight here from the Heckmondwike Haemorrhoid Society Annual Dinner,' she announced, cheerfully. 'Although it's not actually a dinner ... more of a stand-up buffet.'

Thus the tone was set and she went straight into Fanshawe the Farting Phantom, displaying her banjo-playing expertise between each vulgar verse, to the delight of the audience, or ninety per cent of it. Her routine was brought to a climax with a lusty rendition of 'The Convent Wall' about a drunk who was caught by the Mother Superior as he was urinating against the wall of her convent. The audience loved Sylvia and their reception of her brought a broad smile to the face of the manager, who fully intended taking all the credit for the rearranged programme. As she came off, he took her back on to the stage with him, urging the audience into more applause.

In the meantime, Maggie and Charlie had arranged a one-hour routine which began with Maggie singing solo for three numbers before Charlie joined her. Most of the audience had seen their act before but few had seen Maggie in her prime. A hush descended on the house as she went into her opening number. 'Yesterday' by Paul McCartney. Charlie was watching from the wings and felt a sense of excitement as he detected, just here and there, her old magic.

She finished on 'Don't Give Me Roses' and the audience were on their feet as Charlie walked out. Forty-five minutes later they were on their feet again applauding Fish and Chipperfield as they left the stage, shouts of 'More' ringing in their ears. Charlie turned to Maggie, 'It's you they want, love,' he said, and led her back out. The audience went quiet as the band played the opening bars of 'Don't Give Me Roses', for the second time that evening. This time Charlie was certain it was there.

'Did you feel it?' he asked as they walked back to the dressing room together, leaving behind a cheering audience.

She was hoping he'd mention it, but she wanted to be sure they were talking about the same thing.

'Feel what?' she asked.

'You know ... the hook in your voice.'

'Yes,' she said. 'I felt it, but I couldn't seem to keep it there. It's as though my voice isn't strong enough.'

Charlie squeezed his wife's hand as the specialist came back into the room with a set of X-rays.

'I've compared these with the original X-rays and a lot of the damage seems to have repaired itself.' The man smiled and took off his glasses to wipe them, before examining the X-rays once again. 'However,' he went on. 'There are certain things which may need a tweak to help things along. Things which an operation would put right.'

'Is it a big operation?' asked Charlie.

The specialist leaned back in his chair and knitted his long fingers together, drawing Maggie's attention to them. These fingers could well be poking about in her throat before much longer. She gave a shudder.

'It's more of a delicate operation,' said the specialist. 'But it should give long term benefits.'

'But my voice seems to have improved lately,' argued Maggie. 'Hasn't it Charlie?' she looked to Charlie for confirmation.

Charlie nodded. 'Her old voice seems to be coming back.'

The specialist smiled. 'I'm afraid I can't comment on that. Your problem is in no way life threatening, so the decision is up to you. However, bearing in mind your profession, I'd recommend you have it done sooner rather than later.'

As they drove home from the hospital, Maggie didn't say a word. Her mind was racing. There were things she had to do to put her life in order. And a proper order in which to do them, the most important things first. The fourteen years they'd spent on the road together had been good. They'd travelled halfway round the world and their bank account was healthy. But there was still a hole in Maggie's life; an emptiness that she'd learnt to control since that horrible scare with Charlie. That had put things into perspective. Charlie pulled up outside the house and turned to her, love shining from his gentle brown eyes.

'Well, Mrs Chipperfield?' he asked. 'What do you think?'

'I'll have the operation,' she said. 'But first I want a baby.'

Chapter Twenty-Seven

September 1977

Daniel Aylesbury-Took replaced the receiver and looked up at the headmaster's sympathetic face.

'It's hard to know what to say at a time like this, Tristan,' said Mr Fellows.

'I prefer to be called Daniel, sir,' said the young man in front of him. 'My names are Tristan Daniel, of which I much prefer Daniel, but my friends have abbreviated this to Dan, sir.'

The headmaster stared at the young sixth former, not quite knowing what to make of the situation.

'Were you close to your father, er . . . Daniel?'

'Not really, sir. I hardly ever saw him.'

'Bad business though, all the same.'

'Yes, sir. I think I ought to go home, sir. Mother will probably need me to help with the arrangements. She tends not to handle crises too well, sir.'

The headmaster nodded his agreement to this, inwardly proud of the stoicism the public school system had bred into these boys, despite it being primarily a school for the artistically gifted. At Lambourne Wells, the talent was nurtured but any artistic temperament very much frowned upon. Small children were often reduced to tears during their first few settling-in weeks. A make or break period, at the end of which many a precocious talent was rejected as unsuitable.

There had never been anything precocious about Tristan Daniel Aylesbury-Took. The sudden death of his father had now made him a very wealthy young man. The worst part was reacting to the sympathy which would be heaped on him by his friends and foes alike. He didn't need sympathy. He felt no more remorse at the death of his father than he would for one of his father's estate workers.

Daniel stepped from the taxi and stared up at the crumbling stone edifice above him. Took House. Built in the early eighteenth century by one of his ancestors, who had apparently made his money from trade with the Far East, Africa and the West Indies. The infamous Triangle Run having played a large part in the creation of the Took fortune. A fortune which had ebbed and flowed down through the generations, mainly ebbing, until his grandfather, Lord Miles Took, had taken the reins. An astute businessman, he'd bought a munitions factory in 1913, which he sold in 1918 and re-invested in London property. He unloaded his whole portfolio in the late twenties and invested in United States property just after the Wall Street Crash, when prices were rock bottom. Only part of the noble lord's business acumen had been inherited by his now deceased son.

The late Lord William Aylesbury-Took, Daniel's father, had been a chancer, who had recently boosted the faltering family fortune by some shrewd but risky dealings in the property market. Having seen London property prices double in 1972, it struck him as fortuitous that there hadn't been a simultaneous boom in his home county of Yorkshire. Using his enormous influence and money from various impressionable overseas banks, he'd bought large tracts of development land all over the north of England. When the boom moved north as he anticipated, he sold it on to developers desperate to jump on to the housing gravy train. Within eighteen months, he'd trebled the money, which he considered good business, as the money wasn't his in the first place.

He was a man with little capacity for affection, for his wife, his son, or anyone for that matter. He vent his biological urges discreetly on expensive prostitutes, much to the relief of Lady Audrey, who didn't want troubling too often in that department. He was in the company of one such lady at his London flat, when a heart attack struck him down. The lady in question was quickly paid off and sent on her way by one of his business colleagues, and a statement made to the press that he'd died alone at the age of fifty-two.

The Took Corporation now owned property all over the world, including the four thousand of North Yorkshire's finest acres, on which Took House stood. And Daniel was the sole heir. So why did he feel unsuited to the job?

Lady Audrey came to the door with Michael, who may well have enjoyed the title of butler in more formal times, but formality wasn't one of Lady Audrey's strong suits. She employed Michael as housekeeper, manager, chauffeur and companion. The only other live-in employee was Ethel, an ancient cook, who'd lived there since she was a girl. Various staff came in on a daily basis, to clean and attend to the various needs of a house of that size. The running of the estate was the responsibility of an estate management company, a subsidiary of the Took empire.

Lady Audrey hovered behind Michael as he opened the door to her son. He gave a half bow in deference to Daniel's new status as his employer.

'Please don't do that, Michael,' insisted Daniel. 'I'm not the bloody queen.'

Michael smiled briefly and stepped aside to let the young man past. His mother took him in her arms and hugged him to her.

'Thanks for coming so quickly, Daniel. It was a hell of a shock. I'd only spoken to him on the phone a couple of hours before he . . .'

'I know, Mother,' comforted Daniel. 'It was a shock to me as well.'

Arm in arm they walked into the drawing room. Much of the original drawing room furniture was stored elsewhere throughout the rambling, forty-five room mansion. Audrey had replaced it with more comfortable furniture. William's feet sank into the deep pile carpet, imported at no little expense. Several deep leather Chesterfield chairs and a five seater settee surrounded a large rosewood coffee table. In one corner was a cabinet containing an ultra modern music centre with quadrophonic speakers discreetly positioned about the room. In another corner, a large television set stood elegantly silent, beside a well-stocked bar in carved oak, guarded on the other side by a suit of armour, much older than the house itself; now having to suffer the ignominy of holding a bottle of brown ale in one gauntlet and a bottle opener in the other.

Complementing all this was the original Adam fireplace, above which was a portrait of a female Took ancestor, sitting with two wide eyed children, painted by Sir Joshua Reynolds. Portraits of the male ancestry were given less prominent positions elsewhere in the house, due mainly to the inherent ugliness of the subjects. An ugliness not shared by Daniel, whose dark good looks were at odds with the painted gargoyles peering out from the darkened walls of his ancestral home. Daniel sat down in one of the chairs, looked around him and then at his mother.

'How much of this will be left?' he asked, 'after the vultures have picked over dad's bones?'

Lady Audrey gave a wry smile. 'Enough,' she replied. 'There'll be death duties, other taxes I suppose.'

'And accountants and solicitors . . . and creditors.'

'Creditors?' asked Lady Audrey, surprised. 'What would you know about your father's creditors?'

Daniel gave her an awkward smile. 'Oh, just something I heard at school. You know how these rumours fly around.'

'No, I don't,' said his mother. 'And I hope you put whoever was spreading these rumours firmly in his place.'

Daniel shrugged. 'I suppose all will be revealed when the will's read out. I assume dad's accountants will have brought his affairs up to date before that's done.'

It was his mother's turn to shrug. 'I imagine so,' she said, uncertainly. She sat quietly for a while, staring at nothing in particular. Daniel allowed her her silence, having little understanding of what it must feel like to lose a husband after over twenty years of marriage; her life companion. He suspected the loss might have been cushioned somewhat by his father's prolonged absences, which Daniel tended to think had been longer than necessary.

'There's something I have to tell you, Daniel, which may come as a bit of a shock,' she said at last, turning her pale face to his. Hers was the plainest of faces – and try as he might, even Daniel could see no beauty in it. She was fifty years old, but by no means a well-preserved fifty. Her face was lined and her skin beginning to hang loosely about her jowls with small clusters of liver spots high on her cheeks. Her grey hair was expensively cut and permed but had sadly lost the battle to enhance the rest of her. Wide in the hip and narrow across the bust, she was already walking with the stoop of old age. The dowager's hump. But

Daniel saw kindness and love in her, and that was all that mattered in a mother.

'What is it, Mother?' He was bracing himself for bad news about his inheritance, which he suspected might be severely diminished by his father's creditors. 'If it's about my inheritance, don't worry. He who expects nothing, will not be disappointed. That's my motto.'

Lady Audrey smiled at this. There didn't seem to be a greedy bone in the boy's body.

'No, it's not that,' she said. 'In a way it's more serious than that. We ... I mean your father and I, were going to tell you just before your eighteenth birthday, but his death has brought that time forward.'

Daniel was overcome with curiosity. 'Mother, will you please spit it out, what on earth is it?'

She was struggling to find the words. 'You see ...' she began. 'You see ... you can't inherit your father's title. That goes to your Uncle Robert.'

Daniel was stunned by this. 'Uncle Robert? How ... why?'

Lady Audrey took a deep breath. 'Because you were adopted.'

'Adopted?' he repeated, as though he didn't understand the meaning of the word.

'When you were a tiny baby we adopted you. I couldn't have children of my own, that's why you have no brothers or sisters.' She grabbed at his arm. 'But that doesn't mean we didn't love you just as if you were our own,' she emphasised.

Daniel took his arm away, trying to digest this news.

'Adopted? Good lord!' He looked at her and shook his head. 'You mean you're not my real mother?'

'Of course I'm your mother,' she protested tearfully. 'No mother could love a son as much as I love you.'

'But ... not my *real* mother. Not my biological mother ... so, dad wasn't my biological father either.'

Lady Audrey said nothing, she just watched him with something approaching fear in her eyes. Fear as to how he might react to such a shocking revelation about himself.

'Your father left the bulk of his estate to you, including the house,' she said, hoping to soften the blow she'd just struck.

Daniel nodded, 'That's nice,' he said. 'What about you? What's he left you?'

'He left me comfortable. I'm afraid you're not allowed to sell the house while I'm alive. This is to be my home until I die.'

'Quite right too,' nodded Daniel. 'But I don't inherit his title,' he said. 'Mother, this is going to take some getting used to. Do you mind if I go out for a walk?'

'Of course not, take all the time you need.'

It was the day after his father's funeral and Daniel was still becoming accustomed to the new state of affairs. Lord Aylesbury-Took's study had always been sacrosanct. Daniel couldn't remember ever having been in there. While his father was away on business it was always kept locked and his father took the key with him. With more than just a little curiosity, Daniel turned the key in the lock.

It was a largish room, perhaps twenty feet by fifteen. One wall was completely covered in books. Some in sets, obviously there for effect, others piled up haphazardly. Paperbacks, magazines, old newspapers and catalogues.

The dark oak desk was large and empty save for a single telephone. A television set stood in one corner, and a poorly stocked bar in the other. The noble lord had never been much of a drinker, on the other hand a large humidor stood on the bar counter, well stocked with huge Havanas. The desk drawers were all locked but the keys in Daniel's hand would solve this problem. He wasn't sure what he was looking for. His mother had been very cagey about his biological parents. Apparently his father had died before he was born and his mother had died shortly after of leukaemia. That's all she knew.

The first three drawers he opened contained items of complete disinterest to Daniel. Stationery, a copy of Wisden, company seals, various photographs, a desk diary, a book on estate management and various girlie magazines, which under other circumstances would merit closer scrutiny. A fourth drawer contained several letters which, on examination, appeared to be quite intimate and all written by ladies of dubious morals. They neither surprised nor shocked him, his father had never been a devoted husband. Still, no need for his mother to see them. He locked the drawer and took the key off the key ring, with the intention of destroying the letters at a more convenient time. He failed to notice the corner of a ledger sticking out from beneath the letters. Things might have turned out so much better for him had he spotted it.

The bottom left hand drawer was the last one he opened and inevitably the one to provide a few answers. The first thing to draw his eye was a silver medal. He picked it up and turned it over in his hand, reading the inscription. 'For Bravery in the Field'. Unaware of its significance he slipped it into his pocket. Also in the drawer was a folder containing just two sheets of paper. One, a letter from someone in Harrogate, whose signature he couldn't quite make out, dated 1st March 1960:

> Dear Lord and Lady Aylesbury-Took,
> I must thank you for your gracious hospitality last weekend and I am delighted to inform you that there are four infants due in the coming weeks. I enclose details of the mother – and father if known, the most promising being number four on my list. Excuse the impersonality of using numbers, but for obvious reasons I cannot divulge the identity of the parents.

The second sheet contained just a few typewritten lines.

1. Baby due end of March: Mother, twenty-nine years old, good physique, dark hair, grey eyes, reasonably good looking, average intelligence, bright personality. Father unknown.
2. Baby due middle of April: Mother, twenty-one years old, slightly overweight, plain looks, hair dyed blonde (probably brown), brown eyes, dull. Father unknown.
3. Baby due middle of April: Mother thirty-two years old, slim, average looking, fair hair, blue eyes, quite intelligent. Father unknown.
4. Baby due beginning of May: Mother nineteen years old. Very pretty, excellent physique, brown hair, brown eyes, very bright, extremely talented singer. Father, of Italian extraction, also talented singer, intelligent and highly attractive. Maternal grandfather, holder of the Military Medal.

Daniel stared at the list with disbelief. Selected for his pedigree. It was as if they'd been browsing round a stud farm for something suitable. In a rising temper he stormed out of the study in the direction of his mother.

Chapter Twenty-Eight

December 1977

The view from the hotel window wasn't inspiring. There's nothing inspiring about Nottingham in December. Maggie was thirty-six years old and her life was slipping by. They were there for a week, supporting Davy O'Connell in the Sherwood Theatre Club.

A sparrow hopped on to the window ledge, unaware of the still figure, gazing out from the other side of the glass. Her thoughts were on the grimy little back street they still called home. They had enough money saved to buy a decent house practically outright, but Charlie was happy with Hope Street.

'Let's face it, Maggie. We're only home three or four weeks out of every year,' was his standard argument.

She often wished she hadn't bought the place. What a rash thing to do. She would probably have had her old voice back if she'd gone along with Charlie. But it wasn't losing her voice that caused her depression, nor the house, nor the work. She loved the work. Their act was polished and slick and funny. She'd enjoyed that, especially the cruises. Their act was tailor-made for cruising.

Not a day had gone by without her thinking about Danny. He'd be seventeen now, all grown up. What did he look like? Did he know he'd been adopted? Would he ever try to find her? They'd been trying for a baby for over a year now. No way would she jeopardise her future baby by having an operation on her throat. Unexpected things happened in operating theatres. Things which might affect her chances of becoming pregnant. An illogical process of thought, but one she wouldn't be budged from, much to

Charlie's frustration. Maggie smiled as the sparrow noticed her, and flew away.

'I wish I could fly away,' she said, as the bird disappeared over the rooftops.

'What?' inquired Charlie, looking up from his book.

'Oh, nothing. I'm just bored, that's all.'

Charlie put down his book and walked over to her, slipping his arm around her waist and pulling her to him. 'We could have another try for Chipperfield junior if you like,' he suggested, innocently.

'That's another thing,' sighed Maggie. 'I think I should see a doctor. I'm sure I should have fallen by now.'

Charlie didn't release his grip. 'Maggie,' he asked gently, 'are you worried that something might have been damaged when ... you know?'

'When I was raped, you mean? I've no idea. I wouldn't have thought so, but you never know.'

'I'll make an appointment with the doctor as soon as we get back to Leeds,' said Charlie.

They were sitting expectantly in the surgery, waiting for the doctor to return with their file. Maggie didn't know what she'd do if the doctor told she couldn't have a baby. The doctor gave a quick smile as he entered the room. He was carrying a slim, buff coloured folder which he placed on his desk and opened, rubbing his bearded chin as he read the contents. He looked up at Charlie.

'I understand you had mumps when you were in your mid twenties,' he said.

'That's right,' confirmed Charlie.

The doctor held him in his gaze for a second and nodded, more to himself than to Charlie.

'And was there any inflammation of the testicles, at this time?' he asked, clinically.

Charlie blushed slightly and looked at Maggie. 'Er ... yes. They were ... it was ... quite painful.'

The doctor nodded sympathetically. 'I'm afraid it damaged your reproductive system, Mr Chipperfield.'

'Damaged? What do you mean by damaged, Doctor?' asked Maggie. 'Exactly how damaged is he?'

251

The doctor looked from one to the other. 'There's no easy way to say this,' he said. 'I'm afraid you're sterile, Mr Chipperfield.'

'Me? You mean I'm the one at fault?' gasped Charlie.

'There's no fault in this, Mr Chipperfield. I suspect your condition was caused by your having mumps as an adult.'

'So . . . so I can't have children then?'

'I'm afraid not, Mr Chipperfield.'

Charlie hadn't had much to say for himself since hearing the news. Every time Maggie broached the subject he deflected her.

'I need to get used to the idea, Maggie. I don't expect you to understand, because I don't understand myself. Just give me a couple days, I'll be okay.'

I'm sure you will, thought Maggie. But what about me? Will I be okay?

But it was Maggie whom Charlie was thinking about. Sterility meant little to Charlie, Maggie meant the world.

Maggie stood at the scullery door and surveyed the world beyond. Vera and Denis had long since moved out, their names having arrived at the top of the council housing list. To her shame, Maggie had never been to visit them in their three-bedroomed semi on the Moortown Estate. She'd always meant to, but she'd always been too busy.

Mr and Mrs Patel were her neighbours now. A gentle Hindu couple who'd arrived direct from the Jewel in Queen Victoria's Crown with two small children and an aged parent who didn't speak a word of English. Nor did he venture out much. Preferring to while away his declining years listening to sitar music on a wind-up gramophone. This was a source of some annoyance to the neighbours on the other side who, unlike Maggie and Charlie, had to endure listening to the same three records for fifty-two weeks a year.

Charlie had tried to relieve the situation by giving the old man some of his old unwanted 78s, after which the sitar music was interspersed with Denis Lotis and Ronnie Hilton. The neighbours on the other side saw no improvement in this, and by way of cheap revenge gave the man Jim Reeves's Greatest Hits. Charlie swiftly retaliated with a Leonard Cohen LP and the old man died within three days.

Maggie smiled briefly at Mrs Patel, who emerged in a colourful sari to hang out some equally colourful washing. It was the early summer of 1978 and Maggie's state of mind had become perilously close to a total breakdown. For the most of their marriage she'd always assumed that at some stage she'd settle down and have children and she hoped that this would ease the loss of Danny. It was this knowledge that enabled her to cope with things. The year they'd spent trying for a baby had started out as the most enjoyable part of her marriage, and had ended as the most miserable.

'I'd like to move away from here.'

Mrs Patel turned round, not quite having heard what Maggie was saying and not sure if the remark had been addressed to her. Maggie was staring into space, so Mrs Patel turned away. Charlie had heard and came to stand behind her. He'd cancelled all their bookings for the next month to give Maggie a chance to come round. But it was going to take more than time. His wife was holding herself and rocking backwards and forwards, tears pouring down her cheeks. Charlie knew he'd be of no help, but he had to try. He loved Maggie as much as ever and seeing her like this was hard to bear.

'If that's what it takes, love, we'll start looking round tomorrow.'

She went rigid in his arms. 'If that's what it takes?' there was deep scorn in her voice. 'I wish it was that simple.' She shook herself free of him and walked in the house. Charlie gave Mrs Patel an embarrassed smile which she failed to return. He was sure she blamed him for the death of her father-in-law. Shaking his head at the impossibility of life, he followed Maggie inside.

Chapter Twenty-Nine

'Could I speak to Laurence please?' Charlie tapped his fingers hopefully on the table. There were two Prestwicks in the Leeds telephone directory, neither of whom had even heard of Laurence Prestwick. The one Prestwick in Bradford had been disconnected, so Charlie had enlisted the help of Directory Enquiries and spread his net out to Harrogate. A smart town, teaming with professional people.

'Laurence?' at least the woman on the other end hadn't instantly denied knowledge of anyone called Laurence.

'Yes, Laurence Prestwick. My name's Chipperfield, we were at medical school together,' lied Charlie.

'I'm sorry, but he doesn't live here any more.'

'Oh, dear . . . I don't suppose you know where I could get hold of him?'

'Is it urgent?'

Charlie forced a laugh. 'It is actually . . . he owes me half a crown from 1952.' His joke was met with silence. 'Well, it's not desperately urgent,' he went on. 'I was in the area and I thought I'd look him up. I haven't seen him for going on twenty years.'

'Mr Chipperfield . . . you know he was struck off don't you?'

Any doubts Charlie might have had about this being the right Prestwick were now dispelled. 'Er . . . yes. I had heard something. Are you his, er . . .?'

'Wife?' she finished his question for him. 'Ex-wife . . . we divorced ten years ago.' She was warming to Charlie's easy manner. He didn't sound like a friend of Laurence. By and large

254

they were an intense, humourless lot. His friends struck him off just after the BMA did.

'And is he still living in Harrogate?'

'The last I heard he was living in York, working for a pharmaceutical company. I wouldn't put money on him still working there though. He's not on the phone either.'

'I don't suppose you have his address do you?'

'Hang on a minute.'

He heard her riffling through an address book, humming to herself. Charlie was wondering if divorce from Prestwick had lifted her spirits. She came back on the line, 'It's a York address, 4 Ashleigh Court.'

'Thanks Mrs . . .?'

'It's still Prestwick. I hung on to the name for our daughter's sake.'

There was a silence as Charlie digested the implications of a man with a daughter of his own, doing what Prestwick had done to Maggie. He suspected that Mrs Prestwick was reading his thoughts.

'Word of warning,' she advised. 'Don't mention him being struck off. He'll clam up tighter than a duck's arse, which pretty much describes his attitude to money, come to think of it.'

Charlie was amused at such coarse terminology coming from an obviously cultured woman.

'He's a bit skint is he?'

'Skinflint's more the word – mind you, I don't suppose he's all that well placed financially at the moment.'

'Oh dear – why's that?'

'Well – I did hear that he'd lost his job – and he's apparently got a drink problem. So I suspect that if you catch up with him he'll end up owing you more than half a crown.'

'Oh, right – thanks for all your help Mrs Prestwick.'

'Don't mention it.'

Charlie put down the phone and congratulated himself on his swift detective work. The two main Leeds hospitals had no trace of him, but ten minutes on the phone had located the disgraced obstetrician.

Maggie was upstairs in bed, not wanting to talk to anyone, not even Charlie. They were in separate bedrooms now and Charlie was hoping against hope that her illness could be cured by tracking down her lost boy. There was no doubt in his mind what her problem was.

He parked his Cortina opposite the block of low-rise, brick-built flats where Prestwick was living and looked across at number 4. A ground-floor flat with drawn curtains. Probably permanently drawn to prevent passers by inspecting the mess within. Charlie could identify with this. There was a light on inside when he arrived, which went out almost immediately. A man emerged from the front door and Charlie shook his head. No way could this be Prestwick.

He'd figured Prestwick to be in his mid to late fifties, but this man looked like a poorly preserved seventy year old. Although quite tall, he carried himself badly, walking with short, quick steps, his eyes concentrating on the ground in front of him. Despite it being a warm June evening, he wore a dark, heavy overcoat and a Homburg hat. In one hand was a plastic carrier bag and in the other was a furled umbrella. Charlie looked at the sky, wondering if the man knew something he didn't. The evening sun shone down from a clear sky as Charlie got out of his car and followed the man.

Despite the man's many quick steps, Charlie had to walk at a leisurely pace to maintain his distance. A pub sign came into view, The Racehorse Arms, conveniently situated opposite the Knavesmire, York's famous racecourse.

After stopping to light a small cigar, an awkward exercise that involved hooking his umbrella over his arm and wedging the carrier bag between his knees, the man turned into the pub door. Charlie followed him in.

'G and T Larry?' inquired the barman, not waiting for an answer before he jabbed a glass into one of the optics.

Larry? The name threw Charlie for a second, before he realised what Larry was short for. This was his man all right. The only man who could tell him where Maggie's son was. Everyone else he'd approached had clammed up as soon as he asked. But this man knew.

Up to now Charlie had been playing everything by ear. How should he approach it? Should he ask him straight out where Danny was? Offer him a bribe? He certainly looked as though he could use a few bob. Whatever approach he adopted, it had to work. This man Prestwick was his only hope. This broken wreck of a man could save Charlie's marriage. Mrs Prestwick's advice was very much to the forefront of his mind. 'Don't mention him being struck off.' A glimmer of an idea came to Charlie. He did a deliberate double take of Prestwick, enough for Prestwick to notice.

'I'm sorry,' apologised Charlie. 'It's just that you reminded me of someone I once knew.'

The barman handed Prestwick his gin and tonic.

'Here, I'll get that,' offered Charlie. 'And a pint of bitter for me please.'

Prestwick made no protest. He obviously had no scruples about strangers buying him drinks. Charlie held out a hand. 'Charlie . . . Charlie Jones.' He decided at the last second not to reveal his name, lest Prestwick made the connection with Maggie.

'Good evening, Mr Jones,' acknowledged Prestwick shaking Charlie's hand. His voice was cultured and his vowels well rounded, not cultivated within a hundred miles of Yorkshire. 'Are you here for the racing?'

Charlie had the good sense not to be drawn unnecessarily into a discussion on a subject he knew nothing about. He had enough lies up his sleeve, without complicating matters.

'No, no,' he laughed. 'I don't know the first thing about horses.'

'Neither does Larry,' laughed the barman. 'So whatever yer do, don't listen to any of his tips.'

'That was a cruel jibe,' protested Prestwick.

The barman leaned across to Charlie. 'Do you know the best way ter stop a runaway horse?'

Charlie grinned and shook his head.

'Get Larry ter stick a fiver on it,' chortled the barman.

Charlie laughed louder than the joke merited, Prestwick joined in, but his heart wasn't in it. Charlie decided that humour didn't figure very much in this man's makeup.

'And what do you do for a living, Mr Jones?' inquired Prestwick.

Charlie saw no harm in telling the truth, people were always interested in musicians. 'I'm a musician,' he said.

He had Prestwick's interest now. 'Musician eh? Which instrument . . . no, don't tell me, let me guess . . . you're a guitarist.'

257

Charlie smiled and shook his head. 'I play guitar but it's not my main instrument.'

'In that case,' went on Prestwick, 'you're a percussionist.'

'Correct,' laughed Charlie.

'I knew it,' said Prestwick, with a look of triumph on his face. 'You have the look of a drummer.'

'I'm not a drummer,' said Charlie, mysteriously, arousing a look of curiosity on Prestwick's face. Charlie decided to give him time to guess. Prestwick's curiosity turned to realisation, he jabbed a finger towards Charlie.

'You're a pianist!' he exclaimed.

Charlie grinned and nodded. Prestwick turned to the barman. 'You see,' he explained. 'Most people think that percussion is just drums, but a percussion instrument is any instrument played by striking it.'

'Right,' said the totally uninterested barman.

Prestwick shrugged and motioned Charlie over to a table. 'Join me, young man, away from this philistine.'

Charlie finished his pint and pushed the glass back across the bar. 'I'll just have a shandy please . . . I'm driving. And another G and T for Larry . . . make it a large one.'

'He'll sponge off you all night if yer let him,' warned the barman.

'Don't worry. I'll make him pay.'

The pub was filling up with regulars. The racegoers would arrive the following day, when the regulars would desert to the Horse and Groom round the corner and out of immediate sight. The greetings Prestwick received could in no way be considered hearty. A curt nod, an occasional 'hello', one 'hello Larry', but nothing to identify him as a popular member of the drinking fraternity. Prestwick was someone whose company people endured, rather than enjoyed. Only the most personable of spongers ever achieve popularity in public houses. But Prestwick didn't care, for that evening he'd found a new friend, an amusing musician no less. What's more, an amusing musician who bought him drinks.

Without a hint of embarrassment he allowed Charlie to ply him with drinks as his conversation became more animated. Charlie was at the bar for the fifth time, staring back at his companion, who had taken a newspaper from his carrier bag and was studying the racing page intently.

Charlie went back with the drinks. 'Studying form?' he asked. Prestwick winked at him. 'It's more of a science. I don't bother much with the horses, more of a dog man myself. I have an aptitude you see. It's all based on the dog's physionomy. Dogs are easier to read than horses.'

'I see,' said Charlie.

Prestwick gave a grin, displaying an array of long, nicotine stained teeth.

'Ah, but you don't see. Now, if you had my medical background you might understand.'

'You're a medical man?' asked Charlie, feigning surprise.

'Oh yes,' said Prestwick, boasting now. 'Top of my profession. Would still be there now had it not been for a stupid young girl.'

Charlie felt a surge of excitement, which he contained immediately. 'Ah,' he sympathised. 'A woman ... I've been down that road myself.'

Prestwick leaned across to him and whispered conspiritorially. 'I doubt if you've been down as far as me.' He sat back. 'I doubt if anyone has. The bitch brought my world tumbling down like a house of cards.' His speech was slightly slurred now. Charlie skilfully pressed home his advantage.

'Oh, I don't know,' he argued, intending drawing Prestwick into a contest about who had suffered most at the hands of women. 'I lost a job with the Northern Philharmonic due to a woman.'

'Northern Phimharlo ...' Prestwick couldn't get his tongue around the word. 'That's classical isn't it? I didn't realise you were a classical pianist.'

'Was,' lied Charlie. 'Studied in Paris for three years. Anyway ...' His mind was racing ahead of him, trying to make his story sound plausible. 'I had a bit of a fling with the first violinist ... got her pregnant actually.'

'No harm in that,' said Prestwick.

'Not when she's the conductor's wife,' said Charlie, warming to his story. 'I tried to persuade her to have an abortion, but she wouldn't hear of it.'

'Aha!' shouted Prestwick, drunkenly, causing people in the pub to turn round. 'My point exactly. Silly bitches don't know what's good for them.'

'Anyway I got the sack,' moaned Charlie. 'Can't get decent work for love nor money.'

'Aha!' shouted Prestwick once again. 'It could be me telling the story.'

'What?' asked Charlie. 'You got the boss's wife pregnant?'

'Ah . . . no, not exactly.' Prestwick leaned over once again. 'I was an obstetish . . .' he took a breath and tried again, failing as before. 'I was a baby doctor.' He looked very deliberately around the pub to make sure no one else was listening, then back at Charlie. 'I arranged an adoption for a young whore and she accused me of tricking her into it.'

Charlie nodded sympathetically.

'Of course you know what whores are like,' Prestwick went on. 'One minute she tells me she wants the baby adopting, the next minute she's screaming she's been set up. Of course, the lily-livered bastards at the BMA took her side, struck me off. The bastards! And here I am . . . a broken man.'

'Struck you off!' exclaimed Charlie. 'That's not fair. It's like me. We work our bollocks off for year after year to get to where we are, then . . .' he took a large gulp of shandy. 'Do you know what it is? I'll tell you what it is . . . it's jealousy, that what it is. And I'll tell you something else . . .'

Charlie paused to take another swig. Prestwick's eyes were fixed on him, wallowing in his new friend's pity. 'Tell me what?' he asked, impatiently.

'What?' said Charlie, 'I'll tell you what, you find out who your friends are, that's what.'

'Oh, I agree with you there. Like rats leaving a sinking ship, that was my friends.'

'Mine and all,' agreed Charlie. 'Even people you've done favours for. Hey! Tell me if I'm wrong, I bet them people who adopted that baby never thanked you for it.'

'Thanked me? Thanked me?' laughed Prestwick scornfully. 'The bastards turned their backs on me. Lord and Lady Fucking-Arseholes. Scared of the fucking scandal. Scared of what their stuck up friends might say.' His coarsening language had people turning round in disapproval.

'What were they? Some sort of nobility?' asked Charlie. 'I bet they had a stupid name . . . all posh people have stupid names.'

Prestwick burst out laughing. 'Lord and Lady Aylesbury bloody Took!' he exclaimed. 'If that's not a stupid name I don't know what is.'

Charlie joined is laughter. 'Aylesbury bloody Took? Is that one hyphen or two?'

Prestwick laughed even louder at this. 'Hey!' he chortled. 'Their bastard son will have inherited the lot now, thanks to me. I read in the papers how the noble lord had died. It'll be a bit of a turn up for the books if I tell him his mother's a common Bradford whore . . . should be worth a few quid that, shouldn't it?'

'Tell you what, I'll come and help you. We'll split the money. Where do the bastards live?'

Prestwick was being swept along by the whole idea of blackmail. It appealed to his sense of retribution, someone should pay for his demise. 'Took House,' he said. 'That's where they live. Up in North Yorkshire somewhere. Went there myself once. They couldn't do enough for me when I told them the pedigree of the child they were getting.'

'Pedigree? I thought the mother was a whore?' queried Charlie. He could sense twitching ears all around him, Prestwick was unaware of how loud he was talking.

'She was a singer, which is the same thing. They all put it about, these showbusiness girls.' Prestwick grinned knowingly at Charlie. 'You should know, I bet you've had your share, good-looking fellow like you.'

Charlie forced a smile, but it wasn't easy.

'She was a looker if I remember rightly,' continued Prestwick, 'as was the father, or so I was assured. An Italian singer. She claimed he raped her . . . maybe you remember, it was in the papers at the time.' He gave a short laugh. 'Rape,' he said scornfully. 'More than likely she raped him.'

'So, about this pedigree?' pressed Charlie, closing his mind to any anger he might feel. He needed as much information as he could. 'You mean this Lord and Lady Aylesbury-Took wanted a good-looking child and that's why they were so keen on this girl's?'

'In a nutshell,' agreed Prestwick. 'I couldn't just fob 'em off with any old sprog. A good-looking boy child would alter the Aylesbury-Took strain for the better. They were both as ugly as sin, you see. I'm sure there's a few Took relatives running tomorrow over at the Knavesmire.' He laughed at his little joke, before continuing. 'They were people of influence. Gave me all sorts of promises to further my career.' He stared

gloomily into his drink. 'In the end they abandoned me ...
bastards!'

Charlie nodded. 'Just like you abandoned the girl. Tricking her
into having her baby adopted. No wonder the BMA struck you
off,' he spoke loud enough for the people around him to hear.
Prestwick's drinking companions.

Charlie finished his drink and stood up to leave, noting with
some satisfaction the looks of disgust on the faces of the drinkers
all around. Prestwick swayed in his seat, unaware of his new-
found infamy.

'I think you might need to look for another pub,' advised
Charlie as he left, well pleased with his day's work.

Chapter Thirty

Maggie had been watching the spider for days now. Rarely stirring from her bed, she'd watched it weave its intricate web in the corner of the ceiling and wait patiently for a fly to come along and fall into the trap. The victim had arrived while she was asleep, a big fat fly, as big as the spider itself. It was now being slowly encased in the spider's silken thread. For the thousandth time she felt a pang of guilt.

Guilt, as she compared her own sloth to the industry of the spider. Then she smiled to herself. Had she been as energetic as the busy creature above her, she'd have swept his web away the instant it appeared. He was capitalising on her lethargy, and good luck to him.

Charlie was out, which was a relief. She didn't want him popping his head around the door and asking if she was okay. She would have been okay but for him. He should have known that mumps in adults can cause sterility. He should have had checks before they got married, at least she'd have had the choice. Typical Charlie, act first, think later. Typical man come to think of it. Every man she'd ever known had let her down. Every single bloody one of them.

Her father had been away when she was a child. The vague memories she'd had of this period had been contented ones. She had no bad memories of her dad's first year at home. Then her mother had died. The one person in the whole world she'd ever felt secure with had died. And what had her dad done? Just when she needed him most? He'd gone to pieces, that's what he'd done.

He'd left her to care for Danny. Mrs Bradford had been great, but Danny had always turned to Maggie when the chips were down. But she hadn't been there when Danny had needed her most, and why? Because that day her dad had needed her as well.

And what did her dad do when Danny died? When her baby brother, who'd taken her mother's place in her affections, had died alone? Her dad had gone to pieces again, only worse this time, taking to drink, losing his job, asking her to leave school before she took her O Levels. She'd felt so sad as a child, unable to understand why. Plenty of other children had lost dads and brothers in the war, but none seemed to carry the burden as heavily as Maggie.

Every man she'd ever known had let her down. That bastard Dudley in Bridgefield House. Prestwick, who'd tricked her into giving her baby away. He was the worst. In many ways she hated him even more than Tony Martini who'd raped her. Albert Drake might have robbed her of money, but Prestwick had robbed her of so much more. He'd robbed her of her happiness.

Was there such a thing as a man who could take care of her emotionally as well as materially? For years she'd looked upon Charlie as this person. He was kind and funny and loved her deeply. He'd helped her to cope with what had gone on before. His love and the busy life they'd led had helped, but there'd always been a void, an emptiness. At some stage she hoped to fill the void with a child of their own. Hope being the anchor that stops you drifting away on the tide of despair. And Maggie's anchor had been cruelly taken from her.

By Charlie.

Charlie had mentioned adoption, but the very word turned her stomach. Her own child had been taken from her by the adoption people. She wanted no more to do with them. She'd screamed at him for his lack of understanding, his sheer stupidity. That was when he'd moved into the other bedroom. It was as though her life was being controlled by outside forces. She was unable to make things happen. Things happened *to* her, not because of her.

Here they came again, the tears. Why couldn't someone make it all go away? Where are those bloody pills the doctor prescribed? Antidepressants . . . God, the very name of them made her feel worse. It was an effort to unscrew the top off the bottle. Oh shit! They were all over the bloody floor. Well they could just stay there. She took two small brown pills and lay back. The tears flowing down either side of her face on to the pillow.

Now she needed a pee, bloody wonderful ... even getting out of bed was a monumental effort. Sleep was all she wanted. While she was sleeping she wasn't thinking or crying. But she couldn't sleep in a wet bed, things hadn't got so bad. Not yet anyway.

She eased herself from the bed and padded into the bathroom next door. He'd left the seat up again. Probably did it on purpose, just to annoy her; well, he'd bloody succeeded.

As she sat there, it occurred to her that a bath wouldn't go amiss. She couldn't remember the last time she'd had a bath. But it was too much effort. She looked in the mirror at this pasty, tear-stained, jaded face with straggly unkempt hair, staring back at her. God! No wonder she had no control. Who in their right mind would take any notice of what she had to say? Why on earth would Charlie want to make love to her? She'd stiffened every time he'd approached her. It was a big enough effort just getting through each day without having to find the energy for that sort of thing. Or even for talking. Of course, Charlie had adopted the typical man's attitude. Just because she didn't want sex, it meant she didn't love him. He never said this in so many words, but she knew what he was thinking. Let's face it, if he really loved her he'd leave her alone. Christ! She had enough to cope with, just having to be alive every day with nothing to look forward to. Maybe she should leave Charlie. The idea had been crossing her mind with greater frequency, each time it had more appeal. She just wanted to be left alone.

Her and the spider.

It was dark when she awoke, dark and quiet. Charlie can't be back yet. Even when Charlie was sitting quietly, she could sense he was in the house. He wasn't a quiet person wasn't Charlie. He'd hum or whistle or just fidget. The clock on the dressing table said twenty past ten. So where the hell was he? Leaving her on her own like this? He'd been out all day.

She tried to remember where he said he was going. York, that was it – no – he went to York yesterday, God knows why. So where was he now? He went out that morning saying he'd keep in touch if he was going to be late and she'd said, 'Don't bother'. Why did she say such stupid things? The phone hadn't rung all day. Mind you, if it had she wouldn't have answered it. Too much effort, trailing downstairs and having to talk to someone she didn't want to talk to. A car pulled into the street, she held her breath, hoping it would pull up outside their house. It stopped all right but where? The car door opened and slammed shut. Please let it be Charlie, please let him bang his way in and start whistling, like he always did. This time she wouldn't tell him off about it for waking her up. But it was a door further down the street that opened and shut, leaving Maggie sad and disappointed. The clock ticked on.

Charlie was happy with his work of the last two days, especially with what he'd seen that evening. The problem now was to persuade Maggie to venture outside the house. He looked at his watch as he pulled up into the street, five to midnight. He wasn't unduly worried. She certainly wouldn't be worried, so why should he be? If he had thought she might be worried he'd have given her a ring, but she wouldn't have answered the phone, so why bother?

He let himself in as quietly as he could, and brushed his elbow against a pan handle protruding from the cooker, knocking it to the floor with a clatter. Maggie awoke from her disturbed doze. Charlie! He was back, thank God. For an hour and a half she'd been worrying about him. Her mind painting the blackest pictures of what might have happened.

Charlie grimaced as he picked up the pan, then as quietly as he could, he tiptoed upstairs. Cursing to himself as each step creaked under his stockinged feet. Why don't they creak for anyone else?

'Charlie? Is that you?' called out Maggie, who had no doubt who it was.

'Yes, love.' Charlie popped his head around the door. 'Are you okay?'

'You're late,' she remarked. It was half a statement of fact, half an admonition.

Charlie walked in and sat on the bed. 'Sorry about that. I was going to ring, but it'd have meant you getting out of bed.' He leaned over and kissed her on her forehead.

'Where've you been?' she was genuinely curious. The first time she'd shown any interest in him for a long time.

'I've been organising a bit of a surprise.'

'I don't like surprises.'

'You'll like this one. But you'll have to get out of bed tomorrow night to see it.'

'I'll see.' She smiled at him in the dim light shining in from the landing. The first smile he'd had in a while. He kissed her forehead again and left her.

She spent all the next day wrestling with her curiosity. Charlie was relying on this. No way was he going to tell her what the surprise was. He tempted her with titbits.

'It's the best surprise you've ever had in your life.'

'If you don't tell me I'm not going.'

'You wouldn't want to miss out on this, I promise you.'

His ruse worked. By six the following evening she was out of bed and dressed to go out.

'You look lovely, Mrs Chipperfield,' complimented Charlie.

'Don't push it, Charlie.'

'Just telling the truth, that's all. No harm in that.'

'Where're we going?'

Charlie grinned boyishly and tapped a finger against his nose. 'All will be revealed in due course. Just get into the car, we've a long drive ahead of us.'

The drive to Lambourne Wells took them along a maze of narrow country roads, deep in the East Yorkshire countryside. The trees were alive with the bright foliage of summer, birdsong coming in through the open windows as Charlie cruised easily along, whistling to himself. Maggie looked at his profile. Not bad for a man the wrong side of forty. A pleasantly handsome man, easy to look at, easy to talk to – and madly in love with her. So what had she been thinking of? Moments of lucidity such as this were becoming rarer in Maggie and it frightened her. Frightened of what she might do in a moment of madness.

'I do love you, you know,' she said suddenly.

Charlie turned and smiled, his hand closing over hers. 'I know you do, love,' he replied. 'I just find it hard to see you like this. My lovely Maggie, all twisted up inside.'

'I can't help it!'

Charlie sensed the defensiveness in her voice and quickly changed the subject. A sign saying Lambourne Wells 1½, came to the rescue.

'This is it,' he announced, nearly there.

The road dipped down through a tunnel of trees, opening out into a pretty village. Built in soft, East Yorkshire limestone, all interesting pinks and yellows and browns and reds. The eroded

267

stone provided the perfect grip for climbing flowers, now in full bloom, covering almost every house in the village. Along one side of the road ran a shallow stream, twinkling in the evening sunshine; home to a family of swans, gliding along in majestic formation.

'I don't think I've ever seen anything quite as pretty as this,' remarked Maggie.

'What? Not even Hope Street?'

Maggie smiled, then a thought struck her. She knew what his surprise was . . . and she wasn't going to like it.

'I don't want to leave Hope Street, you know. Not even to live in a place like this.'

'Blimey!' commented Charlie. 'You've changed your tune. I thought you hated the place.'

But he hadn't been put out by what she'd said. This meant she was wrong, he hadn't found them a house in this village. So what was it? They drove past a very inviting pub.

'I wouldn't mind going in there,' she said.

Charlie wrestled with his common sense. It had been ages since she'd shown an interest in anything but lying in bed. But if he took her in the pub it might give the game away. The people from last night would remember him and start talking. No, best to drive on.

'I'd like to, but there's no time,' he said, smiling to himself at the memory of his visit to the pub the previous evening.

His journey the previous day had taken him from Took House in the top left hand corner of Yorkshire, across to Lambourne Wells, a few miles from Robin Hood's Bay on the east coast. Took House was situated near Scarrisbrooke village and it was in the village pub that Charlie found out all he needed to know about Danny.

The landlord had given him a welcoming smile as Charlie surveyed the selection of beers. 'Dunt know what ter do with itself, does it?' he commented, looking over Charlie's shoulder at the undecided sky beyond the taproom window.

'Pardon?' queried a puzzled Charlie.

'Dunt know whether ter rain or shine,' elaborated the landlord. 'What's it ter be, young man?' As part of his publican's patter, he called everyone under the age of seventy 'young man'. Customers beyond that age simply thought he was taking the piss and told him not to be so bloody cheeky.

'Pint of Theakstons please,' decided Charlie.

The landlord nodded his approval of Charlie's choice.

'I'm looking for Took House,' he asked, as he handed over his money.

'You're a bit late, mate,' replied the landlord. 'I reckon his lordship's had his bones picked clean by now.'

'His lordship? Oh, I suppose you mean the late Lord Aylesbury-Took. No, it's his son I was inquiring about.'

The barman's laughter infected a couple of the closest drinkers. 'You'll not get nowt out of him,' he chortled. 'Got his head screwed on right, has young Daniel.'

Charlie felt a surge of excitement at the sound of Danny's name. Daniel was obviously more befitting his elevated status, but at least they'd stuck to the name Maggie had given him, so they couldn't be all bad.

'I don't suppose you'd know if he was at home right now?'

One of the other drinkers, a flat-capped man with a local accent, answered his question for him. 'Doubt it. Most probably be at that school of his.' He looked at his companion for confirmation. 'It's not school holidays or owt, is it?'

'Shouldn't be surprised,' said his friend. 'They get more holiday than schooling nowadays . . . mind you,' he added, with a wink at the landlord. 'I hope they're teaching him how to keep his todger in his trousers.'

'There's many a parent in this village'll give yer no argument here,' laughed the flat-capped man. 'Dan Juan, that's what some calls him.'

'Bit of a lad, is he?' inquired Charlie, brightly.

'You could say that,' said the flat-capped man, holding out his hand. 'Jack Hargreaves . . . and this is Sid Taff.'

'Pleased to meet you, gents,' said Charlie affably.

'Nice lad though,' said Sid, as though not wanting Charlie to get the wrong idea about the young man. 'It's just that he's not what you'd expect the son of a lord to be. He comes in here on piano nights and sings the filthiest songs. God knows where he learned them. Don't think the lad's eighteen yet, neither.'

'He'll learn them at that school of his,' said Jack, turning to Charlie to expand on his explanation. 'It's a sort of artistic school for toffs. Theatre an' painting an' stuff. Evidently yer average toff thinks it's more of a preparation for the sort of life they end up leading.'

'Tell you what though,' butted in Sid, 'he's got a right voice on him has young Dan Took.'

'Dan Took,' repeated Charlie. 'Not much of a name for a nob.'

'It's not his proper name,' said the landlord. 'What's the lad's full title, Jack?'

Jack clutched his lapels theatrically, before announcing, 'Tristan Daniel Aylesbury-Took ... or as he calls himself, The Honourable Dan.'

Charlie laughed, he was beginning to like the Honourable Dan or Tristan Daniel Aylesbury-Took or Dan Took – or Danny Fish, as the case may be.

It was from there that he tracked his quarry across the whole width of Yorkshire to Lambourne Wells School, where he'd stopped off at the Lambourne Arms to glean further information. Daniel Took's reputation was known to the regulars, who all had a different story to tell. Of village girls deflowered and filthy songs sung and the papier mâché penis on the church steeple.

'It was never proved it was young Dan though,' cautioned the landlord.

'No ... it were never proved it wasn't neither,' argued a customer. 'Poor bloody vicar had to leave after that. Fancy having to look up at that thing and see your own face staring back down at you from the business end of a giant dick! Worst part about it was he took his wife with him. Pretty little thing she was as well.'

'Rumour had it that young Dan had been fooling around with her an' all,' added the landlord.

Charlie was beginning to warm to Daniel, but the most valuable piece of information he'd gleaned that night had sent him hurrying to the school to watch the first-night production of the end of term musical, *West Side Story*. And this was what he was bringing Maggie to see.

Maggie frowned as they swung past the school gates. 'Lambourne Wells School' was all it said on the board at the entrance, apart from the principal's name, which she didn't catch.

'Okay, you've got me beat, Charlie. We're here and I still haven't a clue why.'

Charlie smiled, 'I'd rather you worked it out for yourself,' he said, mysteriously. 'It's a sort of high class stage school and we've come to watch the end-of-term production.'

'Are we allowed to be here? Shouldn't we be parents or something?' asked Maggie, reasonably.

'No one will ask. They'll assume we're either parents or someone in the business looking for talent.'

After driving a quarter of a mile along the tarmac drive, the school came into view, an impressive building in an impressive setting. Built of soft, pale stone, eroded by two centuries of coastal wind, it had been originally the country seat of some wealthy landowner with more money than sense, judging by the array of follies scattered around the grounds. Charlie could see Maggie staring at them. A fifty-foot chimney growing out of a lawn, a pagoda and a gigantic stone elephant were just three she could identify. Others poked their mysterious tops over trees and hedges. As Charlie unselfconsciously parked his Cortina between a Bentley and an XJ6, Maggie took out her makeup case and adjusted the vanity mirror behind the sun blind. She'd spotted the competition mounting the wide steps and converging on the pillared entrance to the school. Although still very much in the dark as to the reason for her being there, she saw no reason not to give of her best.

Parents milled about the spacious entrance hall, saying 'hello' to other parents they'd seen before but couldn't quite put a name to. Lots of people saying, 'Hello there' and 'Is it really a year since we saw you last?' while they racked their brains to remember names. Women sizing up each others' dresses and figures and hair and thinking, 'What does she think she looks like? Wearing a short skirt at her age?' Men doing double takes of Maggie and wishing their wives looked half as good; and women following their husband's gawping eyes, envious of this woman's natural poise and grace and wondering whose mother she was.

Maggie looked up at ragged banners hanging from the the high, vaulted ceiling and at the portraits on the wall. All dark with age and all of miserable looking men who should have known better than to waste their money on such vanity.

'The theatre's this way,' said Charlie, taking Maggie's arm and working his way through the crowd.

'Theatre?' queried Maggie. 'You mean they've got their own theatre?'

'Oh yes, quite a nice one as well.'

Charlie led her up a sweeping marble staircase, along a wide corridor leading to a set of double doors, outside which was another smaller crowd of people, waiting to meet their sons or daughters or just not ready to take their seats. Excusing themselves, Maggie and Charlie entered the theatre circle and sat in the front row.

'What a smashing little place,' commented Maggie. 'It's as big as the City Varieties.'

'Slightly bigger apparently,' said Charlie. 'Six hundred seats. Four hundred downstairs, two hundred up here.'

'Charlie,' said Maggie. 'What the hell am I doing here? And don't say wait and see or I'll throttle you!'

'Wait and see.'

Somehow the excitement, or the mystery had cast away her gloom. Her depression had lifted slightly, replaced by intense curiosity. Charlie was hoping it would last and that events wouldn't take a turn for the worse. He hadn't planned beyond this moment.

The lights went down and the curtain came up on a set which wouldn't have disgraced a West End theatre. An eight-piece orchestra, whose average age was around sixteen, struck up from the orchestra pit with great panache as the modern day *Romeo and Juliet* got under way. Maggie laughed at 'Gee Officer Krupke', her favourite song from this show, but her attention was taken by the young man playing Tony, the reluctant member of the Sharks who'd fallen in love with Maria, the sister of the leader of the Jets. There was something about him that she couldn't put her finger on. Something about his voice that seemed familiar. Something about the way she sensed Charlie looking at her every time the young man sang. She looked in her programme at the name Daniel Aylesbury-Took.

There was a hush in the theatre as he began to sing 'Maria'. This was the one everyone had come to hear.

Maggie knew that voice. It was a light baritone, much deeper than her soprano, but the similarity was uncanny. The hook that had been so brutally throttled out of her all those years ago was alive and well and down there on that stage. A shiver of realisation racked her body. The whole reason for Charlie taking her there became gloriously apparent. She turned to Charlie, her eyes flooding with tears.

'Oh my god, Charlie!'

Charlie squeezed her hand, unsure of what to say. Worried what she might do. She returned his squeeze with a vice-like grip.

'It's him, isn't it, Charlie?'

Charlie took a deep breath. 'Yes,' he said, quietly. 'That's him, that's Danny – that's your son!'

Maggie could scarcely catch her breath, giving Charlie some cause for concern. He peeled her fingers from his hand and placed his arm around her as the song reached its climax. She was sobbing audibly, people in the stalls below were turning round and looking up at her. The song finished to thunderous applause, the type of reception that had been accorded to Maggie in her heyday. Her eyes were glued to the young man standing centre stage holding hands with a dark haired young woman. Maggie applauded her son longer and louder than anyone until she was the only one left clapping. Daniel tried to shield the floodlights with his hands as he looked up in her direction and smiled his appreciation but the light was too bright for him to see the expression of joy and confusion on his mother's face. She spoke without turning her head away from her son's smile, her voice hoarse with emotion.

'Charlie, oh Charlie – I don't know what to do.'

Charlie held on to her and kissed her hair. 'You don't do anything, love. You must try to bide your time. I only found out about him myself yesterday. Better not tell him who you are just yet, there's a lot to find out before we drop that particular bombshell. Let's wait until the end of the show and see if we can get backstage. If anyone asks, we're agents.'

As the show went on, Maggie regained some of her composure, realising the wisdom of Charlie's advice. There were six curtain calls with Daniel taking the final one. The two of them sat for a while as the theatre emptied, giving Charlie time to tell her all he knew and how he'd tracked her son down. Then, with deep determined breaths, they stood up and made their way backstage. No one bothered to ask who they were as they mingled with the excited artistes and parents alike. Maggie and Charlie threaded their way over to her son. Her heart almost leapt out of her body as she got close to him. Apart from his dark complexion, there was little of his father in him. He was a Fish alright. Tall and slim and handsome enough, but more like her dad than Tony Martini. Thank God for that.

273

It was a moment she'd never dared hope for. She held out her hand to her son, who took it readily. Happy to talk to the most beautiful woman in the room, a woman who looked vaguely familiar.

'Hello,' she said, amazing herself with the control in her voice. 'I'm Maggie Fisher and this is my husband, Charlie Chipperfield.'

'Maggie Fisher!' cried Daniel. '*The* Maggie Fisher? Of course you are! My voice coach has some of your old records. You were what he calls a natural, untutored talent. Keeps going on about how good you'd have been if he'd got his hands on you.'

'Well now, there's a thought,' laughed Maggie. 'I must meet your voice coach and give him a piece of my mind.'

'Oh! Sorry. I didn't mean it like that. What I meant was ...' Daniel's face was crimson with embarrassment.

'I was joking,' interrupted Maggie.

Daniel smiled at his mother, displaying even white teeth from a mouth she longed to kiss, just as she had all those years ago, when he'd been taken from her.

'There was always something about your voice that got to me,' went on Daniel.

'We called it "the hook",' said Charlie.

'Yes, that's what it was. I used to try and copy it.'

'I think you've managed it,' said Charlie. 'By the way, sorry to hear about your father.'

'Oh, right, thanks,' said Daniel, awkwardly. 'Hardly saw much of him, actually.'

Maggie was at a loss what to do or say. Charlie was right, this certainly wasn't the time or the place to be dropping bombshells on the young man. People were pulling at him, wanting to talk to the star of the show. Maggie knew she didn't have much time. A thought struck her. A way to quickly break the ice.

'I believe your parents and I had a mutual acquaintance,' she said, mysteriously. 'A man who made a huge difference to all of our lives, including yours.'

It was Maggie's erstwhile fame that blocked Daniel's mind from seeing what to others might have been obvious. He only saw in Maggie a voice he admired and a face from a record sleeve that looked far too young to be his mother. Maggie looked a whole generation younger than Lady Audrey. For her to turn out to be his

274

mother would be too impossible for him to contemplate, so the thought never crossed his mind. He waited for her to continue with her revelations, but she'd said all she wanted to say at that point.

'Come on,' insisted Daniel. 'You can't leave me in suspense like this. Who was this man, and what did he do that was so momentous?'

'His name was Prestwick,' answered Maggie. 'You might want to ask your mother about him.'

Daniel shook his head, baffled at all this. But there was method in Maggie's madness. She gave him one of Fish and Chipperfield's cards.

'And once you've had a chat with your mother, you might want to give us a ring,' she added with a smile.

Daniel was both dazzled and puzzled by this beautiful woman. Someone grabbed his arm to whisk him off to meet their parents. Maggie managed to kiss him on his cheek before he disappeared into the throng. She turned to Charlie.

'Thanks, Charlie,' she said, inadequately.

Charlie hugged her to him, then guided her out of the dressing room area on to the dimly lit stage.

'From what I've seen and heard of him, he sounds like a lad who won't turn his nose up when he finds out he's from a humble background,' he said. 'But we don't know anything about him yet. Maybe he doesn't even know he's adopted. We have to tread carefully.'

'I know ... but there's nothing that can stop him being my boy is there?'

'Nothing in the world,' agreed Charlie.

A huge weight seemed to have been lifted from Maggie's shoulders. Up to that night she hadn't known whether her son was happy or sad, clever or stupid, in good health or a sickly child ... or even still alive. She held Charlie in her arms and kissed him, passionately.

'I'm so sorry, Charlie,' she whispered. 'Thanks for doing this. You don't know what it means to me.'

'I thought you'd be pleased,' grinned Charlie. 'At least you can't moan at me for not giving you a child. I tell you something else as well ... he can sing a bit, can't he? And he didn't get that voice from his dad.'

275

'Do you think he's as good as I was?' asked Maggie, curiously.

'I'd have to say "yes" to that.'

'Good, at least I've given him something.'

'I suspect you might be giving him a lot more in the future,' forecast Charlie.

Chapter Thirty-One

In his father's will Daniel had been left the bulk of the estate and along with it, the bulk of the debts. On top of these had been a variety of hidden debts, revealed to him via the visits of stern looking men relaying messages from their bookmaker bosses. Daniel had taken advice on these and had been told that although he was not legally responsible for such debts, it would be as well to take such creditors seriously, as they had unique ways of enforcing payment.

With the bravado of youth, Daniel had written to each of the bookies and offered to accept responsibility for half his father's proven gambling debts, on condition that there was enough in the estate to pay such a sum and that the offer would be withdrawn at the first hint of threatening behaviour. All threats would be reported to the police.

Around a third of the claimants had what appeared to be genuine IOUs to back up their claims and grudgingly accepted his offer of part payment. The other two thirds were either trying it on or were genuine creditors who had trusted his father's word. Daniel had no way of knowing which was which, so he chose to refute their claims, hoping they'd just give up and go away.

Since becoming a car owner, Daniel had spent his weekends at home with his mother. The considerable debts brought to light by his father's death had all been paid. Part of the estate had been sold on the advice of his father's business advisors and Daniel had painlessly settled his father's provable gambling debts by selling the Reynolds portrait he so detested. He was called upon from time to time to sign various documents which the shrewd Lady Audrey vetted beforehand, but it was obvious to him that he was never meant to be a businessman. It was the Sunday after the end of term show.

'I never thought the family business was in my blood, Mother,' said Daniel. 'And from what I've learned about from my parents, the biological ones that is, I suspect my life might well follow a different path from my Aylesbury-Took antecedents.'

'I rather thought that might be the case,' smiled Lady Audrey. 'It was my idea to send you to Lambourne Wells, you know. As soon as I heard you sing in your prep school choir, I knew you had a talent that needed to be nurtured.'

'You know, Mother,' pondered Daniel. 'The oddest thing is that I think I might always have known. I've always thought there was a piece of me missing somehow. I used to look at father and the rest of the Aylesbury-Tooks and wondered where I fitted in.'

'You fitted in just beautifully, darling.'

Daniel's anger upon seeing the list of possible babies was now forgotten. Lady Audrey had explained her situation. How she desperately wanted a child she couldn't have herself, and what was wrong with being a bit selective about it? They were having breakfast, the first opportunity Daniel had had to talk to his mother since his meeting with Maggie and Charlie.

'I understand you know Maggie Fisher,' he said, through a mouthful of toast. 'She was at the show the other night.'

'How many times have I told you not to talk with your mouth full,' scolded Lady Audrey. 'Don't they teach you table manners at that school?'

'Sorry, Mother . . . and no they don't.'

'Who do you say I know?'

'Maggie Fisher. You know, Maggie Fisher the singer.'

'Never heard of her,' her voice was wavering.

'You must have, she was quite big in the fifties. She knows you . . . ah!' he remembered Maggie's exact words. 'Correction,' he said. 'Apparently you have a mutual acquaintance.'

'Mutual acquaintance? Did she say who this mutual acquaintance was?'

'Someone called, Prescott I think.'

'Prescott? Man or woman?' she asked.

'Man . . . hang on . . . his name was Prestwick. Mr Prestwick.'

Audrey's face stiffened noticeably, enough for Daniel to spot it. 'You do know him, don't you?'

'Yes,' she admitted. 'As a matter of fact I do. But I've still no idea who this Maggie Fisher is,' she was lying now, and was most uncomfortable.

'Who is he exactly?' pressed Daniel.

'He's the man who arranged the adoption.'

Audrey needed time to think this one through. How had Maggie Fisher tracked her son down? Why had she come back into their lives? As if she didn't know. The boy had come into money.

'You mean the man who made the list out?' Daniel still had the list in his room. He made a mental note to take another look at the signature.

Lady Audrey nodded reluctantly. She couldn't figure out why Maggie hadn't made herself known to him immediately. Perhaps there was method in her madness. Perhaps she was prepared to keep quiet for a price.

'She's apparently still in showbusiness, with her husband, nice chap,' remarked Daniel, casually. 'They call themselves Fish and Chipperfield,'

'Really? Society entertainers, are they?' she said, sarcastically.

'They gave me a card, just in case we ever wanted to contact them.' He handed the card over to Lady Audrey, who looked at it with a studied disinterest.

'I might go out for a drive after breakfast. Fancy coming with me?' he asked.

She looked at him and smiled. 'Sounds lovely, darling, but there are things I need to attend to.'

Maurice Jarrow, better known as Morrie, was an unhappy man. He'd been unhappy since the death of Lord Bill, as Daniel's father had been known in the betting fraternity. Morrie had taken many very large, private bets from Lord Bill, and when the noble lord had won, Morrie had always honoured these bets and had paid out very large sums of cash. Just prior to his death, his lordship had had a long run of bad luck and had run up a considerable debt, running into six figures. This was a gentleman's debt, with nothing in writing, so it was bad news to hear young Daniel's decision not to pay out debts not backed up by paperwork. Morrie understood the logic behind Daniel's decision, any old Tom, Dick or Harry could come along claiming money, and plenty had. But Morrie wasn't any old Tom, Dick or Harry. Morrie was a man with many mottoes and 'Let the sins of the fathers be visited upon the sons' was a recent addition. Morrie had a very efficient team of collectors, and this team had been given instructions to collect Morrie's money in full.

They'd been waiting for him for two hours in a car parked fifty yards from the gateway to Took House. They already knew what sort of car to look out for, a red MGB. The driver started his old XJ6 up as soon as Daniel swung into the road.

A few minutes later, Daniel spotted the big Jag in his mirror, flashing its lights, impatient to pass. He edged his sportscar over, so that his nearside wheels were just clipping the verge of the narrow country lane. The Jag drew alongside and Daniel glanced across, to see who the impatient driver was. As he did so, the bigger car swerved into his, forcing him off the road into a ditch, where he banged his head violently on the windscreen and sat there, dazed. His engine still ticking over.

He saw a hand reach into the car and switch the engine off, then he was roughly dragged out. The same person held him down as someone else blindfolded him and tied his hands behind his back, then he was dragged up the bank and thrown unceremoniously into the boot of the Jag.

After what seemed an interminable journey, the car came to a halt and Daniel waited for the boot to be opened, so he could at least stretch his legs. His discomfort overcoming any fear he might have had of what was happening to him. He was a tall young man and the cramped confines of the boot were causing him immense discomfort.

His heart sank as he heard the car door open and shut, then footsteps, then a door opening and closing, then nothing.

It was mid-afternoon when Michael answered the telephone at Took House.

'I'll see if her ladyship's available,' he answered, placing the telephone down and walking with measured step into the drawing room, where Lady Audrey was watching the wrestling on TV.

'It's a policeman on the telephone, madam, will you take it in here?'

'Yes thank you, Michael,' she said. Her brow creasing into a slight frown when he revealed the identity of the caller. She picked up the cream telephone from the table beside her.

'Yes?'

'Lady Aylesbury-Took?' inquired the policeman, uncertainly. Not sure of what tone to use when addressing the nobility.

'Yes.'

'This is the police at Scarrisbrooke. We've found a car registered to your son in a ditch about a mile from your house.'

'My son's car . . . is he hurt?' she blurted out.

'He wasn't in it, madam. It's just been abandoned.'

'My son . . . where is he? Do you know if he's all right?'

'There's no sign of him, madam. But we've no reason to think he was hurt. The key's not in the ignition, he may have walked off to find assistance.'

'Oh! Yes, of course,' she said, her panic subsiding. There was a reassuring logic to the policeman's thinking. 'He probably swerved to avoid something and landed in a ditch. Is there much damage to the car?' she asked, 'it's his pride and joy, you know.'

'A few dents, nothing major,' said the policeman. 'Would you like me to arrange for it to be towed to a garage?' This wasn't a service normally offered by the police, but Lady Audrey was no ordinary client.

'I suspect my son's already done that, but thank you for the offer anyway.'

'If there's anything you need, don't hesitate to ring.'

Lady Audrey put the phone down and sighed. She knew Daniel would be all right, but it would have done no harm for him to have rung her. She'd be worrying needlessly now until he got in touch, at which time she'd give him a piece of her mind for causing her to worry. Michael came back in.

'Is everything all right, madam?'

'I think so, Michael. The police have found Daniel's car abandoned in a ditch about a mile away. There's no sign of him and the key isn't in the ignition, so I expect he's all right. I just wish he'd have rung that's all. He's so thoughtless at times.'

'I believe it's called being a teenager, madam.'

'Quite,' smiled Lady Audrey.

Maggie sat in front of the dressing-table mirror and assessed the damage of the past few months. She'd put on weight through comfort eating, there were fine lines fanning out from her eyes and grey circles beneath them. But worst of all, she spotted grey intruders infiltrating her glorious chestnut hair.

281

'You'll have to go,' she told them.

'What have I done now?' inquired Charlie.

'Not you, these damn hairs. I'm going grey.'

'Think yourself lucky,' consoled Charlie. 'I'm going bald. Every time I wash my hair, the plughole's bunged up.'

Maggie turned to look at him as he sat on the bed reading the *Green Final*. 'Are we middle aged?' she asked, suddenly.

'Are we heck middle aged! Middle age doesn't start until you're . . .?'

'Forty?' she suggested.

'Middle age is a state of mind,' he protested. 'You and me are two of nature's perpetual juveniles.'

Maggie turned back to the mirror. He was half right, Charlie was still a juvenile, and thank God for that. This was to be their first night out in many weeks, the start of Maggie's rehabilitation into society. Just a Sunday evening drive into the country, maybe a drink at a pub, but for Maggie it was a milestone. The phone rang downstairs.

'I'll get it,' said Charlie, putting his paper down and swinging his long legs off the bed.

Maggie sighed as he clumped downstairs, making more noise than anyone she knew. Certainly any adult.

'Hello! Chipperfield's Circus,' he announced, cheerfully. She wished he wouldn't do that, you never knew who it might be. His voice suddenly became serious, Maggie couldn't make out what he was saying. She got up and went to the door, listening from the top of the stairs; the other person was doing most of the talking. All she could hear from Charlie's end of the conversation was restricted to the occasional 'yes' or 'I see'. Eventually she heard him say, 'Right, I'll tell her,' and then, 'Give me your number, Lady Aylesbury-Took, and I'll get back to you.'

Lady Aylesbury-Took! Maggie felt a shiver of apprehension. What was Daniel's adoptive mother doing ringing them up?

'What is it?' she almost shouted, as Charlie mounted the stairs.

'It's weird,' he said, sitting down on the bed, with Maggie hovering anxiously over him. That was Lady Aylesbury-Took, Daniel's adopt . . .'

'Yes, I know who she is, get on with it!'

'Well,' he said, trying to make sense of what he'd just heard. 'Apparently he's been kidnapped.'

'Kidnapped?' cried Maggie. 'Why would anyone want to kidnap my Danny?'

'Why does anyone kidnap anyone?' said Charlie, answering his own question. 'For money. Your Danny's a wealthy lad. It seems that someone wants a bit for himself.'

'Oh my God! Has she told the police?'

'That's just it,' replied Charlie. 'Apparently not. They warned her not to. She's hysterical. I don't think she knows what she's doing. But don't ask me why she rang us, because I don't know.'

'Because I'm his real mother, that's why,' decided Maggie. 'Daniel must have told her he's met me. He must have given her our phone number. If she needs help, then who better to turn to than me?'

There was a logic in there somewhere. Charlie could have argued, but he knew better. 'I think she'd like us to go over there,' he said. 'I told her I'd speak to you and ring her back.'

Michael answered the door and oddly enough seemed to recognise them. He gave a faint nod of his head, saying, 'Her ladyship's in the drawing room, if you'd follow me.'

The gravity of the situation prevented either of them finding much of interest in their elegant surroundings. Lady Audrey got up to meet them as they entered the room.

'Thank you for coming so quickly,' she said, shaking both their hands. 'I'm afraid I'm at my wits' end.'

'So am I,' said Maggie. 'It's like a bad dream. I assume you know who I am?' she asked.

'Yes . . . I know who you are,' confirmed Lady Audrey, wearily. 'You're my son's mother. Daniel doesn't know it yet, and I would appreciate your not telling him the instant you set eyes on him.'

'There's a time and a place for everything,' replied Maggie. 'Eighteen years ago he was stolen from me, and the minute I find him, it all happens again.'

Charlie interrupted the conversation. 'Lady Aylesbury er Took . . .'

'Please call me Audrey,' she said.

'Audrey . . . what's the situation right now?'

She sighed and shook her head. 'The situation is that I'm waiting for something to happen . . . a phone call probably . . . I don't know how these things work.'

Maggie was sitting in the chair facing Lady Audrey. A million questions buzzing in her head. 'Tell me about the adoption,' she said suddenly.

Audrey was slightly taken aback. 'What exactly do you want to know?'

Maggie saw no reason to spare Lady Audrey's anguish. For all she knew, Audrey could have been in it with Prestwick. She fixed her with a hard stare. 'You'd better start from the beginning ... and when I say beginning, I mean eighteen years ago, when you adopted him.'

Lady Audrey returned Maggie's gaze, then lowered her eyes in the face of Maggie's intensity. 'As far as I knew, the adoption was legal and above board, we did nothing wrong.'

'Prestwick was struck off by the BMA as a direct result of his part in the adoption, you must have known that,' said Maggie, coldly.

Audrey's eyes were fixed firmly on her fidgeting hands. This nightmare was getting worse. 'Of course we knew that ... and we spent several awful weeks wondering if our child was going to be taken from us.'

'And given back to his mother?' added Maggie.

'We knew little of the actual BMA proceedings, except that your name was never mentioned. It wasn't until we made discreet inquiries some time later that we discovered your identity. We assumed that the adoption itself was, more or less, with your approval and that the BMA were simply disciplining Prestwick for his callous behaviour.'

'He told me I'd got leukaemia, so that I'd give up my baby. How could I have possibly, more or less, have approved of that?' asked Maggie heatedly

'I'm so very sorry!' Audrey seemed shocked. 'It was over a year before Prestwick was brought before a disciplinary committee, and several more months before we heard what he'd done. By which time Daniel was part of our lives.'

'I wish I'd told Danny the whole story when I saw him the other day,' snapped Maggie. 'Maybe he'd have come home with his real mother. At least he'd have been safe.'

Her words were finding their target with a blistering venom. The whole situation was too much for Audrey. Tears ran down her face, drawing Michael out from nowhere to place a comforting arm around his employer's shoulders. He looked at Maggie and Charlie with disapproval.

'Could you leave her ladyship for a few moments please?' Such was his tone, that the two of them got silently to their feet and walked out of the room.

They stood in the spacious hall at the foot of a magnificent sweeping staircase. Maggie imagined Danny sliding down these as a boy. In her mind she'd always pictured her son and her late brother as looking alike.

'Maggie,' said Charlie. 'When we go back in there, it'd be as well if you forgot your differences for the moment and concentrated on the job in hand. All this bickering's not going to bring Danny back.'

She opened her mouth to argue but he stopped her. 'I mean it, Maggie. Just watch your temper, we all need to pull together on this one.'

He poked his head around the door and Maggie heard him ask if Lady Audrey was all right. No way was Maggie going to apologise for her behaviour, but she was prepared to be civil, purely in the interest of getting Danny back. They both went back into the room. Charlie apologised on her behalf.

'Sorry about that, but you must understand how my wife feels about all this.'

'No need to apologise,' smiled Audrey thinly. Maggie wholeheartedly agreed with this. She sat down once again as Charlie squatted beside Audrey.

'Have you told the police?' he asked.

Audrey sighed and shook her head. 'Why do you suppose I asked you across? I'm in a dilemma. When the abductors rang with their demands, they said they'd kill him if I contacted the police. I didn't know who to turn to. If I'd contacted any of my own friends I'm quite sure they'd have rung the police with or without my say so. Then I thought of you. Daniel told me he'd met you, although he didn't know exactly who you were. It just seemed like a good idea to ring you, don't ask me why.'

'We're glad you did,' said Charlie gently, holding her hand. 'Now, what were these demands?'

Audrey expelled a lungful of despairing breath. 'They want a hundred and four thousand pounds,' she said dejectedly.

'A hundred and four thousand?' Charlie whistled at the enormity of the sum, then a puzzled frown crossed his face. 'That seems like a very exact sort of figure. I wonder where they got that from?'

Michael coughed discreetly. 'I think I may be able to throw some light on that.'

Charlie looked up at him. 'Well?' he asked.

'His late lordship incurred many gambling debts, some of which were honoured by Mr. Daniel.'

'Only some?' queried Maggie. 'Why only some?'

'Because it was difficult to separate the bogus claimants from the genuine ones. So he restricted payment to those who had written evidence.'

'If we'd paid out everyone who turned up on the doorstep we'd have been bankrupt,' explained Audrey. 'We had to draw the line somewhere.'

'In that case,' said Maggie. 'I suggest you draw the line a little further down the page and pay these people off.'

'Do you think I hadn't thought of that?' sighed Audrey. 'I can't pay them off. When my husband died he left a mountain of debts. We had to sell much of what is euphemistically known as the family silver to pay all his creditors. There's little cash left. We couldn't raise that sort of money without selling something else or organising a loan . . . and all this takes time. Besides, only Daniel now owns anything of any real value and without his signature . . .' her voice tailed off as her emotions overtook her once again. She held a handkerchief to her face.

'You know,' said Maggie, looking around. 'It's really hard to believe you can't raise a hundred grand.' There was a hint of petulance in her voice.

'That's the problem,' replied Audrey, sadly. 'If you're not convinced, how are we supposed to convince them?'

Maggie nodded grimly at the woman's logic. Audrey had been right not to call the police. Somehow the kidnappers had to be told what the problem was, and not to do anything drastic until they'd found a way of raising the money.

'Did they say when they'd be calling again?' she enquired.

Audrey shook her head and looked at an ormolu carriage clock on top of the television. It said ten past eight. 'They rang about three hours ago,' she said, confirming the time with her own watch. 'I don't know how these things work.'

'We seem to be left with just two options,' deduced Charlie, pacing up and down. 'We can phone the police and leave it up to them . . . or we can negotiate and see if they'll give us time to raise the money.'

'Trouble is, either way doesn't guarantee we get Danny back in one piece,' argued Maggie. The optimism she'd felt since meeting Danny was dissolving rapidly.

The phone rang and Michael answered on the third ring with a calm dignity, at odds with the panicking faces staring at him.

'I'll see if her ladyship's available, who shall I say is speaking?' he held the phone away from his ear as a stream of invective poured from the earpiece. 'I take it you don't wish to give your name, sir?' he said, with an equanimity that must have had the caller livid. He handed it to Audrey, the caller's voice rasped in her ear.

'Yer got twenty-four hours ter get the money or yer'll never see the lad again!' The phone went dead. Audrey's face drained of the little colour left in it.

'They . . . they want the money in twenty-four hours,' she said, haltingly. 'Or I won't see Daniel again.'

There was a silence in the room as everyone digested the implications of the kidnapper's demand.

'It's a chicken and egg situation,' said Charlie, thinking straighter than the women. 'We can't raise the money without Daniel and we can't get Daniel back until we've raised the money. Maybe if we tell them this, they'll see the sense in it.'

'It sounds like a very big "maybe", sir,' observed Michael, a little too aloofly for Charlie's liking.

There was another long silence and Maggie felt herself regressing into the darkness of depression. Would it not have sounded so stupid, she'd have openly blamed herself for all this. Surely it was too much of a coincidence for this to have happened just as she'd found her son again. The light at the end of the tunnel had been extinguished, as she knew it always would be. How stupid of her to think something good was going to happen to her at last. Her bout of depression had left her with no reserves. She looked around the room. There was something oppressive about the place, she didn't want to be here.

'I want to go home,' she said to Charlie, her voice small and uncertain.

Audrey looked upset at this. 'I'd rather hoped you'd want to see this through with me,' she said, quietly.

287

'I just want to go home,' repeated Maggie, rising from her chair.

'She's been quite ill recently,' explained Charlie.

'Don't make excuses for me, Charlie,' reproached Maggie. She looked at Audrey. 'If I'm not here, perhaps things will sort themselves out.'

Lady Audrey shook her head at Maggie's lack of logic, then nodded to Michael who accompanied Maggie and Charlie to the door.

'Goodbye, Lady Audrey,' said Charlie, uncertainly. 'I'll ring you tomorrow.'

After he closed the door behind them, Michael returned to his mistress. 'I think we ought to ring the police, madam,' he suggested.

Daniel lay there for hours. Sleep didn't come easily but when it did, it was a merciful release from his suffering. A key rattling in the boot lid woke him up.

'Okay! Out, yer bastard and quick about it!'

Daniel's limbs refused to obey the commands of his brain.

'I'm sorry, but I've got cramp,' he said. 'I can't move my legs.'

A pair of rough hands grasped him and pulled him unceremoniously out. He was dragged down a flight of stone steps, across a cold, concrete floor, gagged and tied to a chair.

'With a bit o' luck,' said a rough voice. 'We should be havin' a bit o' target practice at you sometime tomorrow.'

Daniel tried to speak through his gag, but couldn't form any coherent words.

'Don't waste yer breath, lad,' rasped the voice. 'Yer've been kidnapped . . . but yer'll not be going back ter dear old mummy, even if she does cough up.'

The man's words threw Daniel into a panic. He struggled against his bonds, causing the men to laugh at his predicament.

'That's it lad, make the most of it. Even if yer do get free, there's a matter of this cellar ter get out of. That's t' hard part!'

He heard the men walk away, laughing to themselves. A heavy-sounding door slammed shut and a key turned in the lock; then two noisy bolts rattled into place.

Charlie knew they were doing the wrong thing as he drove Maggie home. His wife hadn't spoken a word as they reached the outskirts of Leeds. Charlie was formulating some sort of a plan to drop Maggie off and return to Took House himself. He wasn't sure why, it just seemed better than doing nothing.

He turned the key in the lock and stepped aside for Maggie to walk past him.

'I'm going back,' he announced. 'I think I ought to.'

'Okay,' she replied, quietly.

'Will you be all right?' asked Charlie, concerned.

'I'll be fine, I think I'll ring Sylvia. I haven't spoken to her for ages.'

This didn't sound like much of an idea to Charlie, but he knew better than to say so. 'Right. I'll be off then,' he said, closing the door as Maggie turned her back on him to pick up the phone.

A vague idea formed in his head as he drove back to Took House. It was now turned eleven o'clock. He stopped at a phone box.

'Michael,' he said, in answer to Michael's unflappable voice. 'Michael, it's Charlie, Charlie Chipperfield.'

He heard Michael speaking to Lady Audrey, who perhaps thought it was the kidnappers, then he spoke to Charlie again.

'Yes sir, what can I do for you?'

'Have you rung the police yet?'

'Her ladyship's been deliberating on the matter for some time and had arrived at the conclusion that it's better to involve the police.'

'But you haven't rung them yet?'

'No, sir, not yet.'

'Don't,' said Charlie. 'I'm coming back there. I'll explain then.'

There was a muffled conversation which he couldn't make out, then Michael's voice came back.

'When can we expect you, sir?'

'Within the hour.'

'Very good, sir. Her ladyship awaits your return with interest.'

Charlie rather fancied the idea of punching Michael on the end of his nose when he got back. He pointed his car in the direction of Took House, the vague idea now taking shape.

An hour later Charlie was gratefully accepting an ample glass of cognac poured out for him by Michael; an action which did much to soften Charlie's antipathy towards him. He turned to Lady Audrey.

'Did your husband keep a record of his bets? If he was that much of a gambler, he'd have been hard pressed to keep all his bets in his head.'

'He does have some private papers that we haven't bothered to go through. You know, even after his death it seemed such an intrusive thing to do.'

'I think now might be a good time to start intruding,' argued Charlie. 'It might help if we can find out who these people are.'

Accompanied by Michael, Charlie was shown into the late lord's study and made a bee-line for the desk. Three draws were unlocked, but apart from a ledger containing records of business transactions which might have been of interest to the taxman, there was no record of his bets. The girlie magazines had disappeared.

'What's in here?' enquired Charlie, pulling at the locked drawer.

'I don't know sir, perhaps I should find something with which to open it?'

'Good idea.'

Michael reappeared a few moments later with a large screwdriver with which, to Charlie's admiration, he swiftly prised open the drawer. The letters which Daniel had meant to destroy were still there. Charlie's face dropped, then Michael pointed out a thick notebook hidden underneath the envelopes. Charlie took it out.

'Bingo!' he exclaimed.

The book contained every bet Daniel's father had made over the last five years.

Every six months he'd drawn up a profit and loss account, which had shown him marginally beating the odds up to the year before his death. Bets on the horses, dogs, boxing, football, cricket – even general elections. At the back of the notebook was an accounts section, with lists of debtors and creditors. This was what Charlie had been looking for.

'The hot favourite's Morrie Jarrow,' he announced, as he walked into the drawing room with the ledger beneath his arm. Charlie looked at Lady Audrey. 'Your husband seemed to be using him a lot over the last few months of er . . .'

'Of his life?' suggested Audrey.

Charlie nodded. 'He owed Jarrow over a hundred thousand. Your husband seemed to double his wager each time, to try and recoup his losses . . . only he got in deeper and deeper.'

'He'd have come up smelling of roses had he lived,' observed

Lady Audrey, drily, 'he always did. So, you think this Jarrow person might be holding Daniel until we pay William's debt?'

'It's a strong possibility. I've never had anything to do with Jarrow, but I've heard he's a nasty piece of work.'

'So,' said Audrey. 'Now that we know who he is, why don't we contact the police?'

'Because we don't know for certain,' explained Charlie. He looked at Michael for support and was gratified to see the man nod his agreement. 'I suggest we wait for him to ring again and mention the name Jarrow to the caller. If he knows we know who he is, if nothing else it'll make him think twice about doing anything drastic.'

'That's if it's him,' said Audrey, confused.

'To use a bookmaker's own terminology, I suggest he's the hot favourite,' said Michael.

'Oh, very well,' she said. 'But I doubt he'll be ringing tonight,' she was looking at her watch when the phone rang.

'Took House?' said Michael. He nodded, then handed the phone to Charlie. 'Your wife. Sir.' There was an element of distaste in his voice. In his eyes, Maggie hadn't come up to scratch in this affair.

'Maggie? Are you okay?'

'Not really. Charlie ... Sylvia's here ... will you be coming back tonight?'

Charlie explained what had happened and who he thought was the culprit.

'Morrie Jarrow!' her voice exploded in panic at the other end of the line.

'Maggie, calm down. We've got things in hand at this end.' He listened to her for a few seconds more before she slammed the phone down.

Maggie spun round in her chair and looked at Sylvia. 'Charlie reckons Morrie Jarrow's got my son,' she said, in an empty voice.

Daniel's hands were tied both to the chair and to each other. Releasing them from the chair was fairly straight forward, his fingers easily unravelling the knot. His hands were still tied behind his back and the cellar was pitch black. Dragging the chair behind him, he found a brick pillar, against which he managed to position himself, so that he could rub the rope up against a sharp edge. In minutes the rope snapped, he was free of his bonds and had found a light switch.

His heart sank when he explored his surroundings. Whitewashed brick walls, no windows, just the door his captors had locked from the outside. He rattled it hopelessly, then turned around to survey his prison. There must be some way out. Maybe through the ceiling. Some of the plaster had come away, revealing ancient joists supporting floorboards. If he could prise away the floorboards he'd be able to squeeze through. A blow to the back of his head sent him reeling to the floor. The door, which he'd been too engrossed to notice, had opened and closed again above his prostrate body.

'Seventeen minutes it took him . . . yer owe me a fiver,' said a triumphant voice.

'Bollocks . . . yer should have tied him up tighter, the bet's off.'

A fierce argument ensued, as Daniel lay unconscious on the floor.

A peacock was screeching to its mate from the roof of an adjoining stable block as Maggie rang the bell. Michael answered the door, it was seven-thirty in the morning and he'd had little sleep.

'Have you got forty-three quid for a taxi?' asked Maggie. Much of her earlier dullness seemed to have gone. Replaced by a look of determination, more in keeping with the Maggie of old.

'I'll alert your husband, madam,' said Michael, spinning on his heels and disappearing inside.

The taxi fare was raised with some difficulty. Michael having to chip in a tenner.

'Maggie, what are you doing here?' asked Charlie.

'I had an idea last night,' she said mysteriously. 'Have they rung yet?'

'If you mean the kidnappers, no they haven't.'

'Good, when they do, this is what you say to them.' She outlined a plan that had Charlie looking most uncertainly at Audrey, who eventually shrugged her agreement.

An hour later the phone rang. Michael answered in a tone that indicated everything was all right with his world.

'Took House?'

He listened impassively to the caller's belligerent demands, before replying in wonderfully modulated tones, considering the circumstances. 'What do you think this is, you bloody bastards?

292

Barclays bloody bank? It takes time to raise that sort of cash and as you are holding the only person who can sign for it, how are we supposed to raise such a sum? Tell your Mr Jarrow to give us a reasonable amount of time, and not to be such a bloody moron. I'll thank you to ring back at twelve o'clock.'

He calmly replaced the receiver and looked across at Maggie, who had been listening in on an extension in the hall.

'Brilliant, Michael,' she said.

He then looked at his mistress. 'I do hope my expletives didn't offend you, madam, but I understand it's appropriate terminology when dealing with such people.

'That's perfectly all right, Michael,' Audrey gave him a frail smile. Then to Maggie and Charlie, she added, 'Somehow, you've made me feel a little better. I'm glad you both came back.'

Maggie looked at Michael. 'When you mentioned the name Jarrow, did you notice a reaction? Not much, maybe just an intake of breath?'

'I believe I did, madam.'

Maggie turned to Charlie. 'So did I . . . I'm certain you're right about it being him who's behind all this.'

'So?' inquired Charlie, 'what do we do now?'

Maggie turned to Audrey. 'Audrey, how much ready cash can you raise right now?' she asked.

'I don't know . . . maybe three thousand pounds, no more.'

'That should be more than enough,' said Maggie, picking up the phone. She dialled her own number.

'Sylvia?' she said. 'It's on. They're ringing back at twelve o'clock. They've got to pick him up before then.'

Audrey looked at Charlie. 'Who's Sylvia?' she asked.

'You don't want to know,' replied Charlie, almost as puzzled as she was.

'She's an old friend of mine,' said Maggie. 'In some ways she has a lot in common with you.'

'With me? In what way?' inquired Audrey.

Charlie was about to ask a similar question.

'She has a very er . . . influential family,' explained Maggie. 'By the way, sorry about last night,' she added. 'Us nutters tend to blow hot and cold.'

Chapter Thirty-Two

David Jarrow turned the key in the lock of his father's Burniston Place betting shop. His head was thumping from a major hangover. In the distance, the parish church clock struck ten. The rest of the staff would be arriving in an hour. A morning in bed would have done him no harm, but it wouldn't have been worth the bile his father would have heaped upon him. How he hated being the apple of his father's eye. One day he'd clear off and not come back, just like his two younger brothers had. The promise of the Jarrow empire being handed down to him had ostensibly kept David firmly under his father's thumb, but not for much longer.

His father had gone into bookmaking as a natural progression from being a market trader cum extortionist. Morrie Jarrow had no aptitude for figures, he relied heavily on David for that. David had studied accountancy and would have done well in that profession had it not been for his father. But, what goes around comes around and David's turn was coming. For years he'd been systematically creaming the profits. Leaving enough to make his father satisfied, but nicely swelling David's many and varied bank accounts.

Closing the door behind him, he walked through to the office, where Ronnie and Trevor Tattersall were patiently waiting.

Morrie Jarrow waved to his wife through the window of his Harrogate home. She was pottering about in the garden, good for her, someone has to do it. Morrie hadn't been brought up with gardens, so it wasn't in his blood. It had taken him years to establish himself as a respected member of the community. Marrying Rowena had given him a kick start there, that's why

294

he'd treated her right. In all his married life he'd never laid a hand on her. He bought her a big boring house in the most boring part of a boring town. But he was rarely there, so it didn't matter much. She was no great shakes in bed, but that didn't matter either. There were women whose job it was to provide that sort of service. All in all he reckoned he'd acquitted himself well as a husband, father and pillar of the community. He'd even considered running for the council. The phone rang.

He picked it up and looked at his watch, half past eleven. It couldn't be the lads, they weren't due to ring the Took woman for half an hour. They'd told him about the last phone call they'd made to Took House; how this bloke had answered, cursing his man and calling him a moron. Somehow they'd figured out who it was who had taken Daniel, which was a bit of a worry. But the lad's mother was still in the market for a deal, so she obviously wasn't able to prove anything. It made topping the lad a bit risky. Up until then he'd every intention of killing Daniel, whether or not his mother paid up, much less messy that way. On top of which he had a reputation to maintain. Anyone who even tried to welsh on Morrie Jarrow would know the consequences. He picked up the receiver.

'Hello?' he grunted.

'Jarrow?'

'Yes . . . who's this?'

'We've got your lad,' said a muffled voice.

'What?'

'You bleedin' heard . . . we've got your lad.'

'Which lad? I've got three.'

There was a pause as he heard the rough voice asking someone his name. The caller spoke again, 'says his name's David. If owt happens ter the Took kid, yer'll never see your lad again.'

The phone went dead. Morrie looked at it as though wondering why. 'You bastards!' he cursed.

Had they taken either of his other two sons, he would have had to think seriously about it. But David was the best of the bunch, the only one he could trust. He rang the Burniston Place shop to check, but the news confirmed his fears. The shop was open when the staff got there, but no one was about. David should have been there but wasn't, no message, nothing. As he put the phone down, it rang again. It was David sounding most distressed.

'Whatever they want, Dad, please do it for them. They've got this pickled hand in a jar, that they cut off someone else. If you don't do as they say, they're going to do the same to me. Dad, they're not messing about, they mean it.'

Another voice came on the line, the same voice as before, rough but muffled. 'Don't go worrying about his hand, Jarrow. Yer've got till teatime ter let the Took lad go. If he's not free by then, we'll naturally assume yer've topped him already and we'll send you yer lad's head. Don't mess us about Morrie, yer bastard.'

Still holding the buzzing receiver, Morrie looked at his wife through the window and wondered how he was going to explain this one to her.

Daniel was sitting fearfully on the chair, pondering his fate. He was tired and hungry and thirsty and his head was aching ferociously, with the dual knocks it had suffered. Release from his bonds had allowed him to relieve himself in a corner, far preferable to peeing in his pants, although the smell was becoming a trifle rank. The cellar door opened and two men came in, one wearing a back-to-front balaclava with eye holes cut out and the other a cheap Elvis mask. He felt a surge of hope. They didn't want him to recognise them, this was good. One had a sawn-off shotgun – not so good. With mixed emotions he made no struggle as they tied his hands behind his back and blindfolded him. As he was being bundled up the stone steps to the waiting car he was thinking how a blindfold was good, there were grounds for optimism here.

'Has the ranson been paid?' he asked, curiously. At a loss to figure out how his mother could have raised a sum of any significance.

'Shut yer gob!'

'Right, sorry.' No need to antagonise them, things seemed to be going well.

Maybe I'm only worth a couple of thousand, he smiled to himself grimly as his captors shoved him into the Jaguar boot and slammed down the lid.

After about an hour the car stopped, as did Daniel's heart. He felt that his fate might be decided in the next couple of minutes. The boot lid opened and one of the men ordered him out. But Daniel couldn't move.

'I said get out yer deaf bastard!'

'Sorry, I've got cramp again,' explained Daniel, politely, while doing his best to get out. The man grabbed him and yanked him out, unceremoniously. Daniel dropped to the ground, still blindfolded and tied up. As he lay on the ground, stretching his legs to get the circulation going, he heard the men get back into the car and drive away, leaving him at the roadside, relieved, frightened, blindfolded and trussed up. This time the rope was too tight for him to free himself. Staggering unsurely to his feet, he could hear the occasional car going past. He ventured as near to the sounds as he dared, stopping when his feet left the soft grass and touched the hard road surface. He took a step back and waited until he heard the sound of a car slowing down.

David Jarrow's release was a little less formal. He was pushed from the side door of a stolen transit van, which slowed down only marginally for his painful exit. The van driver looked back at his brother and grinned. It had been the easiest grand they'd ever earned. They were wondering if they ought to ask for a bonus to cover the additional phone call they'd made to Morrie, explaining in grisly detail what they'd been instructed to do to him and his family if ever he attempted a repeat performance.

David rolled on to the footpath, happy to have escaped with a broken arm and a sore head. But nevertheless he was grateful to be alive. His father must have come up with the goods, whatever they were. He was even feeling guilty about stealing money from the firm and had vague thoughts about replacing it as a mark of gratitude for his father's unexpected compassion. A passer-by helped him to his feet and offered to phone the police.

'No thanks, you're very kind, but that won't be necessary,' said David, who, knowing his father, felt that involving the police wouldn't be to his advantage.

His arrival home in a taxi was witnessed by his father through the front room window. Morrie had managed to keep his son's abduction a secret from his wife, but it had been with great reluctance that he'd ordered the release of Daniel Took. It had never occurred to him that the nobility could be so ruthless. He'd been genuinely shocked and disillusioned by Lady Aylesbury-Took's underhand actions.

As David walked through the door into what he hoped were his father's welcoming arms, Morrie unleashed all his pent-up frustration on him. With the flat of his hand he sent the young man crashing to the floor, crying out in pain as he landed on his already broken arm. He looked up at his father standing over him, seething with anger.

'What the hell was that for, Dad?'

'What was that for?' stormed Morrie, out of control. 'What was that for? You've just cost me over a hundred grand, that's what!'

'What? You paid a hundred grand ransom for me?' If this was the case, David was ready to excuse his father's violence.

'Ransom?' Morrie laughed hysterically. 'I wouldn't pay a hundred arseholes to get you back, yer useless pillock.'

David watched his father walk from the room and knew it was high time he followed in his brothers' footsteps and severed his business connections with this man.

Daniel was sitting in a pub in Skipton when Audrey, Maggie and Charlie walked in. He was eternally grateful to the farmer who'd stopped and untied his bonds, despite the man's dark, muttered remarks about young people 'what ought ter have better things ter do wi' their time.' So curmudgeonly was the man that Daniel chose not to enlighten him about his ordeal, but gratefully accepted a lift on the back of his Land Rover. The sacks of horse manure he sat amongst did little to enhance his personal fragrance as he arrived in the thriving North Yorkshire market town, from where he'd rung Took House.

Daniel was in a daze, not only from his painful experience, but also from seeing his mother and Maggie Fisher together. What on earth was going on? After answering all the questions put to him about his ordeal, he asked one of his own.

'Mother, why didn't you want me to ring the police?' He'd been sitting there, nursing a sore head and a pint, wondering about that, ever since his mother, over the phone, had instructed him not to.

'There's a good reason for that,' whispered Lady Audrey, in his ear. Her son's proximity causing her to wrinkle her nose. 'Good Lord! Daniel, you're a bit ripe, if you don't mind me saying so.'

'I rode into town on a truck load of horse shit, Mother,' explained Daniel, mildly put out at such criticism.

'Ah, I see,' replied his mother. 'Now the reason for not

involving the police is that, in order to get you back in one piece, we had to play the kidnappers at their own game. Well, not me exactly ... you have Maggie and her friends to thank for that.' Audrey explained briefly why he'd been abducted and by whom and how they'd got him back.

'Thank you, Maggie,' said Daniel, who could now see why they didn't want the police involved.

'It was a pleasure,' smiled Maggie. 'But first we need to get you to a hospital to have you checked over. We've told them you were involved in a car accident.'

'There's an element of truth in that,' grinned Danny. 'You know, for a while I thought they were going to kill me.' He said it with no acrimony towards his captors.

'It crossed our minds as well, darling,' said Audrey. 'Anyway, I've booked you into a room at the Wharfedale Clinic for them to check you over. Maggie's going with you ... I, er ... I believe she's got something to tell you.'

Daniel's mind was in too much of a whirl to study the implications of his mother's final remark. He smiled at Maggie.

'I hardly know you,' he said, 'but you've been amazingly helpful.'

'Perhaps we'll get to know each other better in the future,' said Maggie, lowering her eyes, lest she betrayed the love she felt for this young man.

Chapter Thirty-Three

Early the following morning, Daniel woke up from a mildly sedated sleep and looked across the room at Maggie, engrossed in a morning paper. It took him a few seconds to figure out where he was and what had happened to him. Maggie looked up, did a double take when she realised he was awake, and smiled at him.

'Morning, Daniel.'

She forced herself to use his more formal name, so as not to add to the confusion.

'Good morning, Maggie.'

She stood up and pressed a button at the side of his bed. 'I'll order breakfast,' she said.

'Full English please,' ordered Daniel. 'I'm starving.'

'Excuse me,' she grinned. 'This is a hospital, not an hotel. You'll get what you're given.'

A nurse entered and stuck a thermometer in his protesting mouth.

'I *was* hoping for egg and bacon,' he said, through a mouthful of thermometer.

'Any nonsense from you, young man,' she said, 'and I'll stick it in the other end, makes no difference to me.'

'He'd like his breakfast,' explained Maggie. 'He's starving.

The nurse looked at the heavily bandaged head of her charge. 'As soon as you've had breakfast, I'll take your dressing off for the doctor to have a look at. I think he might want to keep you in for another day or so, for observation.'

She removed the thermometer from his mouth, nodded her approval of its reading and left.

'If this'd been the NHS, you'd have been on the bus home by now,' observed Maggie, wryly.

'Hey! Don't think I wouldn't prefer it,' protested Daniel. 'At a hundred quid a day, they're not going to chuck me out until they're good and ready.'

A woman came in with Daniel's breakfast. Full English, as anticipated and arranged by Maggie. He looked up at her and grinned his appreciation. She went back, ostensibly, to her paper and allowed him to eat his meal in peace, taking the opportunity to formulate her words for the final time. Daniel polished off the food, double quick.

'You're a bit of a guardian angel, Maggie Fisher,' he commented as he wiped his mouth with a napkin.

'Maybe I'm a bit more than that,' said Maggie, having found the opening she was hoping for.

'More than what?' inquired a puzzled Daniel.

Maggie walked across the room and sat on his bed.

'Daniel, I know you're aware that you're adopted,' she began, carefully.

'Yes, mother told me just after father died. That's why I can't inherit his title.'

'Hmm . . . pity about that.'

'I've got used to it,' said Daniel. His mind was alert now as he looked up at Maggie. 'You're here to tell me something about my real family, aren't you?'

Maggie nodded, 'Yes, I am.'

There was an awkward silence, then Daniel seemed to realise something. 'You and I, we're related aren't we?'

This wasn't going as Maggie had planned. Perhaps these things never did. Her hesitation told him he could be right. Suddenly it all made sense to him. Both of them were singers, both had the same dark colouring, maybe to other people they even looked alike.

'Maggie,' he asked, slowly. 'Are you my sister?'

Maggie didn't know whether to laugh, or hug him, or both. She settled for a kiss on his cheek. 'No, Daniel,' she smiled, 'I'm not your sister.'

'Oh!' He was now puzzled. He felt a strong affinity with this beautiful woman, but it wasn't a physical attraction. Which was not like him at all. Why was that?

'Daniel,' she asked. 'When you were a baby, do you know if anyone gave you a war medal? A Military Medal?'

He frowned. 'I found a Military Medal in my father's desk after he died. I believe it was my grandfather's.'

Maggie took a large envelope out of her handbag and handed it to Daniel. 'It belonged to your grandfather all right,' she said. 'This is the citation that goes with it.'

Daniel read the citation, then repeated the name to himself, 'John Fish'. He looked up at Maggie. 'Where do you come into the picture?' he asked. 'If you're not my sister, are we cousins or something?'

Maggie had played the game long enough. She took a deep breath. 'Daniel,' she said, 'John Fish was my father.' Then looking squarely into her son's eyes, she added, 'I'm your mother.'

Having made her revelation, she froze, not knowing what to expect. Daniel stared at her in disbelief.

'You're joking!' he gasped.

This wasn't the reaction Maggie expected. 'No joke, Daniel.'

'But . . . you're too young!' He sat up, trying to accept the truth of the situation.

'Well, it's very nice of you to say so, but I'm afraid I'm not. I had you when I was just nineteen.'

She took his hands as he stared at her, open-mouthed with shock. 'Maggie Fisher, my mother. Good lord!' He looked down at his hands, now being tightly held by hers, then back up at her uncertain face.

'Good lord!'

'You've already said that,' she remarked, with a gentle smile.

She tentatively took him in her arms. Daniel, at first, was reluctant to respond; but there was real love flowing from this woman, a warmth he'd never known before. He finally allowed himself to go with the flow and rested his bandaged head on her shoulder, knowing the missing piece of his life had at last fallen into place.

Chapter Thirty-Four

Michael pulled up outside number seventeen Hope Street and wondered at the wisdom of allowing his charges out of the car. The denizens of the street looked dangerous to him. This was a whole different world from Took House. Daniel looked through the car window with interest. A scaffold tower had been erected across the road in preparation for yet another loft conversion. The original front doors had all but gone, replaced with an assortment of DIY doors, some with glass panels and bullseye glass for that country cottage look, the effect completed with artificial stone cladding. Cobbles and flags had been replaced with patched tarmac, and the stone kerbs with concrete ones. The old cast-iron gas lamp-posts on either side of the street had been replaced with a single concrete lamp standard which would illuminate the whole of the street with a lifeless monochrome glow. The old flags and cobbles and gas lamps had now become fashionable and much sought after, and were far too good for the Hope Streets of the city. They now paved and lit paths and driveways and patios in the more affluent suburbs. In between the parked cars, rubbish littered the street, a thing unheard of in Maggie's childhood. Where the street had been poor but proud, it was now tatty and neglected.

A group of youngsters peered into the Bentley; an ethnic assortment, from grimy white to shiny brown. One of them knocked on the window, causing Michael to wind it down an inch, to hear what the boy had to say.

'Is this a Rolls-Royce, mister?' asked the gap-toothed spokesman.

Michael chose not to answer. The boy pressed his face against the window, inspected the occupants, then left behind streaks of mucus as he turned to his pals.

'Berritsa Roller! Betcha ten pence!'

A bedroom window at the far side of the street scraped open and a brown female face fired out a stream of high-pitched Urdu in the direction of the children. The yelling went on for quite some time before one of the smaller, medium brown boys turned to his pals, grimaced and announced in a flat Leeds accent, 'It's me mam . . . me dinner's ready.'

'Berrit's norra Roller,' said a bigger girl of around ten, in answer to the previous challenge.

'Yer on!'

The gang all dashed round to the front of the car to effect an identification. Faces screwed up at the absence of any definite Rolls-Royce markings and a fierce argument ensued. Undecided, the gang dashed back to the driver's door.

'It's a Roller, innit mister?'

Michael pressed the electric window switch until it was fully open, leaned out and grabbed the biggest boy by his shirt collar.

'You're the one, aren't you?' he said balefully.

'Eh?' inquired the worried boy.

'You're the one we're looking for. The one who did it.'

'No, I'm not mister . . . honest.' He turned to his pals for support. 'It wasn't me, was it?' Support wasn't forthcoming.

'It must be you,' insisted Michael, menacingly. 'They said you'd walk straight up to the car and cause trouble.'

The gang backed off as Lady Audrey and Daniel suppressed their amusement. Michael released the boy, who turned and shot off like a scared rabbit, followed by his friends.

'Welcome to Hope Street,' grinned Charlie, who had witnessed all this from the other side of the car.

'Hello Charlie,' returned a smiling Daniel. 'Our man's just making friends with the natives.'

'I think your man ought to stay in the car,' warned Charlie. 'A Bentley loses some of its dignity when it's propped up on bricks.'

Thus warned, Michael remained in his seat as Daniel and his mother got out and went into Maggie and Charlie's house. Lady Audrey nodded her approval as they entered the pleasant front room. Maggie and Mrs Patel had been hard at it all morning in preparation for the visit.

Maggie had left a bewildered Daniel in the hospital room when the nurse came in to take off his bandages. She'd left him with an invitation to come and visit her just as soon as his head was okay. A somewhat ambiguous statement under the circumstances.

There were lots of gaps in the story that Daniel needed filling and he suspected the woman he'd called 'mother' for eighteen years might not be too forthcoming in this respect. The detour on the way back from hospital took Lady Audrey by surprise.

'I'm afraid the neighbourhood's gone to the dogs since I was a girl,' said Maggie, looking beyond them into the street, as they entered her home. Then, silently admonishing herself for making excuses about her humble background, she smiled at Lady Audrey.

'Would you like a cup of tea, Audrey?' she asked brightly.

'That'd be lovely, thank you, Maggie, can I help with anything?'

Maggie grinned to herself at the thought of her ladyship making a brew in the tiny scullery. 'No thanks,' she said. 'Charlie's the tea maker in this house . . . Garibaldis okay?'

'Lovely, thank you,' said Audrey and Daniel in unison. Charlie went through to make the tea, unable to figure out what was so special about Garibaldi biscuits.

The four of them sat round a glass coffee table, which Charlie and Maggie, in response to a drunken bet by a fellow artiste, had stolen from the cocktail bar of the Clarendon Hotel in Doncaster. The only crime that Maggie had ever knowingly committed.

The conversation inevitably revolved around the entertainment industry. Daniel wanted to know all about Maggie's earlier career, which she told him about with no little enthusiasm. Until she reached the part when that career came to an abrupt halt. She looked at her son, knowing he needed to be told the circumstances surrounding his conception, birth and adoption. She'd rehearsed this many times with Charlie and now was the time to get it over with.

'Maggie,' began Daniel, then stopped uncomfortably and looked at Audrey. 'Look, I can't simply stop calling you Mother, just because you're not . . .'

Maggie stepped in quickly. 'I'd like you to call me Maggie, and Audrey, Mother. At some stage in the future, if you really want to, you can call me Mum. It'll be up to you.'

'Fair enough, Maggie,' smiled a relieved Daniel.

There was another uncomfortable pause, broken by Maggie. 'You want to know about your father I suppose?'

'Yes please,' said Daniel. 'Mother was pretty vague about him.'

'All I ever knew was that he was a singer and he died in an accident,' said Audrey.

'Did you know *how* he died?' asked Maggie.

'In a fire, I believe.'

'Yes,' said Maggie. 'The same fire that killed my father.'

Maggie's brain was racing. How much should she tell him? How much did he already know? The newspapers had been full of it in 1959. All Danny had to do was dig out an old newspaper.

'So, my father and grandfather were killed in the same fire . . . My God, Maggie! It must have been awful for you,' said Daniel. 'No wonder you had me adopted.'

Maggie stared at him. He'd got hold of the wrong end of the stick, but it made a much better story than the truth.

'Did you love him?' inquired Daniel.

'Who? Your granddad?'

'No . . . I expect you loved my grandfather, he sounds a wonderful sort of chap. I meant, did you love my father?'

Maggie held Daniel's gaze and shook her head. 'Your father was called Patrizio Franciosa, better known as Tony Martini,' she said. 'One of the most successful singers in the fifties.'

'I've heard of him,' said Daniel. 'He sang "Bluebirds over Broadway", didn't he?'

'That was one of his hits,' confirmed Maggie. 'He made a lot of records. Tony Martini was a great singer . . . that's where you get your voice from.'

'I beg to differ,' argued Charlie. 'Daniel gets his voice from his mother.' He winked at Audrey. 'I'm a musician, I know these things.'

'So,' said Daniel. 'You didn't love my father. In that case, I suppose it would be naive of me to ask where I came from.'

Audrey and Charlie held their breath as they looked at Maggie. They both knew how she'd conceived Daniel.

'Euphoria, that's where you came from,' said Maggie. 'I'd just done a great show and Tony Martini was waiting for me in the dressing room with a bottle of champagne to celebrate.'

Daniel smiled and held up his hands. 'All right, I don't want to hear the gory details.'

Maggie stared at him for what seemed like an age. Her mind going back all those years to that night in her dressing room that destroyed her career. Back to her time in Bridgefield House and Prestwick's awful deception, from which Audrey had benefited. Then she looked at Charlie, who shrugged, as if to say: 'It's up to you.'

'Your father raped me,' she said quietly, holding Daniel in her gaze. Daniel said nothing, allowing Maggie to continue. 'He was drunk when I came back into the dressing room and he wouldn't take "no" for an answer.' Tears tumbled down her cheeks as fast as the words tumbled from her mouth. 'He denied it, our agent took his side and when your grandfather found out, he went to see them.'

'What happened then?' asked Daniel. His voice husky with the emotion of seeing Maggie, his mother, so overcome with grief.

'Nobody knows for certain. There was a fire and the three of them were killed.'

Daniel sat for a while before moving round to Maggie's side and holding her hand. 'Actually,' he said. 'I knew most of that already. Rang a chap I know at the *Yorkshire Post* . . . he dug it all out for me. I just needed to hear it from you.'

'You knew?' gasped Maggie through her drying tears. 'You little sod! I've been going through hell trying to work out what to say to you. I changed my mind half a dozen times in the last five minutes.'

Daniel held her hand as she sobbed her pent-up emotions away. Eventually he drew back and asked the question he'd come to ask.

'Why did you have me adopted?'

Maggie looked startled at the suddenness of this question.

'I know it sounds a silly question,' went on Daniel. 'It wasn't exactly the ideal way to conceive a child . . . but, didn't you have any feelings for me?'

'Feelings for you?' Maggie's tears started up again. 'Good grief, Danny! I loved you more than anything in the world. The day they took you away was the worst day of my life . . .' Her voice was breaking with emotion, Charlie took up the story.

'She was tricked into thinking she was dying,' he said. 'So that she'd give her baby away.'

Audrey's face had gone grey. 'I wasn't told any of this at the time,' she explained, quickly. 'Had I known the truth, I'd have returned you to your mother straight away.'

Both Charlie and Maggie knew she was bending the truth a little here, but the pleading on Audrey's face aroused sympathy in Maggie, who had regained some of her composure.

'Audrey's not to blame in any way for all this,' she assured Daniel. 'The culprit was a man called Prestwick. He was struck off by the BMA, but the adoption itself was perfectly legal.'

Maggie realised her explanation was posing some tricky questions, but she decided to let Audrey deal with them. After all, she wasn't as innocent as all that. Daniel stood up and paced up and down the small room, watched by three pairs of anxious eyes.

'I wonder what it is about me that makes people keep stealing me from my family?' he asked, with an air of cynicism.

He stopped with his back to them and looked out of the window, pulling back the net curtains slightly. Three pairs of eyes on his back.

'Tell me, do you think my father killed my grandfather, or was it the other way round?' he asked, peering sightlessly into the street. 'My guess is that the hero killed the Italian.' He nodded, as if to confirm his own assessment. 'So, where does that leave us? My father was a singing star who raped my mother, who was also a singing star - and conceived me. So instead of me being Lord Tristan Daniel Aylesbury-Took, I'm actually Danny Fish, the bastard son of a singing rapist. My grandfather was a war hero, who blotted his copybook by killing my father for what he did to my mother; and my adoptive father, of whom I saw very little, probably bribed someone to tell my real mother she was dying of leukaemia, so that she would give me away to him, because my adoptive mother couldn't have children of her own.' He turned and looked at Audrey. 'Have I missed anything out, Mother?' he asked.

It was certainly a stark assessment of the reality of events, thought Maggie, alarmed at the hostile tone of his voice. Despite what had happened, she didn't want him turning on Audrey.

'I told you,' said Maggie, quickly, 'Audrey's not to blame in any of . . .'

Daniel held up his hand to stop her. 'I know what you said, Maggie. But I'd like my Mother to tell me the truth, for once.'

Audrey had determinedly recovered her composure. Her upper lip remained firmly in its aristocratic position, after all, she was still the matriarch of the Aylesbury-Took family.

'Your father didn't bribe anyone,' she almost snapped, forcing Daniel on to the back foot for a moment. 'At the worst he made a few extravagant promises to Prestwick to ensure we got the pick of the crop, so to speak. I thought if I had to adopt I might as well introduce a more comely strain into the family. I'm aware of my own un-prepossessing appearance and your father was no oil painting either.' She stood up to put herself on level ground with Daniel. 'When the BMA findings were made public, both your father and I were shocked when we heard what Prestwick had done. So much so that your father washed his hands of the awful man.'

'How convenient!' blurted Maggie, unable to help herself. 'Did it ever occur to you to ask how I felt about losing my baby?'

Audrey's upper lip was under serious strain now, as she turned to take on this new adversary. 'Yes,' she admitted. 'It did occur to me, but ... but I was too frightened to find out the truth. I'd convinced myself that you were better off without the child and probably didn't want him anyway. After all, you were unmarried ...' Her lip collapsed under the pressure. She stood in the centre of the room and wept for the first time in many years.

'I'm sorry, Maggie,' she sobbed. 'But I loved him so much, I ...'

Maggie stood up and put a forgiving arm around her. 'It's okay, Audrey,' she sighed, with a shake of her head. 'It'd have taken a saint to have given him up.'

The two women held on to each other, each relieved that the truth was out at last. Daniel, now dismissed from the conversation, stood there, amazed.

'Oh, so everything's all alright then is it?' he asked.

'Never mind, Danny,' said Charlie, placing a consoling arm around the young man's shoulder. 'It could have been worse.'

'Could it? How could it be worse?'

'Well,' said Charlie, stuck for an answer. 'You could have been a tenor ... I hate bloody tenors.'

The sheer stupidity of Charlie's comment brought a look of amazement to Daniel's face. His mouth began to quiver as he looked at Charlie grinning at him. He returned Charlie's grin with one of his own. Charlie and Daniel stood there laughing as Maggie and Audrey wept on each other's shoulders.

Epilogue

February 1979

Charlie was almost as nervous as Maggie as he stood in the wings and watched her stand centre stage behind the curtains. Eyes closed, taking slow, deep breaths as she listened to the compére announce her. Daniel stood behind Charlie and was probably the most nervous of the three. After all, this was his professional début.

Daniel had fortunately finished his A Levels before the trauma of his kidnapping, otherwise he may not have got the A and two Bs he ended up with. But it was probably a waste of a good education. If anyone was destined for a life on stage, it was Daniel.

His voice coach had been shocked to hear of the operation Maggie had been contemplating.

'How can a surgeon possibly know where the magic comes from?' he pointed out, forcibly. 'An operation like that could finish your career for good. Training is what your voice needs. How long is it since you had singing lessons?'

'Well, not since my school choir and they weren't exactly lessons.'

'Shall I come to you or will you come to me?' he asked. 'The school doesn't take up all my time.'

Maggie had driven across to Lambourne Wells once a week for four months, at the end of which time, her old voice had been miraculously restored.

'I think it was on its way back anyway,' said Charlie, somewhat ungraciously. An attitude perhaps brought on by the guilt he felt at trying to persuade Maggie to have the operation. He'd written a song for her and Daniel. One of many he'd written over the years, but somehow he felt that this was a bit special. 'Where Have You Been All My Life?' had a poignancy which would hit those in the audience who knew the story behind Maggie and Daniel's reunion ... and this was just about every person in the audience at the Bradford Alhambra.

Maggie opened up with 'Don't Give Me Roses', for which she took tremendous applause. Her voice was as strong as ever, as was the elusive hook.

'Ladies and gentlemen,' she said, as the applause died down. 'As my husband seems to have found himself another woman,' she paused as a ripple of laughter drifted towards her. The audience had already been well entertained by Charlie and his new partner. 'I thought it only right and proper,' she continued, 'that I get myself another feller.' The women in the audience voiced their approval of this. 'And ladies,' she said. 'If you're going to get another feller, why not get one who's young and handsome?' This sentiment met with more noisy approval. 'Ladies and gentlemen ... would you welcome on stage, for the first time, my lovely son, DANNY FISHER!'

As Daniel walked out to warm applause, Charlie felt a dig in his ribs. He turned to Sylvia Tattersall, the other half of his new act, Tatty and Chips.

'Fingers crossed Sylvia, here goes.'

The orchestra struck up the opening bars that Charlie had written, in what he hoped had been an inspirational hour in the tap room of the Crimea Tavern. As Maggie began to sing, he knew the song was right. And when Daniel's voice joined in with a magical harmony he also knew that Fish and Chipperfield were a thing of the past. But he didn't care. Wherever Maggie went this time, Charlie would be with her. He was her agent, songwriter, manager and lover. An indispensable combination. His role as agent also gave him leave to book Tatty and Chips as support act wherever Maggie went. Daniel, in time, would follow his own glittering career, but it would do no harm for his mother to give him a boost.

'If I may say so, Mr Daniel,' commented Michael, as he drove the Bentley through the grim streets of Bradford. 'I've scarcely heard a singer of your age with such a mature and accomplished voice.'

'Thank you, Michael,' grinned Daniel.

311

The smile on his face had been there since he came off stage to an explosion of applause. The same smile was mirrored on the faces of both his mothers. It had been the best of nights. A night that had seen the start of one career, the resurgence of another and the start of an hysterical new comedy act.

'It's like being in a car with a bunch o' Cheshire bloody cats,' commented Sylvia. 'Drop me off at home would yer Michael, love.'

'Very good, madam,' said Michael.

'How do you like your new home?' inquired Maggie.

'It'll do till summat decent comes along,' answered Sylvia.

'Cheeky! It did for me for thirty-seven years,' said Maggie. 'All my life I lived in that house. I was sorry to leave. There's a lot of memories stored up there.'

'Well, if you don't like living in Took House, Michael can always drop you off with Sylvia,' suggested Daniel, tongue in cheek.

'Well, I suppose they weren't all *good* memories,' conceded Maggie. 'Anyway, it's a mother's job to make sacrifices. It's only right that both mothers should be with their son. Besides, three's a crowd ... I reckon your Roy wouldn't thank me for muscling in on the happy home ... wouldn't you agree, Mrs Bradford?'

'You keep well away from my toy boy, Mrs Chipperfield, or me brothers might just have ter pay you a visit.'

'I thought your brothers had retired from er ... public relations,' said Charlie. 'I thought they were running a security firm.'

'They are,' said Sylvia. 'And when my brothers look after a firm, it stays looked after.'

The rest of them nodded their agreement to this, especially Daniel, who knew whom he had to thank for his rescue from abduction and probably worse. The deeds to number seventeen Hope Street had been Maggie's gift to Sylvia for arranging things, her brothers having settled for hard cash. All in all it was a satisfactory outcome, insofar as it left Maggie and Charlie homeless and with little alternative other than to accept Daniel's offer of a permanent suite of rooms in Took House. Officially, Lady Audrey had no say in the matter, apart from it being her suggestion.

Roy Bradford came out into the street to greet his new wife and bent down to wave to the occupants of the limousine. His eyes lingering wistfully on Maggie. Roy and Sylvia had hit it off the first day Maggie had introduced them, backstage at the Batley Variety Club. Sylvia fell in love with his decency and lack of guile – unheard of qualities in the men she'd known. Roy had simply fallen head over heels in love with her. He knew her history and accepted it. 'It doesn't matter how many have gone before,' he'd said to her, 'so long as I'm the last . . . that's what counts.'

He was currently working out his notice at Openshawe's, with a view to becoming a roadie to Maggie and company.

After they'd said their goodnights, Maggie turned to Lady Audrey, sitting beside her. 'Will you be putting the kettle on when we get in, Audrey love, my throat's parched after all that singing.'

'Oh dear! . . . I don't actually think I know where the kettle is,' said Lady Audrey.

'I reckon you and Maggie have a lot more in common than you think,' commented Charlie. 'I just hope you don't start ganging up on me. Still, I'll have Danny and Michael on my side, that should even things up a bit. What do you reckon, fellers?'

'I fear we would be outnumbered, sir,' replied Michael, pointing the Bentley towards their new home.